Praise for Richard Matheson

"The best novel I read last year."

—Stephen King
on *Journal of the Gun Years*

"The author gives his story a credibility and
honesty unusual in the genre."

—*Publishers Weekly*
on *Journal of the Gun Years*

"Breathtaking . . . first-rate . . . impossible
to put down. Mr. Matheson has done something
remarkable: with a single novel he has placed
himself in the front rank of Western novelists."

—Richard S. Wheeler,
author of *Virgin River,*
on *Journal of the Gun Years*

Also by Richard Matheson
from Tom Doherty Associates

The Beardless Warriors
Button, Button (The Box)
Duel
Earthbound
Hell House
Hunted Past Reason
I Am Legend
The Incredible Shrinking Man
Journal of the Gun Years
The Gun Fight
The Memoirs of Wild Bill Hickok
Nightmare at 20,000 Feet
Noir
Now You See It . . .
The Path: A New Look at Reality
7 Steps to Midnight
Somewhere in Time
A Stir of Echoes
What Dreams May Come

JOURNAL of the GUN YEARS

GUN YEARS

|AND|

The GUN FiGHT

RiCHARD MATHESON

A TOM DOHERTY ASSOCIATES BOOK | NEW YORK

This is a work of fiction. All of the characters, organizations, and events portrayed in these novels are either products of the author's imagination or are used fictitiously.

JOURNAL OF THE GUN YEARS AND THE GUN FIGHT

Journal of the Gun Years copyright © 1991 by RXR, Inc.

The Gun Fight copyright © 1993 by RXR, Inc.

All rights reserved.

A Forge Book
Published by Tom Doherty Associates
175 Fifth Avenue
New York, NY 10010

www.tor-forge.com

Forge® is a registered trademark of Macmillan Publishing Group, LLC.

ISBN 978-0-7653-9316-6

Our books may be purchased in bulk for promotional, educational, or business use. Please contact your local bookseller or the Macmillan Corporate and Premium Sales Department at 1-800-221-7945, extension 5442, or by e-mail at MacmillanSpecialMarkets@macmillan.com.

First Edition: April 2017

Printed in the United States of America

0 9 8 7 6 5 4 3 2 1

CONTENTS

JOURNAL of the GUN YEARS

Being CHOICE selections
from the *Authentic*,
never-before-printed
DIARY of the famous
gunfighter-lawman
CLAY HALSER!
Whose deeds of *daring*
made his name a by-word
of TERROR in the Southwest
between the YEARS OF
1866 and 1876!

For:

William Campbell Gault, William R. Cox, Henry
Kuttner, Les Savage, Jr., Joe Brennan, Hal Braham,
Malden Grange Bishop, Chick Coombs, Dean Owens,
Bill Fay, Willard Temple, Frank Bonham, Todhunter
Ballard, Wilbur S. Peacock, and all my other friends
in the Fictioneers.

Happy memories.

BOOK ONE

(1864–1867)

It is my unhappy lot to write the closing entry in this journal.

Clay Halser is dead, killed this morning in my presence.

I have known him since we met during the latter days of The War Between The States. I have run across him, on occasion, through ensuing years and am, in fact, partially responsible (albeit involuntarily) for a portion of the legend which has magnified around him.

It is for these reasons (and another more important) that I make this final entry.

I am in Silver Gulch acquiring research matter toward the preparation of a volume on the history of this territory (Colorado), which has recently become the thirty-eighth state of our Union.

I was having breakfast in the dining room of the *Silver Lode Hotel* when a man entered and sat down at a table across the room, his back to the wall. Initially, I failed to recognize him though there was, in his comportment, something familiar.

Several minutes later (to my startlement), I realized that it was none other than Clay Halser. True, I had not laid eyes on him for many years. Nonetheless, I was completely taken aback by the change in his appearance.

I was not, at that point, aware of his age, but took it to be somewhere in the middle thirties. Contrary to this, he presented the aspect of a man at least a decade older.

His face was haggard, his complexion (in my memory, quite ruddy) pale to the point of being ashen. His eyes,

formerly suffused with animation, now looked burned
out, dead. What many horrific sights those eyes had be-
held I could not—and cannot—begin to estimate. Whatever those sights, however, no evidence of them had been
reflected in his eyes before; it was as though he'd been
emotionally immune.

He was no longer so. Rather, one could easily imagine
that his eyes were gazing, in that very moment, at those
bloody sights, dredging from the depths within his mind
to which he'd relegated them, all their awful measure.

From the standpoint of physique, his deterioration was
equally marked. I had always known him as a man of vig-
orous health, a condition necessary to sustain him in the
execution of his harrowing duties. He was not a tall man;
I would gauge his height at five feet ten inches maximum,
perhaps an inch or so less, since his upright carriage and
customary dress of black suit, hat, and boots might have
afforded him the look of standing taller than he did. He had
always been extremely well-presented though, with a broad
chest, narrow waist, and pantherlike grace of movement; all
in all, a picture of vitality.

Now, as he ate his meal across from me, I felt as though,
by some bizarre transfiguration, I was gazing at an old
man.

He had lost considerable weight and his dark suit (it, too,
seemed worn and past its time) hung loosely on his frame.
To my further disquiet, I noted a threading of gray through
his dark blond hair and saw a tremor in his hands completely foreign to the young man I had known.

I came close to summary departure. To my shame, I
nearly chose to leave rather than accost him. Despite the
congenial relationship I had enjoyed with him throughout
the past decade, I found myself so totally dismayed by the
alteration in his looks that I lacked the will to rise and cross
the room to him, preferring to consider a hasty exit. (I dis-

covered, later, that the reason he had failed to notice me was that his vision, always so acute before, was now inordinately weak.)

At last, however, girding up my will, I stood and moved across the dining room, attempting to fix a smile of pleased surprise on my lips and hoping he would not be too aware of my distress.

"Well, good morning, Clay," I said, as evenly as possible.

I came close to baring my deception at the outset for, as he looked up sharply at me, his expression one of taut alarm, a perceptible "tic" under his right eye, I was hard put not to draw back apprehensively.

Abruptly, then, he smiled (though it was more a ghost of the smile I remembered). "*Frank*," he said and jumped to his feet. No, that is not an accurate description of his movement. It may well have been his intent to jump up and welcome me with an avid handshake. As it happened, his stand was labored, his hand grip lacking in strength. "How *are* you?" he inquired. "It is good to see you."

"I'm fine," I answered.

"Good." He nodded, gesturing toward the table. "Join me."

I hope my momentary hesitation passed his notice. "I'd be happy to," I told him.

"Good," he said again.

We each sat down, he with his back toward the wall again. As we did, I noted how his gaunt frame slumped into the chair, so different from the movement of his earlier days.

He asked me if I'd eaten breakfast.

"Yes." I pointed across the room. "I was finishing when you entered."

"I am glad you came over," he said.

There was a momentary silence. Uncomfortable, I tried to think of something to say.

He helped me out. (I wonder, now, if it was deliberate;

if he had, already, taken note of my discomfort.) "Well, old fellow," he asked, "what brings you to this neck of the woods?"

I explained my presence in Silver Gulch and, as I did, being now so close to him, was able to distinguish, in detail, the astounding metamorphosis which time (and experience) had effected.

There seemed to be, indelibly impressed on his still handsome face, a look of unutterable sorrow. His former blitheness had completely vanished and it was oppressive to behold what had occurred to his expression, to see the palsied gestures of his hands as he spoke, perceive the constant shifting of his eyes as though he was anticipating that, at any second, some impending danger might be thrust upon him.

I tried to coerce myself not to observe these things, concentrating on the task of bringing him "up to date" on my activities since last we'd met; no match for his activities, God knows.

"What about you?" I finally asked; I had no more to say about myself. "What are you doing these days?"

"Oh, gambling," he said, his listless tone indicative of his regard for that pursuit.

"No marshaling anymore?" I asked.

He shook his head. "Strictly the circuit," he answered.

"Circuit?" I wasn't really curious but feared the onset of silence and spoke the first word that occurred to me.

"A league of boomtown havens for faro players," he replied. "South Texas up to South Dakota—Idaho to Arizona. There is money to be gotten everywhere. Not that I am good enough to make a raise. And not that it's important if I do, at any rate. I only gamble for something to do."

All the time he spoke, his eyes kept shifting, searching; was it *waiting*?

As silence threatened once again, I quickly spoke. "Well, you have traveled quite a long road since the War,"

I said. "A long, exciting road." I forced a smile. "*Adventurous*," I added.

His answering smile was as sadly bitter and exhausted as any I have ever witnessed. "Yes, the writers of the stories have made it all sound very colorful," he said. He leaned back with a heavy sigh, regarding me. "I even thought it so myself at one time. Now I recognize it all for what it was." There was a tightening around his eyes. "Frank, it was drab, and dirty, and there was a lot of blood."

I had no idea how to respond to that and, in spite of my resolve, let silence fall between us once more.

Silence broke in a way that made my flesh go cold. A young man's voice behind me, from some distance in the room. "So that is him," the voice said loudly. "Well, he does not look like much to me."

I'd begun to turn when Clay reached out and gripped my arm. "Don't bother looking," he instructed me. "It's best to ignore them. I have found the more attention paid, the more difficult they are to shake in the long run."

He smiled but there was little humor in it. "Don't be concerned," he said. "It happens all the time. They spout a while, then go away, and brag that Halser took their guff and never did a thing. It makes them feel important. I don't mind. I've grown accustomed to it."

At which point, the boy—I could now tell, from the timbre of his voice, that he had not attained his majority—spoke again.

"He looks like nothing at all to me to be so all-fired famous a fighter with his guns," he said.

I confess the hostile quaver of his voice unsettled me. Seeing my reaction, Clay smiled and was about to speak when the boy—perhaps seeing the smile and angered by it—added, in a tone resounding enough to be heard in the lobby, "In fact, I believe he looks like a woman-hearted coward, that is what he looks like to me!"

"Don't worry now," Clay reassured me. "He'll blow himself out of steam presently and crawl away." I felt some sense of relief to see a glimmer of the old sauce in his eyes. "Probably to visit, with uncommon haste, the nearest outhouse."

Still, the boy kept on with stubborn malice. "My name is Billy Howard," he announced. "And I am going to make . . ."

He went abruptly mute as Clay unbuttoned his dark frock coat to reveal a butt-reversed Colt at his left side. It was little wonder. Even I, a friend of Clay's, felt a chill of premonition at the movement. What spasm of dread it must have caused in the boy's heart, I can scarcely imagine.

"Sometimes I have to go this far," Clay told me. "Usually I wait longer but, since you are with me . . ." He let the sentence go unfinished and lifted his cup again.

I wanted to believe the incident was closed but, as we spoke—me asking questions to distract my mind from its foreboding state—I seemed to feel the presence of the boy behind me like some constant wraith.

"How are all your friends?" I asked.

"Dead," Clay answered.

"*All* of them?"

He nodded. "Yes. Jim Clements. Ben Pickett. John Harris." I saw a movement in his throat. "Henry Blackstone. All of them."

I had some difficulty breathing. I kept expecting to hear the boy's voice again. "What about your wife?" I asked.

"I have not heard from her in some time," he replied. "We are estranged."

"How old is your daughter now?"

"Three in January," he answered, his look of sadness deepening. I regretted having asked and quickly said, "What about your family in Indiana?"

"I went back to visit them last year," he said. "It was a waste."

I did not want to know, but heard myself inquiring none-theless, "Why?"

"Oh . . . what I have become," he said. "What journalists have made me. Not you," he amended, believing, I suppose, that he'd insulted me. "My reputation, I mean. It stood like a wall between my family and me. I don't think they saw me. Not *me*. They saw what they believed I am."

The voice of Billy Howard made me start. "Well, why does he just *sit* there?" he said.

Clay ignored him. Or, perhaps, he did not even hear, so deep was he immersed in black thoughts.

"Hickok was right," he said, "I am not a man anymore. I'm a figment of imagination. Do you know, I looked at my reflection in the mirror this morning and did not even know who I was looking at? Who is that staring at me? I wondered. Clay Halser of Pine Grove? Or the *Hero of The Plains*?" he finished with contempt.

"*Well?*" demanded Billy Howard. "Why *does* he?"

Clay was silent for a passage of seconds and I felt my muscles drawing in, anticipating God knew what.

"I had no answer for my mirror," he went on then. "I have no answers left for anyone. All I know is that I am tired. They have offered me the job of City Marshal here and, although I could use the money, I cannot find it in myself to accept."

Clay Halser stared into my eyes and told me quietly, "To answer your long-time question: yes, Frank, I have learned what fear is. Though not fear of . . ."

He broke off as the boy spoke again, his tone now ven-omous. "I think he is afraid of me," said Billy Howard.

Clay drew in a long, deep breath, then slowly shifted his gaze to look across my shoulder. I sat immobile, conscious

of an air of tension in the entire room now, everyone waiting with held breath.

"That is what I think," the boy's voice said. "I think
Almighty God Halser is afraid of me."

Clay said nothing, looking past me at the boy. I did not
dare to turn. I sat there, petrified.

"I think the Almighty God Halser is a yellow skunk!"
cried Billy Howard. "I think he is a murderer who shoots
men in the back and will not . . . !"

The boy's voice stopped again as Clay stood so abruptly
that I felt a painful jolting in my heart. "I'll be right back,"
he said.

He walked past me and, shuddering, I turned to watch.
It had grown so deathly still in the room that, as I did, the
legs of my chair squeaked and caused some nearby diners
to start.

I saw, now, for the first time, Clay Halser's challenger
and was aghast at the callow look of him. He could not
have been more than sixteen years of age and might
well have been younger, his face speckled with skin blem-
ishes, his dark hair long and shaggy. He was poorly dressed
and had an old six-shooter pushed beneath the waistband
of his faded trousers.

I wondered vaguely whether I should move, for I was
sitting in whatever line of fire the boy might direct. I wondered vaguely if the other diners were wondering the same
thing. If they were, their limbs were as frozen as mine.

I heard every word exchanged by the two.

"Now don't you think that we have had enough of this?"
Clay said to the boy. "These folks are having their breakfast and I think that we should let them eat their meal in
peace."

"Step out into the street then," said the boy.

"Now why should I step out into the street?" Clay asked.
I knew it was no question. He was doing what he could to

calm the agitated boy—that agitation obvious as the boy replied, "To fight me with your gun."

"You don't want to fight me," Clay informed him. "You would just be killed and no one would be better for it."

"You mean *you* don't want to fight *me*," the youth retorted. Even from where I sat, I could see that his face was almost white; it was clear that he was terror-stricken.

Still, he would not allow himself to back off, though Clay was giving him full opportunity. "*You* don't want to fight *me*," he repeated.

"That is not the case at all," Clay replied. "It is just that I am tired of fighting."

"I *thought* so!" cried the boy with malignant glee.

"Look," Clay told him quietly, "if it will make you feel good, you are free to tell your friends, or anyone you choose, that I backed down from you. You have my permission to do that."

"I don't need your d——d permission," snarled the boy. With a sudden move, he scraped his chair back, rising to his feet. Unnervingly, he seemed to be gaining resolution rather than losing it—as though, in some way, he sensed the weakness in Clay, despite the fact that Clay was famous for his prowess with the handgun. "I am sick of listening to you," he declared. "Are you going to step outside with me and pull your gun like a man, or do I shoot you down like a dog?"

"Go *home*, boy," Clay responded—and I felt an icy grip of premonition strike me full force as his voice broke in the middle of a word.

"Pull, you yellow b——d," Billy Howard ordered him.

Several diners close to them lunged up from their tables, scattering for the lobby. Clay stood motionless.

"I said *pull*, you God d——d son of a b——h!" Billy Howard shouted.

"No," was all Clay Halser answered.

"Then *I* will!" cried the boy.

Before his gun was halfway from the waistband of his trousers, Clay's had cleared its holster. Then—with what capricious twist of fate!—his shot misfired and, before he could squeeze off another, the boy's gun had discharged and a bullet struck Clay full in the chest, sending him reeling back to hit a table, then sprawl sideways to the floor.

Through the pall of dark smoke, Billy Howard gaped down at his victim. "I did it," he muttered. "I *did* it." Though chance alone had done it.

Suddenly, his pistol clattered to the floor as his fingers lost their holding power and, with a cry of what he likely thought was victory, he bolted from the room. (Later, I heard, he was killed in a knife fight over a poker game somewhere near Bijou Basin.)

By then, I'd reached Clay, who had rolled onto his back, a dazed expression on his face, his right hand pressed against the blood-pumping wound in the center of his chest. I shouted for someone to get a doctor, and saw some man go dashing toward the lobby. Clay attempted to sit up, but did not have the strength, and slumped back.

Hastily, I knelt beside him and removed my coat to form a pillow underneath his head, then wedged my handkerchief between his fingers and the wound. As I did, he looked at me as though I were a stranger. Finally, he blinked and, to my startlement, began to chuckle. "The one time I di . . ." I could not make out the rest. "What, Clay?" I asked distractedly, wondering if I should try to stop the bleeding in some other way.

He chuckled again. "The one day I did not reload," he repeated with effort. "Ben would laugh at that."

He swallowed, then began to make a choking noise, a trickle of blood issuing from the left-hand corner of his mouth. "Hang on," I said, pressing my hand to his shoulder. "The doctor will be here directly."

He shook his head with several hitching movements. "No sawbones can remove me from *this* tight," he said.

He stared up at the ceiling now, his breath a liquid sound that made me shiver. I did not know what to say, but could only keep directing worried (and increasingly angry) glances toward the lobby. "Where *is* he?" I muttered.

Clay made a ghastly, wheezing noise, then said, "My God." His fingers closed in, clutching at the already blood-soaked handkerchief. "I am going to die." Another strangling breath. "And I am only thirty-one years old."

Instant tears distorted my vision. *Thirty-one?*

Clay murmured something I could not hear. Automatically, I bent over and he repeated, in a labored whisper, "She was such a pretty girl."

"Who?" I asked; could not help but ask.

"Mary Jane," he answered. He could barely speak by then. Straightening up, I saw the grayness of death seeping into his face and knew that there were only moments left to him.

He made a sound which might have been a chuckle had it not emerged in such a hideously bubbling manner. His eyes seemed lit now with some kind of strange amusement. "I could have married her," he managed to say. "I could still be there." He stared into his fading thoughts. "Then I would never have . . ."

At which his stare went lifeless and he expired.

I gazed at him until the doctor came. Then the two of us lifted his body—how *frail* it was—and placed it on a nearby table. The doctor closed Clay's eyes and I crossed Clay's arms on his chest after buttoning his coat across the ugly wound. Now he looked almost at peace, his expression that of a sleeping boy.

Soon people began to enter the dining room. In a short while, everyone in Silver Gulch, it seemed, had heard about Clay's death and come running to view the remains.

They shuffled past his impromptu bier in a double line, gazed at him and, ofttimes, murmured some remark about his life and death.

As I stood beside the table, looking at the gray, still features, I wondered what Clay had been about to say before the rancorous voice of Billy Howard had interrupted. He'd said that he had learned what fear is, "though not fear of . . ." What words had he been about to say? Though not fear of other men? Of danger? Of death?

Later on, the undertaker came and took Clay's body after I had guaranteed his payment. That done, I was requested, by the manager of the hotel, to examine Clay's room and see to the disposal of his meager goods. This I did and will return his possessions to his family in Indiana.

With one exception.

In a lower bureau drawer, I found a stack of Record Books bound together with heavy twine. They turned out to be a journal which Clay Halser kept from the latter part of the War to this very morning.

It is my conviction that these books deserve to be published. Not in their entirety, of course; if that were done, I estimate the book would run in excess of a thousand pages. Moreover, there are many entries which, while perhaps of interest to immediate family (who will, of course, receive the Record Books when I have finished partially transcribing them), contribute nothing to the main thrust of his account, which is the unfoldment of his life as a nationally recognized lawman and gunfighter.

Accordingly, I plan to eliminate those sections of the journal which chronicle that variety of events which any man might experience during twelve years' time. After all, as hair-raising as Clay's life was, he could not possibly exist on the razor edge of peril every day of his life. As proof of this, I will incorporate a random sampling of those entries which may be considered, from a "thrilling" stand-point, more mundane.

In this way—concentrating on the sequences of "action"—it is hoped that the general reader, who might otherwise ignore the narrative because of its unwieldy length, will more willingly expose his interest to the life of one whom another journalist has referred to as "The Prince of Pistoleers."

Toward this end, I will, additionally, attempt to make corrections in the spelling, grammar and, especially, punctuation of the journal, leaving, as an indication of this necessity, the opening entry. It goes without saying that subsequent entries need less attention to this aspect since Clay Halser learned, by various means, to read and write with more skill in his later years.

I hope the reader will concur that, while there might well be a certain charm in viewing the entries precisely as Clay Halser wrote them, the difficulty in following his style through virtually an entire book would make the reading far too difficult. It is for this reason that I have tried to simplify his phraseology without—I trust—sacrificing the basic flavor of his language.

Keep in mind, then, that if the chronology of this account is, now and then, sporadic (with occasional truncated entries), it is because I have used, as its main basis, Clay Halser's life as a man of violence. I hope, by doing this, that I will not unbalance the impression of his personality. While trying not to intrude unduly on the texture of the journal, I may occasionally break into it if I believe my observations may enable the reader to better understand the protagonist of what is probably the bloodiest sequence of events to ever take place on the American frontier.

I plan to do all this, not for personal encomiums, but because I hope that I may be the agency by which the public-at-large may come to know Clay Halser's singular story, perhaps to thrill at his exploits, perhaps to moralize but, hopefully, to profit by the reading for, through the page-by-page transition of this man from high-hearted exuberance to hopeless resignation, we may, perhaps, achieve some insight into a sad, albeit fascinating and exciting, phenomenon of our times.

Frank Leslie
April 19, 1876

September 12, 1864

We are still here in this Valley, I think we will be here For Ever with those Secesh Boys keep us boteled up, the Sholder Strapps say we are at a Place called Al Mans Swich wer ever that is, I do not no, all I *Do* no is the Army of the Patomic is siting here, siting here and those Secesh Boys piking us of like Pigins on a log, I hate siting, siting, I feel tyd down like a prisner and I wish we just *Go*!! I hate to feel tyd down, by G———. I hate it! I think if we woud Go and Go Hard we woud thro those Jony Rebs back to Jef Davis Back Porch, that woud be the *End* of it, I rely feel that, *Do* it, *Do* it, dont just Sit Here like lumps, we her to suport the Artilery but all we are suporting our own rer ends while we *Sit* here!! Why think it all out, just GO!!!

My frend from New Jersy Albirt Jonson (I think that is a rong speling his Last Name) he took a Minie Ball in the rigt side this afternoon, it put him in grate pain, was holering and crying Some Thing awfil that I did feel sorry for him he was feeling so bad, it must have hurt like H———, poor Albirt. So a few of us Boys caried him Behind The Lines, we finily fond a waggin going North and placed him on it, caried him away poor fello, he was bleding Some Thing ferce, I hope he makes it—And as if that was not enogh the salt beef and patatos gave us last nigt made a bunch siker than Dogs, how we did "cast up acounts" over the Hill Side and down the Creek was Some Thing awfil!

How Ever at the start I did not feel sik but as more and more my comrads got sik after a time I did to and went the same road.

It did not make me feel beter to get a note from Mother, you woud think I took a trip for pursonel plesur here in Vergina insted of figting a D———War! Why doesnt She leave me be not alway Scolding me as poring linamint into a sore with Ever Lasting Heranging, why did I leve the Farm when there is so much Work to do there, why did I enlist in the Army of the Patomic when there are lots of soldirs who can figt the War but No, no, no "Not enogh Good Men At Home" to help take care of ther Familes, My Lord She goes on and on and on, no wonder He went off to California (My Father) I think the Army of The Se-cesh less to face than *Her*, I mean I Rispect her and all but why does She never stop Heranging me, I am in a D——— War for G———'s sake, not for pursonel plesure!! Well that is that and we had beter move soon or I take my Rifel and go at those Rebs all my self and mean so in *Ernest*!!

September 14, 1864

Yesterday, this time, I thought we would be here forever. The problem this way: the Secesh Army planted solid on the Heights and regardless how our batteries fired at them— our cannons burning hot!—were so much dug in it did no good at all. This is a "key spot" Lieutenant Hale said; the Rebels need to hold it At Any Cost and no matter what we did, they held.

We started rushing them, charging the heights, bayonets in fix position, but a volley of fire burned at us and we were forced back in defeat, half dead and wounded on the field. Only our artillery at them saved any at all though it did hit some of our boys too. It was a bloody attack that was no use. I had 60 rounds of lead pills which, when it was over, I was down to 17 and I do not know if I had hit a soul, the smoke so heavy you could not see through it the boys in Grey were hid so.

At three o'clock this afternoon Lieutenant Hale collected a group—eight in all—and led us up the far slope of the Valley to "harass" the enemy. He said, "Come on, boys! Today we have a chance to fight our way to Glory!"

He was right, we *did*! It was a battle out of H————but I came out without a scratch. I think my life is charmed because, when we charged up that slope, though it was far to one side, shot and shell ploughed up the ground in all directions; it was flying hot and heavy. Minnie Balls were buzzing all around us like swarms of angry bees! I felt the *wind* of them and some went by my ears so close they made me jump but not a one could touch me!

By when we reached the top, there was only three remaining, George Havers, me and some fat man from New York State that I had not met. (How he climbed that slope not being blown to his Maker I will never know!) We got behind a fallen tree and, from that point, through clouds of smoke, could see the Grey lines clear as day. I said to Havers and the fat man we must fire at the Secesh batteries, but they were none too keen to lift their heads as bombarding shot was fierce and Southern Sharp Shooters doing their best to kill us!

So I had to do it my self though Havers, to admit the truth, did fire a shot or two. Mostly, it was me how ever and the first time I got value from the Sharps I picked up last month from the body of a killed Confederate. Lord All Mighty, how that piece can do! I aimed first for the Sharp Shooters, those I could see, and it was like I could not miss. I had 30 lead pills in my sack and there were not too many wasted! I shot at Battery Crews I saw and they fell also; Rebs were going down like sitting birds! I lost count at twelve what with smoke and noise and being worked up, I fell in what you might say was half sleep. I kept firing and firing and Havers screamed, "God, boy, you hit *another*! God, boy, you hit *another*!"

When the firing at our lines grew thin, our boys came charging up and took the Heights and it was all because of me that we could whip them! Now they are on the run and I am happy as a clam at high water! I can say it if I want, no one will read this.

That is for now. I am glad I took this Record Book from a dead Rebel officer last week. I believe I will keep writing in it regular because . . .

Jim Brockmuller told me some boys have come across a Moonshine Still the Greys were running so there is going to be a lot of Liquid Joy tonight!

September 16, 1864

Early morning—the boys are sleeping off the battle for the Moonshine Whiskey Heights. I believe our officers were wise to let us drink after what we went through yesterday; anyway more fellows came to drink than expected—good news does travel fast!—and no one got enough to hear the owl hoot. It made our bellies warm though and our heads some light.

I can not sleep for thinking of the man I met last night. His name is Frank Leslie, a Reporter for *The New York Ledger*. He had heard about my part in the battle and came to ask questions to write about it in his News paper. I can not get over it. A story in a News paper read by thousands. About *me*. The folks in Pine Grove will be some surprised to read it, I imagine. Specially Mother: may be she will sing a warmer song now. And Mary Jane. It thrills me to think about her reading what I did. I would not show her this Record Book (or show it to any one) but if a News paper man wants to write about me I can not stop him. So long as I do not have to see or talk to all those people who read it; I want to be *Private* Halser all the way. But I do not object to a story in a News paper.

After he had introduced him self to me, Mr. Leslie said that several of the boys had "witnessed my heroic action" (as he put it) specially Private George Havers, Mill Town, Pennsylvania; that was nice of George, I thanked him later.

"He tells me that you turned the tide of battle almost single-handedly." Those were his words. It happened that I shot down nineteen Rebels, killing eleven including two officers, "throwing such confusion and dismay into the Southern ranks that they began to waver," as Mr. Leslie stated it. (I wrote down that hill of words soon after, so not to forget them.)

"Tell me, Private Halser," Mr. Leslie said. "What were you feeling during that engagement?"

"I was not feeling any thing," I answered. "I had little time for feeling."

"You felt no fear?" he asked me with surprise.

"No, sir," I told him. I explained that I do not know what that particular "emotion" feels like; he was even more surprised to hear that. May be I am odd, I fail to know. I was not even able to "build up" what I did. I suppose that was a dumb thing but I did not want to lie to him; not for a News paper. I had to tell him, in all truth, that I have had a lot of targets more hard to hit in my life. I agree they were not shooting back (which counts for *something*) but they were a H———of a lot smaller and moving faster.

"To what do you refer?" he asked. Lord, to talk so savory!

I told him when I was a boy in Pine Grove (that made him smile because I believe he thinks I look like a boy now, though nineteen) I had to supply my family with meat, my father being dead. (I did not reveal the truth about

Father as I do not believe Mother would be pleased to see it printed in a News paper.) Any way, with five brothers and one sister plus Mother that was some degree of meat to provide. So I had to learn to shoot All Mighty Straight All Mighty Soon or we would starve to death once Father was gone. Specially with the cock-eyed Ballard I had to use; it drifted like a d————boat!

I told him how I learned to shoot when I was ten. He was right surprised by that. I can still see the expression on his face as he said, *"Ten?"*

"Yes, sir," I answered. "I was small for my age and all the bullies in the country side had them selves a frolic on me. I was black and blue so much some people thought I had a unknown disease."

I went on to tell him that, for Xmas 1855, my Uncle Simon gave me his worn out Maynard for a present and I made use of it first rattle out of the box. I practiced regular and it was some hard doing as well as my chores because I had to keep firing the same lead balls again and again. I did so, how ever, and in not too much time I learned to down a small bird on the wing.

"That was when I gathered all the bullies of the area to watch me shoot," I said to Mr. Leslie. "After that, the black and blue spots started fading."

We talked a while more and, at last, he asked what I planned to do with my self after the war was over. I told him I am not certain save one thing—I will not let my self be tied down but will live a fast, exciting life of some kind, that is for dead sure!

March 9, 1866

Another day gone off where ever days go when they end. It is some hard to recall when life had some excitement. H———, it is some hard to believe it *ever* had excitement. Here I am at home, the farm, the d——— chores—when I do them—Mother at me all the time to do more, do more. I have got to get out of here soon, I *mean* it.

I am sitting by candle light, writing in my Record Book. It started good in the War but is some thing to make a man sleep now. I feel tied down with ropes. I want to get away but Mother tells me (enough times to bury me) there are things I must take care of, I am the man of the house, she needs me, the family needs me, may be if Father had not run off to California—words, words shoveled at me night and day.

I feel my life is wasted. I am stuck here on this d——— farm in this d——— community, I agreed to marry Mary Jane come Spring; I do not even know how that took place, I swear I never said the actual words, "Will you marry me?" but, some how, it has happened. I do not know where we would live; Mother no doubt expects on the farm. I would not want that but do not like the thought of trying to work in Pine Grove either. I mean I love Mary Jane and all but feel sick inside to see myself a married man and father growing old in this dead place. What else can I *do* though?

Well this: I am thinking of leaving Pine Grove to go out West. We hear each day, it seems, how much is going on out there. There are new chances and all manner of excitement. I have got to give it serious thought.

March 11, 1866

Just helped Ralph to bed. He is a good lad and I do not think will tell Mother what happened tonight at the *Black Horse Tavern*. It was good luck she was sleeping when we got home or I would be on the taking end of a "word hiding" right now I am certain; not to mention what poor Ralph would have to endure, being younger.

Ralph came to town to fetch me as Mother was angry at my absence all day and knew I was somewhere in Pine Grove drinking and playing cards as I do, so she sent Ralph to bring me back for a "good talking to" as she likes to call it—several hundred times a week.

I was playing Seven Up with several of the boys when Ralph came in. He walked behind my chair and said, "I have been looking for you, Clay."

"Good, you found me," I told him. "Now go home." I had been drinking my fair share of whiskey and, what with losing cards, was feeling not to happy with my lot.

"Mother says she wants you to come home," Ralph said.

"Tell Mother I will come home when I am ready," I responded. "Now get out of here."

The other boys piped in and said the same, for Ralph to clear out, he was ruining the card game.

Ralph is not easy to push, how ever, and kept on ragging me. Mother says the north field needs plowing out for rocks, you promised long ago to do it. Mother says the roof is leaking and one of the windows. Mother says we need meat and on and on.

Finally, he started pulling at my sleeve and riled me proper, so I gave him a shove and he slipped on a wet spot on the floor and landed on his elbow. I guess it hurt something bad for he began to cry even though he is sixteen. At which the boys at the table started jibing him for being a Cry Baby. I told them to "lay off" but they continued doing so.

At this, Ralph got all wrathy—he has the Halser temper like us boys all do—even though he is as skinny as a corn stalk. He jumped up and to the table where he slapped the cards from Bob Fisher's hand, who had been the worst one, pretending to be Ralph and crying like a infant.

This got Bob Fisher good and mad so he got up and, when Ralph had a swing at him that missed, he punched Ralph on the nose and made it bleed.

I could not let that happen to my brother so I dropped my cards and jumped up. Bob turned just in time to get it on the jaw from my fist and go flying back, falling over Ralph.

This made Hannibal Fisher mad to see *his* younger brother hit so he jumped up and hit me on the head. I returned the favor, punching his left eye so he fell across the table we were playing on and knocked the cards and money all to H———.

Every one got wrathy then and I was fighting four of them. Ralph was on my side, I guess, but little help. Every time he tried to give me aid, I got an extra blow or two because he hindered more than helped. I did the best I could, gave my share of hits and bruises, but there were too many what with Ralph no help and soon the two of us flew straight out through the bat wing doors and landed on the street. Ralph had bleeding from his mouth and nose. My head was ringing but I tried to make him stay outside so I could go back in and give a better account of myself, but Ralph insisted he would go along and we would "clean" the place out. I decided it was wiser to forget it, talked him out of it. He is a good lad but a bad joke as a fighter.

It is sad when a tavern dog fight (which I lose) is the best thing I have known in months!

March 14, 1866

I have just come back from Mary Jane's house and feel I have to say I am some low, fiendish being straight from H———!

That poor, sweet Angel of a girl deserves a better fellow than me. I love her dearly and admire her and she is ever kind to me—so why do I feel like a trap is just about to clamp shut on me? What is wrong with me? What is wrong with living here in Pine Grove for that matter? It is . . .

H———and brimstone, I can not even finish that remark! Pine Grove is the dullest, dumbest place on God's Green Earth! I have got to go out West! I need to make my mind up—*do* it! I am not afraid to go, that is not it. It is because I do not want to make Mary Jane unhappy. Not to mention Mother who keeps talking of the wedding all the time now and how Mary Jane and me will share the farm and if I want to I can build a separate house and we will all be together—GOD! The more I think of it, the worse I feel!

Does Mary Jane complain how ever? No, not her. She is so sweet and understanding. She is an *Angel* and I know she had other offers. Why does she want *me*? She is such a fine person yet wants no more than to be Mary Jane Halser, make a happy home for me, bear and raise my children and live her span by my side. What is wrong with that?

I have got to resolve my mind soon. I can not do this to her. Am I the master of my life or not? Do I want a life of excitement or not? *Am I going to go out West or not*?

If only some thing would make up my mind for me.

March 21, 1866

I can not believe it, looking back. It came so sudden and without a hint.

I was in the *Black Horse Tavern* playing Seven Up with several of the boys. Also in the game was Scoby Menlo, son of Truman Menlo, owner of The Pine Grove Mercantile and Shipping. I had not seen much of Scoby since the War but heard he was a hot head and a scoundrel; several of the local girls were got "in trouble" by him and their families paid off by his father.

I soon found out the truth of the report about his temper. I am not the coolest head around but he was worse. I had enjoyed a winning streak and built my pile to more than forty dollars. I was feeling good, thinking Mother would be pleased to see the money; I would claim it was an old loan paid to me or unexpected money from my Army pay.

Menlo was feeling other wise from me. His face got redder as we played. He slammed his cards on the table when he lost, and cursed, and drank his whiskey down like water.

Finally, it came. He glared at me and said, "I think some body at this table cheats at cards."

It did not take a college man to know he meant me since I was the only one who had a winning pile. I tried to ignore it though because I felt so good; I was some whiskey laden as well.

It did not end at that how ever. Shortly later, Menlo spoke again. "No one wins so much at cards unless they cheat," he said.

I could not pretend I did not understand those words and felt a low fire catching in my belly. "If you mean me," I said, "not only are you dead wrong but I want you to apologize for what you said."

He made a snorting noise like that was some joke I had spoken. The fire in my belly rose, I looked him in the eye and told him, "I believe you heard."

He stared at me, his cheeks a little redder now. I noted how his eyes reminded me of Beulah's (our pig) and considered telling him so.

"Yes, I heard," he said.

"Then do what I ask," I said.

"Apologize to you?" he answered with a sneering smile. "A card cheat?"

"You say that one more time," I told him, "and I will wipe the floor with you."

His face looked white now; I recall how fast the color left his cheeks. "Wrong," he said. His voice was shaking. *"I am going to wipe the floor with your blood."*

At that, he unbuttoned the front of his coat so I saw the handle of a six-shooter under his belt. He started reaching for it.

As quick as thought, I knew all talk was ended for there was no point in telling him I was not armed because he meant to kill me where I sat. That so, I leaped up fast and dived across the table at him, grabbing at his right hand and, by fortune, getting it before he could pull the gun free. He fell back on his chair, me on top of him, and we began to wrestle on the floor, he trying hard to get the gun so he might shoot me dead. I said nothing as we struggled for the will to murder was as clear as writing in his eyes.

I do not know how it happened but the gun went off like thunder; still inside his trousers and he screamed in pain. I jerked back and I saw a red stain at his stomach, spreading on his shirt so fast I knew the wound was fatal. Menlo tried to stand but had no strength to do it and he sat down, weak, his right hand over his stomach. He made a sound like he was going to cry. "You b——d," he said. "You killed me."

Moments after, he slumped back on the floor, cold dead.

I stared at him, heart beating so hard it hurt my chest. I had never killed any one face to face and it was terrible to know I had.

No one made a move. I can not guess how long we stood, silent as a cemetery, looking down at Menlo and the puddle of blood around his body.

Then Donald Bell (the bar tender) said some thing about the Constable. At his words, I felt an extra blow of fright inside my heart because I knew Scoby's father having so much power, he would see me hang for sure.

I turned and ran outside to jump on Kit. I rode home in a lather and told Mother what happened. She was no help to me, only saying, "I knew it. I knew it—" following me around the house while I gathered some clothes and my Record Book and flung them in a sack. I told her I had to take Kit but she did not seem to hear my words. She kept saying, "I knew it. I knew it—" like that would help me. I felt sick to hear her so uninterested in what happened and gave up trying to explain.

I did not want to wake my brothers or Nell so kissed their cheeks as they slept and turned away from them. I tried to kiss Mother but she pushed me off, looking angry though tears ran on her cheeks and saying those words again. I came close to tears my self at that. "Well, good bye then!" I shouted. "If that is all I mean to you!"

I wanted to stop at Mary Jane's house to explain what happened but, near Pine Grove, I could see an armed pursuit preparing and was forced to pull the horse around and gallop for the Wabash River.

I have stopped to rest Kit for a while and write this down by moonlight; I will be an easy target if they see me.

God have mercy on me, it is done now. I am off the

plank and have to swim alone. I wondered what will happen to me. Will they over take and capture me? Will I hang for Scoby's try to murder me? Where will I go now?

D———! The answer is so clear, I feel a fool for even wondering.

West!

July 12, 1866

I am in Morgan City, Kansas. I have only the dinero (which means money, I learned) to sleep tonight and buy some food but still feel *good*. This place is Alive! It may be just a dirty trail town but I never saw the like, so Pine Grove seems as far away as Russia!

There is one Main Street. On each side sit saloons, gambling houses, dance halls, cafes, theatres, stables, horse trade corrals, stores, hotels. Not one building looks like it will last a year, all give the feel of being built last week.

And the men and women! Every kind a person could imagine. Cow boys with their Ten Gallon hats, merchants in their white shirts, buffalo hunters in their bloody ones, gamblers in their fancy duds, the street seems never empty of them! Also women like I never saw in Pine Grove. Dance hall girls and actresses and "worse," not many high tones here though you see a few. But I like them all and like this town! It took me long to get here, had to sell my saddle, then sell Kit, work at different jobs but here I am and mean to stay.

I know that I am going to find a life of excitement now!

July 14, 1866

Did not have one shin plaster in my pocket so have taken work in a saloon, *The Red Dog*. I am clean up man and—may be—relief bar tender. It is not what you would call a "fancy" position but beggers can not be choosers—as Mother liked to say—and I am in the begger group all right until I earn some dollars.

The regular bar tender is a tall, thin fellow, Jim Clements by name. He gave me a dollar of his own to find a place to live so I am going to take up in a boarding house run by a Mrs. Kelly, not bad.

I start tonight.

July 16, 1866

I can not believe it! I have seen it happen after only four days here!

I was talking to Jim Clements while behind the bar; just brought out a tray of glasses from washing them. I told him how exciting Morgan City was compared to Pine Grove and he nodded at my words.

"Yes, that is how it is in cow towns," he observed. "All this H——— raising is common because these towns are made so cow boys can blow off steam at the end of cattle drives."

"I never saw so much going on," I said, "not since the War."

And that is G——d's truth! Cow boys crowd the streets by hundreds, some big drive having ended. They fill saloons and gambling houses and what Jim calls "Pleasure Domes"; that is a funny name for crib houses.

"These cow boys have a lot of 'pent up' action in their blood," Jim said. "They want to have them selves a blow out before riding out for more long months of hardship on the plains." He reminds me, by his words, of that reporter in the War, what was his name? I will look it up, hold on.

Frank Leslie.

Any way, we talked on and I told him that I like the West a lot but cow boy life did not appeal to me.

"No, a man has to have a taste for it," Jim admitted.

We went on some more about Morgan City. Since its money comes from "walking beef" as Jim referred to them, and from the men who "walk" them, no one aims to see the town "domesticated" as Jim called it. Even the peace officer is told by Main Street owners not to step on cow boy toes.

His name is Hickok called "Wild Bill." It seems I heard of him but I am not sure. Jim says he came out from Illinois and was the scout for a General named Custer. Jim says he (Hickok) has built him self a reputation as a man to be accounted for in any "show down." Still he does not make efforts to preserve the peace except for may be outright murder. Which occurs a good bit here, Jim said. "A word and a blow too often turns into a word and a shot—" was how he put it.

And, of all strange things, he said it and—in *seconds*— that very thing took place in front of me!

A big, tall, ugly cow boy started arguing with some man Jim said (later) worked in a livery stable down the street. I could hardly believe what they argued about. Like this—

"And I say cows is stupider—" The cow boy.

"And *I* say *horses*—" The livery stable man.

"Well, what do *you* know?" said the cow boy. "I *live* with the G——— d——— stupid critters and I say horses can read *books* compared to cows!"

"Well, I take *care* of horses night and day and nothing on this whole wide world is dumber than those G————d———— buzzard heads!" the other man replied.

I thought it all right and funny and was chuckling (so was Jim) when, in a flash, the two men started cursing at each other, then shoving, then the cow boy pulled his gun and shot the livery stable man right in the chest. There was a cloud of dark smoke but I saw the livery man knocked back on the floor. The cow boy fired his gun so close it set the dead man's shirt on fire.

I admit I stood behind the counter like a statue. I know what killing is. I shot those soldiers in the War and, though not intended, had to do with Menlo's death. But that was over *something*; Menlo called me a cheat at cards and made the threat of wiping the floor with my blood. This was over *nothing*, the brains of cows and horses for G————d's sake! Still the livery stable man is no less dead than if there had been reason to it.

Jim has seen this kind of thing before, it was clear: he filled a stein with beer and leaned across the counter to dump it on the dead man's shirt, then did the same again and put the fire out. All the time he did, the ugly cow boy was glaring around like daring any one to say him wrong.

Jim was first to speak. "You better clear out or you'll likely be arrested, charged, and hanged," he said.

The cow boy did not like to hear this; he looked like a red-faced savage, I believe the blood lust had got into him. "Don't tell me to clear out," he said.

"You better pull your freight," Jim told him. His tone was peaceful and did not seem distressed but there was a look in his black eyes that did not mean well for the cow boy, I believed.

The cow boy did not see the look. "I am warning you, you skinny, no account b————d," he said.

"Would you rather I sent for Hickok?" Jim asked.

"Sure, you yellow-livered son of a b———h," the cow boy said. "Get somebody else to help you."

Jim only looked at him. The cow boy had a mean smile; he was full of "forked lightning." "If you had the guts of a pig, you would meet me outside, man to man," he said.

"Is that what you want?" Jim asked.

"Come outside and I will meet you smoking," was the cow boy's answer.

Jim did not reply but reached beneath the counter and picked up a .41 revolver kept in case of someone trying robbery. The cow boy twitched, then stepped back, Jim slipping the gun beneath his waistband and, with no word, heading for the bat wing doors. The cow boy looked some stupid watching; I think he was amazed that Jim accepted him. Then he cursed, and spat, and said "All right!" and swaggered for the doors.

I hurried after them and got a spot outside the door.

It did not last long. Jim and the cow boy stood about nine feet apart on the street off the plank walk, looking at each other. The cow boy said, "You b———d! *Die!*" and grabbed down at his gun. Jim reached for his, the cow boy pulled first but was shaking, I believe. There was a roaring shot from his gun, then another from Jim's and, for moments, I could not see clearly for the cloud of powder smoke. Then I saw the cow boy on his knees, thrown back. He made a sound of pain and fell to his right side, cursing, and dying.

Jim incurred a powder burn across the left sleeve of his shirt. He rubbed it as he walked past me, saying, "Never leave the counter untended." I watched in awe as he returned to his spot and put the .41 away, started pouring whiskey for a customer. He is a chunk of steel and anyone who strikes him will strike fire, that is sure.

I could never be as brave as that.

August 9, 1866

It has been a slow few weeks. I am beginning to think excitement is not ahead of me after all. The job is boring at the *Red Dog*; there is nothing to it which I do not mind but it is dull. If Jim was not there I feel I would move on.

I like him though and believe I can account him as my friend. He does not say much of him self but I have learned he comes from Pennsylvania, fought in the Army of the Potomac, incurred a shrapnel wound at Gettysburg (has a scar on his back, he told me), never married, is a loner.

He is nice to me. I do not know how old he is (thirty-five may be) but he is like a sort of father. He has bought me dinner twice, gives me good advice on how to get by, and there was the day we took that ride together on rented horses I liked a lot.

Still, life in total is dull. I almost feel the way I did in Pine Grove. Morgan City is a wilder place but not that wild; that cow boy thing I saw is all there was. I am twice now to the Golden Temple but did not like the girls each time, they are too rough and out spoken for my taste, also one stole a dollar from me, I am sure. Jim says what can you expect from them?

Now what?

August 11, 1866

Finally some thing different in my life.

Last night was my night off so I went to the Fenway Circus which has stopped in Morgan City. I was much pleased by the chance as I have not done much of pleasure since arrival having to collect hard money after taking part in that game of Black Jack I was lucky to come out of with my teeth.

Any way, I was excited and went running down the street to town edge where the circus was set up. In dashing on the grounds, I bumped into a tall man in a black suit and, as luck would have it, it was no man else but Hickok, a tall fellow with drooping mustache, not bad looking—but what a temper! I thought, first, he was going to shoot me, then kick or hit me but he settled for a "dressing down" my ears have not heard since that Sergeant, training for the War. Hickok has more than guns in his arsenal, he has cuss words in such number and array as few men possess and I believe he used them all on me at once.

I did not like it, made me simmer some but, after all, he is the Marshal and had two guns. I had nothing. If there had been a weapon in my pocket, I might not—H———, what am I saying? I would have "called him out"? Not likely for his pale blue eyes are not too pleasant as they bore at you, so I let him have it out and took it all without a peep. As said, I did not like it, who does to have your skin flayed off by someone's tongue, still what could I do?

When he turned and stormed away from me, I took a breath; which was how I saw a woman nearby, smiling at me. I suppose she saw the whole event. I did not think what to do until she said. "Don't let him bother you. He has a hard job and his nerves are rubbed thin."

At that I smiled back and we introduced our selves. She said her name was Hazel Thatcher, she and her husband are performers with the circus, doing bare back riding. She was fine looking I saw, with a head of red hair very handsome. We had a chat, quite nice, then she held her hand out, said she hoped I would enjoy the show. She seemed to hold my hand a little longer than I would suppose but decided that was imagined.

Enjoy the show I did! Well worth each penny of the dollar and fifty cents though I have little dinero to spare. I confess I spent a good deal of the show looking for the arrival of Hazel Thatcher and, when she arrived, all the time she was performing staring at her in her costume which was less than eyes could believe! She is one grand figure of a woman, that is certain, every curve complete. Her costume, as noted, brief as law will bear and all the men went crazy over her, whistling and stamping; no louder than a certain party in the front row, initials C.H. She is graceful as a bird as well. She and her husband, Carl (mostly her, he seemed less lively), did leaps, and somersaults, and capers on the back of a galloping horse to much thunderlike clapping; my palms were red and stinging after they went off.

Following the performance, I sat a long time in the tent, not wanting to depart, savoring the show like some kind of feast I was digesting. In truth, I hoped (did not admit to my self at first) that Hazel Thatcher would appear so I might tell her I thought she was a fine acrobat and beautiful lady. She never did show up though and, at last, the workers told me to be on my way, they had to "strike" the tent.

I went outside, the grounds were dark and no one anywhere in sight. I strolled across them and, in walking around a wagon, of all things, came upon Hazel Thatcher and her husband. I saw then why his movements were not lively in the show—he was drunk, she leading him, one arm around him; I could smell his breath from feet away.

I felt embarrassed to come on them in that way but Hazel Thatcher seemed pleased to see me, asked right off if I would help her take her husband to their wagon.

I said I would be glad to, grabbed his left arm while she held his right. His legs were made of rubber it appeared and various times he almost fell. He kept muttering, "This is not necessary—" in a kind of dignified voice; but it *was* necessary since he would have toppled if we had not held him up.

"This is very nice of you," Hazel Thatcher told me as we led her husband.

I still was embarrassed. "I am very glad to help," I said.

"This is not necessary," said her husband.

"He has been feeling pain from a broken leg which never healed right," Hazel Thatcher told me. "That is why he drinks a little more than good for him."

I nodded.

"This is not necessary," said her husband as he almost fell again.

It took a while to get him up the steps of their wagon and I wondered how the man was able to perform in such a state until Hazel Thatcher told me he had started drinking heavily after the show was ended and I recalled that I had sat inside the tent long enough for a minister to paint his nose.

At last we got Carl Thatcher on his bunk and he went off to sleep, was snoring in a second. Hazel Thatcher thanked me and I said that I was pleased to be of service, started to back out of the wagon when she asked me to help her light the hanging lantern which I did.

I confess to being raptured by the sight of oil light on her face. Her skin is very white and clear, eyes green as jade with long red hair falling on her shoulders. I have never seen a woman so beautiful in all respects. I stared at her, she smiled and touched my cheek. "You are very handsome," she said.

I had no reply, I felt a stupid boy again. Hazel Thatcher smiled (what teeth!) and asked if I would care to have a cup of coffee with her. Well, to tell the world I would have said "yes" if she asked me if I cared to have a cup of poison with her. "Yes, thank you," I replied.

She told me sit down at the table (very small) and I did while she removed her cloak. She looked around then, I had made a gasping noise because she still had on her costume and the sight of her white shoulders and bosom tops caused me to catch my breath. She smiled at me, leaned over and kissed my cheek (she did!). "You are very sweet and young," she said, those were actual words. I remember shivering though far from cold.

I did not hear her words too well as she prepared the coffee, I was too entranced in looking at her, I mean close up she was so remarkable to look at, she made me feel (the only word that catches it) *hungry*. I did not hear the snoring of her husband which was loud, I was so much fascinated by her looks, the truth is I have never seen the like, not ever.

What did she say? (I said nothing, a staring lump.) I think she said her husband once was a star performer in a Europe circus, drank occasional but not much. His wife was killed in an accident during a performance and he had lost interest in life, began to drink for real because he thought her death his fault. The circus let him go, then another, and he ended up in the United States where he took a job with another circus, his reputation as a bare back rider ahead of his reputation as a drinker, in this country any way.

He kept on drinking and that circus let him go and the next one hiring him was Fenway Circus where he met Hazel Moore (her previous name). They married and, for some while, he seemed better, taught her all the bare back tricks and things looked bright. But he started "hitting at" the whiskey vat again and now is hanging by a thread since he managed to be close to sober for performances and Fenway is a small circus any way. (I guess I did hear almost every word in spite of staring!) So it was not his leg he drank for, I learned.

Hazel Thatcher told me all these things without a single cruel word and I do admire her for that, not tearing at her husband who could not defend himself but being thoughtful of the reason for his weakness.

I would not say more if I was telling this to some one but this is my own Record Book and no one will ever read it being my private concern. So I continue and reveal that Hazel Thatcher (I feel dumb to call her full name as things are) asked me if I cared to have a "jot" of whiskey in my coffee which I said I would not mind. We talked and talked (I do not remember much of that, mostly she asked questions, where I came from, what I had done, what I planned to do) and it was not too long before she added coffee to our whiskey, then forgot the coffee all together.

By then, my head was numb, the wagon seemed to move some under me and, in the lantern light, I thought Hazel the most matchless woman in the world and told her so.

I remember she was holding both my hands on the table, tears in her eyes. "Oh, Clay, it is so hard to be without a man because my husband only cares for drink," she said.

"I'm sorry, I am sorry," I told her.

She drew my hands closer to her self, it was a small table so I could lean further. "I am so lonely all the time," she said, tears rolling down her cheeks.

"Oh, I am sorry," I said. I wanted to say I would take care of her but even roostered as I was, I knew my self to be a clean up man in a saloon and no more.

"Thank you, my dear," Hazel said. She lifted my right hand to her lips and kissed it. Then she kissed my left hand. Then she leaned forward at me. "Please," she whispered.

What I was feeling at that time! I bent forward and her warm, red lips pressed to mine, I tasted her breath, then again and harder; I have never had a girl (woman) kiss like that.

I jumped a little as she pulled back, pushing up the table

where I saw she hooked it up, then, with a sigh, fell against me and held my arms and we were kissing fierce, my arms around her and her lips came apart and—Oh, I must pause!

All right, to the finish. (I will burn this Record Book before a human soul shall read it!) We kissed and kissed and Hazel drew down her costume so her b——s were bared, all white and heavy and, before I knew it, we were on her bunk, both n——d as our days of birth. G——— in Heaven, she is such a gorgeous female and her body is—well, private Record Book or not, I can not put it down what happened. All I will say is I lost my head and every thing and did not even care her husband was asleep and snoring only several feet away from us, the wagon rattling, rocking as we—did not even *care*!

I remained with her until the middle of the night and four times "claimed" her; or did she claim me? She is some fiery person, those two girls in The Golden Temple seem like dull goats. To be honest, it was the first time I could think of Mary Jane and not feel bad because I know she could not give me any thing what Hazel did because she is a different sort; I will not go into fine points but I *will* say Hazel—

(*Here I must omit three paragraphs which, in their vivid clinical description, are unsuitable for the general reader. F.L.*)

I returned to my room at nearly five o'clock and slept like two men in a grave yard. Now it is past one o'clock, afternoon, I have to go to work soon but must write down what I remember.

I suppose she is much older than me but I love her. I love Hazel Thatcher and can not wait 'til I see her again!

Later: same day. It appears that many things can happen at the same time.

When I went to work tonight it was to find the *Red Dog* burning. Jim was across the street, watching it so I walked over to him to ask what happened.

Much to my surprise, he told me he had set the fire him self! He said the owner of the *Red Dog* (Mr. German, I have not met) played poker with him last night and lost a pile but did not care to pay it honest there fore hired some trail bum to bushwhack Jim. The trail bum was stupid, missed, and Jim "took care" of him, then went to the saloon, threw down oil lamps, setting them ablaze. He said he would shoot Mr. German like the cur he is (if he could find him) but it would likely bring on wrath from Hickok who is paid by men like Mr. German so he set the saloon on fire instead.

I asked Jim what he meant to do now for employment. He replied he planned "returning to an earlier pursuit"— stage coach driving, said if I am half the rifle shot as I have told him (clearly he does not believe it) I could hire out as guard.

I might do it but for Hazel. I would rather have a job so I can stay nearby her. I admit the idea does appeal to me— being guard, I mean. But Hazel first and fore most.

August 12, 1866

What did I write the other day? Let me look. That many things can happen at the same time. What I meant—a person's life goes on and on the same and then, no warning, every thing is changed.

Now another. I went to the circus to see Hazel, took a while to get her to my self because of Carl, he was not very drunk tonight. I told her about the coach guard job and said I did not mean to take it for I wanted to be with her, asked her to find out if there was some job I could do with the circus so we could be together when ever Carl is drunk or may be she might think to leave him some time if it worked out, her and me.

We were out behind the tents and Hazel was so quiet I wondered what was wrong and asked. I heard a sound of her swallowing in her throat, that is how still it was. Finally, she drew a long breath in and said, "I can not let you do that, Clay."

I failed to know what she was meaning.

"Don't you see how painful it would be for me to have you around when I am married to Carl?" she said.

I began to say again about her may be leaving Carl but she pressed hard against me, hugging me. "Oh, no, my darling," she declared. "You have your own life to lead."

I tried to answer but she went on. "You are much too bright to waste your life being a circus roust about," she said.

"I don't mind," I told her. "It will be—"

"No, no." She shook her head, then kissed me on the lips. "I can not permit it. You have a full life ahead of you."

"But, Hazel—"

"Please, my darling, no," she said.

"But I love you," I told her. "I want to be—"

"And *I* love *you*," she said, "with all my heart, Clay. That is why I can not do this to you."

"But—"

"For another thing, I am too old for you," she said.

"No," I said, protesting. "We could—"

She stopped my talking with another kiss. "No, no," she said. "I could not bear to see you looking at me as the months went by and you began to see me as I am."

"As you am?—you *are*?!" I asked; I was so worked up by then I could not speak a proper English.

She held me tight, I held her tight. "Just remember me as one who crossed your path," she said.

"But, Hazel!"

"No, no," she said, and kissed me once more. "Go quickly," she told me. "And do not look back."

She was the one who went quickly, with a sob, into the night. I stood there feeling sick. I wanted to run after her and make her change her mind but I was not able to move, I felt my legs were anvils.

I do not understand. She says she loves me and I love her; isn't that enough? There is an aching in my chest; I wonder if hearts really break. Oh, G———, I feel so miserable! Is poor Hazel in her wagon now, crying? Does her heart ache too? She is doing this for Carl, I know it. She is sacrificing her self for him, so bravely.

I will never be the same again.

September 14, 1866

My hand is shaking as I write this, still weak from what happened but I want to put it down while still fresh in mind.

What did I say a few months back?—several times while writing in this Record Book, it seems. That I wanted excitement? Well, I have got it and double.

In truth, I never thought the like would happen. My writing in this book has been enough to put a reader (if there was one) to dead sleep. First it was exciting to ride the driver's seat with Jim, armed with pistols and my new Winchester (I am glad I got it rather than carrying a shotgun as suggested by some including Jim), but soon the jolting on my backside and eating dust became a pain.

Also nothing happened, I mean *nothing*. We picked up passengers and shipment, carried them from place to place, stayed overnight at road ranches, or long enough for meals, changed teams at relay stations, traveled thirty-five miles about each eight hours and that was it. The closest to excitement came that time I thought a road agent was stopping us and got ready for action to find out it was a cow boy whose horse had stepped into a chuck hole and broke its leg so had to be shot leaving him afoot. That was my excitement since I started in August as noted in this Record Book.

Again, as in the *Red Dog*, if it was not for Jim I would have quit. But I have written endless of his skill and han-

dling as much as eight "ribbons" at once, and skill at cracking the whip so close he can remove a small fly from a
horse's ear never touching the ear. Also have written endless of our talks, and how we know each other well, and
are good friends so no more of that.

We were talking when it happened, coming down a
grade from Black Rock Pass about seven miles from Fort
Dodge. As I recollect, we were discussing Hazel. I was
telling Jim I had recovered from the pain but still feel
Hazel is a fine woman who is sacrificing herself for her
husband.

"Yes, I know the kind," Jim said and I could tell he
understood.

I noticed then that he was glancing around. "What are
you looking for?" I asked.

"Not for. At," he answered.

I looked around but did not see a thing. "At what?" I
asked.

"Twenty or so Cheyenne," he answered.

I felt my heart bump at these words and looked around
more carefully. I saw some movement in the distance;
horses and riders it appeared.

"Did they just show up?" I asked.

"No," Jim told me. "They have been trailing us all
afternoon."

I was amazed to hear that, which makes it certain I will
never be a stage driver or guard of any value. I felt a fool
to hear it but pretended not by asking Jim why the Red
Skins did not rush us if they wanted to—they had us beaten
in numbers.

"They will probably make their move before we get
much closer to the Fort," he said.

His words came true before another fifteen minutes
had gone by. I felt myself shiver as the Red Skins started

riding in at us, galloping their ponies. I raised my rifle but Jim said wait 'til they were closer which I did.

Soon the Cheyennes—twenty-one—were galloping across our path and moving in a line like a traveling circle which, in time, they started to draw in like a noose around our coach. I raised my Winchester again but Jim said not to waste my powder as the "breech clouts" were still not close enough to us. I thought they were; they were no further than those Secesh soldiers I was able to hit during the War, still it is true these targets were moving more.

"Pass down mail sacks to the people and tell them to barricade them selves," Jim told me. He cracked his whip and the team of six (I wished there were eight) leaned forward in their traces, moving faster.

I put my rifle in its boot and started handing down the mail sacks to the four passengers, telling them—as Jim told me—to look to what ever weapons they might have as it was likely they were going to have to defend them selves.

Before forgetting, I must put down that, though this was the first time I have been in mortal danger since the War (the event with Menlo happened too fast for me to feel anything), the emotion I had in those long ago days came rushing back full force—no fear what ever; I felt keyed up and anxious for the battle to commence. It is only now I see how dangerous it was and find it strange I did not feel it as such.

Then I was all pitched up for the fighting. I remember shouting at those Red Skins as they rode in their moving circle, getting closer and closer. "Come on, you b——s!" I yelled. "We are ready for you!"

Finally, they did—with a series of blood-curdling "whoops"—and the battle was on! "*Now* start firing!" Jim shouted. "And show me how good you are!"

It was a fierce battle because those Red Skins do know how to ride and they can duck while riding which makes shooting at them not an easy task. They also shoot not bad for savages; I wonder where they got their rifles and who taught them.

Jim drove the coach as fast as the team could pull it, cracking his whip across their heads so that it sounded like the firing of a pistol. The coach creaked awful as we sped; there was a woman passenger inside who screamed in fright. The rocking and skidding did not help my shooting either, nor the shooting of the passengers; I do not believe their firing hit a single Red Skin.

So it was up to me and I must say I did all right! I kept on firing at those Cheyennes and that Winchester is some good weapon! No matter how those Indians galloped or dipped or ducked, I kept on hitting them one by one; I think it all took place in only minutes too, though noisy minutes what with the thunder of the hooves, and wheels creaking, and the woman screaming, shots and howling Savages, it was a scene straight out of H————! Yet even so I gave seven of the Red Skins one-way tickets to their Happy Hunting Ground, finally—I believe—impressing Jim with what I told him I could do but he had never seen me do. For he yelled and whooped him self and even laughed once which I hardly ever hear him do.

The last Cheyenne I got appeared to have a charmed life for he kept on riding at us with a lance to throw. I kept missing and the woman in the coach was screaming out of her mind before the Red Skin was only ten feet or so away and I was able to shoot him off his horse. He went tumbling and another Cheyenne pony trampled on him. After that, the Indians slowed down and gave up; may be he was Chief or some thing though he had no Head Dress on.

Speaking of charmed lives, mine held up; well, almost. In the War, despite the Minnie balls around me and many explosions, I was not touched. This time, with only twenty-one Red Skins, I took an arrow in my right leg underneath the knee which is odd because I never felt it 'til the Cheyenne left us be. By then, how ever, I had lost some lot of blood (my boot was full of it) and things began to swim around me so I almost toppled from the seat to my death, I am sure, under heavy wheels. Jim grabbed me by the belt and held me from falling while he drove. That is one I owe him as he no doubt saved my life.

He also may have saved my leg (the Doctor said) for, when the Indians had moved off, Jim stopped the coach to bind my leg and "cauterize" the place the arrow went in. He broke off the back part of the arrow, pulled it out, then opened a bullet and poured its powder into the wound. It is lucky for me I was almost "out" any way for if I knew what he was going to do I would have given him a fight. Because when he set fire to the powder, I had a pain as I have never known in all my life, and screamed just like that woman (I am not ashamed to tell it), and passed out cold. Jim put me in the coach, my leg wrapped with his bandanna and drove me to the Fort where now I am.

I am writing this from bed. The Doctor says my wound is not too serious but I will be "out of action" for a while.

September 19, 1866

Jim came in to see me, brought some candy and a news paper to read. There is a little story in it of the "Indian Attack On Stage" and how a "Mr. Cley Halsem" shot some of the "pursuing Savages" to help "save the day." Give credit to that Cley Halsem, he is one fine shot, who ever he is.

Jim said the company has replaced me as guard on his run which does not please me but he said he talked them into giving me a post as helper at the Blue Creek Way Station. The work will not be hard, they told Jim, odds and ends, and when I have recovered from my leg wound I will get back my job as guard, I hope with Jim again; he says he will request it.

I start at Blue Creek next Monday so guess all is well for now.

Little did Clay know. F.L.

October 8, 1866

Another rotten day. Leg hurts like H————. Zandt knows I have been hit there by an arrow but does not seem to care a D————, has me on my feet constant, day and night. He woke me up last night after sleeping only two hours, said a coal oil lamp exploded in the Station house, wanted me to clean the mess. I tried to tell him I was tired having worked since six o'clock yesterday morning but he shoved me hard and said, "I vant it *now*, vare stayin?—(what ever that means) so had to rise to do it. He is a real b————d for certain.

October 10, 1866

I swear he did it on purpose, knocked that deck of cards all over the floor just to make me pick them up.

October 11, 1866

He yelled at me in front of all those people because some one had knocked the soap on the dirt instead of putting it on the dish outside as if it was my fault. I know he did it to "show off" in front of two lady passengers to make them think how big a man he is. I hate him.

October 13, 1866

I think my leg is getting worse. I limp more now than when I came and it aches some thing fierce, some times bleeds a little, cracking open. You think that means a d————to Zandt? "Vat are you, *cripple*, Halzer? *Move!*"—and shoves me on the back.

Lying here, never more "washed out" in all my days. A spider crawling on my leg, I am too tired to brush it off.

October 14, 1866

Heard today, from a passing driver, that, before I came, there was a Mexican named Juan who was helper. Zandt made his life so miserable he took off one night without pay or belongings, never has been seen again. I can understand. I would leave my self but my leg is hurting terrible and I could not walk. I would not steal a horse, that is too dangerous out here, better kill a man than steal a horse. I do not have enough dinero to buy a stage ride out allowing Zandt would let me go. So what can I do?

He rags me some thing awful. Mother was a angel compared. He limps like I do but worse when I am around with people watching. If it was not for my d————d wound I would go at him full tilt. The way it is, I will be lucky if he does not ruin my leg for life.

I can not go regardless but if I could I do not think I would; that would be running from him and I will never do that from a bully.

Oh, the H————.

October 16, 1866

Too tired to write. Zandt has been at me all day. I have been working like a mule since five o'clock this morning, now is past eleven at night. I must *sleep*.

October 17, 1866

Some thing new, worse. I am ready to do some thing *hard* in return, I swear I am. Leg aches like a tooth ache but I can not pull it out like a tooth can be.

Today, when the afternoon run from Leonardville came by, Zandt grabbed me in front of every body and wrestled me, threw me on the floor. I landed on my left elbow which is swelling and now also aches. D——— him any way! I wish I could pump lead into him like I did those Cheyennes! He is too big to fist fight. G——— d———, he is a son of a b———!

October 19, 1866

I do not know how much more I can stand. I feel close to murder. Zandt is the worst bully I have known in my life. Menlo was a comrade compared. Zandt does all these things:

1. He over works me.
2. He under feeds me.
3. He makes fun of my limp.
4. If I feel sick or weak, he mocks me.
5. He shoves me around and hits me on the back a lot.

6. He rags me in front of passengers and wrestles me, knowing I am too weak to resist.

7. How to say this? There is some thing "odd" about him. When he is not ragging me or bullying and has a few drinks "under his belt," he puts an arm around me, hugs me like a girl and says I am "a good-looking young fellow." Once touched me in a certain spot.

I made it certain I will not stand for this. That only makes him wrathy and he throws me around some more. Today he flung me down so hard my leg wound cracked again and blood leaked out.

I am getting close to some thing and do not like what I feel close to. I will not run off no matter what, like some cur with my tail between my legs. Yet I am not strong enough to give him back his own "brand" of medicine.

Some thing has to break.

What Clay could not have known, which I have now established, is that Emil Zandt had been an officer in the Prussian Army and been dishonorably discharged for attempting "liaisons" with certain of the more youthful men in his command.

Additionally, it should be noted (since Clay does not), that Zandt was a giant of a man, some six feet four or five inches in height and weighing in excess of two hundred and fifty pounds. As stated earlier, Clay Halser was no taller than five feet ten and, at the time, because of his hampered convalescence, weighed at least a hundred pounds less than the hulking German.

Lastly, it is noteworthy to observe that Clay rejected the notion of retreat; typical of him. In retrospect, it seems that, surely, there was some way he might have backed off from the situation. As it turned out, although his conse-

quent action is understandable (if not justifiable), it forged
yet one more heavy link in the chain which was, one day,
to hold him fast in its tangled length.

October 23, 1866

It is ended and I am not sorry. If I fry in H———— for it, I
will not say that I am sorry for what happened.

It started as the night stage from Stockdale came in so
the passengers could warm them selves and eat some food.
It was bitter cold with whistling wind and people came in
quickly, stood before the crackling fire and warmed their
bodies while I helped prepare the food and drink.

As always, Zandt began to "put on" for the passengers,
the women mostly (there were two), showing them how he
could rag me as he chose. He had been drinking all the
day and put his hand on me once, which I knocked off so
his face got red with anger; he was in a black mood.

He was never worse, pretending to the passengers he
was a rogue and full of fun instead of the b————d he was.
He kept punching my arm and slapping me on the back,
knocking me off balance, being "jovial" as he said.

When every one was eating, he began to wrestle me
and hold me tight to make me look the fool I was, so
helpless in his arms. His face was red and white in patches,
and his whiskey breath steamed on my face, and made
me sick.

I got so mad I twisted hard and was able to break free
which surprised him, I believe; he did not realize I was
some stronger in spite of little sleep and food.

"Zo," he said. "You are ze little *worm* tonight." He
laughed to show the people he was playing at a game but
I knew he was not playing, not from the look in his red
pig eyes, like Menlo. I had never noticed 'til then.

He moved at me and I backed off. *"Zo,"* he said. "You think you can outvit me."

He reached for me but I slapped his big, fat hand aside. This made him frothy that I gave him back so much because it hurt his pride; he did not like to have me giving back what he liked "dishing out." He kept moving at me and I told him leave off, I did not want any more.

That made him crazy, I believe, to hear me talking up in front of all those people, mostly the women. He lunged at me and I dodged side ways, knowing if he caught me he would do his best to hurt me and could squeeze so hard with me in his arms he might crack my ribs.

"Oh, leave the young man alone," one of the women said.

That got all Zandt's bristles up for sure. He did not pretend he was all jovial now. He looked as mean as he was feeling and that was much. He began to stalk me around the room, ignoring any one who said to stop.

He jumped at me, I side stepped but he stuck his leg out so I tripped. I fell down on my right leg and the pain was like the arrow sticking in there when it happened and the powder being burned there. I cried out and he laughed at that. "Vot's the matter, little boy, *hurt* your self?" he said.

I pushed to my feet and he stepped in, started pushing me around, jostling me, and slapping me across the shoulders, "straight arming" my chest, and knocking me backward 'til I hit the wall. By then the pain in my leg was crazing me and, as he stopped in front of me, I made a fist of my right hand and hit him in the face as hard as I could.

That broke the dam. Jumping at me with a curse, he started squeezing me so hard I could not breathe and knew I would pass out. There was nothing I could do, so had to jerk my knee up at his ———— and hit him there as hard as possible. He cried out, backing off, and clutching there

in spite of ladies watching. "Zon of a b———," he muttered, "zon of a b———."

He leaped at me but I jumped to the side and he fell on
his knees, slipping. The pain of that was too much for him
and he bellowed like a bull. Staggering up, he turned away
from me, at first to my surprise, then cold dismay as I saw
where he headed—to the counter where he kept his horse
whip underneath.

Snatching it up, he shook it loose, glaring at me with his
pig eyes, breathing heavy.

"Put that away," the stage coach driver said. "There are
passengers here."

Zandt gave no attention to him, his eyes intent on me. I
started easing toward the door but he was shrewd and cut
me off, a mad smile on his lips. *"Zo,"* he said. "You want
to *run?"*

I knew he had me and I wondered what to do. I can not
say I was afraid but knew that he could cut me to shreds
with that whip of his.

The stage coach driver moved at him. "Zandt, *stop* this,"
he declared.

The next instant, Zandt had brushed him aside like a
child and the driver was flying across the room to almost
crash into the fire place.

"Now, *girl man*," Zandt said, and began to flick the whip
as he stalked me like his prey.

I did not say one word, knowing it was useless. I kept
my eyes on him as he came nearer.

"Now I crack your crust, you little scum," he said.

The whip end shot out, snapping like a pistol shot near
my face.

"Stop it!" cried a woman which made Zandt the mad-
der; now his face was closer to purple than red.

He started cracking out the whip end harder, snapping

it closer and closer. I tried to grab it but it only tore a chunk of skin from my palm. The passengers were all up from the table now and backed against the wall, several calling for Zandt to stop which he would never do at that point.

Suddenly, the whip end lashed across my neck and I felt fiery pain.

"*Got* you, girl man!" Zandt cried; I never saw a look so wild, not even on the faces of those Cheyennes.

The whip end snapped again and tore a piece of shirt arm off me and the skin beneath. Fury made *me* crazy now and I began to hurl things at him, dishes, candle holders, fire irons, stools, any thing I could lay hands on. Some hit him, making him more angry yet. The whip cracked faster and faster, tearing at my clothes and body so it felt like slashes of a red hot poker on my flesh.

When the whip end caught me on the cheek and gouged out skin, I lost my mind, it made my right eye hurt so much. With a cry that sounded like some wounded animal, I raced across the room and dived across the counter. Scrambling down some feet, I reared up quick and grabbed the shotgun off the wall. Zandt thought me still where I had disappeared behind the counter and he cracked his whip there, ripping out a piece of log wall.

He was turning to me when I fired both barrels to hit him straight on in the chest and stomach so he fell back with the cry of some dumb brute and, I believe, was dead before he landed.

In the deathly stillness following, all the people stared at me. I did not say a word. I felt a little sick but I was glad that Zandt was dead and still am glad. I put down the empty shotgun and poured my self a drink of whiskey though my hand was shaking so much I could hardly manage.

I regret the need to kill another man who did not have a weapon—unless one thinks the whip such. But there was nothing else I could do, I had to save my self, he would have blinded and crippled me. Every one in that room said I had a right to defend my self so I do not feel worried over that. I will surrender myself to the hands of the law and feel certain of a fair trial under the conditions of what truly happened.

November 19, 1866

I have not been "up" to writing several days. It is not my Record Book was taken; I have kept it hidden under my shirt. No, the reason I have not been able to write is I am so shocked by what has happened all I did was sit and stare in dumb amazement at the wall.

I am to hang.

Hang.

I can not believe it even now that I have put the words in my own hand. I sat in my cell day by day waiting for the judge to come so my trial would take place. No one (certainly not me) believed I was in danger. Even the Marshal—a man named Dolan who is kind to me—believed the trial would be short and in my favor.

No.

The trial was short all right but not in my favor. I had no defense, it turned out. Not one of the passengers or driver or guard who saw what happened at Blue Creek that night were any where near, so all the judge could see was that I shot a "Un-armed" man with a double shotgun charge; so I was guilty—murder—now to hang.

Hang!

I am still in a daze about it. My head feels numb, my stomach seems empty like hollowed out. In less than two weeks, the hang man will be here and I will drop, my neck will—J——s! It is not fair! I did not murder Zandt! If I had not shot him, he would have whipped me clear to death! That is no guess but certain! I am not the kind to kill a man in cold blood! I am *not*! I shot those soldiers in a War, I made Menlo shoot him self by accident (in self defense) and that is *it*! No murders. None. I was defending my self. *Defending* my self!

Oh, to H——— with it! To G——— d——— H———with every body!

November 21, 1866

I have got a cell mate, a Texan near my age. His name is Henry Blackstone and he told me he has been "in jug" a lot of times. He was found guilty of robbing a store and murdering the clerk which he claims he did not do for the good reason he robs only stage coaches.

He also seems entertained by my anger. He says he has no bad feelings against me but finds my "distress an amusement" because I believed I would get a fair trial.

I was reading about the trial in the *Riverville Clarion* today, raging at the lies and half lies in the story. To read it, you would think I was a heartless brute who decided it would be a good joke to kill Zandt. Finally, I flung the paper off from me but Blackstone only smiled, lying on his bunk. "Do you really expect to find the truth in a news paper?" he asked. He shook his head. "You never will, old fellow." That is what he calls me.

He seems so calm and easy going about every thing, it is hard to believe he is, also, sentenced to hang.

November 24, 1866

I talked with Henry today; he says to write in my Record Book to say Hello. To *who*?

Any way, he says we have no chance of beating the hang man's noose so might as well "accept our fate." He says that young men like us never have a chance because the world is against us. I never thought of it before but, when you think about what brought me here, it was not justice, that is sure. Coming west because of Menlo is another thing. Henry says it was a "bad break" as in a game of pool, nothing more. We are the kind of people who get bad breaks all the time, he says; that is just the way it is and nothing we can do about it. Even G——— does not care what happens to people like us.

I hate to believe that but what else can I do? It seems to make sense when you think what has happened to me. The only thing left is to die "without a murmur" Henry says; show the dirty b——s we will not crack in front of them.

I think I would rather try to break free on the day they mean to hang me, force them to shoot me down so death comes fast.

November 25, 1866

No, I will not die without a murmur! I am going to scream out curses at the b——s! I will tell them what I think about their G——— d——— d justice!

November 26, 1866

Henry and I talked today of cutting our arms some how and cheating the hang man and "justice" but decided it was better to let them see how brave men can die.

November 27, 1866

I have decided not to make a sound, just stand there glaring at every body, showing how low I think they are.

But there is the hood. How can I glare at them . . . ?

November 28, 1866

I intend to *scream* at them, the stinking b———s!

November 29, 1866

One of the prisoners is sick (a Mexican) and there is fear that he has come down with small pox. There is a panic rushing through the town; we see them in the street talking of it. A small pox "epidemic" (Henry's word) could wipe out the town. It would not be the first time such has happened.

I hope it does. That is what *I* would call justice. Let the whole d——— town go with us!

November 30, 1866

I could not believe my ears when Henry offered to take care of the sick prisoner. He told the Deputy his father was a doctor so he knows what to do. The Deputy has gone to ask Dolan if it is all right. The Mexican's cell is a mess, smells awful.

I suppose Henry feels if he is going to "swing" any way, he might as well die by small pox as by "strangulation" (another of his words). I think I would prefer the rope as faster.

"I thought you said your father was a cow boy," I asked him a few seconds ago.

"I did," he answered, smiling.

He is very odd.

Later. Still feel dizzy from the speed of it. I feel I may wake up and find it is a dream. I have had dreams like it every night lately which is why it seems unreal.

It went like this. The Deputy came back to say that Dolan had accepted Henry's "generous" offer. Henry said (to me) he knew they would ahead of time because it would give them some chance to "isolate" the disease, as he said, where if they had to go near the Mexican them selves or leave his cell uncleaned, the small pox might spread.

The Deputy took out his gun and pointed it at Henry as he unlocked the cell door. Henry smiled and held his hands up in the air, saying, "I am not going to try to escape."

"I know you are not," the Deputy replied.

He took Henry to the Mexican's cell and unlocked the door. Henry went inside the cell and leaned across the Mexican who was lying on the bottom bunk. The Deputy remained in the door way of the cell, gun in hand.

Henry put his palm on the Mexican's brow and felt the

skin. He made a humming noise and shook his head. He put his fingers on the man's neck and prodded. Then he whistled softly and looked around at the Deputy. "Yes, it is small pox all right," he said.

The Deputy got a look of dread and took a step back, lowering his gun.

The next instant, he was knocked back by the wooden slopbucket which Henry had, some how, got hold of and hurled through the door way. The Deputy cried out in surprise (and, I must add, disgust) and lost his balance, falling against the cell door on the other side.

Before he could recover, Henry leaped across the space between them like a panther; I have never seen a person move so fast who never seemed to want to move at all. Snatching up the fallen gun, he laid the barrel sharp across the Deputy's skull and knocked him senseless.

He took one breath, then grabbed the Deputy's keys, and ran back to our cell. He unlocked the door and flung it open, grinning at me. "Time to make tracks, old fellow," he said.

I admit to being so surprised by what happened I could not move, staring at Henry.

"You want to *hang*?" he asked.

He did not have to say another word. Pulling on my boots, I shoved the Record Book under my shirt and left the cell. We ran to the Marshal's office where, as luck would have it (for Dolan, Henry said), he was out at lunch. We each took a rifle, Henry a Sharps, me a Winchester, I pushed a Colt under the waist of my trousers and we went outside, Henry wearing the Deputy's jacket, me a blanket wrapped around me for the cold.

There was a horse tied up down the walk and we took it, riding double out of town. I find it a joke now that I hesitated about stealing it, thinking it is bad to steal a horse out here. Then I realized I was supposed to "dangle" any way and could not be hanged twice, so rode the horse without another thought. By fortune (and the cold) no one much was outside in the street and we rode from town without a hitch, trotting the horse first, then galloping when we were out of town.

It was a strange feeling to be free and a wanted man at the same time. Still, the joy of having clean air (even icy cold) in my lungs and being in the open weighed over the bad. I had to laugh and seeing how my breath steamed like a kettle made me laugh harder. Henry asked me what was funny and I told him after all the trouble he went to getting us out, we might both die of small pox any way.

"He does not have small pox," Henry told me.

"But I heard you say . . ."

"That was to trick the Deputy and turn him off from what I was planning," Henry said.

"Then what *does* the Mexican have?" I asked.

"Chicken pox," Henry answered. "People always get the two mixed up."

"How do you know that?" I asked.

Henry smiled and told me that he rode once with a doctor who told him all about it. "Before I robbed him, of course," Henry said.

May be it was not that funny but it struck me so and made me laugh until tears ran down my face.

Then I asked him how he could know it was chicken pox all the way from our cell. He said he couldn't. "That is the risk I took to get a chance at breaking out," he told me.

That sobered me so I asked him what if it *had* been small pox.

Henry smiled. "Old fellow, that is the game we play," he said. "You never know what card you will draw."

I write this in a hut we came across, thank G——— because it is so cold outside. Henry is asleep. (He smiles in his sleep.) He says we might as well team up a while as both of us are "fugitives" from the sentence of hanging. I can not see a better idea. He saved my life so I owe him some thing in return.

Besides, he seems a steady person all in all.

One of the more ironic statements in the journal. F.L.

So began a new phase in the life of Clay Halser, his period of adventuring with Henry Blackstone.

Blackstone was a strange, young man, a unique product of his times. On the face of things, he seemed as light-hearted a person as Clay had ever known. According to Clay's entries during this time, Henry Blackstone smiled almost constantly. (As noted, Clay even saw him smiling in his sleep.) Nothing seemed to bother him. Yet something festered underneath. The War and his background scarred him in some way Clay was never to truly comprehend. Behind the beaming countenance and pleasantries, there lurked a violent amorality.

Clay was witness to this in the first community they reached, and it is an interesting insight into his sense of values that he would not condemn Blackstone's action, even though he clearly disapproved of it.

December 8, 1866

Henry killed a man today. I do not know what to make of it. He saved my life and he is certainly good company. Still, I feel uneasy in his presence.

Here is how it happened.

We reached this town at two o'clock in the afternoon.

It was terribly cold (still is!) and we were glad to reach some shelter. The town is called Miller's Fork and I guess it is in Kansas although we have ridden far enough South to be in the Nations, I believe.

We had some money Henry had taken from the Marshal's office when we escaped and we went to have a bath and get our clothes washed. We had a nice sleep in a warm bed, then a hearty supper of steak and eggs, then a few drinks at a saloon. Henry said that all our needs were now accounted for except for one and suggested that we make our way to the nearest w——— house for an evening of "dalliance," as he called it. I agreed and we asked the bar tender where to find one. He told us and, after one more glass of whiskey, we headed in that direction.

It was our misfortune—actually, it was the man's misfortune—to run into a huge man coming out of the w———house as we were going in. He reminded me of that b———Zandt because he was so big and ugly in his manner.

"Well, what have we here?" he said. "Don't tell me you two boys are going *inside* this place?" He blocked our way and looked amused.

Henry only smiled and asked him if he would kindly get out of the way.

"I don't think that two young boys like you should go in *here*," the man said, laughing. "I am going to tell your Sunday School teacher you are sneaking off to 'cat cribs' when her back is turned."

"Get out of our way, please," Henry told him.

"Oh, no. You are too young."

Those were the last words the man ever spoke in this world. I did not notice Henry drawing. The first I knew, a shot was roaring in my ears and the big man was falling on the ground with lead in his chest. He twitched once and was dead.

Henry looked at me with a smile. "Let's go in and find some women now," he said. He did not seem concerned about the man.

I thought we should run for it but Henry gave three dol-

lars to one of the w——s and she told the town Marshal
that the man had drawn on Henry first and Henry had
killed him in self-defense. Which may be the case, I suppose, in fairness to Henry. His eyes may be quicker than
mine and maybe that man was just about to go for his gun.

We stayed at the w—— house for the evening but I
did not enjoy it much because the killing had disturbed
me some. It seems to me that Henry shot that man without a thought and never gave a hint that he intended doing
so. I owe Henry my life, that is certain. Still, I am a little
restless about his way of thinking.

Later: I asked Henry before he went to sleep why he had
killed that man. I was not easy about asking but had to
know.

Henry was not disturbed by the question. "I asked him
to get out of the way and he wouldn't," he answered.

He explained to me that he can be so cheerful all the
time because he never lets anger stew inside him. He told
me that, if he had been Zandt's helper, he would have shot
him the first day, in the back or in the front.

"Never bear a grudge, old fellow," he told me. "If a
stranger starts to rile you, kill him right away. That way
you get it 'out of your blood' so to speak and are not poi-
soned. I am not talking about friends, of course."

I was glad to hear that as I guess (I hope) I am a friend
of his.

*The entries in Clay's journal through the winter and
into the spring of 1867 are cut from the same cloth. Constantly in Henry Blackstone's company, he began to
manifest that infirmity of character which had turned
him toward indolent pursuits instead of honest labor following the War. He never worked, drank a good deal,
learned to play cards almost like a professional and*

generally caroused through the Indian Nations, Texas, and New Mexico. When things were lean, he was not above a crack at highway robbery, on at least two occasions assisting Henry Blackstone in stagecoach holdups.

None of this is stated as condemnation for he, later, more than compensated for these youthful digressions from the law. It is merely noted to "flesh out" the picture of the young man he was at that point—becoming fully acclimated to the Western mode of life but yet to earn—or be given the chance to earn—the opportunity to prove himself a law-abiding citizen.

An illustrative entry follows.

February 22, 1867

Almost "bought it" tonight. The two of us have never been in such a tight before. How we got out of it, the Lord alone knows.

We were playing poker with some Mexicans on the outskirts of town. I don't even know the name of it except to say we are in Texas.

Henry and I were winning like there was to be no end to it. It was after midnight when he and I began to realize (we think alike, it seems) that, short of some miracle, those Mexicans were not going to let us leave the game except with empty pockets and slit throats.

It was not a cheerful situation to be in, a sod hut on the high ground near a muddy river with the only light a candle on the table and our only "companions" five Mexican b——s who would steal pennies off their Mothers' dead eyes.

Henry moved first. Fortunately, I know how he does things now so when he yawned and stretched, I felt my muscles snap to, ready for the play.

It came fast. Shooting out his hand, Henry doused the candle flame and flung himself to one side of his chair. I did the same. The dark hut was a scene of shouts and curses. Fiery gun explosions followed and I felt the hot wind of lead around me. Henry dove through the window opening a second before I did.

It was good luck for us that the moon was not in sight but bad luck that some s——— of a b——— had taken our horses while we were playing cards.

"The river!" Henry said and we legged it down that slope as fast as we could.

By then, those Mexicans were out the door and shooting after us. I discovered later, to my surprise, that those were the first shots they had gotten off. The shots inside were snapped off by Henry, trying to kill a few of them before we lit out. When I told him that the slugs almost got me instead, he laughed and reminded me that a miss is as good as a mile.

We reached the river bank a few yards ahead of the Mexicans and plunged into the current which was COLD!! I pulled out my revolver and fired off a few shots at the Mexicans but it was too dark and the river current very fast. I held my gun so I wouldn't lose it and we fought our way to shore a distance down the bank, it might have been a half mile.

We found ourselves near the town and ran toward it to steal some horses to replace our own. Our clothes got stiff before we reached it and we moved like wooden creatures held by strings. Then, when we were cutting out two horses from the first house, a pack of hounds came at us. They tore at us insanely, ripping open our clothes and skins. The seat of my trousers was torn out and my rump bit hard. Henry shot one of the dogs and we got on the horses and rode, not bothering to look for saddles.

That was the most agonizing ride in the history of my

life! My behind was bare and bloody, freezing cold and pounded to a pulp on that horse's bony back. I think I picked a nag that had not seen a square meal for a month or else was ninety years of age for I felt every bone it had.

As if that was not enough, the Mexicans caught sight of us and took out in pursuit. They would have caught us too if a storm had not come up.

Lightning crashed and I saw clouds like black mountains in the sky. Thunder began and then more lightning. A tornado of wind commenced that not only almost blew us off our horses' backs but almost blew our horses over as well. Finally, hailstones as big as peaches started pounding us before it started raining so hard that it was like riding underneath a waterfall. I swear I thought the Lord above was punishing us for the life we were leading.

Henry must have thought the same thing (though not as seriously as me) for he looked up at the sky and shouted, "Well, old fellow, about the only thing you ain't seen fit to hit us with tonight is *boulders*!"

At that moment, we were riding through a draw and several boulders from above started rolling down at us. We barely managed to escape them. I was scared white but Henry laughed as hard as I have ever heard him laugh. He tipped his hat to Heaven. "Called me on that one, didn't you?" he shouted.

We are taking shelter in a cave now, drying out our clothes over a fire. Henry is asleep as I write. I thank the Lord I keep this Record Book on my person now and did not leave it in my saddle bag.

What Clay refers to as a "bad chill" (probably pneumonia) plus complications from his still not completely healed shoulder wound compelled him to slow the frenetic pace of his schedule and take a job on a New Mexican ranch, first as cook's helper, later as a cowhand. Out of

friendship, Henry kept him company and the arrangement
worked out reasonably well until late September when
Henry shot one of the cowhands over a card game in the
bunkhouse. Forced to flee, he left the ranch accompanied
by Clay who had, by that time, regained his health.

September 22, 1867

I am on the run again with Henry. He killed Ned Wo-
odridge last evening while they were playing poker. He
said that I did not have to light out with him as it is his
own trouble but I decided that I owe it to him still.

The chase was not too bad. We got away from the cow
boys who were led by Baxter. (*The ranch's foreman. F.L.*)
We did get a shock as we were riding though. Suddenly,
our horses reared back, terrified, as it appeared that we had
galloped straight into an Indian witch!

It turned out to be a dead papoose. We had ridden into
an Indian burial ground without knowing it. The papoose
had been tied to a tree but the fastening had come loose
and the body swung to and fro. It was a grisly sight with
its face shriveled up and staring at us, looking very strange
with all the beads and ornaments attached to it.

We rode another hour or so and came upon the camp-
ground of a group of men, outlaws as it turned out. To my
surprise, Henry said hello to their leader Cullen Baker.
They have ridden together in the past.

I have heard about this Baker. Everyone says he is a
murderous "desperado" but he strikes me much like Henry.
He does not seem aware of his renown and is affable. Like
Henry, he smiles a good deal.

I do not know what to do now. Henry has declared that
he intends to join forces with Bonney and ride with him
again. I do not believe that I am up to living that kind of

life again. It is exciting, sure enough, but hard to sleep, never knowing when John Law might pick you up. That time in jail, thinking I was going to hang, was enough for me. I do not want to be a cow boy or a cook's helper, that is for sure. Neither do I choose to be "gallow's meat."

September 23, 1867

It seemed today as if it wasn't going to matter whether I decided to ride with Henry or not!

All of us were riding up a hill and I was thinking how to let Henry know that I was going to split up with him when we heard a noise in the distance that sounded like rolling thunder. The difference was it made the earth shake underneath us.

As we reached the top of a hill, we saw what was causing the noise. Hundreds of stampeding buffalo chased by several dozen Comanches. Seeing us, the Red Skins left off chasing buffalo and started after us. Deciding that caution was the better part of valor, we turned tail.

Those Indians rode too well for us, however, and it became clear that a stand would have to be made. Spotting a deserted trench house in the distance, we rode like H—— until we reached it. Leaping off our mounts, we pulled them inside and slammed the door shut just before those Red Skins reached us.

I can not say if they were drunk or crazy or what but those Comanches sure did want our hides for supper! They kicked and hammered at the door and dove in through the window. Only our constant, accurate fire kept the battle on an even keel. There must have been twenty-five to thirty of them and they just kept coming at us like they were determined to kill us to the last man.

Once, in a lull that lasted a few minutes, I heard a bugle call and told the others, with excited pleasure, that the Cavalry had come to save us. They laughed and said it was an Indian doing it who had, likely, stolen the bugle from a dead Cavalry man. "They like to blow bugles," Henry told me. "It fires them up."

I guess it must have for the next attack came right away. It was a mean one. We fired our guns until they were burning hot to touch. Indian bodies were stacked all over. Our horses screamed and bucked, knocking their heads against the roof of the house. There was so much powder smoke that it was hard to see or breathe. The Comanches yelled, and pounded on the door, and jumped in through the window even though it just meant jumping into lead. I must have shot down seven or eight of them. You did not have to have good aim either. You could not miss them.

Finally, they had enough I guess and what was left of them rode off. (Which was a good coincidence as we were down to nine more shots between us.) Two of Baker's men were killed and nineteen Indians, six inside and thirteen around the house. One of our horses was also killed but, I am glad to state, my "charmed life" has reported back for duty as I did not get so much as a scratch.

When we were leaving—Henry riding double with Cullen—I decided that it was as good a time as any to declare myself and told Henry that I had made up my mind to get myself another ranch job. This is not true but I did not want to tell him that his mode of living is not to my taste any more.

He did not take it hard, only smiling and saying, "Sure thing, old fellow. Good luck to you—" as he rode off. I thought our parting would make him a little sadder than that.

I am sad about it. Even though Henry is a strange person,

he had always been a good friend to me and I am sorry I could never repay his favor by saving his life. I do not suppose I will ever have the chance now.

Adios, Amigo! It has been good fun but our paths go off in different ways now.

About a week later, Clay came upon the camp of an old man with a small herd of cattle. The man had been lying in his bedroll for three days and was close to death.

October 2, 1867

I buried the old man today. He did not have much of a chance to live, I think. I took care of him as best as I could and he seemed grateful. He said that I could have his herd of cattle if I would write a letter to his son in Missouri and tell him what had happened. I promised that I would. The old man's name was Gerald Shaner.

Now I am a cow boy once again. I can not seem to get away from it. I hate those long horns like the plague and now I have to nurse a herd of them across the plains. I say "a herd" but there are only twelve of them! I say "I have to nurse" them but, of course, I don't. I could let them wander off to live or die but that would not be smart. I can use the money they will bring me so I am going to drive them to Hickman which is about a hundred and twenty miles southwest of here and hope to sell them. That is my plan.

As indicated earlier—and a leitmotif throughout Clay's account—his plans "gang aft astray." Judging from a percentage viewpoint, one might declare that Clay's plans were altered by outside influences more than not. This fact strengthens my contention that he was, indeed, a "product" of his times, being led with almost preordained in-

evitability toward his destiny. This is not to say that he did not have a mind of his own or make decisions on his own. Yet, caught up by the violent wave of the period through which he lived, he could do little more than "keep his head up," swimming short distances in various directions even as the wave bore him on toward his appointment with fate.

The next entry of note occurs almost two weeks later as he nears Hickman with his herd of nine cows, two of them having been lost to Indians, one to a pack of wolves.

October 17, 1867

I came up on the camp at sunset yesterday, the men there working for a ranch called The Circle Seven.

Their foreman, a man named Tiner, was affable at first, inviting me to light and have some food. I accepted gladly and counted myself fortunate to have come this way. He told me that Hickman is just a day's ride away and I decided that I was a lucky fellow to have made it.

Then he surprised the H——— out of me by telling me that, since I was new to these parts and a "one-man spread" I only had to pay them ten dollars to move my herd across their range. He told me this was Circle Seven land and strangers were required to pay for its use.

I was angered by this and told him I did not have a one-bit piece to my name. This did not disturb him. He said that I could pay my way across with one of my cows.

"How can you rake me down like that?" I asked him. "You know that I can get more than ten dollars for one of those cows."

He said that he was sorry about that but that, if I wanted, he could have the cow cut in half or thirds and take ten dollars worth of it for payment.

Something about the way he said that riled me good. I

got up and mounted. When he told one of his men to cut out a cow, I told him to keep his d——d hands off. He paid no attention to me and sent the man to do what he had ordered.

I suppose I am crazy but I got so mad at this, I saw red. I told that cow boy to stay the H——— away from my herd. He acted as if I wasn't even talking and started after one of my cows. I pulled out my rifle and shot the ground up by his boots.

That did it royal. The next second, lead was flying and I was forced to ride for my life. I tried to drive my herd off on the run but wasn't very far before they caught me and shot my horse out from underneath me. I had to leg it to a pile of rocks and take cover. It was almost dark by then and although I took a shot or two at them, I don't believe I hit a single target.

Now it is morning and my herd is gone and so are all the Circle Seven men as well. I have no horse so it looks like a long walk ahead for me. If I ever run across those cow stealing b——s, I will let air into them so help me G———!

No further entry appears for five days. Clay's walk across the New Mexican prairie must have been an arduous one. Cowboy boots are hardly designed for hiking (he knocked the high heels off the first day so he could move more easily), and Clay, though healthy, was not accustomed to walking great distances. By the time he reached the property of the Arrow-C ranch, his feet were swollen, blistered, and bloody. He was taken into the ranch by one of the cowboys, fed, and put up for the night.

The following day, he met Arthur Courtwright who probably had more to do with what Clay Halser became than any other individual.

I have decided to stay at the Arrow-C and work for Mr. Courtwright.

He is about the nicest gentleman I have ever met and I like him a good deal. He is British and has only been in this country for nine months. He is twenty years older than me but we talk the same lingo. He makes a body feel at ease and has charm enough to talk the birds out of the branches. He seems to have taken a shine to me, I am glad to state. I spent most of the day talking to him.

He told me that his family is a "venerable" one. (I think that is the word he used.) He said that they go back in English history and were, at one time, famous, and rich. Now, although the fame in history is still intact, their riches have faded. He took what was left of the money and "came to The New World to recoup the family fortune" as he put it.

A Hickman man—named Charles McConnell—who Mr. Courtwright met in St. Louis convinced him that this area was ideal for his purposes. Taking McConnell's word at face value, Mr. Courtwright came here, bought this ranch and started a supply store with McConnell in Hickman.

Since coming here, however, he has discovered that the "path to wealth" is not to be an easy one. There is a man named Sam Brady who controls the entire range, holding the best springs, streams, water holes, and grazing lands which makes his ranch (The Circle Seven!) the most powerful around.

I asked Mr. Courtwright why the small ranchers did not join forces to break Brady's "strangle hold." He answered that, until he came here, Brady owned the only supply store in Hickman. Either the ranchers went along with him or they got starved out.

Now that Mr. Courtwright and McConnell have a "rival" store, the tide is changing but it is just beginning to change. Most of the small ranchers are buying their supplies from the Courtwright-McConnell store now and Sam Brady is beginning to hurt. Mr. Courtwright fears "a major conflict" some time soon. He hopes to avoid it but doesn't know that it is possible.

I got the feeling that he feels a little doubt about his partner although he never said it in so many words. I don't even *know* McConnell but I feel doubt about him. I mean, why didn't he tell Mr. Courtwright he was sticking his neck on a chopping block by coming here?

I don't know why Mr. Courtwright told me all these things. He said that he could trust me and asked if I would stay and help him. I said I would be glad to do so and would never stand back in a tight place. I would help him even if it was just because he asked, I like him that much.

But for a chance to get back at those Circle Seven b———s, I would take a situation in H———!

What Clay did not realize was that, by taking employ at the Arrow-C he was doing just that; taking a situation in H———.

So he began to work for the Britisher Arthur Courtwright whom he came, quickly, to revere. Clay never mentioned his own father or expressed any sense of loss at never having had a father-son relationship. It seems clear, however, that, in Courtwright—who, by all reports, was a man of infinite charm, patience, and wisdom—Clay found the father he had never had.

He also found, within the month, the young woman he was, consequently, to wed.

Mr. Courtwright was kind enough to take me with him to-day into Hickman where we had Thanksgiving dinner at the home of his partner, Charles McConnell.

I cannot say I like McConnell worth a d——— although I would never say this to Mr. Courtwright if my life depended on it. I think McConnell is not to be trusted. I found out, to my surprise, that he was, at one time, Sam Brady's lawyer! This is not what I would call a good "omen." If a man can turn on one he can turn on another. If he ever proves to be false to Mr. Courtwright's trust, I will kill him.

That would not be so easy to do however. I do not mean as a physical act. (McConnell is a weak tub of a man.) I mean it would not be so easy to do because of his daughter, Anne, who I met today.

I don't trust myself any more where it comes to the heart but I have the feeling that I could fall in love with Anne McConnell very easy. There is something about her that reminds me of Mary Jane Silo. (It is hard to believe that it is getting close to *two years* since I saw her last!) She is very pretty and has a gentle smile that pleases the eye.

I must not let myself be fooled however. I thought I was in love with Hazel Thatcher. What is more, I have had many females since (all w——s) and may not have the ability to feel an honest emotion.

I do feel *something* though—and something powerful. I hope I am not fooling myself to believe that she feels something too. I can not believe, however, that the looks and smiles she gave me were without meaning.

I *do* believe that her father does not care for me. When I was looking at his daughter, I noticed him frowning. I guess he knows that I am only a common ranch hand and wants more for his daughter. Because Mr. Courtwright is his partner though and Mr. Courtwright likes me, Mc-Connell can't say anything right out.

I don't believe that Mrs. McConnell noticed anything of what passed. She is Anne's stepmother and seems very re-tiring in nature.

Clay's ability at character analysis deserted him on this occasion as a later entry makes vividly clear.

December 14, 1867

God All Mighty, what a strange H——— of an afternoon!

Mr. Courtwright sent me in to Hickman to deliver a mes-sage to Mr. McConnell. He was not at home but Mrs. Mc-Connell was.

It is not often that you smell whiskey on a lady's breath. A w———'s yes but not a lady's. I smelled it on Mrs. Mc-Connell's breath however. Her eyes had a faraway look in them and she moved oddly.

I did not know what to say when she told me to come inside the house. I thought, at first, she meant for me to sit and wait until her husband got home so I could deliver the message to him personally. On second thought, that did not make much sense but, by then, I was already in the house.

Mrs. McConnell embarrassed me by offering me a drink of whiskey. I said no thank you and she had one any way. I sat on the sofa which she told me to do. I tried to be po-lite and make conversation with her but it was hard.

Too late I remembered Hazel Thatcher and that night in the wagon as Mrs. McConnell put her hand on me. I don't mean on my *hand* either! I was so surprised I must have turned into a statue!

She started saying things to me that I can not put down even if this *is* a secret journal! I mean I never heard such talk from a female, not even a w————! I tried to get up and excuse myself but she wouldn't let me. I know I was blushing because my face felt as though I was holding it a few inches from a red hot stove.

Then she cursed and pulled open her dress and buttons popped all over. She had nothing on underneath and I near to froze when she held her bare b——s in her hands and told me to————!

I couldn't even speak I was so startled by the turn of events! She was grabbing me and telling me she wanted me to——her right there on the sofa in the full light! I swear to G————, fighting those Comanches was a sight easier than fighting off that woman.

To top it all, Anne came in just then! Seeing her, her stepmother cursed something awful, then ran upstairs and slammed a door. I stood dazed and looking at Anne, believing that she was going to tell me to get out of the house and never come back.

To my surprise, she asked me to sit down. She was blushing too as she sat across the parlor from me and told me that her stepmother is "ill" and that she would honor me if I would not say anything about what had happened as it would break her father's heart. I agreed and, shortly after, left. When I did, she kissed me on the cheek and said that she was grateful to me and hoped that we might see each other again under "more pleasant circumstances."

I take back what I said. I *do* love Anne McConnell. I believe that I must ask for her hand in marriage.

It is going to be d————d awkward though. I mean, for G——'s sake what am I supposed to say the next time I see her stepmother? It is such a dreadful problem, I can not even ask Mr. Courtwright what *he* would do though I am sure that he would give some good advice.

December 15, 1867

A few lines remaining in this, my first Record Book that I found on the belongings of that Confederate officer more than three years ago.

I am going in to Hickman in a few days to pick up some supplies for Mr. Courtwright. While I am in town, I will buy myself another Record Book.

BOOK TWO

(1868–1873)

If the purpose of this work were to present a story of young love in the West, circa 1867–68, a modest volume in itself would be prepared from this period of Clay's life during which he came to know and love Anne McConnell. Like all young men in any given period of history, Clay rhapsodizes endlessly about his loved one's beauty, and charm, and the total wonderment of their feeling for each other.

Whenever he was not actually working for his employer, Clay was seeing Anne or dreaming of her, filling countless pages in his second Record Book (sixty-eight in all) with youthful outpourings.

As to his "courtship" of Anne McConnell, it consisted, as courtships usually do, of walks and rides together, dances attended, visits at the McConnell house or at the Courtwright ranch. Clay says nothing more of Mrs. McConnell except to note that he almost never saw her after the unsettling incident in the McConnell parlor. Doubtless, she remained to herself whenever there was any possibility that their paths might cross.

Anne's father continued to object to her relationship with Clay but never strongly enough to make a difference—especially when it started to become apparent that Courtwright's feeling for Clay was that of a man for his son which, of course, considerably illuminated Clay's potential as a son-in-law.

All in all, this was a time of happiness for Clay. He had found a home, a father, a bride-to-be, and a potentially stable future. So wrapped up was he in these individual pleasures that he even forgot his animosity toward the Circle Seven ranch, feeling that "fate" had more than compensated him in other ways.

As indicated, however, this is not a story of young love but a tale of mounting violence in which Clay was to enact a bigger role with each succeeding year.

Accordingly, we skip, in time, to August of 1868 when Brady made his first clear move to break Courtwright's increasing control of the small ranchers in the area.

August 12, 1868

The "conflict" Mr. Courtwright foresaw when I first met him seems to be beginning.

This afternoon, Sheriff Bollinger came out to the ranch with a warrant for Mr. Courtwright's arrest. It has been obvious to all that Bollinger is Brady's pawn but no one thought he would make it as clear as this.

Bollinger told Mr. Courtwright that Brady was claiming ownership of the Arrow-C. He said that Brady had a paper from the ranch's former owner which signed over the ranch to him in payment for a debt. Mr. Courtwright explained to the Sheriff (I would have chased him off the ranch) that this was "ancient history" as he called it. He said that the former owner had never filed for the land whereas he had. This made Brady's paper "invalid." Bollinger allowed as how that might be true but Courtwright had to come and face trial any way.

I told Mr. Courtwright (taking him aside) that he should not surrender himself to the Brady forces but he said that he had no fear as he was in the legal right and they would not dare to hurt him openly.

I did not like it. There was no reason why this claim on

the ranch should be brought up again. I suspected Bollinger and followed him and Mr. Courtwright at a distance.

My suspicion proved a true one. I saw Bollinger draw his revolver and point it at Mr. Courtwright. Later, Mr. Courtwright told me that Bollinger said the warrant was only a ruse. There was to be no trial because he was never to reach Hickman alive. When asked what had happened, Bollinger was going to say that Mr. Courtwright had tried to escape and that he had to shoot him.

He will never say it now, by G——! He will never say another lie to anyone. I grabbed my rifle and aimed as fast as I have ever aimed in my life. Before he could pull the trigger, I blew him off his saddle. It was a lucky shot. I got him the first time.

I rode down to Mr. Courtwright who was very white and shaken. I told him that, from now on, I would not let him put himself in such danger. He did not argue with me. All he kept saying was, "I had no idea they would try a thing like this."

A month later, a second "arresting party" rode out to the Arrow-C, led by Bollinger's brother who had been appointed as the new Sheriff.

September 13, 1868

Brady made himself as clear as day this afternoon.

Mr. Courtwright, Tom (*the foreman of the Arrow-C. F.L.*) and I were having dinner when a group of riders pulled up at the ranch house. Tom and I put on our guns and went outside to see what was going on.

It turned out to be *another* Sheriff Bollinger (the former one's brother has been made the Sheriff) and four of his

Deputys. He said that he was here to take in Mr. Courtwright for the murder of his brother.

"You are not taking any one," I told him.

"I will take him a corpse or a living man," he answered.

"Take *me*," I said, "for *I* am the one who shot your
brother."

He looked at me in surprise. Later, Tom said that, even
though I am twenty-two years old, I look like a boy and
this was what set back Bollinger. "*You*?" he said.

"*Me*," I said. "As I will shoot down any s———— of a
b———— who tries to murder Mr. Courtwright."

Bollinger started cursing at me but Tom told him to get
off the Arrow-C unless he was prepared to sling lead for
the privilege.

Bollinger said no more. He looked at us a while, then
pulled his horse around as did his Deputys. Something
warned me that he had some other play in mind so I said,
low, to Tom, "Pretend to turn away."

We did that and, from the corners of my eyes, I saw Bollinger go for his gun.

"Down!" I cried and threw myself across the porch,
snatching out my revolver. Tom ducked behind a porch
chair and lead started flying. Tom and I had the advantage
being in the shadows of the porch. Tom brought down one
of the Deputys, and I killed another, and wounded Bollinger. The group took off at high speed. I am sure they
will be back.

Mr. Courtwright had been watching at a window. He
told me afterward that he was much impressed by my "instinctive prowess" (his words) with the hand gun. He said
that I should practice at it and become "adept" as I am certain to be one of Brady's "principal" targets now.

I have never thought about the hand gun much. I have
used it, of course, but never given it consideration as a
weapon, preferring the rifle. I can see, however, that there

are times when one must defend himself at close quarters and a rifle is useless for that.

I suppose that I had better practice some and try to get a little better.

"I suppose that I had better practice some and try to get a little better."

With these simple words, Clay embarks on his brief career as one of the deadliest gun fighters ever spawned by the frontier. I am certain that he had no conception of his future when he wrote those words. Thinking, no doubt, that he was, merely, developing a skill that would help him to protect his employer, he could not have dreamed of the violent path down which he would be led by this mastery.

A mastery he acquired with almost consummate ease, I would add. Where other men might have had to practice for years, Clay became incredibly "adept" in a matter of months. Possessed of near to preternatural reflexes (eyewitness accounts of his gun battles verify this time and again) and a virtually infallible sense of direction, he discovered that his ability increased by leaps and bounds as he learned "to start my lead pump fast."

Learn he did, using a five-month period of stalemate between the Brady-Courtwright forces to refine his natural skill at drawing and firing accurately at high speed. Although he learned to do this ambidextrously, he elected—after much experimentation—to confine himself to the "cross" draw, wearing his scabbard on the left side, the butt of his revolver reversed; he preferred, at this time, a Single Action, .41 caliber Colt.

That he soon would have use of this newly developed skill was a fact not lost on Clay as he wrote, during the winter of 1868, "There is going to be powder burned soon."

March 23, 1869

I am writing this on a piece of brown paper that I took from the store a while ago. Later on, I will write these words in my Record Book.

We are under siege. It has been going on since morning. We are in the grain house out in back of Mr. Courtwright's store—Mr. Courtwright, McConnell, Benton, Stanbury, Grass, and myself. All the rest are dead and Mr. Courtwright's store is nearly burned to the ground. This is the first time I have had a moment's breath since morning. It is only for a moment too. We will have to make a break for freedom soon or die.

Bollinger (that b———!) and his men waited until we were in Hickman. He must have been planning this for months. It came as a surprise to us since we had been looking for an attack on the ranch.

We were in Mr. Courtwright's store getting supplies when Bollinger came in and said I had to surrender myself for the murder of his brother. I refused, naturally. This did not appear to surprise him. He said that he had done his duty now and whatever happened afterward was on our heads. He left the store and, five minutes later, the firing began.

Bollinger must have had thirty or forty men out there because the lead came flying hot and heavy, breaking all the windows and making Swiss Cheese of the walls. I grabbed Mr. Courtwright and pulled him down behind the counter. He never showed fear. I admire him the more for that. He has behaved with courage all day long which is more than I can say for that sniveling son of a b———, McConnell!

Any way, although we were much outnumbered (there were nine of us to begin with), we kept Bollinger's forces off because of our accurate rifle fire. I got a Winchester Repeater from the rifle cabinet and was able to hit many living targets in the next few hours. Once again, my "charmed life" is in evidence and, although things look grim, I feel full of cheer and am confident that we will get out of here safe and sound.

About four o'clock, we had lost three men and decided to retreat to the grain house which is made of stone as the fire set by Bollinger's men was getting too hot to bear. While we were running, poor Tom took a slug in the back of his head and died in a second. He was a brave man. The rest of us got into the grain house alive although Grass and Benton are wounded, Grass in the right leg, Benton in the left thigh.

It is almost dark now and we are going to have to make a run for it shortly. If we can get to the ranch we will be all right.

Later: We are at the ranch. Mr. Courtwright has a slight wound in his arm but is otherwise untouched. I have no wounds at all.

We broke out after six o'clock. It started raining and the fire started smoking quite a lot. As wind began to blow the smoke across the yard, we ran out, one by one. I was close behind Mr. Courtwright as we dashed across the yard and over the wall. There was a perfect hail of lead but we were untouched except, as I said, for a slight wound to Mr. Courtwright's left arm. Poor Glass was killed however and Stanbury is a prisoner.

So is McConnell but I don't give a d———— about that. He refused to leave the grain house, crying and pleading with us to surrender so the "bloodshed" would stop. Finally, I shoved him in a corner and we took out.

After making the wall and going over it, we ran through the back alleys and found some horses tied up in front of

The Latigo Saloon, which we quickly "commandeered" and used to ride back to the ranch. Mr. Courtwright says that he will send them back tomorrow, which shows what an honest man he is even at such a time.

I do not know what he is going to do now. The store had more than two-thirds of his money in it and is a total loss. He says that he will not give in to Brady though for which I admire him even more. Still, what is he going to do?

I do not know how I am going to see Anne now as I can not ride into Hickman any more without risking life and limb.

As for her father, I hope they hang the b——— by his——! He is a miserable coward and nothing more.

What Clay did not know at the time was that McConnell, after being captured by Bollinger, was given a choice of helping Brady deal with Courtwright or being killed. Being, as Clay accurately appraised, "a miserable coward and nothing more," he quickly agreed to help Brady in order to preserve his own existence.

March 27, 1869

I am writing this before I leave for Hickman. I may not come back alive but I do not care as long as I get whoever is responsible for Mr. Courtwright's death.

I had been up for two straight days on guard and had fallen asleep in exhaustion. While I was asleep, McConnell rode out to the ranch and told Mr. Courtwright that Brady wanted to parley in town and declare a truce. (Benton told me this.) Mr. Courtwright had been terribly upset since the attack on his store and wanted to believe that what McConnell said was true. Immediately, he had his horse saddled and started into town beside McConnell.

When I woke up and found that Mr. Courtwright was gone, I saddled fast and rode for Hickman, feeling a cold weight in my stomach because I knew, somehow, exactly what had happened.

I found Mr. Courtwright at the bottom of a draw, his body riddled by lead. There were hoofmarks all around the spot and I calculate that four men must have been in on the murder, one of them McConnell.

I brought Mr. Courtwright's body to the house and, I confess, spilled hot tears every foot of the way. I have never known a finer man in my life and say openly that I loved him and respected him as I would love and respect a father. D——— his killers! I will find them if it takes me twenty years! And if I die in getting them, that is all right too.

I am leaving now. G——— help those who murdered Mr. Courtwright for vengeance is riding after them.

Later: I rode to Hickman and went first to the McConnell house. Anne opened the door when I knocked and told me that her father was not there.

I did not believe her and pushed inside. I searched the house from top to bottom and found him hiding in the cellar. He had a Derringer in his hand but did not pull the trigger, knowing that he was a dead man if he did.

I told him that I wanted to know who had been with him when he murdered Mr. Courtwright. I heard Anne gasp when I said that, then she said no more.

McConnell started crying and begging for his life. He swore that he had had no notion that Brady meant to murder Mr. Courtwright. I yelled at him and asked him what in H——— he *did* think Brady meant to do! He could hardly answer me, he was so scared. He swore on his

Mother's grave that he had not drawn a gun but had ridden off when he saw the three men waiting to kill Mr. Courtwright.

I asked him who they were but he would not tell me, saying that his life would not be worth a plugged nickel if he told. I put my Colt against his forehead and swore that I would drench the cellar wall with his brains if he did not answer. Anne began to cry and grabbed my arm. I pushed her off and told McConnell again that I would kill him if he did not tell me who the men were.

He answered that the three hired by Brady were not from Hickman. He said that they have been staying at the hotel but he did not know if they were still in town.

I was going to kill him where he stood but Anne was pleading for his life and, despite my fury, I could not make myself kill her father in front of her eyes. I left the house and went to the hotel. The clerk told me that the three men were not checked out but were not in their rooms. I went to the cafe but they were not there either.

I found them in *The Latigo Saloon*. They were standing at the counter, drinking and laughing, bragging about the "Limey" they had "put to rest" that afternoon.

As soon as they said that, I pulled out my gun and pushed in through the bat wing doors, firing and snapping as fast as I could until the gun was empty. They did not expect me and not one of them had time to draw, but I do not feel remorse about murdering them the way they murdered Mr. Courtwright. One of them was wounded, lying on the floor. I reloaded my revolver and stepped over to him, putting a ball between his eyes as he begged for his life. I left the three of them dead and rode back to the ranch.

There is nothing left now but to leave. I can not ask Anne to go with me and doubt that she would if I did ask. I feel numb inside. It is impossible for me to believe that everything has changed so much. A week ago, my life was perfect. Now everything is ended and the world seems black to me.

I will leave in a . . .

Anne just left. She rode out from town to beg me not to leave. She said that she and her father will testify on my behalf. I do not believe that McConnell will do anything of the kind no matter what he told her. I *do* believe Anne though. She said that she will tell the jury at the trial exactly what her father said about Brady making him go out to invite Mr. Courtright into town for a parley and how the three men were waiting on the trail to murder him instead.

Still, I am not sure. Brady still controls the town. If I surrender myself to Sheriff Bollinger, what is to prevent them from murdering me as well? It is true that, if I run, I may be running from the law until I die and I do not want that. Anne believes that I will be acquitted and says that she will marry me afterward and we will leave Hickman.

I do not know what to do. To give myself up to Bollinger would be like putting my head in a noose. There must be some other way.

The "other way" Clay chose was to surrender himself to the military post at Fort Nelson (two miles outside of Hickman) hoping, by this stratagem, to stay out of Brady's hands while, at the same time, remain on "the right side" of the law.

It soon became evident that he was not, in this way, to escape Brady's influence. The commander of the fort—a Captain Hooker—turned out to be one of Brady's "under-the-table" confreres who saw to it that Clay was imprisoned in a "bull pen" stockade, a small open area surrounded by high walls on which sentries were posted twenty-four hours a day. They "ironed" Clay—put shackles with chains on his ankles and wrists—and kept him staked to the ground all day every day, no matter what the weather. During this period, two toes on Clay's right foot became frostbitten, then gangrenous and had to be amputated by the post surgeon.

The trial was endlessly—deliberately, I feel—postponed in the hope that Clay would die of natural causes prior to the need for a trial. When his dogged will kept him alive, the trial was started.

Clay was forced to walk to the courthouse and back, the ankle irons rubbing at his skin until the flesh was lacerated, bleeding and infected. All hope deserted him as, first, McConnell, then Anne, left town without testifying on his behalf as promised. The trial was brief. Clay was found guilty of murdering the original Sheriff Bollinger and sentenced to hang.

Now in the custody of Bollinger's brother, he was mercilessly abused until he told a fellow prisoner that he anticipated hanging "with pleasure" so that his "torment would end."

One night in February, 1870, Bollinger, raging drunk, burst into Clay's cell and beat him almost senseless. He had just received notification from the office of the territorial governor that every man involved in the Brady-Courtwright War had been granted amnesty. Under the circumstances, Bollinger did not dare to murder Clay and, having beaten him savagely, threw him on a horse and sent him packing.

Barely conscious, slumped and bleeding on the saddle, Clay rode off into the darkness, heading toward the next phase of his life.

May 17, 1870

I have been in Caldwell now for two weeks. It is no great shakes of a town but it will do for a while. My money is holding out all right. I win a little at cards and lose a little. I can probably get by for several months without a job. I do not care to work right now. I am not in much condition to do so. I have not learned to walk very well yet with those two toes missing. Also, my ankles are weak and I get stiff in my back when the nights are cold. I am in great shape for a man of twenty-five years.

I am sitting in my room, writing in this book again. I decided to give it up after leaving Hickman. I did not care enough about day to day living to keep a journal on it. Now I feel a little better so I will start writing again.

I will not try to fill in the details of what happened to me after I gave myself up at Fort Nelson. (*The facts about this period were told to me by Clay, in person, at a later date. F.L.*) I will start here at Caldwell with a "new slate." Not that I am a new *anything* myself. Leg wound, shoulder wound, missing toes, rheumatism, (I suppose that sounds like a poem!) from lying on that d——d ground so many days. It is amazing I can deal a hand of cards.

This town reminds me of Morgan City. It is similar in nature except for more permanent residents—about seven hundred. Morgan City only had four hundred. The look is the same, however, and the purpose. Caldwell is a cow town. I am told that more than a quarter of a million head of cattle move through its stockyards during shipping season.

The providing of entertainment for the men who drive the herds is Caldwell's main business. On South Main Street are four solid blocks of saloons, gambling and dance halls, fleabag hotels, cafes and w—— houses. The population of this "infamous zone" (as some old galoot I was drinking with called it) consists of w——s and horse thieves, drunks and murderers, cappers, deadbeats, and pickpockets, and close to a hundred gamblers, members of the so-called "circuit." It is a grand place to bring your mother for a visit.

If I could become good enough at cards to make a living, I would be pleased to join the "circuit" myself.

As the concluding sentence of this entry demonstrates, Clay, in his early days in Caldwell, despite a revival of his sense of humor, seemed to be retrograding toward that mental state which had given him trouble following the War and during his period of adventuring with Henry Blackstone.

Devoid of ambition, he passed his days without accomplishment, rising late and spending his afternoons and evenings playing cards and keeping company with the denizens of the four-block area along South Main Street.

This situation continued until one night when, while playing cards in an inebriated condition, he lost almost every cent he had and was forced to face the prospect of earning his keep once more.

While in this state, he took a conversation with some never-to-be-identified bartender and took a fateful step in the direction of the career which was, soon, to make his name a byword in the West.

July 9, 1870

I have been thinking over seriously what that bar tender told me last night.

He said that Caldwell has no law to speak of. Not that this was much of a shock to me. It is clear the town is not conducted on the order of a Sunday School. Still, I did not realize that the Marshal—a man named Palmer—has no control at all, being merely a pawn in the hands of the local "merchants" who pay his salary, allow him to stay alive.

From what the bar tender said, Palmer is a coward and will do anything to keep from following the former Marshals into Boot Hill. (Four in all.)

The man in charge of everything is named Bob Keller. He is the owner of the *Bullhead Saloon*—the biggest in the town—and the president of The League of Proprietors—a fancy way of saying "saloon owners."

I asked the bar tender if there are any Deputy Marshals and he said that there are not. I am thinking of applying for the job. If I can get in "on the deal" it will be fine with me. I am sure there is enough money floating around to keep me from starving. I am also sure that they could use a good man with a gun to help them keep the peace during shipping season.

As is evident from this entry, Clay's motivation for desiring to become a Deputy City Marshal in Caldwell was hardly of the highest caliber, being more in the nature of a search for an easy meal ticket than an ambition to foster law and order. (At the same time, it is not surprising that Clay had no respect for the principles of law and order in the West, having been "stung" by them more than once.)

At any rate, learning a week later that the position of Deputy Marshal was one which was handed out by the town council, he headed for the courthouse to consult the head of said council, Mayor Oliver Weatherby Rayburn.

July 11, 1870

I took a stroll to the courthouse after lunch today. It is a raw pine structure on the edge of town.

There was a dried-up old man on the porch as I arrived. He was sitting on a rocking chair, moving back and forth. He looked a hundred years old. His derby hat was too big for his shriveled head.

I asked him if he could tell me where to find Mayor Rayburn. The old geezer answered that he was "said dignitary." (His own words.) I will try to remember the words he used for he could sure spit out a power of them.

"May this ancient worthy inquire what he can do for you, young man?" he asked.

I told him I had come to apply for the job of Deputy City Marshal.

"If it is suicide you seek," he replied, "why not drink or——— yourself to death for it is infinitely more pleasant to pass on that way than with an aggravated case of lead poisoning."

It took me several moments to haul that in and sift out the sense of it. Then I told him that I did not intend to commit suicide but planned to rock on a porch myself some day, my old head shaded by a derby hat. I said that I did not choose to do manual work and was not good enough to be a professional gambler. (The fact that I was applying for a job was proof enough of that!) As I had some skill with the gun and did not buffalo easy (I told him) I figured I would not do too badly as a Deputy Marshal. I assured him that I did not plan to cause a wave of goodness and light to wash over Caldwell but only wanted a "bread and butter" position.

He allowed as how he "apperceived my point of view" but could not promise that Marshal Palmer would receive the news of a new Deputy Marshal with smiles and songs. "Not to mention Bob Keller and the League of Proprietors." He said that he liked me, however, and would appoint me if that was what I really wanted but that staying alive afterward was my problem.

I accepted and, I must say, for the first time since the attack on Mr. Courtwright's store, I felt a "tingle" of excitement. I hold that tingle precious after more than a year of deadness and would have gone on even if the job was not a paying one.

The mayor swore me in and told me to report to Marshal Palmer, who would more than likely be found at the *Bullhead Saloon* playing cards and drinking as a good, obedient peace officer should.

I went to the *Bullhead* and found the Marshal who is a rednecked, heavy man. I introduced myself and told him that I had just been appointed as his Deputy.

I can not say that my news went over big. Palmer looked at me as if I had just come crawling out of the nearest rat hole. The men who were playing cards with him seemed amused to hear it though, chuckling a good deal among themselves. One of these was Bob Keller, a big man with dark curly hair who, I guess, you would call handsome. All he had to say was that I limped kind of bad and did I think I could make my rounds without falling down?

I told him that I thought I could and Marshal Palmer got his voice back long enough to tell me I could take the night shift starting at six o'clock and lasting until midnight.

I played the whole hand like a farmer with hay seeds in his hair and I am sure they think I am some poor lad who has gone demented. From the way they started laughing when I left the saloon, I expect it was the joke of the year for them. This amuses me as I know what they do not— that they have got something on their hands a little more than expected. Not that I am going to turn on them and try to be a Big Man. But neither am I going to let them hurrah me. If they give me enough respect to get by on I will play along with them.

After I left the saloon, I took a walk around the South Main area, checking every entrance, front and rear, of every building. After that, I spent the last of my money on a shotgun and a saw which I took to my room. I have cut the barrel short and will take it with me on my "rounds."

I have also cleaned my revolver with extra care and spent about thirty minutes practicing my draw. I was pleased to see that I am not as creaky as I expected.

Now I am ready for my first time on the job as Deputy City Marshal of Caldwell, Texas. I do not think I will have too much trouble when they find out I am not planning to step on any toes.

Later: The job is not going to be as easy as I thought. I was prepared for a little trouble but not for what happened.

Promptly at six o'clock, I began to walk (limp) my rounds. I had pinned the badge on my shirt and, I must say, got many goggle-eyed stares from people I passed on South Main. I guess I am the first new "law man" they have seen in a month of Sundays.

All went well for about an hour. Then I heard the sound of gun shots coming from the *Bullhead Saloon* and, running over, saw what appeared to be a drunken cow boy staggering around inside, firing his revolver.

I say "what appeared to be a drunken cow boy" for, on the verge of going in, I got a prickling on the back of my neck and decided that I wasn't going to go in by the front way after all. I ran around the building as fast as I could and went in through the back.

My hunch proved correct. The drunk was only a ruse. Waiting in a front corner was a second man, gun drawn and cocked. The picture was clear to me. While I was trying to arrest the cow boy, the second man would give him back action and disarm me, maybe even kill me if I resisted.

Seeing this, I stepped in from the back room and held my revolver pointed at the second man, my shotgun at the first. "If you boys are itching to meet your Maker, now is the time to do it," I told them.

At that, the play was turned. That cow boy was no drunker than I was. He and the second man dropped their guns on the floor and raised their arms at my command. I glanced at Bob Keller who was sitting at a nearby table. (Palmer was "elsewhere.") I smiled and said, "Your boys will have to do better than that."

I do not know why I did not let it go at that. Bob Keller laughed and said that I had caught those men fair and square and there would be no more "horseplay" at my expense. He invited me to join him for a drink and I could tell, from his expression, that he expected me to do it.

I guess I am strange but I would rather have died than give him satisfaction at that point. He just *knew* that I was going to feel relieved and have that drink with him to be everlasting grateful for his kindness.

The look on his face when I told him that I couldn't have a drink with him until I had put the two men in jail was something to keep me warm on winter nights! His mouth fell open and he looked as if he had been kicked in the stomach by a mule.

He caught himself and smiled but I had won the hand and he knew it. He did not say any more as I marched those b——s to jail and locked them up.

That was not as easy to do as it is to write. It took me twenty-five minutes to find the key to the cell. That jail looks as though it hasn't had a cleaning in years, its only prisoners being spiders. I will have to clean it up, I can see. I had to laugh when the "drunken" cow boy sat on a cot and made a cloud of dust rise from the mattress that caused him to cough until his face was red.

Well, I have done it now. I could have "won over" Keller, I believe, but I had to do it my own way. Maybe I can settle things with him later. Right now I am sure he would be happy to see me take a one way ride to H————on a runaway horse.

All in all, a good day!

It is worth a comment, at this juncture, to point out Clay's intuitive ability to "smell" a perilous situation.

From a practical viewpoint, there can have been no logical reason for him not to enter Bob Keller's saloon when he saw what appeared to be a drunken cowboy firing indiscriminately.

Only if we look toward that sense which is "beyond the senses" can we explain Clay's action. This "extra" sense seems to have been part and parcel of the makeup of every successful gun fighter of that period. It is as if they had built in antennae which enabled them to "pick up" impulses of danger whether they were visible to them or not. This ability served Clay in good stead many times in the years to come.

As to his intention to "settle things" with Bob Keller, this was not to be, the entire situation altering radically the following day.

July 12, 1870

Things have sure moved fast since I had that talk with Mayor Rayburn yesterday!

I was in the jail this morning, sweeping up, when Palmer burst in, fortified by a breakfast of whiskey. Obviously, Keller had given him the word because he tried to order me to let the two men go and, when that didn't work, told me I was "discharged."

I know this kind. McConnell was exactly like him, all bluff and bluster and jelly for a spine. I told him he had better go back to Keller and tell him he had failed to follow orders properly. (It seems, no matter what my intentions, I end up "crossing swords" with Keller!)

Palmer started losing nerve and yelled at me in a voice that started sounding like a woman's. "You get out of here!" he cried. "No one wants you! Get out, d———it!"

I reached out and ripped the badge off his vest.

"No," I said. "*You* get out before I kick your——— to Kingdom Come."

He turned as white as a snowflake and left the office, moving backward. The next I heard, he had saddled up and ridden hell bent for leather out of town. I guess he knew his life was worthless from the moment he had failed to follow Keller's orders.

I finished cleaning the jail and took another walk to the courthouse. The good Mayor was still in his rocking chair. I think he has taken root there. I told him that since the position of City Marshal of Caldwell had been "vacated" unexpectedly, I was applying for the job.

He looked at the Marshal's badge which I had pinned to my shirt and nodded. "Since there seems to be no throng of applicants waiting to compete with you," he said, "I guess that your availability will decide the issue." (Lord, how that man can spiel!)

Then he leaned forward in his chair and said, "Young fellow, take it easy now and maybe you will see the Autumn."

I walked to the *Bullhead* and went inside. Keller was in his room so I went up and knocked on the door. He was with a woman and didn't like being disturbed. When I told him I was the new Marshal, that topped it. "The H——— you are!" he said.

I guess I could have made some effort to unruffle his feathers. That was the time for it. There is something about him that rubs me the wrong way though. No matter what I mean to do, every time I see his face, I could not say a kind word if my life depended on it.

And it may.

The facts now stated were told to me by Clay at a later date, there being no way he could have known about them at the time.

After he had gone to Keller and informed him of his new status as City Marshal, Keller went storming to Mayor Rayburn who, not surprisingly, was also on his "boodle roll." He ordered Rayburn to get rid of Clay but Rayburn, old and tough—if not above whatever financial chicanery he could get away with—replied that Keller would have to do it himself. There was no point in Keller arranging the "advent" of a new Mayor either, he added, because the new one might be even less cooperative than he.

He told Keller that it was better to leave well enough alone. Clay was far superior to Palmer and, during their peak season, a dependable Marshal would be valuable to "hold the cover on the boiling pot." As for Clay's antipathy toward Keller, that would pass and things would simmer down.

This proved to be an error in judgment on Mayor Rayburn's part. He did not take into consideration—perhaps the concept was beyond his limited intellectual means— the inimical chemistry between Clay and Keller.

Sometimes, two men cannot get along no matter what the circumstances. Why this is so is grist for a full-scale study in itself, being a matter of so many infinitesimal details and their admixture that no "pat" solution can possibly be advanced as to why such a clash occurs.

That it does occur is evident. Clay and Keller probably

*could not have made peace with each other if they
tried. Some fundamental alienation existed between the
two which, in time, resulted in one more step of the
progression—or, some would say, retrogression—of Clay
toward his ultimate station as one of the West's most noted
men of violence.*

*Clay's initial days as City Marshal in Caldwell were not
easy ones. His journal entries made it clear he felt compelled to prove that his authority was valid. With Keller
doing everything in his power to thwart this effort, it
turned out to be an onerous one indeed.*

*Clay began to experience, for the first time in his life, the
uncomfortable sensation of knowing that his life was in jeop-
ardy twenty-four hours a day. Shots burned by him in the
night, fired from alleys or darkened windows. Near accidents
occurred with horses, wagons, and falling objects. On at
least one occasion he found ground glass in his food, on
several others, scorpions in his bed, once, a rattlesnake.*

*This proved to be a far cry from the sort of excitement to
which Clay responded. His "tingle" soon degenerated to
a cold sweat, his pleasure at having achieved the position of City Marshal fading steadily. His nerves began to
fray, his temper shortened.*

Then, one day in September of that year . . .

September 7, 1870

Got a nice surprise today. While I was making my rounds,
I ran into Cullen Baker and several of his cronies coming
out of a saloon. He did not recognize me right away, seeming to see only the badge which made his features harden
when I addressed him.

Then he remembered me and we shook hands. I invited

him into the saloon for another drink but he said that he and his boys had to be on their way. I think his feeling toward me was unfriendly even though I tried to make him feel at home.

That is not important though. What is important is that, when I asked him where Henry was, he said in Kellville recovering from some minor buckshot wounds. Kellville is only forty miles away!

I have sent a letter with the evening stage and hope that Henry will receive it soon and answer me. I asked him if he would like to come to Caldwell and be my Deputy. I told him that I realized he had no love for the law (nor do I) but that being Deputy would be a good "cover" for him so that he could be safe from any warrant put out for his arrest. Also, I wrote that if he wanted action, this is the place to find it as a daily food.

G———, I hope he comes! It would be grand to see the "old fellow" again! It would also be a relief to have someone like him backing me up. I am getting tired of being alone. It is not good for the nerves.

The passage of several weeks of silence just about convinced Clay that either Henry had not received his message or did not choose to reply, feeling that Clay had betrayed their friendship by becoming a "law man." In this, he underestimated Henry. To Blackstone, friendship was the only verity to be respected. He had no regard for anything else, least of all the law. It did not matter to him, therefore, which side of it he lived on. If "going honest" was what his friend requested, he would be pleased to do so.

September 23, 1870

Henry has come! G———— d———— but it is good to see his smiling face again! He has not changed a bit!

I was leaving my office when he came in.

"Well, old fellow," he said, "here I am."

I was so happy to see him I gave him a bear hug. He laughed and said to take it easy because his buckshot wounds were giving him a little bother.

I apologized and shook his hand. (*Wrung* his hand is what I did!) I had no idea how much I needed someone. When he told me he had come to be my Deputy, I felt a heavy weight fly off my back.

We talked a while and he told me what he had been doing since I last saw him. It was not much different from what he and I had done. How he can look so unchanged living like that is amazing to me.

He told me that he had read about my "exploits" in the Brady-Courtwright War which surprised me as I did not know that the papers in New Mexico had written about it. (How could I have known *anything* being staked to the ground every day?) He said that he had stopped in Hickman to say hello but found that I was gone. I told him all about it and he said that if he was ever back that way, he would shoot Bollinger for me.

I took him to the courthouse and told Rayburn I wanted Henry sworn in as my Deputy. Needless to say, the Mayor was rocking. He never even slowed down as he swore in Henry.

Henry and I walked back to South Main and went into the *Bullhead*. There, I introduced him to Keller. While that was still fresh in his craw, I told him he was going to have to move his faro tables out of the back room and put them in front where I could keep an eye on them. A lot of cow boys have complained to me that they were fleeced. His is not the only place that does it naturally but, since he is the biggest (and my favorite victim!), I figured an example should be set.

I really had the b——— off his balance today! To begin with, he is not sure at all how far he can push me. On top of that, Henry bothered the H——— out of him! I can see why. Henry looks so young—younger than me now—and standing there, smiling like he does, with a shotgun cradled in his arms, he must have set Keller's teeth on edge.

Maybe I imagined that but, whatever the case, they carried those tables into the front room and Henry and I left. We went across the street to the Palomino House and I bought him the biggest steak they had. Lord, but it is good to be together with him again!

Keller, now more anxious than ever to dispose of Clay—though unwilling to attempt the job himself—began to work on Lieutenant Alfred Gregory, the hot-tempered son of the General who commanded Fort Morgan, a nearby military post.

Gregory was well known in that area as a troublemaker. Handsome and arrogant, the victor in a score of past gun duels, he provided the ideal pawn for Keller's game.

Telling Gregory that Clay had voiced hostility toward him, he enhanced the plot by implying that the talk about Clay's prowess with the hand gun was without substance, no one ever really having seen him use it. As for the stories circulated by Henry Blackstone regarding the "murderous swath" Clay had cut through the Brady-Courtwright War in New Mexico, they were obvious fabrications put forth by Blackstone, with Clay's blessing, to bolster Clay's position as Marshal.

The first encounter between Gregory and Clay came about as follows.

November 19, 1870

I was standing at the counter in *The Virginia Saloon* tonight, having a drink with Henry when Lieutenant Gregory came in.

I knew as soon as I saw him that he had made up his mind to test me. Even as he started toward me, I made up *my* mind to try something I had never done before.

He stopped behind me and I turned to face him. Henry did not turn but watched us in the mirror. Knowing he was there gave me confidence that no tricks would be played on me.

"What do you want?" I asked Gregory.

"I want to know if you are really as fast with a gun as I have heard," he replied.

"There is only one way to find out," I said.

"That is why I am here," he answered. "I intend to prove to every one present that you are nothing but a bag of wind."

"Prove away," I told him.

"And after you are shot down, I am going to cut out your tongue and make you eat it before you die."

"Sounds as though you have quite an evening planned," I said. I did not look around but I knew Henry would be smiling at that.

Gregory waited.

"Well?" I asked. "What are you waiting for? If I am to have my tongue for a late snack, we had better get to it."

"Fill your hand," he said.

"I will not pull down on you first," I told him.

"You are a coward then," he said.

"No," I answered, "I am just too fast for you and think it only kind to let you take first crack."

That did it. I saw him start to draw in his eyes, long

before the message reached his hand. I did not give him any time but snatched out my Colt and laid it across his skull as hard as I could. He went down like a sack of grain.

I finished my drink. Then Henry took one of Gregory's legs and I took the other and we dragged him out of the saloon and down the street to jail.

He opened his eyes as I was locking the door of the cell. I never saw such hatred in a man's face, not even Keller's. He told me that the next time we meet, the only possible exchange between us is one of lead.

I believe that I will not be able to buffalo him a second time and will keep my eyes on him in word and action.

Henry said that he did not know why I did not kill Gregory. I told him that I wanted to see if I could buffalo him as I had never done that to a man before. Henry asked me if I wanted him to kill Gregory in the cell but I told him no. I think he would have done it too.

Henry is as strange as ever.

The "show down" between Clay and Lieutenant Gregory came following a blizzard.

I wonder if the reader is aware of the fantastic violence of the so-called "Norther" of the plains. If not, it might not be amiss to append here a brief description of same selected from an article written by myself some years ago.

"The sky is a sunless gray and a deep, incredible stillness fills the air. Horses and cattle are restless, snorting and moaning in anticipation of something terrible about to happen.

"Suddenly, their breath goes white, all warmth swept from the air as a cloud of white appears on the horizon. Soft and fleecy-looking, it approaches quickly, rising and spreading. Soon the wail of wind is heard, the icy juggernaut drawing closer and closer.

"In the flash of an instant, it hits, a brutal "Norther"—blinding, smothering waves of fine white snow. Livestock turn their backs to it, covered, in seconds, by a blanket of white. Men, women and children rush for shelter, unable to breathe outside, their nostrils clogged by freezing, driving grains of snow, their eyes stung and blinded.

"The wind increases steadily, an Arctic banshee howling across the land. Nothing can be seen but one, continuous, glittering whirl of particles. Powdery snow rushes over everything. Great drifts begin to form. Horses and cattle shiver helplessly, their mouths and eyelids frozen shut, icicles hanging from their jaws."

Such a blizzard hit Caldwell in December of that year leaving in its wake a vast, white, mantling silence.

Soon afterward, the incident which became popularly known as "Snowballs and Lead" occurred.

December 20, 1870

Henry and I were in the office, sitting by the stove, when we heard some horses stop outside. I was comfortable and sleepy so I asked Henry to see who it was.

He got up and went to the window.

"Gregory," he said.

That woke me quick enough. I got up and went over beside him.

Lieutenant Gregory and three men, one of them a Cavalry Sergeant, were just dismounting. They saw us looking at them but made no sign that they had. Their breath steamed as they stood outside, waiting.

"We have to go outside?" Henry asked.

"Don't you want to?" I said.

"No," he replied. "It is too cold. Can't we just shoot them down from here?"

"Henry," I said. "We are law men. We are supposed to *not* shoot people if we can."

"I thought you said this job was going to be fun," he replied. I glanced at him. Naturally, he was smiling.

We looked at Gregory and the three men for a while. I guess they thought we were trying to figure out a way to get out of it.

"If we can keep from going out a little longer," I said, "they will freeze to death and we will not have to face them."

"I hope so," Henry said. "I hate to go outside when it's cold."

"Well," I said after a few more moments, "we had better go out anyway."

We put on our coats and hats but no gloves.

"The odds are not good," I said. "If we can keep from shooting, we had better do it."

"Anything you say," Henry told me but I knew that he was hoping there would be gun play. There is a difference in his smile when he is ready for action. I did not notice it in the old days but I do now.

We went outside and stood on the plank walk facing the four men across the hitching pole. There was snow on top of it and I scooped up some and started packing a snow ball while we talked.

"Well," I said, "don't you think it is a little cold for this sort of thing?"

"Don't worry," Gregory said, "you will be frying in H———— pretty quick."

"Has it ever occurred to you that *you* might be the one to fry?" I asked.

"No," he said. "It is going to be you and your G———— d————d, grinning Deputy."

I looked at the other men. They did not seem as sure of the play so I decided to work on them. If I could separate them from Gregory, there would be less of a problem.

"You boys look sensible," I said. "Why are you here? This is not your ruckus."

None of them spoke but I could see, clear enough, that not one of them wanted to fight.

"We are not here to listen to you, you yellow b————," Gregory said. I saw him pull back the flap of his coat and start to draw and I let fly with the snow ball. It was a risk but it worked. The snow ball hit him on the hand and knocked his revolver into the snow.

The Sergeant knew what I was trying to do right away. It is strange how he and I seemed to understand each other without a word between us while, after seven months of talk, Keller and I are further apart than ever.

Any way, the Sergeant understood that I was trying to avoid spilling blood and, as quick as he could, he snatched up snow, rolled a ball and heaved it at me. It hit me on the chest and splattered over my coat.

That opened up the situation fine. Those other men were glad to grab up snow and, in a matter of seconds, the air was thick with snow balls flying back and forth. Everybody started laughing. Henry got a real kick out of it and laughed louder than any of them. We started having a H———— of a good time and I figured I had saved some lives.

Henry broke it. I do not know if it was an accident or not. I am afraid it wasn't because Gregory had called him a G———— d————d, grinning Deputy. Henry kept throwing snow balls at him. Gregory was not returning them but he was not shooting either even though he had picked up his gun and put it back in its scabbard. He was smart enough to know that it wasn't four to two in his favor anymore but two to one in ours.

As I say, Henry broke it. First, he knocked off Gregory's hat. That was not too bad as I had lost my hat as well as the Sergeant and one of Gregory's other men. But then Henry hit Gregory full in the face with a snow ball and blood started spurting from Gregory's nose as he staggered back. It must have hurt him something terrible.

"You G——— d——d s——— of a b———!" he cried. Suddenly, he did not seem to care what the odds were for he snatched at his revolver.

I guess that was what Henry was waiting for. He out-drew Gregory and shot him dead between the eyes.

In that moment, all the fun and laughter ended. The three men went for their revolvers, I drew mine and gun fire exploded all around. It did not last for more than five or six seconds, I believe. When the cloud of black smoke drifted off, Henry and I were still on our feet, untouched, but, except for us, only the Sergeant was still alive and that was because I had tried to knock him down without kill-ing him.

I put my Colt away and moved to the Sergeant. The snow was red with his blood.

"I am sorry it went this way," I said. "You saw I was try-ing to avoid it."

He nodded but could not speak because of pain. I helped him to his feet and started leading him down the street toward Doctor Kiley's place. Henry went with me.

As we passed the *Bullhead*, Keller and some other men were standing outside. Keller glared at us, disappointed that we were still alive.

"The next time you talk anybody into coming after me," I told him, "I will come gunning for you after I have killed them."

He did not say any thing. He jumped as Henry kicked some snow across his legs and shoes. He would not fight though. Henry kicked some more snow at him and he backed away. When Henry picked up snow, Keller went into his saloon fast. Henry threw a snow ball after him which sailed over the bat wing doors. I hope it hit him on the back of the head but I doubt it.

The next time I *will* go after him, the miserable s———— of a b————. The Sergeant died tonight. It is a waste of a good man. I promised him that I would write to his wife in St. Louis. I wish I knew what I could say to her that would make it easier.

The duel in the snow was the first gunbattle of Clay's to be publicized to any extent.

While some notoriety had attached itself to his part in the Brady-Courtwright War, word of it was not as widely promulgated as word of this particular encounter.

Why this is so is anybody's guess. My personal feeling is that the details of it had a certain extra color to them: a good-looking young Marshal trying to avoid bloodshed by attempting to convert a moment of sanguine threat into one of schoolboy jollity and, failing that, making it obvious that the attempt had not been motivated by cowardice by revealing himself to be a deadly gun handler and, with his Deputy, killing three men and fatally wounding a fourth, all at close range.

Whatever the reason, the story of "Snowballs and Lead" spread around the country like wildfire, catching the fancy of a man who, more than anyone, was to catapult Clay's name into national prominence.

April 17, 1871

Henry and I were having breakfast at the Palomino House when this dude came in and walked over to our table.

He introduced himself as Miles Radaker, the editor-publisher of a New York City magazine called *The Current Observer.*

I asked him what he was doing so far away from his home digs.

He told me that he had come out West for a number of
reasons. The main one was to meet me.

"What for?" I asked.

"You are too modest, sir," he replied. "Do you not
realize that your name is on everyone's tongue back
East?"

"Why?" I asked.

"Because of your heroic exploit in the snow," he said.
"Not to mention your daring accomplishments during the
Brady-Courtwright War on which I have been doing con-
siderable research."

"Is that right?" I said.

"That is pre-eminently right, sir," he replied. (He and
Mayor Rayburn ought to get together!) "People back East
are entranced by frontier activities and read every word
about them they can lay their hands on. And you, sir, are
just the sort of man they want to read about."

He sounded weird to me so I did not have too much to
say to him. I left, soon, to go to the office. Henry stayed
behind. I wish I could have hidden underneath the table and listened. Henry said, later, that he started telling Radaker one "whopper" after another about me. For
once in his life, he said, he did not smile but kept a serious
face.

For instance, Radaker asked him how many men I had
killed.

"Well, sir," Henry answered, "not counting Rebs and Indians, seventy-five. No, make that seventy-six. I forgot the
one he shot this morning before breakfast. He likes to do
that as it sharpens his appetite."

How he could keep a straight face through that I can not
imagine. When he told me all the crazy things he had said,
to Radaker, about me, I laughed until my sides ached.

What is most amazing, Henry said, is that Radaker believed every word!

Here, Henry Blackstone (and Clay) revealed his basic naivete.

I know Miles Radaker and, if there is one quality he does not possess to any degree whatsoever it is gullibility. Obviously, Blackstone, thinking he was joshing Radaker, was, in fact, being joshed himself. I have no doubt that Radaker knew that Blackstone was "stretching the truth," but did not care since this was exactly the sort of material he was looking for. The more outrageous the lies, he knew, the more they would work to his advantage. To Blackstone, he may have appeared gratifyingly agog. Actually, I am sure that Radaker was mentally adding up the dollars to come even as he listened, openmouthed and "credulous," to Blackstone.

All unknowingly, therefore, thinking that he was only joking, Henry Blackstone began to build that structure of fictional absurdities upon which Clay was soon to climb to fame's precarious heights.

Let me be clear on this. Clay was *as I have presented him; to all intents and purposes, fearless in a dangerous situation and, without a doubt, deadly with a six-shooter. He was* not *the Godlike figure all the stories make him out to be. No human being ever could be such a figure and Clay was human; very human.*

The first articles in Radaker's magazine appeared that summer.

July 9, 1871

That dude, Radaker, was not joking when he said that he was going to write an article about me in his magazine.

Today, the stage brought in a copy of the magazine with the article in it. Radaker sent it to me. It is a caution sure enough.

Henry read it to me in the office this evening. I had already looked it over but the true foolishness of it was not apparent until Henry read it aloud.

"This Halser," he read, "has one of the handsomest physiques that I have ever had the pleasure to observe. His shoulders are incredibly broad and taper to a narrow waist at which hangs his brace of 'forty-fives,' ever ready for action."

I was trying to get some paperwork done and I told Henry to shut up. *Brace of forty-fives!* Radaker must have been blind not to see that I only wear one gun and it is a .41.

Henry would not shut up. "There is grace and dignity in his manly carriage," he read on. "His face is exceptionally well-fashioned by the Creator's art, his lips thin and artistically sensitive, his nose a strong, aquiline promontory, his eyes as gentle as . . ."

Henry snorted and almost fell off his chair, which was leaning against the wall. ". . . as a woman's!" he said.

I had to laugh. *"Will you shut up?"* I said.

He would not. There were tears rolling down his cheeks as he kept on reading. "One would not believe that these two gentle orbs have pointed the way to dusty death for scores of frontier miscreants. [That word really tied his tongue in a knot.] But, as they say on the border: When Halser shoots, it is to kill."

"Shut up!" I yelled and threw my hat at him. He fell off his chair and landed on the floor, kicking his legs he was laughing so hard.

I have thought about it all day and, I must say, it is not only amusement I feel. I suppose I can not blame Henry for telling those whoppers to Radaker. He meant no harm and, even if he had not told them, Radaker probably would have written the article any way.

Still, I am displeased. The article makes me sound foolish. I may not be a Great Hero but I am not a fool. And I *have* done *some* of the things he wrote of in the article. It is just that they are lost in all those lies.

Two facts become apparent from this entry:
One: Clay resented the exaggerations, being honest enough to recognize them for what they were.
Two: This resentment was equally directed at the fact that the article tended to obscure those of his achievements which were true.
In brief, he did not mind being placed in the limelight but wanted facts to put him there, not fancies.
I speak from firsthand knowledge when I state that Clay was not immune to the gratification of being celebrated. In the early days of his newborn renown, he was not at all adverse to being famous, only to being famous for the wrong reasons.
The possibility that this spurious acclaim might be a source of danger did not occur to him.
About that time, an old acquaintance returned to his life.

July 25, 1871

Got a nice surprise today. The Fenway Circus has come to Caldwell.

I was in the office when the wagons rolled by. I did not see Hazel but I saw the name of the circus.

After having dinner, I took a stroll to the edge of town where they were setting up the tent. Seeing my badge, Fenway thought I was there to make problems but I told him that he was welcome in Caldwell and asked him if Hazel and Carl were still with his show.

He said that they were but that Carl was now a ground worker and Hazel has another partner for the act.

He told me where to find her wagon and I went there. Carl was working, helping to set up the tent. I walked right by him but he did not recognize me. He looks terrible. He must be drinking more than ever.

I knocked on the door of the wagon and Hazel asked who it was.

"Clay Halser," I said.

She was silent long enough to tell me that she didn't remember my name. Then she said, "Clay!" and pulled open the door. She had been drinking some herself. Maybe that was why she didn't recall me.

I went inside and we kissed each other. She had only a thin robe on and the way she pressed against me I could feel every soft part of her.

She said that Carl would be working for hours and she bolted the door and took off her robe less than a minute after I got in the wagon.

I was worried about Carl but she said not to be as she took my clothes off. She said that even if he came in while we were "at it" he would not say a word. She takes care of him now, providing him with whiskey and a place to sleep. (Never her bed anymore.)

I had forgotten how good it was with her. Nancy and Myra at Mama Wilkie's place are not bad but nothing special. Hazel is special. I hope the circus stays here for a long time.

She is impressed that I am the City Marshal in Caldwell. She hinted that she is getting tired of circus life and of Carl and that a man "in my position" could use a "help mate."

I suppose that is true but I do not think that Hazel is the one. She is still married to Carl for one thing and, even if she was not, I do not think that I would care to make her Mrs. Halser. She is starting to look a little "worn at the seams" as they say and she is so willing to get into bed with me that I suspect she has gotten into bed with many other men too.

I wonder if it would make any sense to write to Mary Jane. I guess not. I am sure she is married already.

I would write to Anne if she had not betrayed me. I still have a warm place in my heart for her despite her treachery. Maybe treachery is too hard a word for what she did. What difference does it make? I will never see her again.

Any way, Hazel will save me the money I usually spend at Mama Wilkie's!

At this point, I can break in personally, not only to comment on Clay's journal but to carry forward the story for a period of time.

In the summer of that year, I traveled to Caldwell to interview Clay. Having read Radaker's outlandish article, I recognized the unbelievable figure presented as being none other than the present day (exaggerated) version of the young soldier I had interviewed near the end of the War.

I persuaded my editor (I worked, at that time, for The Greenvale Review) *to let me travel West, speak to Clay and prepare a series of articles which, while no less fascinating, would be more factual and, therefore, more acceptable to the intelligent reader. Fortunately, I was able to convince him—because of personal experience—that Radaker's article was not completely false, only colored to a ludicrous extent. I assured my editor that a more realistic approach would prove even more popular; that, within the boundaries of truth, Clay had accomplished many things well worth recording.*

I was witness to such an occurrence one afternoon while talking to Clay in a saloon. A cowboy (later identified as the one who had pretended to be drunk on Clay's first night as Deputy Marshal) walked up behind Clay, drew out his revolver and pressed it to the back of Clay's head.

"Now I got you, Mr. Marshal Big Time Halser," he said. "Let me see you get out of this tight."

While I observed in speechless dread, Clay replied, "Now, Jim, that is not your way. You are not the kind to take a man's life without giving him a show."

I do not know which aspect of the situation shocked me more—the sight of that cowboy with the muzzle of his revolver pressed against the back of Clay's head or Clay's incredibly calm voice. He might have been ordering dessert in a restaurant!

"We have no reason to be set against each other, Jim," he said. "We both know it is Keller who wants me dead because I am trying to prevent him from cheating men like you in crooked card games. You and I have every reason to be friends so why not put up your gun and sit down to split a bottle of champagne with me?"

I cannot put down every word Clay said because, in truth, I cannot remember them. The words above I wrote from memory that very evening. Even at that, I could not remember every word because there were too many of them—although the foregoing conveys the "gist" of their import. Clay kept telling the cowboy, over and over, that he was a person of honor who would not murder a defenseless man; that Keller was the one behind the situation and that there was no reason for the cowboy and Clay not to be the best of friends; finally, that Clay would be honored if the man would sit down with him and split a bottle of champagne. In the deathly silence of that saloon, Clay must have spoken without cease for a good twenty minutes before the cowboy pulled back his revolver and put it away.

At that, Clay moved for the first time, turning casually to the bartender and ordering a bottle of champagne. This was brought to the table where Clay poured some for me, the cowboy and himself. What is more, I swear on the Bible that there was not so much as a tremor to his hand!

He toasted the cowboy ("You are the right stripe of man, Jim."), had a few glasses of champagne, exchanged several jokes, then left.

I followed him to his hotel room.

"Who is it?" he asked when I knocked on the door.

I told him and he unlocked the door to let me in.

He had just taken off his coat and vest and was in the process of removing his shirt. He might have just come in from standing in a rainstorm, it was so sopping wet.

"That was inspiring," I told him.

Clay smiled. "Perspiring," he said.

Notwithstanding, I was genuinely impressed and made haste to convey that feeling in the first of my projected series of articles for the The Greenvale Review.

When it appeared in the magazine a few months later, I was appalled by the changes made. It had been enlarged upon and, like the Radaker article, conveyed a general tone of grandiloquent hero worship. What I had intended to be an honest appraisal turned out to be merely another slice of lurid journalism.

Infuriated, I resigned my position with the magazine and vowed never to attempt such an article again. (Unfortunately, by then, I had already sent in two more which were, also, "doctored" beyond recognition.) I apologized to Clay, who accepted with grace. Again, however, I could see that, while amused by the article's excesses, he could not help but be affected by the fact that all those sumptuous words were about him.

I remained in Caldwell for a number of months, working for the local paper, (The Caldwell Gazette) *a position which Clay acquired for me.*

It was not my intention to remain in Caldwell indefinitely but to stay there only long enough to collect an adequate amount of material regarding Clay, so that I might prepare a biography of his life. In this way, I hoped to be able to present, to the reading world, a more honest examination of his achievements.

It is to my shame that, to this day, no such biography has been written. (One reason, perhaps, I have prepared this volume.) Nonetheless, the period during which I lived in Caldwell did enable me to observe, at first hand, the rise of the Halser Legend.

After Radaker's article—and mine, I presume—had "started the wheels turning," an increasing number of magazines and newspapers sent representatives to Caldwell to interview Clay. He had "caught on" in the East as a symbol of Heroism. He was Hercules in boots, Samson with "a brace of pistols." (I never did know whether Clay's eventual practice of wearing two six-shooters was a matter of practicality or an unconscious desire to match the descriptions of himself which invariably referred to "a forty-five in each hand, spewing leaden death to all who opposed him.")

At any rate, Clay was plucked from the crowd by the hand of a thrill-loving populace and lifted to a height of dubious fame. Men everywhere began to envy him, women to dream romantically of him. He became an idol to the young.

Much to my uneasiness, I saw that he was starting to acquire a kind of helpless fascination toward the mounting flood of written matter concerning him. It was as if he read the articles and stories with a schism in his mind. For a time, he would be amused by the absurdities of what was written. Then, it seemed, it would rush across him that he was reading about himself; that all those words

*of praise and reverence were about him and no other—
and he would react accordingly.*

*When the novels started to appear, his absorption be-
came indelible. How many men, in their middle twenties,
have novels written about them?—full-length books which
refer to them by name, in which they are involved in one
incredibly heroic exploit after another? Even discerning
their flaws with a clear eye—which he never lost—he
could not restrain an inward sense of pleasure. (Indeed,
had he been able to do so, he really would have been a
Super Being.)*

*Soon, a reaction began to manifest itself and he found
himself becoming edgy and defensive. In essence, his
rationale (though never actually voiced) might have been:
"All right, the articles, and stories, and books are ridiculous exaggerations. Still they are not entirely made up. I
have not exactly been sitting on my hands since leaving
Pine Grove. Some of what they are writing is true.*

"Quite a bit of it, in fact."

I have, deliberately, omitted, from this section of the
story, the many journal entries which detail the day-by-
day problems Clay faced as Marshal of Caldwell. I have
done this primarily because they, largely, duplicate a later
section of this book in which the elements of being Marshal in a "cow town" are more, graphically, covered.

Suffice to say that Clay's conflict with Keller continued
unabated. Keller was never resigned to Clay's position as
Marshal. Clay trod upon his toes on too many occasions,
costing him money.

In addition to this conflict, there was, of course, the main
body of Clay's duties which was to "keep the peace" (as
well as he could) when the masses of cowboys descended
on the town like locusts following their drives to the rail

head. These periods were incredibly demanding. During them, he and Henry Blackstone were forced to be "on call" virtually twenty-four hours a day. Clay made some attempt to ease this situation; by swearing in additional deputies during these times but, almost always, they would quit when the "going" became too hard for them.

About this time, reactions to the laudatory articles about Clay began to occur periodically when cowboys, their courage fired by whiskey, would challenge Clay to gun fights.

On almost every one of these occassions, Clay used, to great advantage, his ability to "buffalo" his would-be opponents. Outdrawing them, he would knock them unconscious with the barrel of his revolver, toss them into jail, and release them the following morning, chastened and, almost always, grateful for his forbearance in not killing them.

On one occasion, however, when a cowboy tried, again, to "take him on" the next day, Clay was forced to shoot him. Fortunately, the cowboy's wound was not severe and, after a period of recuperation, he was able to return to the ranch on which he worked.

Clay ultimately solved the problem almost altogether by initiating a "no guns while in town" policy which, following some inevitable resistance, was generally accepted.

Finally, I have eliminated those entries which mention Clay's renewed dalliance with Hazel Thatcher.

During the time the circus was in Caldwell, he and she "took up" where they had left off in Morgan City. Their relationship was marked by a total lack of growth. Although Hazel suggested, more than once, the advantages she foresaw in a marriage between them, Clay never went along with her. Clearly, his moral standards would not permit him to associate with such a woman in marriage

*although he was perfectly willing to share her company
and bed as long as she permitted it.*

*I might add that I am not able to appreciate how she
could have been described, by Clay, as a "powerfully
good-looking woman." Even allowing for the deterioration which attends "hard" living, I do not see how a truly
"good-looking" woman could have lost so much in her
appearance (between that time and the time they first had
met in Morgan City), as to look the way Hazel Thatcher
did when I knew her. "Coarse" is the only word which
comes to mind.*

*In time, the circus left and there was a rather cool fare-
well between the two.*

*Soon after—as an unexpected dividend of his mount-
ing fame—a relationship more meaningful in Clay's life
was restored.*

March 14, 1872

I am very excited and happy as I write this. I received a
letter from Anne today!

I always hoped that I would hear from her again although I never really could believe that I would.

Now I have and I understand why she did not testify at
my trial.

She explained that, after her father had run out (in the
dead of night while she and her stepmother were asleep!)
her stepmother had run off with another man and ended up,
sick and destitute, hundreds of miles away. She had written
to Anne for help and Anne had traveled to her side to remain with her for several months, nursing her back to health.

She had had every intention of testifying for me but
her correspondent from Hickman—a Brady sympathizer

she eventually discovered—had lied to her about the trial date. When she'd finally learned of my conviction, she had made immediate plans to return to Hickman despite her stepmother's illness.

Then she had been told about the Governor's amnesty and had assumed that I was safe and would wait for her despite the fact that I had failed to answer any of her letters. (I never received one of them and am convinced that they were destroyed before I could.)

Now she has read about me in the newspaper and "taken courage in hand" to write to me. She hopes that I remember her kindly and will come to visit her in Hickman some day.

I still love you very much is the final sentence of her letter.

My G———, I am happy! I have sent her a letter, telling her that I still love her too and want her to marry me and come back to Caldwell with me as my wife.

Things are slow now any way. I can make Henry temporary marshal while I travel to Hickman.

Anne!

Clay received a prompt, overjoyed answer from Anne and immediately prepared to entrain to Hickman.

Since I was planning to return to New York about that time, I arranged my schedule so that he and I could ride North together before going our separate ways.

A minor—yet telling—incident occurred our second day out.

Two young boys, discovering that Clay was on the train, approached him, saucer-eyed, to stare and listen reverently to his words.

Embarrassed by their gaping awe—especially with me sitting beside him and the other passengers observing— Clay resorted to the tall tale, spinning the boys a whop-

*per in which fifty-seven Indians trapped him in a box
canyon with his only weapon a knife.*

"What happened?" *asked one of the boys.*

"I was killed," *Clay answered.*

*His intent had, clearly, been to josh the boys out of their
attitude of hero worship and give them a laugh. Instead,
all he did was confuse them. I am sure that they believed
that Clay had been telling them the gospel truth until his
final words, at which point, for some unexplainable reason,
he had chosen to avoid relating the gory details of how he
had killed those fifty-seven savages with his knife.*

*As they returned to their mother, disappointed, Clay
frowned and said he did not understand. It was the one
time in all the years I knew him that I directed a remark
at him which might have been interpreted as critical.*

"You almost believe some of the stories yourself now,"
I said. "Is it any wonder that they believe them all?"

*Clay and Anne were reunited to discover that the fer-
vor of their love was easily recaptured.*

*Clay remained in Hickman for a month, at the end of
which time he and Anne were married in the community
church and prepared to return to Caldwell.*

*Another telling incident occurred the day they went to
leave Hickman.*

May 2, 1872

I cleaned out an old sore today.

Anne and I were on our way to the train station when I
caught sight of Sheriff Bollinger talking to some men
across the street.

I stopped the carriage and told Anne that I would be
right back. I crossed the street and walked up to Bollinger.

"There you are, you son of a b————," I said. "I have been wondering where you have been hiding while I was in town."

The man is a coward. I have always known that. All the blood in his face disappeared. He stared at me with the look of a man who knows he is about to die.

I did not try to change that look.

"You yellow b————," I said. "Maybe you would like to beat me now."

He raised his arms as though I had said, "Hands up." "I have no quarrel with you," he said.

"Well, I have a quarrel with you," I said. "And I am going to end it here and now. Go for your gun, you son of a b————."

"No," he said. "I have no quarrel with you."

"Either go for your gun or I will shoot you down like the dog you are," I told him.

"You would not shoot a man with his hands in the air, would you?" he asked.

"What makes you think you are a man?" I said. "You are a sneaking cur and a bully, nothing more."

Sweat was running down his face. He looked sick to his stomach.

"Are you going to fill your hand?" I asked. "Or must I murder you?"

"You would not," he said. "You would not."

I was getting tired of it by then. What glory is there in humbling such a specimen?

"Tell these men here that you are a coward and a G————d————d son of a b————," I told him.

He said it right away as if he believed it.

"Now take off your gun belt and drop it in that water trough," I said.

He unbuckled his belt with shaking hands and dropped the works into the water.

"If I ever hear of you wearing a gun again," I said, "I will come back and kill you without mercy."

I turned on my heel and went back to Anne. I think that Bollinger will not be very popular in Hickman now.

While Clay, perhaps, deserved some praise for his restraint in not actually killing Bollinger, he failed to realize, I believe, that, to a large degree (if not entirely), Bollinger was cowed so pitifully by Halser the Legend rather than by Halser the man.

It is, of course, possible that Bollinger, being what he was, might have behaved in just as craven a manner had there not been any articles or stories recounting Clay's deadly skill with a gun.

I very much suspect, however, that the stories had affected Bollinger and that he believed himself to be confronted by some Super Being at whose dread hand he could expect no mercy.

May 9, 1872

This has been the roughest day I have spent in Caldwell since the day Lieutenant Gregory rode into town to kill me.

I have told Anne that it can not happen again but I do not think she believes me. It is too bad it had to take place the first day she arrived here.

Henry did not write to me while I was in Hickman but that did not disturb me. I assumed that he had things in hand.

I had a bad surprise in store when we reached the hotel. Anne and I had been stared at while we were walking from the train station but I figured that it was because they had heard I was getting married and were curious about my wife.

It turned out to be a different story altogether.

Claxton (*the desk clerk. F.L.*) was amazed to see me! He said that every one thought I had left Caldwell for good. I asked him how they could think that. Did they believe that I had made Henry the Marshal?

That brought on the second bad surprise. Henry left town two weeks ago, he told us! (To this moment, I do not know why.) The third bad surprise—a new Marshal had been sworn in by the Mayor!

I got Anne set up in a room and told her I would be back as soon as I had settled things. She seemed upset and I could not blame her. She must have thought that I had made up the whole thing about being Marshal of Caldwell! Now that I look back, she must have thought, for a while, that she had married a mad man!

I walked to the courthouse. For a change, Rayburn was not on the porch, sitting on his beloved rocking chair. I found him inside, in his office and asked him what the H——— was going on.

He looked surprised to see me too. He said that, like every one else, he had thought that I had left Caldwell for good—especially after Henry took out.

I asked him who had told him all this. I should have known.

Bob Keller.

Rayburn told me that the new Marshal was one of Keller's "toadies" just as Palmer had been.

"We will see about that," I said.

"I don't think that Keller is going to be glad to see you," Rayburn told me.

"I do not give a d——— whether he is glad or not," I said. "I am the Marshal and that is the way it is going to remain."

I was seeing red by then. I walked fast as I could to the *Bullhead* knowing that, whoever the new "Marshal" was, he would be there.

He was at that. I found him playing cards with a few of
Keller's other boys. If I had not been so mad, I would have
laughed. It was Nicholson! *(The other man Clay had put
in jail his first night as Deputy Marshal. F.L.)*

He looked pretty d——d surprised to see me. I walked
across the room to the table he was sitting at. He was about
to take a drink of whiskey and the glass was frozen in the
air between the table and his mouth. I knocked it out of
his hand and grabbed him by the shirt front. Hauling him
to his feet, I ripped the badge off his shirt and shoved him
back into the chair.

"If you want it back," I told him, "you will have to take
it from my dead fingers."

I waited for him to draw but was not surprised when he
did not. He started to shake and put his hands on the table, palms down.

"Who in the H——— told you that you could be the
Marshal?" I demanded.

"Mr. Keller," he replied. "He told me that you were gone
for good. I swear I would not have put on the badge if I
had known you were coming back."

I had to believe him because he was so scared.

Just then, Keller came down from upstairs and I walked
over to him.

"If you ever try to pull a trick like that on me again," I
told him, "I will bury you in Boot Hill."

He did not answer me but I could see, in his eyes, that
he was close to the edge.

To make sure he could not back down, I told him that,
from then on, I was going to hurrah him night and day.
"I am going to make a set of rules for you alone," I said. "And
if you break just one of them, I will toss you in the hoose-
gow and throw away the key."

I turned and started for the door, using the sides of my
eyes to keep a watch on him in the wall mirror.

As I expected, I was almost to the door when he reached beneath his coat to draw the Derringer I knew was there.

Before he could fire, I dove to the left and took shelter behind the counter end as the shot roared and a ball tore wood away near my head.

Snatching out my gun, I reached above the counter and fired back at him. I heard chairs scraping back and men running for safety.

"Nicholson!" Keller shouted.

I thought he was asking Nicholson to assist him in killing me and I shouted, "Any man who helps Keller is a dead one!"

Another shot rang out and lead exploded through the wood close to me. I flung myself behind the counter and the bar tender took off. I did not realize, at that moment, that Keller had called to Nicholson to throw him his six-shooter.

Another shot roared and bottles were smashed above me, spilling whiskey on me. I looked up and saw a movement in the mirror. Keller was rushing toward the end of the counter to shoot at me.

I reared up fast. He was just passing by. I saw his head snap around, a look of shock on his face. Then I fired at point blank range and put two balls in his heart. He was flung away from the counter and landed, dead, on the floor, his vest on fire.

I looked around the room but all the others had gone. Keeping my Colt in hand just to be safe, I edged along the wall. I saw the bar tender peering out from the back room and told him to "put out" his boss.

I returned to the hotel. My clothes were dirty and wrinkled and there was a tear in the right knee of my trousers. Anne, who had heard the gun fire, was waiting on the porch of the hotel, looking terrified. I took her by the arm and led her back inside.

"Is this the way it *always* is?" she asked.

I had to chuckle at the sound of her voice. She sounded like a little girl.

"It will simmer down now," I told her.

Simmer down it did. Keller disposed of, all organized attempts to weaken Clay's position ceased and, within the framework of what it was—a "wild and woolly" frontier cattle town—Caldwell assumed almost a tranquil atmosphere. Clay had succeeded in "taming" it.

He had, also, succeeded in creating, for himself, a state of gilt-edged boredom. Violence and tension, he discovered, are like drugs to which a man of his temperament can become addicted.

The articles and stories and books continued, but the situations which inspired them no longer occurred—or occurred in such minor ways as to be without stimulation to him. As in Pine Grove, seven years earlier, he started to become restless and discontented, yearning for renewed excitement to "get his blood moving" again. (Clay's own phrase.)

This situation was exaggerated by the problems inherent in the establishment of a marriage relationship with Anne. Always in the past, Clay had sought out the company of women only when he needed to assert his "male prerogative." He had never been required to make allowances for female tastes or desires. Now, he did, and it is probable that these emotional demands on him caused him to yearn, all the more, for some escape from marital responsibilities. It is even possible that what he sought was an escape from marriage itself, using his desire for action as an excuse to separate himself from the obligations of matrimony. With Henry gone (and unheard from) he did not even have a "crony" to share his troubles with. Card games were out. Drinking was out. Fighting was out.

Accordingly, to Clay's way of thinking, enjoyment of life was out.

When a letter arrived, from the City Council of Hays, Kansas, offering him the job of peace officer, he was immediately eager to accept. The deterrent was Anne. Despite the fact that the offer was, financially, a better one, she was opposed to accepting it. With a baby on the way, she wanted to live in a settled community. Caldwell might not be "exciting" anymore but it was maturing sensibly. As a charter citizen, Clay should be investing in its future, planning toward a quiet, affluent retirement.

It is my personal observation that Anne Halser never understood her husband's needs. A "typical" young woman, she desired a home, a family, and security. While, certainly, no criticism can be leveled at her for aspiring to these age-old desires, at the same time I believe that she should have realized that a marriage to Clay could not possibly bestow these things on her.

Her desire to remain in Caldwell and "live a quiet life" was, undoubtedly, more chilling a prospect to Clay than the prospect of facing those "fifty-seven Indians" with a knife would have been. His entries, during this period, consist, almost entirely, of reasons why the offered job was superior to his present one and why Anne should be able to "see" it.

Where his position in Caldwell brought in a salary of one hundred and twenty-five dollars per month, the new one guaranteed one hundred and fifty. Where the portion of fines he received in Caldwell was ten per cent, in Hays he would receive twenty-five. Where they had to live in the hotel in Caldwell (they could have moved into a house eventually, of course; Clay was "loading" the situation there), in Hays they would be given a house. If Anne was really concerned about the needs of their coming children, she should appreciate the value of the new job.

Anne's reply (unfortunately, for Clay, a devastatingly valid one) was that their main consideration should be the need of their children to see their father remain alive and not shot down in the street.

It took ten months for Clay to win the argument. After their baby—a girl which they named Melanie—was born and Anne could no longer use the argument that she did not want to travel while carrying the child, Clay renewed his attack, now almost threateningly, his boredom in Caldwell having reached a fever pitch by then.

Finally, Anne succumbed although convinced that Clay was making a terrible mistake. An entry made at this time is revealing.

March 14, 1873

Anne is in bed, upset. We have had another argument.

She said something that disturbs me. I can not believe it to be true and yet it bothers me.

I told her that I feel it is my responsibility to bring law and order to Hays as there are not many men who can.

"It isn't law and order you care about!" she cried. "You are just searching for excitement!"

She put her hand on my arm and asked, "Clay, do you *believe* all those stories about yourself? Do you feel that you have to *live up* to them?"

I scoffed at the idea but I am wondering, is it possible?

I do not know. All I know is that I can not go back to what I was. There is only one direction for me and that is forward.

My second book is filled.

BOOK THREE

(1873–1876)

Hays, Kansas, in the year of 1873, was one of the most tremendous "cow towns" on the frontier. Every season, in excess of half a million head of cattle were driven into its shipping yards and more than five thousand cowboys rampaged through its streets.

It was a brutal town, filled beyond capacity with every outcast type of male and female known in the West, all of whom "infested" the massive South Side area—a sprawling conglomerate of saloons, dance and gambling halls, brothels, and honky tonks of all varieties.

It was this notorious zone which was to be Clay's responsibility.

April 4, 1873

Arrived in Hays this morning.

After leaving Anne in the house we are to live in, I was given a ride around the town by a man named Streeter, a member of the City Council.

He showed me the South Side first. It is like the South Main area in Caldwell but about five times as large.

I had to ask Streeter to be shown the North Side of Hays which is beyond the so-called "Dead-line." (The railroad tracks.) This is where all the "respectable" citizens live. I asked Streeter why the house they gave us is not on the North Side and he said that it was on the South Side so that I could be "closer to my work."

The way he said it made it clear that the real reason is that Anne and I are not considered good enough to live among the "gentry." I did not like his answer but did not make a point of it. I may, later.

As the buggy passed the Sheriff's office, I saw him at the window, glaring out at me. His name is Woodson.

"My rival?" I asked.

Streeter told me that I should not be concerned with Woodson.

"The ones to worry about are the ones who control Woodson," he said.

These are the Griffins who, he says, are nothing less than out and out criminals. Criminals, however, who have learned not only to remain within the "good graces" of the law but, actually, employ it for their own purposes.

They are very wealthy, Streeter told me. The bulk of their riches, he said, comes from cattle rustling and stage coach hold ups! No one has ever succeeded in getting the goods on them however. Any one who tries is soon put out of the way. The Griffin "empire," as Streeter called it, has been "well secured" by threats and violence.

In addition to the rustling and the hold ups, like the Circle Seven, the Griffins control all the usable water sources for miles around and require cattle drovers to pay dearly for its use. On top of that, any cows that happen to stray during these drives are quickly picked up, clumsily re-branded and sold back to their original owners. The owners know that they are being "taken" royally but are in no position to object being far outnumbered by the Griffin forces.

As Streeter told me all those things, I could feel that long lost "tingle" returning. I welcomed it back as I would an old friend. I do not believe that this job is going to be more than I can handle but it promises to be one H————of a hot one!

Later: After having lunch with Anne, I helped her to unpack.

She seemed a little more resolved to being here. The house is not bad. It is not as nice as her home in Hickman but it is a big improvement over the hotel in Caldwell.

After I had helped her, I took a stroll to the City Marshal's office. There, I met my Deputy, a man named Ben Pickett.

He is a small, quiet man in his forties (I guess) with a straggly mustache and a stocky build. He is not flashy in any way, looking more like a store clerk than a Deputy Marshal. He strikes me, however, as the sort of man who might be outdrawn and outshot but would "get his man" regardless. I took a liking to him and he seems to like me too.

He showed me this week's edition of the *Hays Gazette*. (The editor, he tells me, is another wheel in the Griffin machine.) The headline shocked me, I confess. It reads KILLER MARSHAL ARRIVING! The article goes on to state that "the well-known, cold-blooded pistol killer, Clay Halser, is arriving this week and all citizens of Hays can now look forward to a sanguinary reign of terror."

I must say that it is strange to read these words. While I certainly do not believe all the other kind of articles about me, I have gotten used to being praised. To see the opposite approach puts a fellow back on his heels.

Pickett told me that I should prepare myself for a good deal more of the same. Obviously, he said, the Griffins want me out of the way since I am the only possible fly in their ointment.

Pickett told me, next, about John Harris, a local gambler and saloon owner. Being strictly a "loner," Harris has always opposed the Griffin "regime" and has supported one peace officer after another. He allows them to use his saloon as their "hang out" and spare armory. While expecting no more than token leniency (since, Pickett says, he runs an honest establishment anyway), the value of having the city Marshal as an unofficial ally has been worth, to Harris, ten per cent of the saloon's earnings. Three per cent of this has, by custom, gone to the Deputy Marshal.

Pickett put this to me in a straightforward way and I replied that I was not against the idea if Harris and I got along. I knew that Anne would not object to the prospect of using that seven per cent to build a "nest egg" for the future.

Pickett took me over to the *Keno Saloon* and introduced me to Harris. He struck me right immediately and agreement was reached. He invited me to take a social drink with him and I said that I would.

When the bar keep brought the bottle to the table, I was delighted to discover that he was none other than Jim Clements!

Harris invited Jim to join us for a drink and we had a nice chat. Harris told me that he has been thinking of approaching various merchants with the idea of "co-sponsoring" a series of prize-fighting matches. Cow boys coming into Hays are always hungry for "diversions," he said. A special entertainment like that could make us all a good raise. He asked me if I would be interested in getting in on it. He said that I would not have to put up any money. My name alone would give the project "stature."

I told him that I would be happy to lend my name to such a venture if it would help. I had a few more drinks with them, then went home, feeling very good. Not only had I met two men who, I believe, promise to make fine friends, but have also gotten together again with Jim. Not to mention the sources of extra income I am finding here.

When I got home, I told Anne that, despite her fears,

Hays is going to be the making of us. "We are going to like it here," I said.

As I spoke, there was a thundering of hooves outside and a body of men pulled up in front of the house. In my shirt sleeves, but wearing my Colt in plain sight, I stepped out onto the porch to see who it was.

It was the Griffin family out in force to take a look at Hays' new peace officer—and, I have no doubt, to try to rattle me from the start.

"Just rode in to see the famous Marshal Halser," said a toothless old man. He introduced himself as Roy Griffin, the head of the family. They all sat on their horses "—measuring me."

I thought that it would not hurt to get the jump on them so I said, "That is very kind of you. If you are planning to stay in town, however, you will have to check your weapons at the jail. It is the new rule."

Roy Griffin made a noise that was, I guess, amusement. "Is that right?" he said.

I did not reply but smiled to show him that I was not cowed by him or his sons and brothers.

"Seems as how the *former* Marshal tried to make that same rule," he said. "As long as we are in town, we might as well pay *him* a visit too. He is out on Boot Hill with the other Marshals."

"I intend to stay right here," I told him, trying to sound unconcerned.

"Bless me, sonny, so did they," he answered.

He pulled his horse around and the Griffins rode off in a cloud of dust. I watched them until they had ridden out of sight, then went back inside. Anne had been watching from the window. She did not have to speak. I knew the question in her mind.

We are going to like it here?

Later: It is almost one o'clock in the morning. I have just gotten Anne to bed.

Relieving Pickett at six, I told him that, starting tomorrow, we would begin enforcing the "no guns while in town" policy. I asked him to go to a printer's shop in the morning and have some posters made.

He left and, after a while, I went out on my first rounds.

The South Side, at night, is like a city in H———, I think—all noise and smoke and flickering light. Partly, it excites the senses, partly it repels them.

I walked through it all as though I owned it. It is the only way to demonstrate authority. These kind of people do not recognize anything but a show of strength.

I gave them all the show they expected. I was wearing my best black suit, my best black hat and boots, a good white shirt with a string tie and my brocaded waistcoat; what they call "gambler's dress." I kept my coat unbuttoned so that they could see the butt of my Colt at all times. (I have decided, after some thought, to stick with a .45 even though it is harder to handle.) It has more "stopping" power.

Wherever I went, I knew that they were watching me. Looking for some sign of weakness. They never saw one. I did not exchange a word with anybody. I merely nodded at people, smiling a little as if the sight of them amused me. No one approached or addressed me.

Until, some hours later, when a gang of cow boys from the Griffin ranch rode in.

Although the "no guns" rule is not to take effect until tomorrow, I decided to "set the stage" by making an example of the Griffins.

I walked quickly to confront them as they were tying up in front of a saloon. I told them that the policy was to surrender their guns when in town and told them that I expected them to obey.

There were nine men in the group. One of them was one of Griffin's sons—I think his name is Jess. He looked at me with a scornful smile and asked if I intended to stand up against all of them.

"If that is what you want," I said.

They did some "tongue skirmishing" with me but I did not back down. Finally, they decided to take off their guns and went into the saloon, leaving their belts slung over a hitching post. As they went inside, they cursed and threatened me under their breath, but I did not object to that as it enabled them to "let out steam."

By that time a crowd had collected and I was glad they had as it gave them the opportunity to see me at work. I dispersed them and they went away.

One of them turned out to be John Harris. He came over and told me that he "admired" how I had handled the cow boys. He did not say so in as many words but I got the feeling that, if the cow boys had tried to resist, Harris would have given me back action.

This impresses me and makes me like him even more. We had a nice chat as he helped me carry the guns and rifles to the jail.

When I got home at midnight, my satisfaction turned to ashes. To my dismay, I found the house dark, its windows shot out and its siding pocked with holes.

I was about to run inside when Pickett came down the street from his house. He told me that Anne and Melanie were safe but that he and his wife had decided that it might be better for her to stay at their house until I had gotten back.

I asked him what had happened and he answered that a group of riders, leaving town, had opened fire on the house. I know d——— well it was Griffin's son and those cow boys.

I went to Pickett's house and got Anne. I told her that no such thing will happen again. She did not argue but I do not think she believes me. The incident really shocked her.

I will see to it that such a thing does *not* happen again. If war is what the Griffins want, I am prepared to give it to them.

Standing back at a distance of time, it is possible to note a thread of what might be termed "over-assurance" running through Clay's entries during this period.

Although he was only one man, he seemed to possess a confidence in his ability which went beyond logic. His standing up to nine men and demanding that they disarm is indicative of this overconfidence.

His writing that he was prepared to declare war on the vast Griffin empire is, while, perhaps, courageous, also somewhat foolhardy.

There seems little doubt that Clay genuinely believed himself to be the equal of any impending situation, however dangerous.

The legend had begun to eclipse the man.

The next edition of the Hays Gazette *described Clay's "brutal treatment" of a "defenseless" group of cowboys. That this group was from the Griffin ranch was not mentioned. Neither was the riddling of Clay's house with his wife and baby daughter inside.*

Clay's wrath at this distorted account was not diminished by the arrival, in town, of one well-shot-up, well-robbed stagecoach.

April 13, 1873

I decided, this morning, that it was time to make a counter move against the Griffins.

Pickett and I rode out to the Griffin ranch, timing our arrival so that they would be at lunch.

Roy Griffin and his brothers and sons came out onto the porch to see what I had to say. I saw their women watching at the windows.

I told them that, from now on, I intend to ride as guard on any stage coach shipment of great value.

I also told them that, if any of them dares to shoot at my house again, I will return the favor without asking permission of the City Council—except that I will use shotguns loaded with scrap iron.

That done, Pickett and I backed our horses away from the house—not from fear so much as a desire to show them how little we thought of them—and rode back to town.

The next move is theirs.

April 19, 1873

Before he left the office tonight, Ben made the suggestion that I reload my revolver daily. He told me that an overnight temperature change, in cooling the gun, can gather moisture in the chambers and cause a misfire.

I have never given it much thought before but I will start to do as he suggests. He made the good point that, considering the hazards of our job, we can not afford the risk of a single bad shot.

I am going on my rounds now.

It is a coincidence that, after writing about the "hazards of our job," I went out and faced one.

Whether it was the "next move" by the Griffins, I do not know. It may have been.

While I was walking past an alley, some one took a shot at me. The lead bit off a corner of my hat brim but did not harm me.

I saw the man running away and started chasing him. After a brief pursuit, I cornered him in a blind alley and, drawing my Colt, ordered him to raise his arms.

I do not think it was bravery so much as panic that made him draw and try to kill me. I wanted to hit him in the leg but there was not time to aim and my instinctive firing took its toll. The man died instantly, a ball entering his body just below the heart.

It was one of Griffin's cow hands.

April 23, 1873

Another lying story in the *Gazette* today. This one tells how "Marshall Clay 'Heroic' Halser" shot down a poor, "un-armed" cowboy after "bullying him unmercifully."

I am trying not to let Bellingham (*the Gazette editor. F.L.*) make me lose my temper. Streeter said that I can not so much as threaten him. I am expected to prove, by "deed," that his words are lies.

I do not know how long I can go along with that. Anne is becoming very upset with the stories. The worst thing is that I am not sure whether she believes me when I tell her that every word is a lie. I guess it is hard to believe that something in print is completely false.

The sentence that bothers her most is: "It becomes more apparent, with each passing day, that Halser has come to

believe all the extravagant myths about his Greatness and
now regards himself as above the law."

We had some words about that.

"Do you believe it?" I asked.

"No. But . . ."

"But *what?*" I asked. "Either you believe it or you don't.
Which is it?"

"I don't know," she said after a while. "I just don't know."

That got my wind up and I replied, "Well, let me know
when you make up your mind."

I am feeling hot under the collar as I write this. I still
love Anne but, I must say, she seems to think a good deal
less of me than I do of her.

I do not believe she has any idea of what it is like to be
in my position. On the one hand, I am swamped with
printed lies that make me sound like the Second Coming
Of The Lord. On the other hand, I am, now, being swamped
with printed lies that make me sound like a cross between
a rattlesnake, an Apache and Emil Zandt!

Somewhere in between these two extremes I am trying
to do my job as City Marshal of Hays . . . but it is not
easy. If Anne knew how simple it would be for me to
"throw my weight" around, she would be shocked. I could
shoot down every man who stood in my way if I chose. I
could horse whip that b——— Bellingham and shut him
up too!

I am not doing any of these things. I think I am showing considerable patience and wish she could see it.

Later: More trouble.

After I left the house, I went down to the bank and
signed contracts which commit me to the prize fight exhi-
bitions. John thinks that we should make a regular thing
of them and I agree.

After signing the contracts, he and I went to the *Keno* for a drink.

We were standing at the counter, talking, when a cow boy came in and approached me.

"Halser," he said.

I looked at him. There was no doubt in my mind that he was there for blood.

"My name is Barrett," he said. "It was my friend you murdered."

"I am sorry about that," I said. "It was . . ."

". . . *murder*," he interrupted me. "And I have come to right the wrong."

Here is a good example of what I was writing about before. If I had chosen, I could have drawn on him immediately. Instead I tried to talk Barrett out of it. As calmly as I could, I explained what had happened.

"What you read in the *Gazette* is a lie," I said. "I did not murder your friend. He tried to kill me from ambush and missed. I chased him through the alleys and, when I caught him, I told him to raise his hands. I was going to put him in jail but he drew his revolver and I had no choice but to defend myself. That is God's truth, Barrett, and I hope you will have the good sense to believe it."

I could do no more. As the Lord is my witness, I did the best I could but he would not accept it. He said that he wanted revenge and nothing else would satisfy him.

At last, I gave up trying and we went outside. By then, I had lost my temper and did not care any more. If the man would not back down from me, what was I supposed to do?

We faced each other on the street at a distance of approximately five yards.

"Your play," I told him.

Despite his air of confidence, he fumbled at the crucial moment. As in his friend's case, I would have liked to wound him. It was too late for that however. I can not control my reflexes that late in the game. I put a ball in his chest which passed directly through his heart. He was dead before he landed on the ground.

There is only one thing that disturbs me. (I do not feel guilty for having defended myself.) The man was very quick with his hand. (I learned, after, that he had won eight gun duels previously.) If he had not fumbled, it might have been a close thing.

Is it possible that his fear of my reputation won the battle for me?

Two observations can be made about this entry.

One: Clay seems, for the first time, to be aware of the possibility that his eminence in Hays might not be based entirely on facts.

Two: One might question Clay's presentation of the incident with Barrett. If the two men were standing together at the counter, would it not have been possible for Clay to "buffalo" him and put him in jail, thus sparing his life? Of course, this may have been impractical. Barrett may not have been standing close enough. Further, Clay might have felt that, even if he did buffalo Barrett and put him in jail, it would only be forestalling the inevitable "moment of truth" between them.

At any rate, more conflict with Anne ensued because of the killing.

Despite Clay's efforts to convince her that he was justified, the incident drove yet another wedge between them.

Even John Harris coming to tell her what had actually happened did not diminish her reaction.

The situation was aggravated further by a special edition of the Gazette, *the headline of which shrieked WANTON MURDER!*

April 25, 1873

Jim has suggested that I tell Bellingham there will be genuine wanton murder if he does not stop printing lies about me.

I confess that I am giving his suggestion serious thought.

I have never been exposed to any thing like this. It is more than criticism. That d——d Bellingham is out to nail my hide to the wall!

The Council told me again that I must not hurt him though.

They called me in this afternoon to let me know that my "image" is "assuming most unfavorable proportions." (A Rayburn remark if ever I heard one!)

"Is all this killing absolutely necessary?" Mayor Gibbs asked.

"No," I said. "It is not necessary at all. I could let them murder me."

That remark did not win any prizes but I did not care. The way things are in Hays, I figure that they need me a H—— of a lot more than I need them. Surviving Marshals do not grow on trees.

Any way, I told them that they could have my badge back if they wanted it because I did not plan to continue as peace officer if deprived of the basic right to keep myself alive.

They backed down as I knew they would. Streeter had to have the last word though.

"We *would* appreciate it," he said, "if you would, at least, *endeavor* to keep the peace with more decorum."

"I will certainly try," I answered. "The next time some one tries to kill me, I will slap their wrist and make them stand in the corner."

I left that meeting in a rage. I am beginning to see what

a pawn I am in the game between the Council and the Griffins.

When Woodson stopped me in the street, I was just about ready for bear.

He told me that he might have to arrest me for the two shootings!

I looked at him as if he were a tarantula about to crawl up my leg. "You do that," I said. "Any time at all." I unbuttoned my coat. "Why not now?" I suggested.

He backed off, holding his hands away from his body. "There is nothing personal in this, Marshal," he said.

"I would not bet on that hand either," I answered, walking off.

An attempt, the following week, to rob the stagecoach of a valuable gold bullion shipment failed as Clay and Ben Pickett rode as guards.

Clay's unexpected presence inside the coach proved to be the difference. His devastating rifle fire augmenting Pickett's routed the attackers, killing four of them. All were known Griffin employees.

Reprisal came the following night.

May 5, 1873

It is almost three o'clock in the morning. Anne has just fallen asleep. I think that we are safe in Ben's house but I am not taking any chances for a while and will stay awake.

It is fortunate that I am a light sleeper. I woke up about midnight and smelled smoke. Jumping out of bed, I found smoke filling the hall. I woke up Anne and got her and Melanie out the front door before the blaze in the kitchen and hall had reached the stairs.

Then I ran back upstairs and started throwing our

clothes out on the roof and then to the ground. Anne hurried to Ben's house and he came down the block and helped me. We got almost all our belongings out. The house could not be saved however. Ben rode to get the volunteer fire fighters but the house was an inferno by the time he rounded them up.

Ben has told us to stay here in their son's room until we find another place. He has been a lot of help tonight and Marion was very comforting to Anne.

After Melanie was asleep, Anne told me that she believes it was a terrible mistake for us to have come here.

"I think we should leave as soon as possible," she said. "We have Melanie's life to consider if not our own."

I tried to be patient with her and assure her that I would settle with the Griffins. (I know they were behind the fire.)

"That would do no good," she said. "There would just be some one else to settle with *you* then. Don't you see that this is more than you can handle?"

I did not care to hear her say that but I did not tell her so. I told her that I had two dependable Deputies (*Clay had persuaded Jim Clements to become his second Deputy. F.L.*) and could handle anything the Griffins chose to throw at me.

"Well, *I can't*," she answered. "I will not be able to sleep a wink now, fearing what they might do to us."

I tried to reassure her but there was no way of doing it. Finally, I had to remind her that I have signed a contract and am bound to respect it.

That made her cry. I put my arms around her and told her that things are not as bad as she imagined. We can find another house, I told her. I reminded her of the money we are going to make—not only from the higher salary and fine commissions but, also, from my percentage of the *Keno* earnings and my twenty per cent of the proceeds from the coming prize fight matches.

None of it helped. She kept crying and saying that Melanie was going to be killed. Finally, to quiet her, I told her that, if things do not settle down by the end of my year here, we will move back East, maybe to Pine Grove. That seemed to satisfy her although she still feels that something awful is going to happen if we do not leave right away.

I know one thing. I am not going back to Pine Grove unless it is in a Pine Box!

May 6, 1873

Well, we are off again.

Anne seemed to settle down a little after last night. Then she saw my journal on the bedroom table and read my last entry.

Now we are further apart than ever. I told her that I only meant that I hate Pine Grove. There are other places we can go, I said. But I think she knows that I do not want to go back East under any condition.

It is just as well she knows it now. She will simply have to learn to accept our life in Hays, that is all. I have a good setup here and am not going to be driven out by those d——d Griffins!

I am sitting on the balcony of the *Hays House* as I write this. I think I had better keep my Record Book in the office from now on.

Down on the stage, men are finishing up preparing the prize fight ring for tonight's match. John is down there with them, telling them what to do.

I have been reading that G——— d——d *Gazette*. Now Bellingham is serializing one of those stupid "novels" about me. He certainly went out of his way to pick the dumbest one he could find! He has added his own bright comments here and there. I do not know how much longer I intend to let him puff. If it were not for the City Council, I would—

Later: D———, d———, d———and double d———!

While I was writing before, Woodson came in with a summons to stop the match.

They have dug up some d———d city ordinance no body ever heard about which says that it is against the law to conduct "an athletic event" within the city limits. I do not know if it is a real ordinance or something they made up just for the occasion. Naturally, they waited until we had gone to all the trouble of getting things ready before making their move!

John and I are all for going ahead and saying to H——— with Woodson, the Griffins and their d———d ordinance. But our "partners" have jelly in their spines and are afraid to tangle with the Griffins so they have run off like a pack of dogs.

The setback is a costly one, especially to John.

Later: After midnight. I have just gotten back from duty.

Another killing. My luck is turning sour, it seems.

Not that I was the one who did the killing but that will not help.

It was after ten o'clock when I stopped at the *Keno* for a drink.

John was playing cards with some men. I had not spoken to him all day because he was in a black mood and I knew that he did not choose to talk. When I came in, he merely nodded his head at me.

As bad luck would have it, one of his opponents was a big cow boy named Ernie. Ernie kept peeking at the discards while they were playing. He was drunk and said that he always did that when he was playing.

John kept telling him again and again to stop monkeying with the dead wood and play cards but Ernie would not listen. He was obviously the kind of man who always goes his own way.

Except for tonight. John got sick of talking to him finally, threw down his cards and raked in the pot (he and Ernie were the only ones left in the hand), telling Ernie to get out of his saloon.

Ernie got mad and demanded his money back. When John told him to go to H————, Ernie pulled a knife on him.

It all happened too fast for me to stop it. (I was across the room at the counter.) I have never seen John in action before. If he pulls a gun like he does a knife, I am certainly glad he is on my side. In a split second, he had thrown the blade into Ernie's chest.

We took Ernie to Doc Warner's place but he died a few minutes after we arrived.

This comes at a bad time. Still I do not see what else John could have done. He was in the right about the game and in the right about defending himself.

Still, knowing Bellingham, I suspect that John's association with me will not be overlooked.

Clay's suspicion proved a sound one.

What he did not foresee was that Bellingham, preferring Clay as his main target, put as much blame on him as on Harris.

HALSER SUPPORTS MURDER! was the headline, the story going on to say that "with sneering defiance of lawful procedure" Clay was permitting "one of his cronies, the notorious gambler-killer, John Harris, to go scot free after having cold-bloodedly knifed to death an un-armed, law-abiding" cowboy.

Clay's temper proved his master on this occasion—
although its outcome proved more confusing than satis-
fying to him.

May 10, 1873

I went to see Bellingham before.

"Come to add me to your list of murders, have you?"
was the first thing he said to me. He said it almost before
I had shut the door to his office.

"I have not murdered any one and you know it," I said,
taking his words at face value.

"I do *not* know it," he replied. "On the contrary, I know
that you *have* committed murder and will doubtless do so
again."

"If I do," I told him, "you are number one on the
list."

"Good!" he cried. "That is my badge of honor!"

"You had better stop printing lies about me or you will
be sorry," I said.

"That's it!" he said. "Threaten me! That is your way,
isn't it?"

I swear to God I could not get through to him. I think
he is loco. If he is afraid of me, he is certainly good at hiding it. I have a feeling that he *hopes* I will kill him!

I have never run across a man like him before. One thing
is certain though. If he is not afraid of dying, threatening
his life is a waste of time. Worse than a waste of time. The
idea seems to thrill him!

I left the *Gazette* office in a stew. I am disgusted that it
turned out that way. My only consolation is that Bellingham is crazy and the words of a crazy man are not as both-
ersome as those of a sane man.

While I was walking back to the office to see Jim, I met Streeter. He told me that the City Council wants me to break off with John.

I told him that, if there is ever a show down with the Griffins, there are only three men in this whole d——d town I can depend on and as one of these is John Harris, I intend to remain in contact with him.

I did not bother telling him that I like John and that John is my friend. He would not have understood.

Later: That d——d crazy Bellingham has come out with a special one sheet edition of the *Gazette*, the whole thing devoted to a story about how I "bullied" my way into his office and threatened his "life and limb." "Nonetheless," writes courageous Mr. Bellingham, "so long as blood shall flow in my veins and breath in my lungs, I shall continue to espouse the cause of truth and justice though it may mean my very existence!"

I am sure now that he would love to be killed. I am also beginning to wonder if the Griffins really do pay him off. If they do, they are wasting their money. I think Bellingham would do it for nothing!

I guess I will have to learn to live with his *Gazette*.

I told Anne about my visit to Bellingham but I do not think she believes a word I say any more. Our life together has become nearly intolerable. I have not touched her for more than a month.

All she says to me these days is that she wants to leave Hays and that, if we don't leave right away, something terrible is going to happen.

Later: Past one o'clock in the morning.
Almost "cashed in" tonight.
While I was walking my rounds, eighteen cow hands

from the Griffin Ranch galloped into town and started shooting up Main Street.

I was too far from the office to get there fast so I started for the *Keno* to pick up a shotgun.

I was running down the alley when three of the cow hands pulled up behind me and ordered me to stop.

I turned to face them. They had me dead to rights, all three of them pointing their revolvers at me.

"Why don't you draw, Marshal?" said one of them.

"Yeah, Marshal, why don't you draw?" said another. "You are so all-fired fast."

"Go ahead," said the third. "Fill your hand. You are the Great Marshal Halser, aren't you? You should be able to get the drop on us, you are so fast."

I knew that I would probably be killed but I was getting ready to take a crack at it when, fortunately, the play was turned. John heard the cow hands' voices through a window inside the *Keno*, grabbed a sawed off shotgun and crashed it through the window, pointing it at the three men.

"All right," he said. "Marshal Halser is ready now. Commence to firing."

Seeing him at the window with that shotgun pointing at them took the wind out of their sails. They dropped their irons and, while John marched them to jail, I took the shotgun and started after the other cow boys.

There is nothing like a few good blasts from a sawed off shotgun to clear a street. I did not even have to shoot any of them.

I owe my life to John now. And Streeter wants me to break off with him!

When I got home, Anne was still awake.

"So you are back," she said.

"What do you mean?" I asked.

"I heard the shooting," she said. "I thought they would be bringing your body home on a board."

"It was nothing," I told her.

I hope she does not hear what happened.

Clay's hope was groundless. Not only did Anne learn what happened but other occurrences began to happen as well.

Clandestine attempts on his life—and, to a lesser degree, on the lives of Pickett, Clements, and Harris—picked up tempo steadily.

It was a rare night when, making his rounds, Clay failed to hear lead whistling by him in the darkness, followed by the sound of running feet and/or the hoofbeats of a galloping horse.

He began avoiding bright lights and dark alleys and took to walking in the middle of the street. He seriously considered Jim Clements' suggestion that he make his rounds on horseback in order to present a poorer target.

He entered buildings by shoving open doors with the barrel of the sawed off shotgun he always carried now, then sliding in quickly to place his back to the wall.

He began to wear a second .45 caliber Colt revolver at his right hip. He purchased a pair of Derringers and carried them in his waistcoat pockets. He was a walking arsenal while on his rounds, prepared to deal with any and all emergencies. He was never again "caught short" as he had been outside the Keno Saloon *that night.*

Day by day, his state of tension mounted. While not actually afraid (his entries make this clear) he did become increasingly nervous until unexpected noises made him jump and minor irritations evoked responses far beyond their due. (His relationship with Anne reached its nadir during this period and several entries indicate that he began "taking up" with one of the dance hall girls.)

His appetite decreased and he began to lose weight. He had difficulty sleeping. His face became haggard and

*lined. All in all, he was a far cry from the lighthearted
young man who had traveled West with such eagerness
seven years earlier.*

The legend had begun to take its toll.

August 20, 1873

This evening started bad and got worse.

While I was preparing to go on shift, Anne watched me
in silence as I put the two reloaded Derringers into my waistcoat pockets and buckled on my pair of reloaded revolvers.

When I started reloading the sawed off shotgun, she
exploded.

"Look at you!" she cried. "You are a one man Army!
How long is this going to go on?"

I did not try to pacify her. I have given up on that. "I
want to stay alive," was all I said.

"Then leave Hays!" she cried.

"I have a job," I said.

"Then *quit* the job!"

We went on like that for quite a while but nothing new
was said.

Then, as I started walking her (and Melanie) down the
block so she could pay a visit to Marion, a young fellow
who had been waiting in the street blocked our way.

He could not have been more than sixteen, a skinny,
mean-faced kid wearing a revolver. I almost knew what he
was going to say before he opened his mouth.

"Are you Clay Halser?" he asked.

"Get out of the way," I told him.

"I hear that you are fast with a gun," he said.

My patience is not much to speak of these days. "*Get
out of the way*, I said," I told him. "Can't you see I have
my wife and child with me?"

That got his back up.

"Are you hiding behind your wife's skirts?" he replied.

"For the last time," I told him, "*get out of the way.*"

"Not until I get my satisfaction," he said. "I have come a long way to meet you and will not be denied."

I had to restrain myself from killing him that instant.

"Go on ahead," I said to Anne.

"Clay," she began.

"Go on ahead," I interrupted her.

"Clay, don't do this," she begged.

"I said, go *on*." I took her by the arm and started her off. She gasped at the grip of my hand, then, without another word, started for Ben's house, crying and not looking back.

Just then Ben came running down the plank walk with a shotgun in his hands.

"All right, drop your gun belt," he told the boy.

The boy smiled with contempt. "Well," he said to me, "no wonder you have lasted so long. You have so much help."

I was almost shaking with rage by then. The expression on his face finished it.

"Go back," I told Ben.

"Clay, let me put him in jail until he cools off," he said.

"*Go back!*" I yelled at him.

He started to say something more, then saw the look on my face and turned away. After he had walked some yards, I spoke to the boy.

"All right, you loud mouth, son of a b———," I said. "You want to try me, go ahead."

His face got tight. "Draw," he said.

"I don't have to draw," I told him. "I can wait. You haven't got a chance in H———."

He didn't either. He went for his revolver but never got it out. I have never been so fast. Before he could clear half his scabbard I had put two balls through his heart. He was dead before he started to fall.

I left him in the street and walked away. As I passed
Ben's house I could see Anne looking at me.

I am sick and tired of that look! You would think I am
a common murderer.

While scarcely a common murderer, it does seem apparent that Clay had, by this time, reached the point where immediate killing was preferable to extended arguments. Completely confident in his ability to handle any armed opponent, he had lost the patience to deal with them in any other way than instant action. Like his guns, he was always "cocked and ready."

He no longer cared about the stories in the Gazette. *He paid no attention to the castigations of the City Council. He openly defied the Griffins to do their worst.*

Reports from other sources at this time confirm the fact that he had become almost brutal in his attitudes.

He was not surprised or even much disturbed when Anne decided to leave.

September 5, 1873

Anne is leaving.

She says that she can not go on living this way.

She says that she does not feel as though she knows me
any more.

She says that I could have put that boy in jail if I had
wanted to but that it was "easier" for me to kill him.

She says that she is going to Hickman to live with her
aunt.

She says that she wants me to go with her but I think
she is saying it because she feels it is the thing to do. When
I reminded her that I have a contract to respect, she did
not argue the point.

She says that she will expect me after my contract expires but I think she knows I will not be showing up.

My feelings about her leaving are mixed ones.

It does not do my "image" any good to have my wife "walk out" on me. I can tell people that she is leaving for some other reason but every one will know the real reason. That part I do not like.

At the same time, I feel as if a weight is being lifted off my back. I love Melanie and will miss her but my life with Anne has become a trial. There is nothing left between us. She does not respect me any more or believe in what I am doing.

It is just as well that she leaves.

Following Anne's departure, Clay began to manifest, even more, the acid temperament which Marshal Hickok had vented on him years before.

He understood that temperament now. The strain of remaining alert for violence which could erupt at any moment of the day or night was wearing him thin.

He installed a bolt on the door of the hotel room into which he had moved.

He never went to sleep without placing crumpled newspaper pages at strategic places on the floor, most of them around the door and window despite the bolt and the fact that the window overlooked a drop of more than twenty feet.

He kept a weapon within easy reach at all times, sleeping with his gunbelt hung across the head board of the bed, a Derringer beneath the pillow.

He held a revolver in his hand when being shaved, concealing it beneath the barber's cloth, his eyes fixed on the wall mirror so that he could keep the doorway under constant observation.

He kept his right hand free at all times, even training himself to use a fork with his left.

He always sat with his back to the wall.

The need to remain ready for action, whether awake or asleep, drained him steadily. Jumpy and in constant need of rest, he began drinking more than usual.

An indication of his mental state is provided by the following entry.

October 27, 1873

Found out tonight exactly what those G——— d——d people on the North Side think of me.

A bunch of drunken cow boys started firing their guns as they were leaving town. That was all right with me. They do it all the time. It is a way for them to let off steam that hurts no body.

Then they rode into the North Side doing it and woke up the people. I rode after them and chased them out.

After they were gone, I saw the people at their windows and standing on their porches.

Not one of them addressed a word to me. They looked at me as if I was no better than the cow boys. No one asked me to chase after them but I did. Now these people looked at me as if I was a hound that had gotten out of the dog house. I almost fired my shotgun into the air to shake them up, they made me so mad. I didn't though. I touched the brim of my hat like a good Marshal should do and rode away.

B——s! I am their hired gun, no more! The strong right arm of the D———merchants! They don't care about law and order! All they care about is making their "pound of flesh" in peace and quiet!

Clay's next problem came from an old source. F.L.

November 5, 1873

Henry Blackstone showed up today. He is staying at the hotel and tells me that he plans to pay me a "nice, long visit."

It is not bad to see him again but I do not have the same feeling about him I had before.

We are just not cut out of the same cloth. He is loyal to his friends, I suppose, but that is all he is loyal to. He had no reason to leave Hickman, it turns out. He had just gotten "bored" with me gone and had decided to "go find some excitement."

He is just not my sort as Jim and Ben and John are. He still looks the same too! It is unbelievable! When I look in the mirror, I see my years and more. But Henry does not look a day older. There is certainly something to be said for not taking anything seriously.

He still smiles all the time and my friends are taken with him. I do not imagine there is any reason to warn them about him. Since they are my friends, Henry will not do anything to harm them.

Still, I wish he was not here at this time. I have enough problems. He hinted that he would not mind being a Deputy and "helping me out" again but I told him that I had two Deputies and did not need any more. That is a lie. I could use *ten* good Deputies. *Good* Deputies though.

I am not sure, any more, that I could depend on Henry in a real tight.

I hope to G——— he behaves himself.

As the foregoing entry makes clear, Clay's attitude toward Blackstone had undergone almost a complete reversal.

Whether this was based on genuine awareness of

Blackstone's potentially dangerous amorality or simply on resentment that time had treated his old friend so easily can not be known. Probably, it was a combination of the two. Clay had been through many harrowing experiences since he had last seen Blackstone. He was simply not the same man Blackstone had known.

Since Blackstone (if we are to accept Clay's word) was exactly *the same person as he had always been, there would, inevitably, have been no ground for a relationship between them anymore.*

Several weeks passed during which Blackstone "behaved" himself. Clay began to feel a little more at ease with his old comrade although he never did manage to achieve the camaraderie they had once enjoyed together. He played cards and drank with Blackstone, spent considerable time with him, reminiscing.

Without mentioning, again, the idea of him being a Deputy, Henry made himself useful to Clay, Pickett and Clements, relieving them off and on to give them more free time. In his almost childlike way, Blackstone was, perhaps, trying to "earn back" Clay's approval so that he could, once more, be Clay's Deputy.

Then, when Clay was actually considering the possibility, Blackstone altered everything.

Well, I am in the soup again with the Council, Bellingham, and every one who has heard what happened.

I have no excuse this time. I can not hold myself blameless because Henry is my friend.

I do not know what to do. I have Henry here in jail but, obviously, I can not keep him here because I owe him my life. Still, when I let him go, there has got to be an outcry heard from here to Texas.

It happened about an hour ago.

Henry was here with Ben, keeping him company. I was sleeping in my room.

Ben indicated his desire for a cup of coffee and Henry told him to go and get one. He said that he would "mind" the office while Ben was gone.

Since every thing was peaceful, Ben accepted the offer and walked down the street to *Nell's Cafe*.

While he was having his coffee, a group of cow boys rode in. They had been on the trail a long time and were in no mood to "be trifled with," a witness later told me. (Ned Young from the feed store.)

Henry went outside with a shotgun and waved the cow boys over to the office where he told them that the policy was to leave their guns at the jail while they were in town.

The cow boys had never been to Hays before and did not cotton to the idea. One of them was particularly against it . . . and against Henry for suggesting it. Mistaking Henry's smile for weakness, he spoke more angrily by the moment.

He was in the middle of an insult when Henry (still smiling, Young said!) blasted him off his saddle with both barrels.

The noise woke me up and I ran to the window of my

room. Seeing a crowd collecting outside the jail, I dressed as fast as I could and rushed down stairs.

By the time I got there, Ben was trying to calm the now disarmed cow boys who were in a lynching mood because of what Henry had done.

To quiet them down, I pretended to arrest Henry and put him in jail. That seemed to satisfy them and they rode away, although I have a feeling that the matter is not closed with them.

I put Henry in a cell, leaving the door open. He sat down on the cot and looked at me.

"For G——'s sake, Henry, why did you do it?" I asked.

Henry smiled.

"He was dirty talking me," he answered.

Later: Almost midnight.

Henry is gone.

I was making my rounds when the same group of cow boys rode into town and stopped in front of the office. I went over to talk to them and they told me that they were in for Henry's hide.

I told them that the law would take care of him and, after a while, they left. I knew they would be back after they had had a few drinks though and I moved Henry to my hotel room, using the back door of the jail to get him out.

Shortly after, the cow boys started gathering outside the jail again, this time with a rope in their hands. I knew that, sooner or later, they would find out that Henry was not in the jail so I got Henry's horse and brought it up behind the hotel. I went up and got him down a back staircase and saw him mounted.

"Thanks, old fellow," he said with a smile. "We are even now."

I am glad he realizes that and hope he does not come back any more. I shook his hand and wished him luck but

I do not want to see his face again. He is pure trouble and I have enough of that already. I should have told him to stay out of Hays but I did not have the heart.

I just hope that I have seen the last of him.

Blackstone's departure, while relieving Clay of concern about his strange, young friend, did not, in any other way, diminish the tension of his demanding schedule.

Seven nights a week, from the hours of six o'clock to one in the morning, he stood duty as City Marshal.

He continued riding guard on all valuable stage shipments, thus completely cutting off this source of the Griffins' income.

He had to live with the mounting disfavor of the City Council and the North Side populace. Even the men and women of the South Side disapproved of his releasing Henry. (No one believed his story that Henry had "escaped," least of all Bellingham, who was in his glory with a florid account of "this new nadir of perfidy" committed by Clay.)

Finally, Clay had to continue living under the day-by-day, hour-by-hour, minute-by-minute strain of knowing that the Griffins wanted him dead and would continue "working" on that problem as long as he remained as peace officer.

About this time, another problem cropped up, Henry's disappearance strangely paralleled by the re-appearance of an old acquaintance.

December 2, 1873

I was having a drink in the *Keno* tonight when a man came dashing in and said that a cow boy had run amuck in *The Yellow Mandarin (one of Hays's largest brothels. F.L.)*, killed one of the girls, wounded two others, and barricaded himself in their room, threatening to kill any one who entered.

I hurried over to *The Yellow Mandarin* where a crowd was waiting downstairs. The room the cow boy was barricaded in was on the second floor in the rear. I went upstairs and started down the hall.

As soon as the cow boy heard my footsteps, he fired a shot through the thin door, shattering the wood. I jumped to one side and missed getting hit.

I removed my boots and edged along the wall, revolver in hand. I pressed myself against the wall outside the room and told the cow boy to come out with his hands up or he was a dead man.

"This is Marshal Halser," I told him, "and this is your last chance to come out alive."

"You will have to take me as a corpse!" he shouted.

"Are you going to let those two girls die as well?" I asked.

"I do not care about them!" he shouted. "They are just a couple of w——s!"

I asked him a few more times to surrender, then fired some shots through the door. He fired three shots back, then was quiet. I took the chance that he was reloading and kicked in the door.

That was almost my undoing. Only the shock of seeing me charging in kept him from killing me, I think. He had a Derringer in his hand but his arm jerked when I came in and he missed me by a hair, knocking off my hat. I answered his fire without thought and hit him in the chest, killing him almost instantly.

Then I put my revolver away and checked the girls. The first one I looked at had died from loss of blood.

The second one was not dead. She was not a girl either. *It was Mary McConnell, Anne's stepmother.*

Later: Mary McConnell is going to live, Doc Warner says. I have put her in a room at the hotel.

I do not know whether to involve myself with her or turn my back.

I do not owe her any thing but I feel that she needs a hand right now.

She looks terrible. She has lost a power of weight and has little left of the looks she had when I first met her in Hickman.

I do not know how long she has been here in Hays. She must have known that I was here. Maybe she figured that in a place as big as the South Side, our trails would never cross.

Now they have crossed though and I feel sorry for her. Even if she is only Anne's step mother, I feel as if there is a family tie. Anne went a good distance out of her way to help her once.

I suppose I can go a little way out of mine to do the same.

December 3, 1873

I spoke to Ben and Marion this afternoon and they told me that Mary McConnell is welcome to live in the small shed behind their house while she is recovering. It is nothing fancy but it is clean and Mary has no place else to stay. G——— knows *The Yellow Mandarin* does not want her and I can not afford to keep her at the hotel.

I will speak to Mary McConnell about it tomorrow morning when she wakes up.

As indicated earlier, the purpose of this volume is to convey, via choice selections from Clay Halser's journal, the unfolding of a phenomenon of these, our violent times: namely, the so-called gunfighter and/or lawman.

If one chose to deviate from this avowed intent, one could (as in the case of Clay's courtship of Anne McConnell) expend considerable space to the relationship between Mary McConnell and Jim Clements.

Indeed, an entire, tragic tale emerges from Clay's journal during this period. While not directly involved, he was close enough to the situation to view it with an acute eye and, while the bulk of his entries continued to concern themselves with his own problems as City Marshal of Hays, he did write many an extended paragraph on the McConnell-Clements liaison.

While Mary McConnell was recovering from the wound she had suffered at the hands of the cowboy in The Yellow Mandarin, *Ben and Marion Pickett behaved toward her with the very essence of that much abused word "Christianity."*

In the beginning, Mrs. Pickett brought meals to the shed and fed the injured woman by hand; bathed her, changed her bedclothes and her clothing. When Mary McConnell had recovered enough to care for herself, the Picketts invited her to share their meals in the main house.

It is, hopefully, not amiss at this point to comment briefly on the Picketts. Despite the more sensational aspects of Clay's life, and the lives of men like him, if we are to recognize the truth of the matter, it is people like the Picketts who are the true backbone of social development in the West. Undoubtedly, men like Clay Halser fulfill a definite need. Still, it is the strain of people represented by the Picketts which truly "tames" a town.

Excluding the fact that Ben Pickett was a Deputy Marshal—a somewhat exotic profession even for that time—his attitudes and those of his wife and their day-by-day behavior proved them to be the type which, in the long run, settles wildernesses and creates progress in barren lands.

It is also evident, by these facts, that Clay, despite his faults, had good taste in friends. Ben Pickett, as indicated, was a solid, stable individual. John Harris, despite his background and profession, was known to be an honest man with a straight-forward, dependable nature. Finally, Jim Clements, for all the rough-hewn simplicity of his moral standards, was fundamentally a kindhearted, generous person.

It was, perhaps, his kindness and generosity which led to his relationship with Mary McConnell. Then again, it may have been no more complicated than the loneliness of a man approaching his forties who feels the need of a permanent female companion.

Whatever the cause, when Clements—stopping by the Picketts' house for a visit one afternoon—was introduced to Mary McConnell, the "die was cast."

Before Clay learned of it, Clements was visiting the Pickett house regularly and developing a warm emotion for Mary McConnell who, in turn, was developing a warm emotion for him. On her part, it may well have been the first genuine feeling she had ever experienced. On the other hand, it may have been a move prompted by desperation as, six years his senior and well on her way toward becoming one of the "dregs" of society, she saw, in Clements, a last chance for regeneration.

When Clay discovered what was going on, he tried,

without divulging Mary McConnell's unseemly back-
ground, to discourage Clements from considering her as
more than a friend. This proved of no avail. For the first
time, there was friction between the two men and, see-
ing that his friend was firm in his intention, Clay backed
off, not feeling justified in interfering beyond a certain
point.

When Clements and Mary McConnell announced their
wedding plans, Clay could do no more than hope for the
best. Using the Griffins as an excuse, he tried to suggest,
to Clements, that he and his bride-to-be leave Hays and
make a "fresh start" elsewhere. When this did not work
either, he gave up trying and, as his final entry before the
wedding states, "crossed my fingers hard."

January 12, 1874

The wedding took place this afternoon, Mary is now Mrs.
Clements and I hope to G——— it works out for them. I
have never seen Jim so happy. He has always been a quiet,
almost not-speaking kind of man who, maybe, cracked a
small grin once in a long while.

Today he was all smiles and like a different person.

Thank G———, I was able to keep him that way. After the ceremony, while Jim and Mary were accepting con-
gratulations and well wishes inside the church, I went out
to get the buggy so they could drive to their new house.

A couple of South Side men were riding by and stopped
to watch as the wedding guests came out. When the men
saw Mary, one of them said, "Holy C———, that is Mary
from *The Yellow Mandarin*!" He was drunk and I heard
him say that he was going to ask her how things were at
the w——— house! He got off his horse to do so.

Just before Jim and Mary reached the buggy, I stepped

behind the man, pulled a Derringer from beneath my coat and jammed it into his back.

"You say one word and it will be your last," I told him.

He turned into a statue and was as quiet as one as Jim and Mary got into the buggy. Whether or not Mary recognized him, I do not know. She did not seem to.

Any way, we all waved goodbye to them and they departed happily. After they were gone, I put the Derringer away. "If I hear about this any where," I told the man, "I will know who started the talk and come gunning for you."

The man swore on his mother's grave that he would never utter a word. I hope to G——— he does not. I really have got to get Jim and Mary out of Hays somehow. It is just too tight a situation. If Jim found out, I do not know what he would do.

Later: After the party at Jim and Mary's house was over, I went back to the hotel to take a nap before going on duty.

As I neared my room, I saw a figure standing by the door and snatched out my gun.

"Don't shoot," the figure said in a weak voice.

It was Henry. He is very sick and may have pneumonia.

I could not very well turn him away so I helped him to take off his clothes and get into bed. I have never seen his body before. It is covered with scars of every sort, souvenirs from his many knife and gun fights in the past.

He seems quite unlike the Henry I have known. He tries to smile but can not do it too well. He has a terrible cough and can not speak too clearly. All I could make out of what he was saying was that no one saw him come into town and if I will only let him stay a while until he feels a little better, he will never bother me again. The only reason I got that was that he kept on saying it over and over until I understood.

I got Doc Warner and brought him to the room. He

said that Henry probably had pneumonia. He gave Henry some medicine and said that he has to stay in bed and keep warm. He is coming back in the morning to check Henry.

I had to leave while I was on duty but I checked Henry every hour or so and he seemed to remain asleep. He must be exhausted. He does not look like a young man now. He looks like an old man with a young face. His skin is almost grey.

I guess I will have to sleep on the floor tonight. I do not want to leave him. Neither do I want to sleep in a room without a bolt on the door.

I am sitting in the chair, writing this. Henry is still asleep. I feel sorry for him. I have never seen him like this. I never realized how slight of build he is. He has lost considerable weight and, between that and that old-young face of his, he looks terrible lying on the bed.

How can such a pitiful looking creature be such a cold-blooded murderer? It is hard to understand. But then a lot of things are hard to understand. Life is not the simple thing I once believed it to be.

The thing which is most confusing of all to me is how I got to where I am. Was it all just an accident? A coincidence? As I look back, it seems that all the events of my life have combined to make me what I am.

Still, there are others like me who are as fast with a gun and have been Marshals. Why were articles and stories not written about them? Hickok is the only other man I know of who may be in the same position. *Why were we picked out?* Was it an accident? A coincidence?

I wish I knew.

Something about the marriage between Clements and Mary McConnell plus his old comrade showing up so terribly ill seems to have compelled Clay, for the first time,

*to try and understand the circumstances which had be-
fallen him.*

*That this frame of mind remained with him for more
than a matter of hours is demonstrated by the following
entry made six days later.*

January 18, 1874

Henry is feeling well enough to sit up. I have almost had
to rope him to the bed to keep him down. He keeps saying that he would like to go out and have a drink and a
game of cards.

Finally, I had to tell him straight out that he could not
go out under any circumstances because of what happened
the last time he was here.

"I am in enough trouble already," I told him. *"Don't
make any more for me."*

Henry smiled and I was shocked to see a trembling of
his lips when he did. "Sure, old fellow," he said. "I do not
want to make trouble for you. You are the only friend I
have."

That made me feel like a low down skunk although I
did not know how to tell him so. I told him that I would
bring a deck of cards and some whiskey to the room later
and we would have a drink and a game.

Later: It is almost three o'clock in the morning.

I should not have brought the whiskey, I suppose, although Henry did seem to enjoy it despite the coughing.
We both drank too much.

He is asleep now. We had a game of cards and he seemed
to enjoy that too. He is so much like a child that it is strange
to me. I feel like his father now, in some ways. It is impossible for me to believe that once we H——d it up along

the border. It seems as if it happened (if it happened at all!) a hundred years ago.

I think I got more good out of tonight than Henry did. After I had had too many drinks, I spent more time "un-burdening" myself than playing cards. I do not know why I did it with Henry except that, really, he is the only one I *could* unburden myself to. Ben and John and Jim are all so strong. If I revealed what I felt to them, they would lose their respect for me.

Any way, the more I talked to Henry, the more loose my tongue got until I could not shut up. Henry listened pa-tiently, nodding his head and smiling like he does. I do not know if he really understands what I feel but, at least, he gave me a good ear for the time I spoke.

I told him that, during the Brady-Courtwright War, I sometimes felt as though I was not a person but a part of a machine. I turned and moved but it was all within the confines of the "mechanism" that controlled me.

In Caldwell, I felt it even more.

Now, here in Hays, the feeling has reached its apex. It is as if the conflict between the Griffins and the Council is a chess game. In between the two forces is a pawn standing in the open, right in the middle and way out in front. That pawn is me and all I can do is wait for some Great Hand to move me to the next position where I may live or die.

"You are not a piece on a chess board," Henry told me when I was finished. "You are a man and can do what you want."

For a moment there, something "sparked" between us. Something that was deeper and stronger than any thing we had ever known in the old days. I do not know what it was and it did not last for more than a second or two.

Henry broke it when he smiled and said, "Don't let them

ruffle you, old fellow. If they stand in your way, shoot them down."

During Blackstone's period of recovery, Clay received a letter from Anne which multiplied, by many times, his darkened mental state.

She told him that Melanie had fallen down a flight of stairs and almost died. She had recovered but was in such a terribly weakened condition that Anne did not dare to leave her for a moment. Accordingly, she had been unable to look for work to help support the child. Since her aunt was not well off to begin with, what little savings she had possessed had gone to medical expenses for the child, and they were in consequent dire need of funds.

Clay sent whatever money he had on hand, which was not much since Anne had taken all their savings when she left. Newly ridden by a sense of guilt, Clay, in his journal entries, pondered endlessly on what to do. Harris was the only one he knew with any kind of money but he did not feel justified in asking him for a loan, the collapse of the prize fight venture having cost the gambler a large sum. Pickett and Clements were worse off financially than he was. Consequently, all he could do was send whatever portion of his earnings he did not actually need to live on and hope that it was sufficient.

It was not. Anne wrote him constantly, making it clear that the amounts he was sending were not enough to cover her modest cost of living plus the continuing medical expenses for Melanie. There was even the possibility, she wrote, that the child might have to be placed in a hospital for extensive surgery. This, added to Clay's other problems, proved a harrowing blow to his frame of mind.

He was at a peak of inner turmoil when Henry, well and restless, turned the situation into total nightmare.

February 16, 1874

Sweet G————, is there no end to it? Henry has done it *again*!

While I was sleeping this morning, he "got bored" (says his note) and, in spite of everything I have told him, left the room and went to the *Maverick Saloon* for a "drink or two and a quiet game of cards."

With Henry there is no such thing as a quiet anything. I do not know if Galwell was as bad as some say. The few times I have come across him he seemed a little arrogant but no more than a lot of young men whose fathers have money.

I do not know. Maybe he was like Menlo but I doubt it. All I know for certain is that, when he started losing money to Henry, he got mad and made a few remarks.

Shortly after, he paid for that mistake with a bullet in his brain.

Henry has fled. I do not know where he is and care less. I *told* him not to leave the room! "Sure, old fellow. I do not want to make trouble for you. You are the only friend I have." *Sure!*

Galwell's father has offered a reward of a thousand dollars for Henry's capture. Right now, I think I would collect it if I could. I am in the dog house with every body. Henry was recognized as the one who "escaped" from jail that other time. Now every one thinks I let him "escape" again. I can look forward to a blast from Bellingham, several from the City Council and a lot of trouble from the South Siders.

D———— Henry! Why did he have to do it? *What is the matter with him any way?*

Later: I have just heard from Henry.

He sent a note to me by a Mexican sheep herder. He is hiding in the Mexican's shack a few miles out of town and needs a horse. He wants me to bring him one and says that he will never bother me again after today.

Later: it is almost ten o'clock.

I have put Henry in jail.

I never saw such a startled look in my life as that on his face when I pulled my gun and told him he was under arrest. He thought that I was joshing him at first. When he saw that I was not, he never said another word.

He is going to have to stand trial for murder. I can not back him up any more. I paid off my debt to him and we are even. I just can not let him go. He is a cold-blooded killer and must be punished.

I am sending the reward money to Anne to use for Melanie. I suppose that, now, every one will accuse me of "selling" my friend for money. Let them think it if they choose. I am the City Marshal and Henry has broken the law. There is no question about it at all. It was out and out murder.

Galwell was not even armed.

The trial of Henry Blackstone was a brief one. The jury found him guilty of murder and he was sentenced to be hanged.

March 5, 1874

I am writing this in the office. I do not know if I have done the right thing or not. I feel that I have but I am not sure. Is there any way to be sure?

It happened about an hour ago.

It is a cold, rainy day so I brought Henry a good, hot

meal from *Nell's Cafe*—soup, and steak, and bread, and pie, and coffee.

When I brought it to the cell and opened the door, Henry smiled.

"Will you sit and jaw with me while I eat?" he asked.

I did not see any harm in it. He seemed calm to me. As he ate, he spoke of different things, mostly his family.

"I hope you will write my Mother," he said to me. "I hate that she should learn I met my end this way but I want her to know. Tell her all that happened. Do not leave out anything."

He talked and talked as he ate. He said he was resigned to his fate and hoped that all the bad talk about him would cease when he had paid his debt and was hanging by a rope, his "soul flung to eternity."

"There has got to be a law," he said. "I see that now. The world would be barbaric if every young fellow lived like me. Now, as the gallows stares me in the face, I recognize what a poor wretch of a person I really am."

I never suspected a thing until, in the middle of a word, he smashed me suddenly across the head with his tray and lunged from the cell.

Dazed, I struggled to my feet and staggered after him. Henry ran outside and started down the plank walk.

If it had not been raining so hard, he might have made it. He started to run across the street to grab a horse that was tied in front of the General Store. He was half way across when he slipped and sprained his leg.

By the time he had limped to the horse and gotten on, I had reached him. I grabbed him by the leg and pulled him off. He fought me like a wildcat but has not recovered from his illness yet and was too weak to beat me. Finally, I got his left arm twisted up behind his back and stuck a gun against his ribs.

It is the only time I ever saw Henry lose control.

"What are you doing?" he cried. "Why don't you let me go?"

I did not answer him which only got him more excited.

"I understand about the reward money!" he cried. "I know you needed it for your baby! But you have *sent* it now! They can not take it back! And no one can blame you if I escape by force!"

I did not answer him. I was still dizzy but also angry that he had pulled such a mean trick on me.

"Clay, I could have killed you if I had wanted to!" he cried. "Don't you see that? *I could have killed you if I had wanted to!*"

He kept saying that over and over as I locked him into his cell. He could not seem to understand why I had not let him escape.

I do not understand it myself.

What made me chase him like that? It would have been simple to let him escape. There would have been an outcry but, soon enough, it would have passed.

Why didn't I let him go then? I know he is a criminal and a murderer and it is my job to keep him under lock and key until he is punished for his crime.

Still, he is *Henry.*

I can see why he does not understand me.

I do not understand myself.

March 9, 1874

This morning came, a desolate one.

Days of rain had ended but the sky was dark and there was a heaviness in the air.

Henry was sitting in his cell, smoking a cigar, when Ben

and I went to get him. He had eaten every scrap of the
breakfast we had brought to him—steak, and eggs, and
coffee, and apple pie.

"I have been listening, for days, to the work men building that contraption out there," he told us with a smile. "I
sure have wondered what it looks like. I am glad I am going to see before I die of curiosity."

I could barely speak. I had been up all night and had
nothing in my stomach because I felt sick.

"I am sorry," I said, holding up the shackles and chain.
"We have to put this on you."

"Oh, that is all right," Henry said.

Ben stood guard with a shotgun while I went into the
cell and put the manacles on Henry's wrists and ankles.
He puffed on his cigar and hummed as I did.

Then we took him outside where Jim was waiting, also
armed with a shotgun.

"Think you boys can handle me?" Henry asked, smiling.

There was a crowd of people present to witness the
hanging. Henry walked through them as if he were taking
a stroll, still puffing on his cigar. He looked at the scaffold
and said, "That is good work. I had an uncle who was a
carpenter. I used to help him some times and I know good
work when I see it."

I took him up the steps and read the death warrant to
the crowd. As I did, I saw Jess Griffin, grinning as if he
were at a circus. I guess it was a circus to him.

I finished reading the warrant and turned to Henry to
ask if there was any thing he wanted to say.

"No, I think that I have said enough for one life time,"
he replied.

He threw away the cigar and got on his knees to pray. I
thought I was going to vomit as I watched him. Henry was
smiling while he prayed.

Then he got up and raised his manacled hands in the air. "Goodbye all!" he cried.

The hang man put the black hood over his head. I felt my heart starting to beat faster and faster. I began to feel dizzy and had to hold on to a scaffold post.

"Draw it tighter," Henry told the hang man. I pressed my teeth together praying that I would not get sick in front of every body.

Then, just before the hang man sprang the trap, Henry cried out again, this time in terror, his voice like that of a frightened boy.

"D——— you, Clay!" he cried. *"You didn't have to do it!"*

I felt as though all the blood in me was rushing out of my legs and into the scaffold as the trap door opened and Henry fell. I heard his neck crack and the sound was like a knife blade plunging straight into my heart.

My God! Henry! *I have killed you!*

Later: Every thing is finished now. I do not care.

I can not remember how I got down the scaffold steps after Henry was hanged. I think that Jim came up to help me but I am not sure. I know that he looked at me strangely. Later on, when I saw my face in a mirror, I knew why. I was as pale as a ghost.

Ben told me to come to his house but I pulled away from him. I walked over to Henry and put my hand on his chest. I could not believe that he was dead. I told Ben that I felt a heart beat and whispered to him that we had to get Henry to Doc Warner before it was too late.

He told me that I was imagining it because Henry was dead.

I turned away and walked to the first saloon I could find. I went inside and bought a bottle of rye and sat at a corner table to drink. I was cold and shaking and the first drink tasted like fire.

I intended to drink until I was unconscious. That was not to be. While I was sitting there, Jess Griffin and several of his friends came in. They stood at the counter and I heard them whispering. Griffin looked at me in the mirror and grinned.

It was all the push I needed. I got up and walked across the room where I started to bait him without mercy, wanting more than anything in the world to kill him. I called him a "mouth fighter" and a "yellow livered son of a b———."

He tried to back down with a joke because he was afraid. I would not let him. I insulted his father and mother and every person in his family. I told him that his mother and his sisters were all w———s. Still, he would not fight. I slapped his face and told him that I would murder him where he stood if he did not have the guts to defend himself.

He started to cry so I could not do it. I took what little pleasure there was in slapping him a few more times, then threw him out of the saloon and went back to my table.

About an hour later, when I went outside and started to cross the street, he tried to ride me down, shooting as he came. He almost knocked me over with his horse. I barely managed to avoid getting hit by leaping to the side and landing in the mud.

He wheeled his horse to gallop back and finish me. Pushing to my feet, I rested the barrel of my Colt across my left arm and, ignoring the hail of lead, brought him down with a single ball through the head.

Jim was the first to approach me after the shooting. He checked Griffin's body, then walked over to me.

"It is war to the knife now, Clay," he said.

"Good," I answered. *"Let it come."*

March 10, 1874

Ben came into the office.

"They are riding in," he said.

"How many?" I asked.

"I count eleven," he replied.

I nodded and looked toward Jim who was buckling on his gun belt. It was just past breakfast, maybe nine o'clock.

We did not exchange words as we armed ourselves. I had told them it was not their fight but they had paid no attention to me. It was their job to help keep the peace, they said. If the Griffins rode into Hays with iron on and my life as their intention, it was their duty to assist me. I should have argued but I could not. I needed them. Three of us together had some kind of chance. Alone, I was a dead man.

We finished getting ready and went outside onto the plank walk. It was a brisk morning with a little wind.

Roy Griffin and his three remaining sons plus his two brothers and five of his hands stopped in the street, looking toward Ben, Jim, and me.

The area was deserted, every one indoors. In the silence, there was a sound of footsteps on the walk and John appeared, carrying a sawed off shotgun. He took a position behind some crates in front of the mercantile store.

"Are you in on this?" Roy Griffin asked him.

"I am," John answered.

"Then get out from behind those crates and fight like a man," Griffin said.

"What is the matter? The odds not good enough for you now?" John asked in a mocking voice.

For a split second, Roy Griffin seemed to hesitate.

"Maybe you would rather back down," I told him.

He stiffened. "You murdered my boy," he said.

"He tried to ride me down and I shot him in self defense," I replied.

"Well, you will never shoot any one else," Griffin said.

For a moment, it seemed as though he was going to draw. Then he glanced at John and smiled. "We will be waiting for you at Kelly's Stable," he said. He pulled his horse around and they all rode down the street.

John came over to us.

"This is not your battle," I told him.

"I am a civilian," he said. "I can join if I want."

The four of us walked down the street to Kelly's Stable. Outside, dismounted, were the Griffins and their cow hands. The eleven of them stood in a line and we stopped to face them at a distance of approximately six yards.

"Surrender your weapons or face arrest," I told them.

"Die, you b——!" Griffin cried, clawing for his gun.

The next instant, the air exploded with a thunder of gun fire. The next, every one of us was obscured by a fog of powder smoke.

It was a scene from H——. The deafening roar of rifles, shotguns, and six-shooters. The fiery muzzle blasts lighting up twisted faces. The screams of wounded and dying men. The gushing sprays of blood. The bodies falling to the muddy ground.

I do not remember how I felt. I acted like a machine. I fired my shotgun, then dropped it, and drew a revolver. I emptied the revolver, drawing the second as I fired. I dropped the first and tossed the second into my right hand to continue firing without halt. I drew one of my Derringers as I fired. When the second Colt was empty, I dropped it and continued firing with the Derringer, drawing out the second Derringer as I did. I did not aim but fired quickly at the figures across from us. They kept falling. Lead whistled all around and the air was filled with the smell of burning powder.

It seemed to go on forever but, I am told, it lasted less than a minute. I lost all sense of what was real. A pistol ball knocked off my hat. Another grazed my right cheek. Several others tore at my clothes.

Otherwise, I was unhurt. John was shot dead beside me. Jim was hit in the chest and fell to the ground. Ben took lead in his shoulder and fell to one knee. Only I was standing, unharmed. As in a dream, I chased the three remaining Griffin cowhands down an alley, all of us reloading as we went.

I caught up with them behind the General Store and we exchanged fire. Not one of their shots came near me but I killed them all.

Then I heard footsteps running up behind me and I spun and fired without thought, killing Ben with a ball through his heart. He had been running to help me.

I could not comprehend what I had done. I knelt beside Ben and felt for his heart beat the way I did with Henry. I could not believe it was real. I was positive that I was going to wake up in my bed and find it all a dream.

I left Ben and went back to the stable yard. Townspeople were beginning to appear. They gaped at all the corpses. I helped Jim to his feet and led him to Doc Warner's office. He was bleeding badly.

When I came out of Doc Warner's, Streeter was there. His face was white. "You are no better than the Griffins," he said.

I walked past him. My legs felt like wood. I went to where John was lying dead, his body riddled with lead. His eyes were open and I closed them. I stood up. The street wavered around me. I thought I was going to faint. I walked down the alley. I was amazed to see that Ben was still there. I started to cry because I knew it was not a dream.

I picked up Ben and carried him to the undertaker's. I put him on a table and sat beside him, holding his hand

and crying. I do not know how long I was there. Marion appeared and sat beside me. I felt as if the insides of my head were going to explode. She sat beside me, holding my hand and crying with me and I was the one who had killed her husband. Eleven men against us and he had survived only to be killed by me.

I am sitting in my room. I still feel dazed. My hands and feet are like wood. My head is numb. I still hope it is a dream. I know it is not.

John is dead because of me. I could have made him leave. I was selfish. I wanted him by my side because I needed him. Now he is dead.

Jim is badly hurt. Doc Warner says that he does not know if he will live.

Ben is dead. I killed him. Eleven men against us. Dozens of rifle and revolver balls fired at us yet he was only slightly hurt. And I killed him. *I killed him*. Without a thought. Spinning like a machine. Firing like a machine. Killing the best man I ever knew except for Mr. Courtwright. Ben Pickett was as true as steel and I killed him. In an instant. Ben is dead because of me. Because of *me*, not the Griffins. I can not believe it. It has to be a dream.

It was not a dream despite the fact that Clay rewrote that sentence sixteen times.

He had just taken part in the most real, *most bloody encounter ever to take place in the West which, later, became known as "Carnage At Kelly's Stable."*

This was the high water mark of Clay's career as a gunfighter. Never again was he to achieve such a summit of deadly efficiency with the six-shooter.

While making allowances for erratic observation, eye witness accounts indicate that, of the eleven men killed in the Griffin force, Clay killed a minimum of seven.

John Harris was killed almost immediately although it

is logical to assume that, armed, as he was, with a shotgun, he took at least one of the Griffin men with him when
he died.

By his own statement, Jim Clements killed two others,
one of them Roy Griffin himself, before a severe chest
wound knocked him to the ground.

Which leaves one life, accountable, no doubt, to Ben
Pickett.

As Clay indicated in his journal, it must, indeed, have
been a scene from H——, fifteen men exchanging shots
as rapidly as possible, using shotguns, rifles, six-shooters
and Derringers. At that close range, violent mortality must
have come with extreme quickness. Estimates of the true
length of the battle run as low as twenty-five seconds,
which sounds perfectly feasible.

The incredible factor—here, we must openly admit, it
seems more legendary than real—was that Clay did not
receive a single wound more serious than a scratch across
his right cheek. How this could have happened when,
clearly, he would have been the principal target of the
Griffin force, is difficult to understand.

Nonetheless, it did happen precisely in this manner.
Perhaps it was because Clay knew instinctively which of
his opponents was more likely to hit him and aimed for
them first. Certainly, he was at the absolute zenith of his
prowess in this battle, a veritable colossus of death,
emptying and dropping one weapon after another, so
rapidly that his fire never ceased for a fraction of a second until his ammunition was exhausted.

Whether the total fury of this encounter was what
changed him will never be known. Surely, it had its affect
on him. Whatever he had been involved in before, no battle could have matched, in brutal intensity, the Carnage
at Kelly's Stable.

More than this, however, it was, doubtless, the loss of

two of his closest friends that ultimately drove the spirit from him. Having just been the instrument of execution for Henry Blackstone, to now have been indirectly responsible for John Harris's death and directly responsible for Ben Pickett's must have been an emotional blow of severe force. Clay's entry, following the battle, seems to have been made by a man almost literally struck dumb by horrified disbelief.

He was never the same again.

March 15, 1874

The Council called me in today.

They told me I was a murderer. A shame to my profession. They said they were not going to renew my contract.

I did not say a word to them. While Mayor Gibbs was ranting, I took off my badge and threw it on his desk. They do not need me now because the Griffins are dead. The pawn has done his job.

On my way back to the hotel, Bellingham approached me. He did not know that the Council was not renewing my contract or that I had quit. He told me that he had "searched his soul" and decided that I represented "true law and order" in Hays and had decided to "switch his hat" and come out in my favor.

If I could have laughed, I would have. After everything he has written about me, to tell me that. I guess he needs another "friend" now that the Griffins are dead.

I felt too tired to hit him so I just walked by him without a word. The way I feel, I could not harm a man if he stood in front of me with a gun in his hand and said that he was going to kill me.

I am tired. I am going to rest. I will get out of Hays as soon as I feel strong enough.

To H——— with this journal. To H——— with every thing. I am going to finish this bottle of whiskey. Then I am going to finish another bottle of whiskey. I am going to drink until I pass out.

I have not told Marion. I am the only one who knows that I killed him. I can not tell her. It would be too awful. I will carry the secret to my grave.

I might add, at this point, that Mrs. Pickett died less than a year after her husband. Accordingly, as far as she is concerned, Clay has carried his secret to the grave.

Following the above, a month went by without another entry. What reports are available indicate that Clay sank into a state of almost total vegetation, sleeping and drinking and never leaving his room except to visit Marion Pickett and Jim Clements and bring fresh flowers to Ben Pickett's grave.

Clements started to recover from his wound in late April, and Clay decided to leave Hays and return to Hickman, hopefully to reconcile with Anne.

The day he left Hays, he lost his final friend.

April 29, 1874

I am sitting on the train as I write this. Hays is many miles behind me. I will never return to it. There is nothing there for me any more.

I was packing my bag when a man came running upstairs and knocked on my door. He told me that Jim had murdered his wife and a seventeen-year-old boy who worked in the General Store.

I rode out to Jim's house. There were some people standing in the street. One of them told me that I had better not go near the house or the "crazy man" inside would kill me.

I walked on to the porch and tried to open the door. It was locked.

"Get away from there," Jim said, inside.

"Jim, it is Clay," I told him.

He was silent for a while. Then he said, "You do not want to see this, Clay."

"Let me in," I replied.

He was silent again. Then I heard his footsteps and he unlocked the door. He was wearing his night shirt and an old robe. His hair was out of place. His eyes looked old.

"She is over there," he said, pointing.

I walked in to the parlor. There was a blood soaked blanket over two bodies. I drew it back and saw Mary's white face staring up at me. Beside her was a young boy. Both of them were unclothed.

Jim came up beside me and looked down at his dead wife.

"She thought I was asleep upstairs," he said. "I found them in here. Mary screamed at me. She said that, since I could not 'service' her, she had a right to find some body else. My rifle was above the mantel. I took it down and shot them both."

He started to shiver and I put an arm around him.

"Listen," I said. "I understand. Get dressed, mount up and leave town."

"I have to be punished," he replied.

"You have been punished enough," I told him. "Get dressed and leave. Start over somewhere else."

He looked at me and, after a while, he smiled sadly and put his hand on my shoulder. "You have been a good friend, Clay," he said.

"Go up and dress," I said. "You can take my horse. It is already saddled. I will not need it anymore."

He nodded. "All right," he said.

I put the blanket over the bodies after he had left the

parlor. I knew that I was helping him to break the law but I did not care. He was the only friend I had left. I was never going to tell him about Mary either.

The shot rang out as I was leaving the parlor. I ran upstairs.

Jim was lying on the bed, dead by his own hand. His Derringer had fallen to the floor. There was a hole in his chest and blood was running across his body.

I almost fell. My legs shook and I could not stop them. I sat on a chair and looked at Jim. After a long time, I got up and left the house. I returned to the hotel and finished packing. Then I went to the railroad station and sat there for two hours, waiting for the train to come.

I have been reading, in the *Gazette*, what really happened at Kelly's Stable. It is strange that I did not notice at the time.

It seems that a group of "hard working cow boys" riding into town for a little "well earned relaxation" were set upon by a "brutal police force in an unprovoked attack." Now the "head murderer" (me) is fleeing town and, under Sheriff Woodson's "upright aegis," law and order will, at long last, return to Hays.

Bellingham does not know it but he is beating a dead horse.

Some people nearby have recognized me. Word of my presence is moving through the car. I do not want to raise my head and see them staring at me. I will just keep writing.

Jim. Ben. John. Henry.

Me.

A week passed without an entry. Then, in Hickman . . .

May 6, 1874

I knew that I was fooling myself.

Anne is not interested in me any more. I think she was just hoping I had some money to give her.

She has received an offer of marriage from the man who owns the lumber yard in Hickman. She is going to accept, she said. She has already gone to a lawyer to get a divorce from me.

Melanie is better. She did not remember me.

Oh, why bother writing about it?

Why bother writing about anything?

Now Clay's last, close human contact had been severed and he was truly alone.

Again, a month passed without an entry. What Clay was doing during that time is any man's guess. In keeping with his past behavior, it is to be assumed that he spent the bulk of his time drinking, gambling, and consorting with the lower grade of female so common to the West.

Whatever he was doing, while he was doing it, the legend was increasing.

In contrast to the Hays Gazette, *the stories about Clay in the Eastern magazines and newspapers continued in an adulatory vein. (Sans my assistance, I am proud to state.)*

The headline for one of the stories recounting the now famous battle at Kelly's Stable reads: SINGLE-HANDED, KILLS SEVENTEEN MEN!

Despite the depths to which his will for life had fallen, his fame was at its peak.

It was a fame completely artificial now. No one in the East had any concept of him as a man. To them, he was untouchable. If there was blood in his veins, it was the blood of gods. Standing on the summit of some frontier Mount Olympus, he looked down, with august superiority, on lesser mortals.

No one realized that he had been thrust upon that mountaintop, condemned to stand alone.

So began the final phase of his life—wherein the legend ruled the man.

In dire need of funds, Clay agreed to appear in a play which was to have its "try out" in Albany, tour the state and surrounding areas, opening, at last, in New York City.

The play, Hero of The Plains, *was the epitome of all the ludicrous tales about him. Nonetheless, the offer from its producer was a handsome one and Clay accepted it rather than accept the various positions of City Marshal being submitted to him.*

June 18, 1874

I am sitting in my hotel room. I have just finished reading *Hero of The Plains*. It is as stupid as any story about me. It is worse.

When I picked up the manuscript at the theatre, the man who hired me shook my hand and said that this play is going to make me more famous than ever.

His name is Budrys and he has produced plays for some years, he told me.

I took the manuscript to my hotel room, took off my coat and boots, and stretched out on the bed to read it.

I was in a low state of mind, but, in spite of that, the play was so ridiculous it made me smile. I began to chuckle as I turned the pages, reading on. Finally, I had to laugh. There is nothing real in the play. I kill hundreds of Indians, and save wagon trains and towns, and shoot down dozens of outlaws and renegades.

Finally, I started laughing so hard, I could not read any more. I started writhing on the mattress, kicking my legs. Tears rolled down my cheeks. I dropped the manuscript on the floor. I was as hysterical as a woman. I pounded on the bed and howled with glee.

Then I realized that I had lost control. I was not laughing any more. I was crying and hitting the bed in fury. I was losing my mind, and I stopped myself.

For the first time in my life, I know what fear is.

Too bad Frank will never know it. But no one will read these words. It is the way I want it. I would not write them otherwise.

Rehearsals of Hero of The Plains *were degrading.*

Clay's entries make it clear how sickened by himself he was.

Standing on a Western street, facing an armed opponent, he had been the very image of steel-nerved deadliness.

Standing on a stage, attempting to mouth the pompous dialogue of the play, he was absurd.

Embarrassed by the words and how he spoke them as well as by the staring actors, he stumbled and stammered. His movements were clumsy and inept. The director, in an agony of prescience, foresaw complete disaster and did not care who knew about it.

Clay foresaw it too but had to continue. A contract had been signed and money paid and he was still a man who honored his obligations.

What neither of them realized was that people would be attending the play for one thing only and that was to see the man who was a myth—the legendary Clay Halser. Whether he was actually portraying himself in a "True Ac-

count Of His Death-Defying Adventures" was beside the point. That he moved and spoke with awkward blundering was not important.

That it was him—*Clay Halser, in the flesh—was all that mattered.*

July 23, 1874

"First Night" as they say!

Sitting in my room. Drunk as a hoot owl. Don't give God d———— about it!

Could not face the audience sober. Drank all day. Came to the theatre half booze blind. They did not know. I can hold it. Stand up. My breath maybe. Who cares? To H———— with them!

Could not remember lines. Kept missing them. Every body laughed. Did not care. To H———— with every body! Whole play falling apart.

Saloon Scene. Supposed to tell my "comrades" about an adventure. Shot down twenty-seven outlaws "six guns spewing leaden death!" *That* again! S——!

Bar tender in play hands me a drink. Thought it *was* a drink. Every one on stage cried, *"Tell us the story, Marshal Halser!"*

Took a swallow of the drink. Spat it all over the stage, on half the actors.

"Who the H———— put cold tea in a whiskey bottle?" I roared.

Audience loved it. Roared back with laughter. Made me grin. Forgot the God d————d play! Said, "I don't tell stories 'til I get some *real* whiskey!"

Thought I was fooling. Was not. Bar tender poured another glass of tea. I poured it on his head. Audience roared.

"*Real* whiskey!" I cried. Audience loved it. "Get him whiskey!" they shouted. They began to chant. "Whiskey, whiskey, whiskey!" as I pounded on the bar.

Some one brought a bottle of rye. Audience cheered. I grabbed the bottle and pulled out the cork with my teeth. Spat out the cork. Audience loved it. Laughed and clapped. Took a swig of the whiskey. *Real stuff.* I made believe it was *hot.* Stamped my foot and howled like a coyote. Audience loved it. Laughed loud. Applauded. Hit of the evening!

I forgot the play. Who needs the play? Dumb thing. Started to tell about Henry and Bill Bonney and us in the trench house. I understand though. Not tell the truth. That is not what they want. They want lies. Made it *two hundred* Indians! Made us only five men! Killed the last fifty Indians with knives and hatchets! Blood up to our knees!

I expected laughter. Gales of laughter. No. They cheered! J——— C———. They cheered! Stood on their feet, applauding. "Standing ovation," they call it. Cheering! *Bravo! Bravo!*

Stared at them like a dumb man. Can not understand. I lied to them! Stupid, dumb, crazy lies! And they believed every G——— d———d word!

To H——— with people!

Whether Clay ever truly understood that the legend had enveloped him is hard to ascertain.

His confusion in this entry seems complete. True, he was drunk when he wrote it, but it is my conviction that he never was truly aware of how he had been victimized by the myth—no, not even to the end. Being a man with a straightforward, logical turn of mind, he seemed, always to attempt to locate some connection between himself and the legend which surrounded him.

He never seemed to comprehend the obvious fact that there was no such connection; that Clay Halser, the man, and Clay Halser, the legend, were two entirely separate entities.

This is, in essence (perhaps), the gist of the phenomenon which destroyed him.

Having succeeded in captivating an audience without adhering to the manuscript of Hero of The Plains, *Clay continued doing so, achieving a kind of freewheeling (and half-drunken) style somewhere in between the play and his own heavy-handed sense of drama—and humor.*

Accordingly, the play became workable and the company began to tour New York and its adjacent states.

Off stage, Clay continued to be a "loner," unable to make friends with anyone in the company. In general, they either regarded him with fearful awe or, in the majority of cases, with superior contempt, believing him to be a poseur and a fraud, a belief no doubt justified in light of his behavior on stage which, of course, was all they knew of him.

Occasionally, he spent some time with various of the actresses in the company but received no comfort from them and no sense of communication.

In addition, the preponderance of "deviates" among the male actors put him off completely and he was compelled, on several occasions, to let it be known that any such approaches toward him would be met with violent hostility.

As a result of all this, he was pretty much left to himself by the other members of the cast and his days and nights were lonely ones, the long, empty hours made palatable by heavy drinking.

The first result of this intemperance occurred in early September.

I am locked in my room. I am afraid to go out. I am afraid to drink and I am afraid to not drink. I am shaking so bad that I can hardly write.

There is the scene in Act Two. A "shootout" between "Black Bart" and me. I always win.

Tonight, I heard him walking up behind me on the street set and I turned.

It was Ben.

I stared at him in horror. "Ben?" I said.

He looked at me. His face was white and streaked with mud and there was blood flowing from his chest.

I screamed and ran from the stage and theatre. I ran all the way to the hotel and to my room. I am sitting here now. I have put a chair against the door and it is locked.

But locked doors can not keep away the dead.

It was the whiskey. I know it was the whiskey. I must not drink so much. I swear I will stop before it is too late.

Ben. Oh, God. Ben looking at me with those sweet, grave eyes. The man I loved and killed. Ben.

Oh, God! I *saw* him!

Firmly believing that whiskey alone caused him to suffer his hallucination, Clay attempted to cut down on his consumption.

An added impetus to this resolve was the fact that the tour was soon to take him near Pine Grove. Despite apprehensions, he hoped that a visit to his hometown would provide him with a needed boost.

It did exactly the reverse.

To his utter disheartenment, he discovered that he had even lost his identity with his own family who, in spite of knowing him all his life, tended to regard him as the super man of violence portrayed in all the articles and stories and not as the young man they remembered.

Mary Jane Silo (Mary Jane Meecham for many years by then) was remote and uncomfortable in his presence. Whatever relationship they had had was entirely a thing of the past and, it seemed to Clay, that past was irrevocably dead.

Indeed, it was as if Clay Halser, the man, was also dead while pretending to be him was this frightening impostor who looked and sounded like him but was, quite obviously, without his soul.

It was in Pine Grove that Clay suffered his second hallucination, one far more terrifying than the first.

October 23, 1874

I have to stop drinking or I am going to lose my mind I *know* it.

It is four o'clock in the morning. I am still cold from what happened.

I was supposed to be in Fort Wayne last night. The "Hero of The Plains" was not there, however. He was here in Pine Grove, drinking.

I should never have come here. I was a fool to think that it would work out. No one knows me for what I am. They have all read the stories and I am unreal to them. Even my Mother does not know me! It was like being with a stranger. My brothers. My sisters. All strangers to me. I thought that Ralph, at least, would see me as I am. All he did was ask about Indians and how many I had killed bare handed. I could not get away from the house fast enough.

I went to *The Green Horse*. It looked different to me. Smaller, more dingy. I sat at the same table where I had played cards with Menlo. I sat in the chair that I had used.

It gave me a strange feeling. Did it all start that night? Was it the beginning?

Some local men came in and gathered around. I tried to be friendly with them but they held back. I was desperate to get a laugh out of them. I thought if I could make myself foolish in their eyes, they would know that I was really just a man after all.

I told them the wildest story I could make up. I told them that I held back a lynch mob of three hundred and fifty people armed only with a rusty, unloaded revolver. I waited for their laughter but it did not come. They wanted to hear the rest of the story! I lost my temper and told them to get away from me.

They scattered like sheep. They were afraid of me. They hated me too. I saw the way they whispered about me. Men always hate what they fear.

I drank by myself. I sat there drinking rye and trying to think what I should do. I could not make up my mind. I do not like it here in the East but I do not want to go back West either. At least men do not challenge me here. There are no boys with pimples on their faces traveling distances to "try" me.

I do not know how long I drank before my brain got muddled. I thought I would rest and I laid my head on my arms on the table. It was late. There was only one other man in the saloon beside myself and that was the bar tender. I guess he wanted to close the saloon but did not dare to tell me to leave.

It is all so clear. I do not see how it could have been unreal. It was so *clear*.

I heard a voice say, "Howdy, Clay."

I lifted my head from the table and looked around. The room seemed to ripple like colorless jelly.

I saw Henry standing in the doorway.

My God, I swear that he was real! I stared at him, a hundred thoughts tumbling through my head. Ben had been wrong! I *had* felt a heartbeat and someone had rescued Henry and saved his life. It was *him*. He had followed me back East.

Then he moved outside and I jumped to my feet. I was dizzy and almost fell. I staggered to the door, calling out his name. The bar tender looked at me but did not say a word.

I pushed through the bat wing doors. "Henry!" I cried. I looked around the dark street but I could not see him?

Fear chilled me. Was he hiding in the shadows, waiting to kill me for what I had done to him?

I threw myself to the ground and looked around. The street ran like water before my eyes. "All right, go ahead!" I told him. "Shoot!"

There was no shot. I looked around. "Henry!" I shouted.

"Here!" he said.

I saw him down the street, standing near a store front.

I pushed to my feet and ran after him. I did not care if he was there to kill me. I deserved to be killed.

When I reached the place he had been standing, he was gone.

I looked around. "Henry, don't hide!" I told him. "If you want to kill me, *do* it! Just let me see your face!"

"Here I am!" he said.

I whirled and saw him standing in an alley. I ran after him. He turned and went away. I ran around a corner. He was standing twenty feet away from me, near a hitching post.

"All right, if you won't draw, I will!" I cried. I snatched out my revolver and fired.

Henry ducked away. I ran to where he had been standing. "Don't do this to me, Henry!" I shouted. "Face me like a man!"

"Clay!" he cried.

He was standing down the street.

I ran after him but he was gone. He was across the street from me. I chased him there and he went into another alley. I cursed and fired at him until my gun was empty. Lights went on in windows. People looked out at me.

I chased him all the way to the graveyard. He stood on a grave and laughed at me. "You will never catch me, old fellow!" he said.

Then he vanished and I fell on the ground, crying. "Henry, please come back," I begged. "Let me see your face."

He can not come back. He is dead. He was not in the doorway or the street or in the alleys. I know that now. He was a vision in my mind. The whiskey again.

Yet it was so clear! I remember what my Gran said when I was a boy. "The dead do walk at times," she said. "When they have need."

Sweet God, *do* the dead walk?

If so—*how many will walk with me?*

After that night, Clay was never to see his hometown again.

Returning to the company, he continued touring with Hero of The Plains.

Approximately one month later, the play opened in New York City.

It was a huge success, not only the "masses" turning out in force but all of "high society" as well.

Clay, just drunk enough not to give a d———— (although, because of fear, he had tapered off his alcoholic consumption), performed with bombastic theatricality and the cheering and applause—albeit partially satirical, I feel—was deafening.

At the time, I was in Kentucky and unable to attend. To this day, I am not sure if I regret it or am grateful. Although it would have been good to see Clay again, I think it would have saddened me to see him making sport of himself.

That night, following the show, he was taken to dinner by Miles Radaker. On this occasion, Clay revealed that underneath the veneer of foolishness he had assumed, there still remained part of a man of ice-grained substance.

November 27, 1874

Went out tonight with Miles Radaker, the man who wrote that first article about me more than three years ago.

I gather he has made a tidy fortune exploiting what he called "The Halser Chronicle." In gratitude, he and his current mistress (he told me that when she had left the table) took me out to dinner.

I should not have gone. It is the first time in my life that I have been in such a "posh" restaurant. I made a fool of myself, not knowing which piece of silver to use, not knowing how to eat with delicacy, and not knowing how to conduct the "chit chat of the elite" as Radaker called it.

His mistress—Claudine—is a beautiful young woman. I think she liked me or was attracted to me any way. Or to the legend, I do not know. What I do know is that it became clear very soon that they were having fun at my expense, pretending to be interested in what I had to say but snickering in such a manner that I knew they took me for a perfect fool. I believe that Radaker truly thought me a country bumpkin who believed all the stories.

I held my temper as long as I could. When they started to make remarks about my clothes and hair, though, I decided to turn the table. I took my Derringer out of my inside coat pocket and laid it on the table between Radaker and myself.

"Here is a game we used to play," I told him. I cocked the Derringer and drew back my hand. "We put our hands on our laps and count to three. The one who grabs the Derringer first gets to live."

Radaker smiled. He seemed amused. "What are you talking about?" he asked.

"A game," I said. I put my hands on my lap. "Put your hands on your lap," I told him. "I will count to three."

"What are you talking about?" he asked. There was a quaver in his voice.

"One," I said.

"Wait a second," he told me. I saw a dew of sweat breaking out on his forehead. "What is this, a joke?" he asked.

"No," I said. "It is a game we played to discover which of us was the real fighter and which could only fight with his mouth."

"All right, all right," Radaker laughed nervously. "Very funny, Mr. Halser. Now put that thing away before it goes off."

"It *will* go off," I said. "In the hand of the first of us to grab it."

"This is not amusing to me any more," he said. There was quite a bit of sweat on his forehead by then.

"It is not supposed to be amusing," I said. "It is a game of life and death. Put your hands on your lap."

"I will do no such thing," he said. His voice shook badly.

"Then I will have to do it by myself," I said. "One."

"Stop this," Radaker said.

"Two," I said.

"For God's sake, are you *mad?*" he asked.

"You had better get ready to grab for it," I said. "Or you are going to die."

"What are you *talking* about?" he asked.

"You are very good with your mouth," I said. "Let us see how good you are with your hand."

"All right, I apologize," he said. "You are very clever."

"One," I said.

"Stop it, stop it," he said. He was sweating hard now and his face was white.

"I will start the count again," I said.

"For God's sake," Radaker began.

"One," I said.

"Halser, if it's money . . ."

"Two," I said.

He pushed back from the table with a whimper.

"Three!" I said. I snatched up the Derringer so fast that he could not even blink before I had it in my hand. I pulled the trigger and the hammer clicked against the empty chamber. Radaker lurched back in his chair and fell to the floor with a cry.

I put the Derringer in my pocket and stood up.

"Good night, Mr. Radaker," I said. "I have enjoyed the dinner. Thank you very much."

I left the restaurant. It was the first time I have felt any pleasure in a long time.

The pleasure is gone now. I am tired of the people back here. I may go back out West after all. Despite the perils, it is, at least, a place where I can breathe my own kind of air.

Four days later, following a night's heavy drinking, Clay's "career" as a stage actor terminated abruptly.

December 1, 1874

I am leaving the show. Tomorrow morning, I am going to catch an early train and start back West.

We had a matinee performance today. There were a lot of children present. I had a headache from the drinking I did last night.

In between each scene, I told the stage manager to tell the spotlight man not to shine it in my eyes because it made my headache worse. He never did it and I got angrier by the minute.

During the first act intermission, I got my Derringer from my dressing room and loaded it.

When the next act started and the spotlight hit my eyes again, I pulled out the Derringer and shot it out.

Then something took me by the hand and walked me to the footlights. I looked out over all the faces in the audience. I saw the children looking at me, and suddenly I could not bear the idea that they thought they were seeing truth on that stage.

I do not remember exactly what I said to them but it was something like this.

"You have been watching nonsense, do you know that? Not a word spoken up here has been a truthful one.

"You have come to see me, Clay Halser, the Great Western Hero.

"Do you want to know what it was really like out there? The truth and not the nonsense you have all been looking at?

"I will tell you.

"There was nothing pretty about it. There was nothing brave and gallant.

"I had a wife and a child but my wife left me because she could not stand facing each day, wondering if I would be coming back for supper on my own two feet or stretched out dead on a board. I was not a *Hero of The Plains* to her.

"I had five good friends but now they all are dead. They did not die like characters in this play. The blood they spilled was real.

"I had a friend named Mr. Courtwright you probably have read about. He was murdered by three hired renegades. I followed those men and when I found them, I did not say, 'Draw, you varmint,' or anything like that. I did not behave like the *Hero of The Plains*. I walked over to the table they were sitting at and shot them down in cold blood because they had murdered my friend.

"I had a friend named John Harris. You probably have read about him. He was a good, honest man. He was shot down by my side and died without a word. There was nothing 'thrilling' about his death. He was just filled with lead. He was not a *Hero of The Plains*.

"I had a friend named Jim Clements. He was brave and honest. He was wounded helping me at Kelly's Stable. He married a woman who had almost been murdered in a w——— house where she worked. While she was recovering, Jim fell in love with her.

"I never told him she had been a prostitute. But, while he was recovering from his wounds, she began consorting with a seventeen-year-old boy. Jim found them together in the parlor and he shot them both dead with his rifle. Then he went upstairs and killed himself with a Derringer."

There was a murmur of shocked voices by then. I saw mothers and fathers rushing their children up the aisles but I kept on.

"I had a friend named Ben Pickett. You probably have read about him. He was a good, brave man and the best Deputy a City Marshal ever had. Do you know how he died? Not at the hands of the Griffins at all. No. *I* shot him. *Me*. I was so worked up by the fight at Kelly's Stable that, when he ran up behind me to help me, I spun around without thinking and shot him dead. I killed my own friend. I was not much of a hero when I did that.

"I had a friend named Henry Blackstone. You probably have read about him. He was a strange, young fellow but a friend of mine. I sold him for money. He could have escaped but I would not let him. I wanted the thousand dollars reward money offered for him. He could have killed me and escaped but he didn't want to hurt me. So they hanged him. He was my friend and I was the one who put the noose around his neck. Do you know what a neck sounds like when it breaks? Like a piece of wood being snapped in two. I did that to my friend, Henry. Then I goaded Jess Griffin into a fight even though he was afraid of me. I did it even though I knew his family would have to seek revenge after I had killed him. And they did and John Harris and Ben Pickett were killed. Because of me.

"That is just a small part of what it was like in the West. I know it is not as exciting as *Hero of The Plains* but that is the way it was and I can not change the facts."

There were a few people who applauded when I left the stage but mostly there was bedlam. People do not like a legend to have flesh and blood.

Budrys said that, if I leave, he will get even with me, somehow. I told him to go to H———.

Later: Budrys really meant what he said, the son of a b———.

I have just finished washing off the blood and am sitting in my room, a power of cuts and bruises.

I feel great!

I was down in the hotel saloon, having a drink, when these three big galoots came in. I was standing at the corner and they stood beside me, two on one side, one on the other. We were the only customers.

"Howdy, Buffalo Bill," the one on my left said.

I did not look at him.

"I said *howdy*, Buffalo Bill," he repeated.

I looked at him.

"Are you talking to me?" I asked.

"I ain't talking to your brother," he said.

"I did not think you were," I replied, "since my brother is not Buffalo Bill, either."

"You *are* Buffalo Bill," he said.

"You are wrong," I told him.

"And you are a dirty, stinking liar who eats s———," he came back. "What do you think of that?"

That was when I realized that Budrys had hired them to take his anger out of my skin.

"Permit me," I said. I finished my drink and put down the glass. I sighed with contentment. Then I knocked that big, ugly b——— halfway across the room with a blow to the jaw that had my fullest cooperation.

The other two lunged at me. I gave one the whiskey bottle right across the face. The other one, I gave a knee in the b——s and a fist in the eye.

By then the first man was back at me and the "battle was joined" as the *Hero of The Plains* used to tell his "comrades."

I do not say it was an easy fight. Those fellows were strong enough and they did put their heart and soul to it. But they were dudes. I mean, a man who has not learned to fight "western style" has not learned to fight.

I used every trick I knew (all dirty) and gave it to them knuckle and skull. By the time I had done with them, those three, poor fellows were stretched out cold and bloody on the floor.

I poured myself a drink and threw it down. It tasted like the nectar of the gods. It was good to win a fight again. I have lost so many in the past year.

"Send the repair bill to Mr. Budrys at the Lyceum Theatre," I told the bar keep. "He will be glad to pay for all damages."

I gave him a smile and left.

Lord, one of my teeth just fell out!

No entries of interest occur for more than a month and a half following the above.

Clay returned to the frontier and began to follow old paths, gambling, drinking, and spending occasional time with the lesser females of the towns he frequented.

As further indication that the legend had, by then, so surpassed the man as to make him literally unrecognizable, the following entry is displayed. Clay was, at the time, in Dawes in the Indian Nations.

January 25, 1875

I was sitting in a saloon this morning when it happened. I was reading the local newspaper. The story of prime interest to me was headlined CLAY HALSER IN TOWN! It told how the "nationally, nay, internationally" famous Marshal-Gun Fighter is "passing through" on his way to "who knows what incredible adventures." I know what. *None.*

Any way, I was reading when there was a sound of gunfire next door. I mean *lots* of gunfire.

I did not intend to find out what had caused it. How ever, a cry went up which, I admit, somewhat stirred my curiosity.

"Clay Halser has been killed!" was the cry.

Every one ran out of the saloon. I got up to follow.

"My God, to view those storied remains," an old man said as I went outside.

"It will be a thrill," I said.

He and I walked to the next door saloon and pushed in through the bat wing doors. There was quite a crowd.

I was lying on the floor, dead.

As a matter of truthful fact, the man did somewhat resemble me. He was dressed in gambler's black and was about the same height and build. There were two pearl-handled revolvers clutched in his hands however. A little too fancy for me.

It must have been one H——— of a shootout. There were an awful lot of holes in that man. I counted five, at first. Blood and people hid the rest from view.

One of the customers was telling how it happened.

"Just came in, mean drunk," he said. "Picked a fight with Bobby there and, by God, Bobby won."

I looked at Bobby. He must have been all of eighteen years of age. He looked like a kid at Christmas, flushed and over joyed.

I moved closer to take a good look at myself. There were seven bullet holes in me. Bobby had taken no chances.

"Should have thought that one would be enough," I said.

The old man was standing next to me. "Against *Halser*?" he demanded. "Are you *insane*?"

I did not argue the point. I left the saloon and went back to the hotel. I think I had better move on. Sooner or later, someone will discover that that body is not quite me. Then Bobby will feel obliged to find the real me and repeat his triumph. Except that he will end up in a pine box. And I am in no mood to start killing again.

I wonder if it would be a good idea to change my name and appearance. I could grow a mustache like Ben's and call myself . . .

Blackstone! that is what I will do.

Henry will live again.

Despite his resolve—which seems to have been a wise one—Clay did not change his name. He grew the mustache but went no further than this in the attempt to prevent others from recognizing him.

Whether this was a result of apathy or ego it is hard to determine. He might have decided not to bother. He might have tried, then given it up. When one spends his lifetime writing and speaking his true name, it is difficult to remember to write and speak a false one however strong the intention to do so.

On the other hand, it may have been ego; a reluctance to remove himself entirely from the myth. It is possible that man and legend had become so inextricably bound by then that he was unable to separate them anymore.

An uneventful month passed by, Clay continuing his life as a gambler. While never a truly accomplished card player, he was good enough to win if his opponents were not of the highest caliber. Remembering past experiences, he saw to it that he never played with members of the professional "circuit." Accordingly, his winnings always exceeded his losses by enough of a margin to support him.

The next noteworthy entry occurred when Clay was in Topeka, Kansas.

February 28, 1875

Maybe I can get by with my "gift of gab" as they say. After accusing others of being "mouth fighters" all these years, it turns out I am not too bad a one myself.

I was having a game of Faro in the *Cimarron Saloon* this afternoon when a gaunt, whey-faced gent came walking to the table on legs as stiff as logs. Oh, God, here it comes, I thought.

"Halser?" he said.

I looked up at him. His face was so white, it could have been dipped in biscuit batter. His hands were shaking. Still, I knew that he had "made up his mind" to face me.

"Before you say another word," I told him, "let me tell you what will happen to you if you do not turn around and walk away from here. First of all, you can not win. You are shaking like a wheat stalk in a wind storm. You will probably drop your gun, assuming you get it out of your scabbard at all.

"On the other hand, I have been a gunfighter for ten years now. (We mouth fighters like to stretch the facts.) I am so fast that you will have three bullets in your body before you can fire one. They will hurt like H———. I can not promise you a quick death either. You might drag on two or three days in utter agony before you die. Is is worth it? You do not look as though you want to die. So just turn around and leave. I will not hold it against you. I will admire you for your ripe good sense."

That poor fellow turned and moved out of the *Cimarron* like a sleepwalker. After he had left, a great laugh went up from all. "Shall we continue with our game now?" I said.

Those idiots applauded me! For a moment, I thought I was back on the d——— stage, doing *Hero of The Plains*.

Later: I am in a strange mood. Part of me is happy and part of me is afraid. The two feelings are mixed and I can not seem to separate them.

Maybe if I write down how they came about, it will grow clear to me why I can not get them apart in my mind.

I went to the theatre after supper tonight. They were performing a comedy called "The Dude Finds Out."

I bought myself a box near the stage because I felt like sitting alone. I brought a bottle of rye with me and had a drink or two as the play went on.

I had not bothered looking at the program so the first I knew of it was in the second act when a character entered who was referred to as "bawdy Aunt Alice."

To my surprise and pleasure it turned out to be Hazel Thatcher.

I was close to the stage (being in the box) but, when she saw me the first time, I do not think she recognized me, probably because of the mustache. Then, during a scene in which she had to listen to a long speech by "Ned the Dude," she peered at me in curiosity. I raised my hand and smiled at her. "Clay," I said with my lips.

She looked delighted and the next few lines she had came out badly.

I confess to being so absorbed in the welcome sight of her that I never noticed what was going on. If I had been a quarter so careless in Caldwell or Hays, they would have buried me ten times over.

The first I knew of it was Hazel looking across my shoulder in dread and breaking the scene by shouting, "Look *out* Clay!"

Before her words were out, I threw myself to the right grabbing at my revolver. A shot rang out close by, almost deafening me. Rolling over as fast as I could, I shot up at the figure in the shadows. He screamed and doubled over dropping his gun.

I stood and put my Colt away, moving to the man who was sitting on the floor of the box, hands pressed across his bleeding stomach, groaning with pain. It was the fellow I had talked out of fighting me this afternoon! I guess the laughter which greeted his departure had been more than he could stand.

Two men came and carried him away, and I said, "Please continue," to the cast and bowed to them. There was applause and the play went on.

I was not as blithe as I sounded. My hands were shaking and there was a cold knot in my stomach I could not untie. Later, I had to step out to relieve my b——s.

I am glad that I survived, of course. I am grateful to Hazel for having saved my life.

But I am shaken that I would have been killed if it had not been for her. I am shaken that I shot the man where I did. In the past, my shots, however rushed, almost never failed to kill men instantly, most often through the heart.

The man will die, of course. He will die exactly as I told him he would—in two or three days, in utter agony. But I told him that to frighten him. I did not really believe it.

Now it is *so*. And I am shaken. Have I lost my skill? How is it possible that he was able to sneak up behind me like that without me hearing a sound? Is it the whiskey again?

I am afraid, but I do not know how to deal with the fear. I feel anxious, and my heart is beating strangely, and my breath is hard to control.

What a thing to happen just as I find Hazel again. For that is what is making me happy. I am going to pick her up after she has changed her clothes. We will have a late supper and, I hope, spend the night together. Maybe I will sleep without the dreams tonight. *(The first reference Clay ever makes to (doubtless bad) dreams. F.L.)*

After the show, I went backstage and we held on to each other for a long time, kissing as though we were hungry for each other. "To have you back," she murmured. "To have you back."

I might have spoken the same words. To have her back. Someone to be with. Someone I know. It makes me very happy.

If only I was not afraid as well.

To rediscover Hazel Thatcher at this point in his life was clearly a moving experience to Clay. So moving, in fact,

*that his eyes and ears endowed Hazel with a charm she
no longer possessed—if, indeed, she had ever possessed
it at all.*

*Time had not been kind to her. The desolate life she had
led made her look far older than her thirty-nine years.*

*Clay never knew it but, some months prior to this meet-
ing, I had run across her in Wichita.*

*She had come up to my hotel room and tried to get some
money from me, telling me that she was Clay's "old
friend" and that she had heard "so much about me" from
Clay and wished that she knew me better "because I was
his friend." Could I loan her ten dollars for a few days?
The poor woman even offered, obliquely, to sell her "fa-
vors" to me for the amount.*

*I wish I could describe the sense of utter corruption she
conveyed to me. She may have been a "handsome" woman
at one time; Clay seems to have thought so, at any rate.
But that night, every second of her dissipated life showed
in her pale, somewhat bloated face, especially in her green
eyes and in the downward cast of her over-painted mouth.*

*That Clay was moved to see her again can only dem-
onstrate the measure of his loneliness.*

*She was more than just a woman to him then. His en-
tries make this clear. She represented, to him, the happy
past which he longed to recapture.*

*As for her, Hazel Thatcher was, doubtless, fully as de-
lighted to see him. Her path had been a downward one
since they had last met. Carl was dead, a victim of alco-
hol poisoning. She drank heavily herself. No longer able
to attract men of any taste whatever, she had been forced
to be content, for the indulgence of her physical desires,
with men of less and less degree, stable hands and the
like.*

*To have Clay reappear so unexpectedly must have
been, to her, like Manna from Heaven. Consequently*

she, no doubt, displayed every last iota of allurement she could manage, not realizing that it was not necessary; that Clay, alone and dispirited, would not have left her for anything.

So, each of them needing the other desperately—neither seeing the other with an eye the least bit objective—they fell into groping resumption of their old affair. Shortly after, Clay became convinced that, this time, it was genuine love and, when Hazel mentioned marriage, he could not resist.

Disenchantment set in quickly.

March 17, 1875

I never knew Hazel had such a sharp tongue. I never saw evidence of it before.

March 21, 1875

Another fight today. Hazel thinks I should take a job as City Marshal somewhere. I told her no.

April 3, 1875

How could I have thought she was beautiful?

Now I know why she prefers to ———— in the dark.

April 9, 1875

I am beginning to think that Hazel is stupid.

April 28, 1875

Hazel said I look like an old man. She said she should have married the stories instead of me.

May 5, 1875

Another battle. She insists I take a peace officer job. I told her that it will be snowing in H———— before I do that.

I am making enough on my gambling to keep going. Of course, when the acting company leaves, Hazel will be without a job.

Unless she goes with them.

May 17, 1875

I am so tired of squabbling with her. I cannot sleep late anymore. She wakes me up each morning with a new complaint. She wants to have children and a home now!

A H———— of a Mother she would make!

May 25, 1875

"Get a job as a peace officer in a *peaceful* town then!" she yelled.

"You stupid b————!" I told her. "Any town that is peaceful does not *need* a peace officer!"

I thought it was going to be so nice with Hazel. It is a nightmare.

June 3, 1875

She wants me to go back on the stage!

"Cash in on yourself, for C——'s sake!" she said.

She has some bright idea about us getting people to give us money so we can start a publishing house. Then *I* will write stories *about myself* and "we will be rich!"

She is such a stupid woman.

June 17, 1875

She called me a "three-toed b———" and I hit her.

June 23, 1875

I told her I might do some mining.

"And in the meantime, what?" she said. "Sleep late every morning? Spend your afternoons and nights gambling while I work?"

She says she is going to quit her job with the play. Let her. There are always w——— houses.

July 4, 1875

Independence Day.

I wish I was independent of Hazel.

July 12, 1875

She read my journal today and laughed at me. I hit her and she scratched my neck until the blood ran.

Then she cried and begged me to take a job as City Marshal. She said that she is getting old and wants a family of her own. She pleaded with me to help her. When I said I would not, she scratched my neck again.

July 19, 1875

I am thinking of leaving Hazel and doing some mining. A man can make a fortune in the gold or silver lodes.

I can not bear to touch her. She does not wash.

July 30, 1875

I am drunk. I am sick of Hazel. I wish I had not married her. We fight all the time. She curses and throws things at me. She hates me because I will not "be a man" and take a City Marshal job somewhere and let her have a home and family.

I do not hate her. I feel sorry for her. I feel sorry for myself. There is nothing in the past. The past is dead. John and Ben are lucky. Jim and Henry are lucky. Mr. Courtwright is lucky. They died in their time.

I have gone beyond mine. I am useless.

What would it have been like to marry Mary Jane and be a farmer in Pine Grove?

So it went from day to day. The marriage was doomed and both of them knew it. Still, they attempted to keep it alive.

With Clay, it was—his entries make apparent—mostly from a sense of loyalty because Hazel had saved his life and was a meaningful part of it.

With Hazel it was—I feel certain—pure and simple desperation. She recognized that, despite their differences, Clay was still her only chance. If they separated, she would go, forthwith, to the bottom, ending up in some trail town brothel. (A fate she has, I fear, suffered by this time.)

The weeks and months dragged by, Clay sleeping until afternoons, then gambling and drinking until the early morning hours; Hazel working in the theatre, then, when the theatre company left Topeka, taking a job as a saloon "girl."

Their life together was increasingly empty and dissatisfying. Both of them drank to excess, their conflicts taking on the aspect of drunken brawls replete with mutual physical violence, the details of which I will not exhibit.

Clay began suffering regularly from nightmares, often waking up, screaming. Several times he experienced further hallucinations, on one occasion becoming so convinced that Henry Blackstone's vengeance-seeking corpse was waiting for him in their hotel room that he would not return there for two days.

Money became a larger problem all the time, Clay's winloss balance shifting to the debit side more often than not. He sold his horse and saddle, his shotgun, his second Colt, finally his Derringers, keeping one revolver for self-defense which, fortunately, he was not called upon to use during this period. If he had been, it is doubtful whether he would have survived because of his inordinate drinking.

Withal, restless, discontented and unhappy, he contin-
ued to maintain his marriage to Hazel, wondering, almost
longingly, when it was going to end.

The one interesting entry during this time has to do with
his meeting of a man who was his equal in fame if not in skill.

September 23, 1875

I was sitting in the *Colorado House* playing poker when a
cheer went up behind me and I looked around.

A tall man dressed in black had entered the saloon. His
hair was long and light-colored and his mustache drooping. It was Hickok.

I returned to my game but knew, from that instant on,
that some one would bring us together, hopefully toward
some violent incident. I made up my mind that—as in
Morgan City—I would defer to him in all things. I was not
afraid of him. I still am not. I simply did not care to face
anyone in a life and death contest. I hope I never have to
face a man in that fashion again.

My apprehension proved groundless. Hickok had no
more desire to clash heads with me than I had to do the
same with him. We were brought together (as I knew we
would be) and sat with each other, drinking and chatting.
I suppose it was a thrill for all those in the saloon to see
two "legends" sitting in the corner.

Hickok is no more a legend than I am. In truth, he has
gone through much of what I have. I feel that he has managed to live with it better than I have but his existence has
been no bed of roses, either.

The first thing I asked him after we were together was
whether he remembered hurrahing me in Morgan City.

He smiled a little. "No, sir, I do not," he said. "However,
I dare say that you understand, now, why I acted as I did."

"I do," I said. "Being a cow town Marshal is not the most relaxing job in the world."

He chuckled at that. "No, it is not," he agreed.

It was a pleasant evening, I must say. I think that he enjoyed it too. Who, more than me, could understand what he has experienced—just as who, more than he, could appreciate what I have been through? I will not say that we "poured out" our hearts exactly. Neither of us are the kind to do so.

Still, we did chat, at length, about our experiences. It is interesting to note the similarities.

Both of us were born in the Middle West and grew up in like ways.

Both of us fought in the War Between The States on the Union side.

Both of us have "tamed" towns only to outlive our usefulness to those towns.

Both of us have achieved national if not world-wide "fame" for the identical reason—an ability to draw a revolver quickly and kill with it.

Both of us have appeared in the theatre in "self-exalting" plays, as he called them. We enjoyed discussing this particularly, laughing at the foolish things to which we were exposed. Our laughter, however, was not untinged with bitterness.

Inevitably, our conversation grew more solemn.

I discovered, to my surprise, that he believes in "life after death," and feels convinced that he has seen the ghosts of several of the men he has killed. His saying that disturbed me and I wonder now if what I have seen was really due to whiskey after all.

He suggested that I acquire and read a book on the subject of Spiritualism. I told him that I would, but I think I would rather not know if these things are true.

He also said that there is a woman here in Topeka who can "communicate" with the dead. That thought really chilled my blood and I changed the subject as soon as I could.

I told him about the man I had seen shot in Dawes. I said that seeing that body riddled with lead had made me aware, for the first time, of the fear and hatred with which I must be regarded.

Hickok nodded. He knew the feeling well, he said. I recall his exact words.

"We are victims of our notoriety," he said. "No longer men but figments of imagination. Journalists have endowed us with qualities which no man could possibly possess. Yet men hate us for these very nonexistent qualities."

His smile was sad.

"Our time is written on the sands, Mr. Halser," he said. "We are living dead men."

I believe that he is right. All this time, I have been telling myself that the skills I have to offer continue to be of value.

Now I wonder if this is so. It may be that the day of the so-called "gunfighter" is on the wane; that, soon, it will be little more than the memory of a brief period in time when masters of the handgun ruled the frontier.

A living dead man. That is what I have been for some time now.

The following night, Clay's marriage ended.

September 24, 1875

I wonder if fate had anything to do with what happened tonight. The facts seem to support the notion. More and more, I have this feeling that my life has been worked out by some one other than myself.

It is the first time I have ever eaten in Waltham's Restaurant.

It is the first time I have ever eaten lobster.

It is the first time I have had a belly ache in such a long time that I can not recall the last.

All these things combined to bringing me back to the hotel room hours earlier than usual.

I found Hazel in bed with some cow boy, both of them drunk.

"*Oh, my God,*" Hazel said when I unlocked the door and came into the room.

The cowboy stared at me in shock.

Then, I guess, he thought that I was going to kill him on the spot because he lunged from the bed and ran across the room, stark naked, going for his gun belt.

I did not shoot him. I kicked over the chair on which his gun belt hung. Then I hit him two or three times with the barrel of my revolver and threw him into the hallway the way he was. His clothes I threw out the window.

Hazel started crying and begging me to forgive her. She said that she was "lonely" with me gone all the time and needed a little "companionship."

I paid no attention to what she was saying. I got my bag from the closet and put my few belongings in. I felt grateful to her. She had made it easy for me to leave.

Not that she wanted me to leave. She kept hanging on to my arm, and crying, and begging me to forgive her, and stay.

Finally, when she saw that I was going to leave any way, she started cursing me and calling me a "no good, three-toed son of a b———" who had lost his "guts." She told me that she has been sleeping with "dozens" of cow boys while I was out gambling. She started to describe to me what she did with them. I had to hit her to shut her up. It was either that or kill her.

I am staying at the *Richmond Hotel* tonight. Tomorrow, I am going to leave Topeka and head West. I hope I never see Hazel again. I have accepted the fact that I am to be alone until the end, however soon or late that may come.

The following day, Clay entrained from Topeka and be-gan his final "tour" of the West, if such a random pere-grination can be called a tour.

He was like a man without a country now, incessantly on the move.

Everywhere he went, the result followed one of two pat-terns.

One: the town was "rough and ready" and, challenged, Clay was forced to talk or shoot his way out of trouble. Twice, he managed the former, once was compelled to per-form the latter. On this occasion, he killed his opponent.

Two: the town was so domesticated that he felt uneasy and out of place. Here, the pressures against his life were replaced by pressures even harder to adjust to—the pres-sures of civilization crowding him out, making him extinct before his time.

He kept moving West.

One town he visited listed him as a vagrant and ordered him to leave within twenty-four hours. Enraged, he tore the notice off its board but, in a day, departed as requested.

In another town, suffering the effects of drink, he had to be hospitalized for two weeks.

In yet another town (Red Hill, Nebraska) he actually committed himself to the job of local peace officer, then, after making his "rounds" for one night, became so ter-rorized by a rise of deep-seated dread within himself that he drank himself unconscious and, following a week-long bout of drinking, fled the town in ignominious defeat, thus ending, before he started it, his resolve to "get back into living."

Finally, eschewing towns altogether, he spent the rest of the winter "grub lining," riding from ranch to ranch and living off them, a welcome guest because he brought, with him, news of the "outside" world. During this time, reverting to an earlier notion, he introduced himself as Mr. Blackstone. Except in one case, no one ever recognized him.

In February, he began to experience eye trouble and, after ignoring it as long as he could, went to see a doctor in Julesberg, Colorado. There, he discovered that he had contracted a venereal infection (probably from Hazel) and was in a median stage of gonorrheal ophthalmia. The doctor did what he could for Clay but told him that, in course of time, blindness was inevitable.

Clay remained in Julesberg for a week, uncertain as to his plans, then, on a sudden impulse, decided to try some mining and left for Silver Gulch.

I will comment no further. The rest of the tale speaks for itself.

April 18, 1876

I have arrived in Silver Gulch. If my eyes hold out, I am in hopes of raising enough money to pay for Melanie's education. I will have it placed in a bank in Hickman in her name. I will make sure that the money can not be used for anything except her education. It is something I will do for her.

This town is certainly a crude place. There is only one, narrow street filled with stumps, boulders, and logs. Dozens of small, ugly saloons line the street, all made of raw pine, as are the gambling halls and w——— houses. The street itself is thick with wagons, houses, mules and ox teams. There seems never a moment when there is not a haze of dust in the air.

I have taken a room at the one hotel here—*The Silver Lode*—a ramshackle building built of cheap, cracking wood. I have cleaned and shaved off my mustache. I look younger but not much.

I am sitting on the bed, making this entry. I am very tired. It has been a long trip and I am bone weary. My old wound is giving me "action" again and feels like a toothache in my right leg. Also, the foot hurts some. It is strange that I can *still* feel those missing toes once in a while when I am really tired!

I am going to take a nap now. Later, I will go out and have some supper and, perhaps, a game of cards.

Later: Back from supper. It is almost nine o'clock. I was going to play some cards but have lost the desire. I am tired and have no energy. I do not see how I can do any mining the way I feel.

What fool idea made me get all dressed, I wonder? My white, ruffled shirt and flowered waistcoat, my black string tie, black trousers, black cutaway, black sombrero and dark calf skin boots. Why here, in this God-forsaken place?

Why do I pretend? I shaved off the mustache and got all dressed up so that I would be recognized. I wrote "Clay Halser" on the hotel register and not Mr. Blackstone. It seems I can not live without recognition. I hate it but, like whiskey, it has become a weakness. Even knowing the pain it brings, I can not stay away from it.

It worked, of course. The hotel clerk had, undoubtedly, told everyone I was in town. When I came down he said, "Good evening, Mr. Halser." People in the street looked at me and some of them said, "Good evening, Mr. Halser." Many were surprised to see that I am still alive. They thought that I had died during the time I was grub lining.

And "he" was pleased. Poor Clay Halser in his gambler's dress, pleased to see that they knew him. Because there is nothing else left for him.

There is less than nothing left. Before I had finished supper, whatever pleasure I felt was taken from me.

Some local merchants approached with an offer of the City Marshal job. I told them I would think it over for a few days. I do not have to think it over for a second. I knew, before they were finished speaking, that I could not take the position. I have no will left any more. What happened in Red Hill is fresh in mind and humbles me. My City Marshal days are over despite my need for money.

Worse than that, my days for courage seem to be at an end too. After eating, I went to a saloon for a drink and a card game. I was told, by the bar tender, that a group of six men (three of them former employees of the Griffin Ranch) are threatening to kill me, saying that I am a murdering dog and back shooter.

I pretended to be amused. Soon afterward, however, I left and came back to the hotel room like a dog with my tail between my legs. I am afraid to meet them. After all the years of . . .

No, by God . . . !

Later: Victory that is not victory.

I am back in my room again. While making the earlier entry, I suddenly became enraged and vowed that I would rather die in a "blaze of glory" than hide in my room like a coward.

I put on my gun and went to the saloon I had been in. I asked the bar tender where the six men were and he told me that they had been hanging out in *Number 9 Saloon:* I left and started down the street followed by some people. At the time, I did not care. I was so mad. Now I know that they were following the *Hero of The Plains*, not a living man.

I went into *Number 9* and placed my back to the wall, unbuttoning my coat.

The six men were standing at the counter. I recognized two of them from the Griffin Ranch. My heart was pounding, but I managed to keep my voice clear because I was angry.

"I hear that you have been making threatening remarks against me and I have come to give you your chance to kill me," I said.

The six men stared at me.

"Well?" I said. "Are you going to start shooting or shall I?"

They did not stir.

"If you are really brave and not just a pack of sneaking curs, you will give me a show right now!" I said.

They were statues.

"*Well?*" I shouted. "Go *on!*" I told them. I have not felt such fury since the night I badgered Jess Griffin. The strange thing is that I do not even know if it was really the six men I was angry at.

"Draw, you ———s!" I told them. I wanted them to fight me more than any thing I have ever wanted. I think I wanted them to kill me.

They would not draw.

"All right," I said. "Unbuckle your gun belts and hand them over."

They did it without a word. I picked them up with my left hand, keeping my revolver in my right.

"In the future," I said, "I suggest you wear skirts instead of guns."

With that I left the saloon amid the cheers of many. I dropped their guns into the first horse trough I came to and went back to the hotel. My moment of "glory."

I am sitting here, cold and shaking. What if they decided

to come and get me? I could not hope to win. They would kill me in seconds.

I am just not up to these things any more. I have lost my nerve. There is nothing left inside me. I am empty.

Later: It is almost four o'clock in the morning.

I guess they are not going to come for me.

I know I can not sleep however.

I dozed off for a little while before and had another dream. A man without a face was drawing on me. My arm and head were like lead and I could scarcely move it. I woke up as death struck.

My mind is a turmoil of thoughts.

I have been thinking about Anne and Melanie. I have been thinking about Mr. Courtwright and those days in Hickman long ago. I have been thinking about Pine Grove and my family and Mary Jane. I have been thinking about Caldwell and Mayor Rayburn and Keller. I have been thinking about Henry and our days together. I have been thinking about Ben, and John, and Jim.

I have been thinking about all these things but I can not believe that any of them really happened. It is not that I can not believe that Henry, and Ben, and John, and Jim, and Mr. Courtwright are dead.

I can not believe that they ever lived.

I feel very odd. Out in the street, it is noisy. I hear some one singing. I hear a man curse. I hear a horse walking by. There is a snapping noise which I can not identify. I sit in this ugly room and think about myself. *Who am I?* I look at my body but it seems to be another man's. I look at my hand as it writes these words, but the hand seems to write by itself. Is it my hand? Are the words my words?

No memory is real. I try to catch one in my mind. They run like water. I can not hold a single, true remembrance.

I do not think they ever existed. I can not believe in any
thing but this room because it is all I can see. I do not think
there is a Hickman, or that there is an Anne, or a Melanie. There is no Hays. No one ever lived or died there. I
did not kill Ben because there never was a Ben. I did not
hang Henry because no one named Henry ever lived.

I run on without purpose. The words I write are the
words of a fool. Who am I to say that nothing is real?
Every thing is real.

I am the one who is unreal.

April 19, 1876

It is after noon. I have slept too late. The pains in my leg
and foot are bothering me. My back is stiff. The air is very
damp.

I am going to get dressed and have some breakfast.
Then I will find out about getting started with the mining. A lot of men are making a good raise here. The hills
are full of silver. There is no reason why I can not get
some for myself.

What a folly if I hit it rich and become a wealthy man!

It looks as though it may rain before the day is over.

More later.

The GUN FiGHT

With much gratitude
I dedicate this book to
Gary Goldstein
for giving me a new literary world to explore.

Prologue

He found them on the morning of the fifth day. It had been difficult to track them down. The range was oven-hot from sunup to sundown, the earth so bone dry and hard, it made hoof prints hard to spot. The heat had worn him down. His canteen was almost empty by the time he reached them, his body feeling seared and weak.

The three men were asleep beside a narrow creek, sprawled exhaustedly on their blankets in the shade of a cottonwood tree. He could make out the form of Aaran Graham, the biggest of the three, a tall, bulky man lying on his right side. The other two were younger, slight of build, lying on their backs, Stetsons shading their eyes.

Benton's gaze shifted to their grounded saddles. All six saddlebags bulged with their contents; what the three men had robbed from the Millersview Bank last Thursday afternoon, leaving behind one dead and one badly wounded teller.

Benton drew in a long, tired breath and dismounted slowly. He really *was* getting too old for this kind of thing. Julia had been on his back for months now. Maybe she was right. Maybe it was time to leave the Rangers and settle down. Still, what else did he know how to do?

He slipped the carbine from its scabbard and started down a dusty slope toward the three motionless figures.

He tried to be as quiet as he could but his boots scuffed unavoidably on the hard soil.

He was glancing at the three staked horses when Aaran Graham jerked awake, twisting around, his half-asleep expression one of startled anger.

"Wake up!" he shouted, grabbing for the holstered pistol lying on the ground beside him.

"*Don't do it!*" Benton ordered, snapping up the carbine barrel. He saw the two younger men sitting up groggily.

Graham paid no attention, clutching at the handle of his Colt and starting to raise it.

Benton's shot hit him in the center of the chest, knocking him backward; he was dead before his body hit the ground.

"*Pa!*" The cry of anguish made Benton's gaze jump to the stricken face of one of the younger men.

Before he could react further, the other young man had snatched up his pistol and fired. Benton grunted in surprise as the bullet struck the barrel of his carbine, knocking it from his grip and numbing his fingers.

Training made him dive to his left, avoiding the young man's second shot by less than an inch. As he fell, his right hand dropped to his pistol. It was free of his holster and being fired before the young man could get off another shot.

The bullet slammed into the young man's chest just above the heart and, with a cry of dazed pain, he stumbled back, eyes already glazed over by the death which took him seconds later.

Benton scrambled to his feet, eyes fixed on the remaining young man who, he saw now, was more a boy than a man. He'd had no idea until moments ago that one of Graham's men was his son.

The boy was staring at his dead father, then at the

other young man who Benton later learned was his older brother.

Benton was never to forget the expression on the boy's face. Stunned and horrified, his eyes wide with total disbelief. The look in the boy's eyes was what Benson would remember most; the look of someone whose entire world had just been shattered.

When the boy's hand clawed down for his pistol, Benton stiffened with amazement. "*Don't!*" he cried, unable to believe what he was seeing.

Only habitual reflex kept him alive; an ingrained mechanism that made him fire without thought, hitting the boy in the stomach. He felt a bolt of shock that his aim had been so poor. It had been, he later realized, the measure of his utter dismay that the boy had attempted such a hopeless move.

The boy had stumbled back and sat down heavily on the ground, a blank expression on his face now. He looked down curiously at his stomach, regarding the pump of blood from the bullet hole as though it were coming from someone else.

Then—Benton felt sick to his stomach when he heard it—the boy began to cry.

"Pa," he murmured. "Henry." He repeated the names over and over, sobbing like a frightened child, tears flowing down his cheeks.

Then, finally, before he fainted, he cried out, once, "*It hurts!*"

Benton sank down on the ground, legs suddenly devoid of strength. He looked at Aaran Graham's body. At the body of Henry Graham. Finally, at the thinly breathing form of Graham's younger son; his name was Albert, Benton later discovered. He knew that even if he tried to get the boy back to Millersview, he'd be dead before they were halfway there.

One week later, Benton brought the three bodies back to Millersview after remaining with Albert Graham for the two days it took him to die.

The first thing he did when he got home was go up to the bedroom, open a chest at the foot of the bed, and dump in his pistol, holster, and belt.

When his wife asked him why he'd done that, he told her that he was finished, that he would never wear a pistol as a weapon again.

3:29 P.M., Millersview, Texas, August 13, 1871.

The First Day

Chapter One

The chaparral bird was running a fierce race with the black roan as it pounded across the hard earth. The long legs of the bird flashed wildly in a swirl of alkali dust, ten yards ahead of the roan's battering hooves.

Off the wide trail, a jackrabbit bounded into the brush with great, erratic leaps. Awakened by the muffled thunder in the earth, a coiled rattlesnake writhed sluggishly and lifted its flat head, dead eyes searching.

The tall roan galloped along the trail, its broad legs drawing high, then driving down quickly at the dust-clouded earth. The spur rowels of its young rider raked once across its heaving flanks and the thick weave of muscles underneath its hide drove it on still faster.

Robby Coles paid no attention to the long-beaked roadrunner skittering its weaving path on the trail ahead. He rode close-seated, his knees clamped against the roan's flanks, his booted feet braced forward and out against the stirrups. Beneath the broad brim of his Stetson, his dark eyes peered straight ahead at the out fences of the small ranch he approached.

The driving hooves came too close and the chaparral bird lunged off the trail, racing into the brush. The roan thundered on, following the twists of the trail, a thin froth blowing from its muzzle. Spur rowels scratched again, the horse leaped forward obediently, past the tall and

spiny-branched cholla cactus, galloping past the first fence
line of the ranch.

Now the rider's eyes focused on the far-off cluster of
buildings that comprised the ranch layout. His thin lips
pressed together into a blood-pinched line and there was
a strained movement in his throat. Was he there? The question drifted like smoke across his mind and he felt sweat
dripping down beneath his shirt collar and realized,
abruptly, how thirsty he was.

Cold resolve forced itself into his eyes again and his
slender hands tightened on the sweat-slick reins. He could
feel the rhythmic pounding inside his body as the hooves
of his roan pistoned against the hard earth. He could feel
the arid bluntness of the wind buffeting across his cheeks
and against his forehead; the abrasive rubbing of his legs
against the horse's flanks.

There were other things he felt, too.

As the hooves of his mount drummed along the trail,
Robby Coles noticed, from the corners of his eyes, the
aimless wandering of cattle beyond the fences. He swallowed hot air and coughed once as the dustiness tickled in
his throat. The ranch was a half mile distant now. Robby
Coles reached down nervously and touched the smooth
walnut of his gun stock. He wondered if he should be
wearing it.

Merv Linken was coming out of the barn, carrying a
pitchfork, when the big black roan came charging into the
open area between the barn and the main house.

At first, the horse headed for the main house. Then the
rider saw Merv and pulled his mount around sharply. Merv
stood watching as the roan cantered over and stopped before him, its flanks heaving, hot breath steaming from its
nostrils.

"Hello there, Robby," Merv said, smiling up at the grim-
faced young rider. "What brings you out in sech a rush?"

Robby Coles drew in a quick breath and forced it out.

"Benton here?" he asked breathlessly, his dark-eyed gaze drifting toward the main house.

"No, he ain't," Merv said. "Matter o' fact, he's to town gettin' supplies."

He saw how the skin tightened across Robby's cheeks and how his mouth pressed suddenly into a line.

"Guess you rode out fer nothin'," Merv said, then shrugged. "Unless you want to set and wait."

"How long's he been gone?" Robby's voice sounded thin and disturbed above the shuddering pants of his roan. He drew out a bandanna and mopped at his face.

"Oh . . . I reckon, since about eight," Merv said. "Said he was—"

He stopped talking abruptly as Robby jerked the horse around and kicked his spur rowels in. The sweat-flecked roan started forward, breaking into a hard gallop before it passed the bunkhouse.

Merv Linken stood there a while, leaning on the pitchfork, watching Robby Coles ride away toward town. Then he shrugged and turned toward the house.

Julia Benton came walking in quick strides across the yard, drying her hands. She was a tall woman, slender and softly curved, her hair a light blond.

"Who was that?" she asked.

"Young Robby Coles," Merv answered.

"What did he want?"

"Got no notion, ma'm," Merv told her. "Just came in, tight-leggin' and asked for the old man."

"Is that all?"

"That's all, ma'm. Reckon he's headed for Kellville to see Mr. Benton now."

They stood silent for a moment, watching from beneath the shading of their palms, the roan and its rider dwindle into the distance of the brush country.

"He's sure bakin' that hoss," Merv said. "Must be anxious to see yore husband."

Julia Benton stood motionless in the hot sunlight, a look of uneasy curiosity in her eyes. She watched until she couldn't see the horse any longer.

Then she went back to her dishes.

Chapter Two

Well, I don't know," John Benton said, with a slow shake of his head. "They may scratch Hardin's name from the black book for now." He grinned briefly. "But I think they'll have to put it back in again."

He raked a sulfur match across his boot heel and held the flare to the end of the cigarette he'd just rolled. He grimaced slightly at the acrid sulfur smell in his nostrils, then blew out a puff of smoke from the corner of his mouth. He shook out the match and tossed it into the sand-filled tobacco box on the floor.

"No," he said to the three men at the bar with him. "Writin' off Wes Hardin because he's in Rusk Prison now— that's a bet I wouldn't take."

"You think he'll bust out?" asked Henry Oliver, the portly owner of one of Kellville's dry goods stores.

"Well, I . . . wouldn't think that either," Benton said, picking the cigarette from his lips and blowing out a cloud of smoke. "He'll try bustin' out, sure enough, but that's quite a place to bust out of. I used to go there quite a few times takin' in prisoners." He fingered his glass of whiskey. "Pretty stiff," he said, nodding once. "I wouldn't think he'd bust out."

"How else can he get out then?" Bill Fisher asked him. "He's in for twenty-five years, ain't he?"

Benton thumped down his glass and smacked his lips as the whiskey threaded its heat down his throat.

"Well," he said, "twenty-five years is the sentence, all right. But there's always paroles. Even pardons."

"Damn right," Fisher replied, nodding purse-lipped and staring into the amber depths of his drink. "They's plenty of folks think Wes Hardin got a bum deal for doin' what he had to do. Ain't that right, Benton?"

John Benton twisted his broad-muscled shoulders a little and scratched once at his crop of darkly blond hair.

"Couldn't say, Fisher," he answered, shaking his head. "They never put me on the case. You know as much about Hardin as I do."

"If they *had* put you on the case, John Benton," said Henry Oliver expansively, waving a thick finger at the tall man, "Mister John Wesley Hardin would have been in Rusk Prison long ago."

"He'd a been in the boneyard long ago," John Sutton added hurriedly, his young voice eager to please.

John Benton only chuckled softly and gestured toward Pat, the bartender, for another drink. He put the cigarette between his lips again and listened amusedly as the men went on discussing the imprisonment of Hardin and the possibilities of his escaping. He nodded once to Pat as the glass was filled, then touched the smooth sides of the glass with his long, sure fingers, a mild expression on his strongly cut face.

"Isn't that so, Benton?" said Joe Sutton, with the tone of a novice seeking ultimate authority.

"What's that, Sutton?" Benton asked.

"I say Wes Hardin killed more men with his border roll than any other way."

The beginning of a smile twitched at the corners of Benton's wide mouth. "As I said," he answered, "what I know about Hardin you could put in a pea shell and rattle."

He stiffened suddenly, his legs going rigid, the amiable expression wiped from his face as Joe Sutton reached down for his pistol. Instinctively, his right hand shot across his body to the spot on his left where his pistol would have been if he'd worn one.

Joe Sutton held out his pistol, butt first. "Show how he does it," he asked, oblivious. "Show how Hardin rolls it."

The tenseness melted imperceptibly from Benton's face, his body relaxed and the movement of his hand continued up smoothly to his glass. The smile returned.

"Sutton, never do that," he said, without rancor. "When a man goes for his gun, he should mean business. You can get yourself killed that way."

Sutton looked blank. "Well," he said, "I know you don't pack no gun and I just thought . . ."

His pistol hand dropped and he looked crestfallen. Joe Sutton was one of the many in Kellville who idolized Benton.

"Forget it," Benton said, grinning. "Just don't want to see you leanin' into a bullet. Here, give it here. I'll show you how he does it."

Sutton handed over the pistol happily and Benton opened the cylinder and spilled out six cartridges on the bar top.

He shook his head. "Sutton, you should only put five bullets in the wheel. You keep the hammer on the empty chamber. That's for safety; otherwise you're liable to shoot your leg off."

Sutton looked rueful again. "Think I'll throw it away," he muttered and a chuckle sounded in Benton's deep chest.

"Just have to be careful," he said.

"You want to use my gun too?" Bill Fisher asked. "Hardin uses two."

"One or two, it doesn't matter," Benton said. "Same in either hand."

The three men and the bartender watched in fascination

as the tall Benton stepped back from the bar and stuck the pistol under the belt of his Levi's.

"Now say I been throwed down on," he told them. "I didn't get any chance to draw my iron. So the man, whoever he is, asks me to hand over my gun. So . . ."

Benton reached down and the men saw him draw the pistol slowly, then hold it out toward them, butt first, his forefinger curled limply in the trigger guard.

"Then—" Benton said.

Suddenly the pistol blurred in their sight as he rolled it backward and, before they could blink their eyes, the sound of the clicking hammer reached their ears.

"You see, you fire with the webbing of your thumb," Benton told them. "Your trigger finger is just the pivot."

"*Jeez.*" An awed Joe Sutton shook his head slowly. "I couldn't even see it."

Benton smiled. "You're not s'posed to," he said. "That's the point, Sutton." The smile faded. "Anyway it's a snaky trick," he said. "When a man's outdone fair and square, he's got no right to cheat his way back to winning."

In the momentary silence, Joe Sutton asked, "Why don't you pack a gun no more, Benton?"

Benton's almost expressionless gaze flicked up at him.

"Don't ask a man questions like that, Sutton," he said quietly. "That's a man's own business."

"Gee, Benton, I'm sorry. I—" Sutton looked apologetically at him.

But Benton was looking down at the pistol, hefting it idly in his palm as if he were weighing the merits of what it represented to him. For a moment, his mouth was pressed into a firm line. Then he shrugged once.

"Oh, well," he said casually. "Here; catch." He tossed the pistol back to Sutton.

Sutton caught it fumblingly in both hands. Benton tossed

his cigarette into the gaboon and shook his head with a wry smile.

"Sutton, you'll have to learn to snatch a gun and set it goin' at the same time." His eyes glinted with detached amusement. "That is," he said, "if you mean to be a real, sure-fire gun shark."

Sutton still looked blank as Benton took a deep breath and threw off his momentary seriousness.

"Throw it here," he told Sutton. "I'll show you."

Sutton tossed the pistol and saw it plucked cleanly from the air and, in the same moment, fired.

"You see?" Benton said, "there's a lot more to gunplay than just a fast draw."

Without seeming to look, he flung the pistol to his left and cocked and fired it in the second his hand caught it.

"They call it the shift," he said. "You'll need that if your shootin' arm takes a slug."

He tossed the pistol back into his right hand and cocked it, the barrel aimed toward the double doors.

The young man who came pushing through them recoiled with a start, his face paling.

Benton grinned and dropped the pistol barrel. "Don't worry, Coles," he said, "nothin' in the wheel but air."

He tossed the pistol back to Sutton again and returned to his drink as the men greeted Robby.

"What time is it, Pat?" Benton asked the bartender.

Pat drew out his gold watch. "About quarter to eleven," he said.

Benton grunted. "Have to be goin' soon. Or the missus will be riding in after me." His smile was inward, seeming to impart a secret pleasure to him as he picked up his glass.

Then he put down the glass and looked aside.

"You want to see me, Coles?" he asked the young man who stood tensely beside him.

"Yes, I want to see you."

Benton's mouth tightened as he heard the sullen anger in Robby Coles' voice. He took his boot off the rail and turned completely.

"What is it, kid?" he asked curiously.

Robby stood there rigidly, unable to control the shaking in his slender body. At his sides, his hands were clenched into white fists and the repressed fury in his face was thinned by apprehension.

"Well?" Benton asked, his brow furrowing quizzically.

Robby swallowed convulsively.

"You better watch out," he said, hoarsely.

The three men at the bar heard the tenseness in Robby's voice and they looked down curiously at him.

"Watch out for what?" Benton asked.

Robby drew in a ragged breath and let it falter through clenched teeth. "Just be careful," he said, his face growing paler.

Benton's left hand raised up as if in a gesture of question. Then it dropped down and he shook his head in small, tight movement. "I don't get you, kid," he said. "What are you trying to say?"

Robby shuddered and forced his lips together.

"Just leave my girl alone," he said, his voice weakening.

Benton's expression grew suddenly blank. He leaned back as if to get a better look at Robby.

"Your girl?" he said, uncomprehendingly. "What does—"

"Well, she told me!" Robby burst out, suddenly. "So I know, I know! You don't have to lie to me!"

Benton's eyes flinted. "What are you saying?" he asked coldly.

Robby swallowed again, a look of sudden dread flaring in his eyes.

"Let's have it, kid," Benton said. "Chew it finer. What's all this about your girl?"

Robby seemed to dredge down into himself for the strengthening of courage. He drew back his lean shoulders and forced out a rasping breath.

"She told me how you been botherin' her," he said in a clipped voice. "And I'm tellin' you to stop."

The anger drifted from Benton's face. For a long moment, he looked at Robby without expression. Then he shook his head once, as if wonderingly.

"You're out of your mind," he said quietly and turned back to the bar with another shake of his head.

Robby stood there trembling.

"Listen, Benton," he said, the anger desperate in his voice, "I'm not afraid of you."

Benton glanced aside. "Kid," he said, "go home. Get outta here and we'll forget what you said. Just don't hang around."

"Benton, damn it!" Robby yelled.

Benton turned brusquely, his face hard with restrained temper. "Listen, kid, I'm tellin' you to—"

He jerked back his head in sudden shock as the white-faced Robby flailed out with his right fist. Flinging up his left arm, he knocked aside the erratic blow.

"What are you—" he started amazedly, then had to ward aside another blow driven at his chest by Robby. His hand shot down and caught Robby's left wrist in a grip of iron.

"Coles, have you gone plumb—"

But Robby was too far gone now. His lips drawn back in a grimace both furious and terror-stricken, he drove his right fist out again and it thudded off Benton's broad shoulder. The men at the bar watched in dumbfounded amazement and Pat came hurrying around the foot of the counter.

Benton tried to catch Robby's right wrist and pin him completely but, before he could, the bunched fist grazed his left cheek, reddening the skin.

"Well, the hell—" he suddenly snapped and drove a short, pulled blow into Robby's stomach.

Robby doubled over with a breath-sucked grunt and fell against the bar, his mouth jerking open as he tried to catch in the air. Benton hauled him up by the left arm, glancing over at Pat who had just hurried up to them.

"All right?" Pat asked and Benton nodded silently.

"Come here," he told the gagging Robby and tried to lead him to one of the tables.

Robby tore away with a whining gasp, then started to buckle and Benton caught him again.

"Come over here with me," he said, the anger gone from his voice. "Let's get this figured."

Again Robby tore away with a sob and backed off, forcing himself to an erect position, hands pressed to his stomach.

"Damn you," he gasped through shaking, blood-drained lips. "I'll get you, Benton, I swear I'll get you."

Benton stood there silently, hands hanging loosely at his sides as Robby turned and staggered down the length of the saloon floor and shoved through the double doors.

After a moment, he shook his head in slow wonder.

"I'll be damned," he said and looked over at the staring men. "I will be damned," he muttered to himself and returned to his still unfinished drink.

"What was on *his* mind?" Pat asked, behind the bar again.

"You got me," Benton said. "It's over my head, *way* over."

Pat grunted and wiped idly at the dark, glossy wood of the bar counter. Down the way, Bill Fisher and Henry Oliver exchanged glances.

"Who is his girl, anyway?" Benton asked curiously.

Pat shrugged. "Got no notion," he said. "Some town girl, I reckon."

Benton made an amused sound and shook his head. "Bothered her," he said. "I don't even know who she is."

"Louisa Harper, that's his girl," Joe Sutton said quickly and the two men, glancing aside, saw that Sutton had edged along the bar in order to join their conversation. Benton's mouth tightened a little but he didn't say anything.

"Her mother's the Widow Harper," Sutton hurried on, oblivious. "Aunt runs a lady clothes store cross the square."

Benton and Pat exchanged a glance and the corners of Benton's mouth twitched, repressing a wry smile. Down the bar, Henry Oliver stretched and told Bill Fisher that he intended going over to Jesse Willmark's Barber Shop for a haircut.

Benton heard him and nodded to himself. "Oh, that's right," he said. "I keep meanin' to get a haircut myself. Missus Benton keeps askin' me and it keeps slippin' my mind." He picked up his glass and emptied it.

"You want me to find out about Robby Coles?" Sutton asked abruptly. "You want me to check for you, Benton?"

Benton looked aside, patiently.

"Listen, kid," he said quietly, "just leave it set, hear? Just forget it."

Sutton looked down gloomily into his drink. "Just wanted to help you," he said.

"Well, you gotta learn the difference between helpin' and stickin' your nose in where it don't belong, kid," Benton told him, without rancor.

Sutton's expression was dully morose. "Didn't *mean* nothin'," he muttered.

Benton clapped the young man on the shoulder once with his broad palm. "Okay, kid, let's forget it. No hard feelin's." He put his Stetson on, then dug into his Levi's pocket for silver.

"Well, I have to drag it," he said. "Lots o' work to do."

The three men at the bar were silent as Benton walked in long, unhurried strides for the doors. They were still silent as he went out. It was only after they heard the sound of his buckboard rolling away from the saloon hitching rack that they turned to each other and started talking.

Chapter Three

Jesse Willmark was sitting in one of his two barber chairs, reading the *Kellville Weekly Bugle*. It was quiet in the small shop, so quiet that the sluggish drone of fat flies could be clearly heard. The only other sound was that of Jesse turning the newspaper pages with idle fingers, his heavyset body slumped lethargically on the black leather cushion.

The wall clock struck eleven with a tinny resonance. Jesse reached into his pocket and checked his watch. He shook his head disgustedly. The wall clock was ten minutes slow again and he'd just had it repaired three years before.

The click of heels near the door made Jesse look up quickly. "*Oh.*" His head dipped once in a nod and he smiled as he pushed up.

"Howdy, Mr. Oliver," he said and slid quickly from the chair, tossing the newspaper onto one of the wire-backed chairs along the wall. "Set you down and we'll get right to it."

Henry Oliver slid out of his waistcoat and hung it carefully on the clothes tree beside his hat. Then, he settled back in the ornate barber chair with a sigh and shifted himself into a comfortable position as Jesse fastened the big cloth around his thick neck.

"Nice day, today," Jesse said automatically and Henry

Oliver mumbled an assent as Jesse picked up the scissors, clicked the blades together his habitual four times, and began cutting.

"Funny thing at the Zorilla Saloon before," Henry Oliver said after a few moments of idle conversation had passed.

"Oh?" Jesse said, eyebrows raising in practiced fashion. "What's that, Mr. Oliver?"

"You know young Robby Coles," Oliver said and Jesse said, "Mmm-hmm," cutting and clipping. "Know his father well. Fine man, fine man."

"Yes. Well . . ." said Henry Oliver, "the boy came charging into the saloon and started a fight. With John Benton."

Jesse's mouth gaped for a moment. "*No*," he said. "*John Benton*? Well, I'll be . . ."

"Yup." Henry Oliver's head nodded vigorously and Jesse held back the scissors until the nodding stopped. "Quite a fight, *quite a fight*. Benton won, of course. Doubled young Robby over with a gut punch."

"No," Jesse said incredulously, snipping and running the comb teeth through his customer's graying hair. "John Benton. Well. What were they fightin' over?"

Henry Oliver crossed his dark-trousered legs. "That's what I don't figure," he said, vaguely mysterious. "The boy accused Benton of—" He looked around carefully. "Of playing around with his girl."

"No! You me—" Jesse's voice broke off, startledly. "Louisa Harper? Playin' around?" His voice rose and fell in jagged peaks and valleys of expression. "I can't believe it," he said, shaking his head. "Strangest thing I ever heard. John Benton. Huh." His nervous right hand clicked the scissor blades in the air and he went on cutting. "Be damned," he said.

"Well you could have knocked me down with your finger," Henry Oliver said. "Surprised the life out of me, naturally."

"Well, naturally," Jesse said, shaking his head, an intent look on his thick-featured face.

"And I wasn't the only one there," said Henry Oliver. "Bill Fisher was there. And young Joe Sutton. And Pat heard too, yes, Pat heard it all. Strange, all right."

Jesse kept shaking his head. "You . . . think it's true?" he asked.

"Well . . ." Henry Oliver's brow tightened. "I couldn't say," he ventured solemnly. "Offhand, I'd say no but . . . well, you can't tell, you just can't tell about those things. I know I wouldn't want to be the one to start a story like that. John Benton's too big a man around here to . . ." His voice drifted off and the shop was still except for the clicking scissor blades.

"Yes, he's admired, all right," Jesse said then as if there had been no lapse in the conversation. "Always thought he's been overrated but . . . well, that's nothing to do with this." He shook his head, cutting absorbedly. "Louisa Harper, huh?" he said. "Now ain't that somethin'."

"Oh," Henry Oliver said, almost grudgingly, his thick shoulders shrugging slightly, "it might be a mistake, of course."

"Sure. Sure, that's right, it could be a mistake," Jesse said, agreeing with a customer.

Twenty minutes later, Henry Oliver walked out of the shop and Jesse sat down again to look at his paper. But he didn't read it, he just sat there staring at the blurred print and thinking about what Mr. Oliver had said.

"Sure," he muttered to himself. "Sure. I can see it; him a hero and all." He licked his fat lips. "Louisa Harper, huh? I wouldn't mind—"

He broke off abruptly as another customer entered.

There was the taking off of the coat, the sitting down in the gilded metal and black leather chair, the tying of the cloth, the comment on the weather, the assent, the plucking up of the long scissors, the tentative clicking of blades.

"Heard about the big fight?" Jesse asked his customer.

"No. When was this?" the man asked casually.

"Just a while ago," said Jesse. "In the Zorilla Saloon. Robby Coles and John Benton."

"No." The man looked up interestedly. "Benton?"

"Yup." Jesse's head nodded in short, decisive arcs as he worked, purse-lipped, on the man's hair. "Had a fight over Robby Cole's girl, Louisa Harper."

"You don't tell me," the man said, face strained with interest.

"That's right," Jesse said calmly. "That's right." His small eyes narrowed. " 'Course it might be a mistake but it *seems* . . . there's been somethin' between Benton and the girl."

The customer's eyes rose to the mirror on the wall and he and Jesse looked at each other with the half-repressed fascination of little boys who believe they have unearthed something of unique prurience.

"*Well*," the man said.

As they went on talking, the sound of their conversation drifted out the door into the air of Kellville.

Chapter Four

Matthew Coles was never on any horse but his chestnut gelding. He did not ride well and was a man who would not let himself be observed doing anything less than perfectly. The chestnut was a mild animal, easily seated, but one which managed to give the appearance of being excitably alert. It was a combination well suited to Matthew Coles who preferred his triumphs to appear hard-won. Thus, satisfyingly, was the gelding added to his list of conquests, which list included also his acquaintances, business associates, wife, and children. Matthew Coles was a man who kept a taut, unyielding rein on every aspect of his life.

It was just ten minutes past noon when he came riding slowly down Armitas Street. At the twelfth stroke of noon, he had risen from the bench of his gunsmith shop, donned his coat and hat, and locked up the shop, leaving in the door window the thumb-worn sign which read simply DINNER. He had mounted the docile chestnut and started for his house where, by God, Jane had better have dinner immediately ready to eat. Precision and efficiency—Matthew Coles was especially guided by these coupled verities.

Mr. Coles was in a particularly sour humor that afternoon. His elder son, Robby, had not appeared at the shop promptly at eight thirty as he was supposed to; as a matter of fact, Robby had not shown up at all. That was an added reason why Matthew Coles rode stiffly, his back a ramrod of irked authority, his face set with dominance defied. He wore black, as always, for it made his five foot ten inches appear taller and, he fancied, made him look unusually handsome for a man in his middle fifties.

As he rode into the alleyway beside the house, he saw his son's roan tied up in back and his mouth twitched angrily. The horse hadn't been rubbed down, it was streaked over with dry sweat. Beneath taut lips, Matthew Coles' false teeth clamped vice-like. Fool!—he raged within. Robby didn't deserve a horse and, by God, if he didn't take better care of it, he wouldn't *have* a horse!

The gelding stopped. Matthew Coles eased his right leg over its croup and let himself down with a grunt. Then he led the horse into the small stable and tied it up near the water trough.

He crossed the backyard with vengeful strides, then clumped loudly up the wooden porch steps, removing his hat as he ascended.

The kitchen door thudded shut behind him and his wife Jane straightened up over the chair in which Robby sat slumped.

"Good afternoon, dear," she said hastily. "I'll get you your—"

"What is the meaning of leaving your mount untended?" Coles asked loudly, ignoring his mouse-haired wife.

Robby looked up, his drained features tensed with nausea. "I was sick," he muttered. "I—"

"Speak up, sir. I can't hear you when you mumble like a child." Mr. Coles hung up his hat with one authoritative motion.

Robby swallowed, grimacing with pain, his hands pressed over the waist of his belt-loosened trousers.

"Matthew, he's ill."

Matthew Coles impaled his small-framed wife with an imperious glare. "Is my dinner ready?" he challenged.

"I was—"

"I've been working," her husband explained with the carefully measured articulation of a harried father addressing his idiot daughter. "I'm hungry. Are you going to stand there gaping at me or are you going to make my dinner?"

Mrs. Coles tried to look agreeable but could not summon the long-lost ability to smile. She turned away and hurried toward the stove.

"Well, sir?" Mr. Coles re-addressed his bent-over son.

"I'm sorry, sir," Robby said, his lips drawn back from his teeth. He groaned slightly and, by the stove, his mother cast a look of anguished concern toward him.

"What's wrong with you, sir?" Matthew Coles demanded. "And where were you this entire morning?"

"I was—" Robby leaned over suddenly, jamming the end of one fist against his pale-lipped mouth.

"Matthew, he's ill," Mrs. Coles said suddenly. "Please don't—"

"This is not your discussion," her husband informed her, face tensed with the expression of a soldier attacked on all sides. "I have an appointment at the bank at one o'clock. I expect to be there exactly on time—fed."

Jane Coles' hands twitched in futile empathy with her upset condition and she turned back to the stove, a hopeless expression on her face.

"Where is the boy?" her husband asked her.

"He's not home from school yet," she answered.

"I can't hear you."

"I say, he's not home from school yet."

"He's *supposed* to be home. I think a little strapping is in order for that young man."

His wife said nothing, knowing that no answer was expected. She went about quietly at her work as Matthew Coles concentrated on Robby again.

"Why weren't you at your work this morning?"

Robby looked up at his stern-faced father with pain-glossed eyes.

"Sir, I expect an answer."

"I went out," Robby said, weakly.

"Out? Out where?"

"T-to . . . John Benton's . . . ranch."

"And what, may I ask, were you doing there?"

"I . . ." Robby swallowed and gasped in air. "I wanted to see . . . to see him."

"About what?"

Robby stared at his father, his lean chest rising and falling with tight, spasmodic movements.

"I am waiting, sir," his father said clearly.

"I . . . sir, I'd rather not—"

"*What was that?*" His father spoke the words in a cold, threatening tone and spots of color flared up in Robby's pale cheeks. His throat moved again as he looked up fearfully into the hard face of his father.

Robby bit his lip. "I had to see B-Benton," he said.

"What about?" Matthew Coles spoke the words slowly, with the repetitious demanding of a man who would not be put off.

Robby looked down at his boots. "Lou-Louisa," he said.

"Miss Louisa Harper?" asked his father, announcing her name as if it were the title of a book.

Robby nodded slowly without looking up.

"And what about Miss Louisa Harper?"

"I . . ."

"Answer me this moment, sir!"

Robby looked up in hopeless despair. "I wanted to f-find out about her and . . . and Benton."

At the stove the father and son heard Mrs. Coles catch her breath. "Robby," she murmured faintly.

Matthew Coles paid no attention. His face a block of carved stone, he caught at the situation as one worthy of his stern attention.

"Make yourself clear, sir," he said firmly and distinctly.

Robby's throat moved convulsively as he stared up.

"Well?"

"Louisa told me that . . . that Benton annoyed her and . . . tried to . . . to—"

"*To effect a meeting?*" His father completed the sentence with imperial outrage, his nostrils flared, his hands clenched suddenly at his sides.

Robby's head slumped forward and a harsh breath shuddered his body. "I guess," he muttered.

Mr. Coles drew back his shoulders slowly as if he were getting ready to gird his loins for a battle with all the forces of evil in the world.

"You saw Benton," he said and it wasn't a question.

Robby nodded. "I . . . yes, I . . . did."

"And what was his defense?"

"He . . . he acted like he didn't kn-know anything about it."

A thin, humorless smile raised the ends of Matthew Coles' lips. "Of course," he said quietly, "that would be what he'd say." He looked down dispassionately at his son's pain-tightened face. "There was a fight," he stated.

Robby nodded and mumbled something.

Then Matthew Coles was leaning over his son and Mrs. Coles was watching her husband with uneasy eyes.

"Miss Harper is your intended bride, is she not?" said Matthew Coles, his voice calm.

Robby looked up quickly at his father and nodded. "Y . . . yes," he said, almost tentatively, as if he suspected that his father was going to throw the admission back in his face.

"Well, then," Mr. Coles said, still calmly, as he straightened up. "What do you mean to do about it?"

In the sudden silence of the kitchen, Robby distinctly heard the frightened sound his mother made. But there seemed nothing visible in the entire room except his black-suited father looking down commandingly at him.

Chapter Five

A little after twelve, the spotted hound raced to the Dutch door and reared up excitedly, its blunt claws scratching at the wood, its hoarse barking echoing in the kitchen. Julia Benton looked up from her pea shelling with a quick smile that drove the tense absorption from her face.

Five minutes later the buckboard came creaking across the yard and braked up in back of the house.

Julia walked over to the door and opened the top half. She saw her tall husband reaching over the iron railing for one of the baskets in the buckboard. "*Hush* now," she told the baying hound.

"Hello, ma," John said, grinning as he came struggling toward the door with his heavy load.

"Hello, dear." Julia pulled open the bottom half of the door and the wriggling hound rushed out, its long tail blade whipping at its flanks. "Howdy, mutt," Benton said as he entered the kitchen, heeled by the excited dog.

Benton set the basket down heavily on the table and straightened up with a quickly exhaled breath. "Am I late?" he said.

Julia nodded, smiling. "The boys finished half hour ago. Sit down and I'll warm you what's left."

"Right. I'll get the rest of the chuck first, though." Benton left the kitchen, the dog prancing and growling happily at his boots. "Easy there, Jughead," Julia heard her husband tell the hound.

A minute later, Benton sat at the table, checking the supply list while Julia warmed his dinner.

"Twenty pounds Arbuckle's," he said, laying down the coffee sack. "Canned cow. Salt. Flour."

"Molasses?" she said.

He nodded with a grunt. "Yup," he said, "black strap." He checked off the item. "Oh, I forgot," he said, "I got you canned peaches. Maxwell just got some in from the east."

"*Oh*," she said, happily surprised, "that's nice. We'll have them Sunday morning."

Benton smiled to himself and worked on the list until Julia put his dinner on the table. Then he washed up and sat down. By the stove, the hound was going back to twitching sleep again.

"John?" Julia asked him while he ate.

"What?"

"What did Robby Coles want to see you about?"

He looked up from his plate in surprise. "How did you know about that?" he asked.

"He rode here first looking for you."

"He did, eh?" Benton sipped a little hot coffee from the mug. "Well, I'll be," he said, shaking his head.

"You saw him in town then," she said.

Benton nodded. "Yeah. Funny thing too," he said. "He was all horns and rattles. Came into the Zorilla Saloon and threw a fist at me."

She stood by the table looking concerned. "But why?" she asked.

He shrugged, food in his mouth, then swallowed. "I don't know," he said. "That's the part that don't make sense. He told me to stop botherin' his girl."

She looked at him silently a moment. "His *girl*?" she said.

"That's right. Came up to me blowin' a storm and tells me to leave his girl alone. Then he throws a punch at me. What do you think o' that?"

Julia shook her head slowly. "But . . . why should he say such a thing to you?" she asked.

"Don't ask me, ma. I didn't even know who the girl was until the Sutton kid told me."

"Who is she?"

"Louisa Harper, Sutton said. Who's she?"

"Louisa Harper." Julia put two fingers against her cheek and stared into space, trying to place the name. "I don't think I ever—"

Suddenly her mouth opened a second in surprised realization. "I think I know," she said.

"What?" he said, still eating.

"You know the girl I keep telling you about; the one who stares at you in church?"

"You *tell* me there's a girl who stares. I never saw one."

"Oh, you wouldn't notice," she said with the affectionate scorn of a wife. "But she does stare at you. And . . . yes, come to think of it," she went on, nodding to herself, "I think I've seen her walking with Robby Coles after church."

"So," he said. "Any more coffee?"

She poured the heavy black coffee into his mug. "You know what I think?" she asked him.

"What's that?"

"I think she told Robby Coles that you pestered her."

"That's right, that's what I said," he answered, nodding. "That's what Coles *told* me she said."

"Well, of course," she said.

Benton looked up at his pretty wife with a grin. "Of course *what*, ma?" he asked.

"Louisa Harper is in love with you."

He stared at her, speechless. "She—"

"In love with you." Julia nodded with a confident smile. "Of course she is. All the girls in Kellville are in love with you. You're their big hero."

"Oh . . ." Benton waved a disgusted hand, ". . . that's hogwash."

She smiled at him.

"That's nonsense, Julia," he insisted.

"No, it isn't," she said with a laugh. "Ever since we moved here everyone's looked up to you. The boys look at you as if you were a god. The girls look at you as if—"

"Why should they?" John said, embarrassed.

"Because you're a hero to them, dear," she said. "You're John Benton, the fearless Ranger, the quick-shooting lawman."

He peered at her until the mock-serious expression on her face broke into an impish grin. "Ha, ha," he said flatly.

"It's true," she said. "To them you're Hardin and Longley and . . . and Hickok all rolled into one."

"That's nonsense," he said. "I haven't worn a gun in town the whole two years we've been here."

"Yes, but they know what you did in the Rangers."

"Oh, that's silly," he mumbled and reached for his coffee mug.

She sat down with her peas again. "Yes, I expect that's what it is," she said. "She's in love with you and she probably dreamed out loud in front of Robby."

"Well, that's stupid," he said in disgust. "If it's true, that is. What's the matter with the girl, doesn't she know any better than that? She has that Coles kid thinkin' I'm a . . . a gallivantin' dude or somethin'."

Julia laughed. "He'll get over it," she said, "as soon as he knows it isn't true."

"How do you know it isn't true?" Benton said, forcing down the grin with effort.

Julia looked up at her husband with soft eyes for a moment, then back to her moving fingers.

"I know," she said, gently.

Chapter Six

gatha Winston walked down Davis Street in the late afternoon, her thin legs whipping like reeds against the heavy blackness of her skirt and the half dozen petticoats beneath. She was a tall, gaunt woman with eyes of jade, and features molded in sharp angles and pinches. She was a hidebound churchgoer who used her self-styled Christianity as a bludgeon on all those not in the accredited fold.

Right now Agatha Winston was on a crusade.

Like a dark bird of vengeance, she swooped down on the small house of her sister, umbrella stem clicking on the plank sidewalk, skirts a vindictive rustle. Mouth a gash, she shoved in the gate and kicked it shut behind her as she clumped and swished toward the porch steps.

Inside the house, the bell tinkled reactively to the wrathful tugging of Agatha Winston's clawlike fingers. She stood tensely before the door, one black and pointed shoe-tip tapping steadily at the porch, the other pressing down a corner of the welcome mat.

There was a stirring in the house. From its depths, Miss Winston heard the voice of her sister calling, "I'll be right there," and then the light sound of her sister's shoes across an inside floor. Through the gauzy haze of freshly laundered curtains, Miss Winston saw her sister's approach.

The door opened. "Agatha," said the widow Harper in surprise.

"Elizabeth," Miss Winston replied with a concise moving of lips.

"Come in, my dear, please," Elizabeth Harper said, stepping aside, her soft, pink face wrinkled in a welcoming smile. "My, what a lovely surprise."

"That's as it may be," declared Agatha Winston. "You may not think so when you find out why I'm here."

The widow Harper looked confused as she shut the door quietly, then turned back to her sister who was driving her black umbrella into the stand like a mariner harpooning a whale. She stood smiling pleasantly while Agatha removed her bonnet with quick, agitated motions.

Agatha Winston lifted a piercing glance up the stairwell. "Where is Louisa?" she asked in a guarded tone.

"Why . . . up in her room, Agatha," Elizabeth Harper said, looking curiously at her sister. "Why do you—"

Miss Winston took her sister's arm with firm fingers and led her into the quiet, sun-flecked sitting room.

"Sit down," she said curtly and the widow Harper settled like a diffident butterfly on the couch edge, one hand plucking at the grey-threaded auburn of her curls. She was forty-four, a gentle woman, helpless in all things.

Agatha Winston looked down grimly at the rose-petal cheeks of her sister.

"I don't suppose you've heard," she said.

"Heard?" The widow Harper swallowed nervously. She had always been somewhat afraid of her elder sister.

"It's shocking," Miss Winston said in sudden anger. "It's just shocking."

Elizabeth Harper looked dismayed. Her hands stirred restlessly in the lap of her yellow patterned calico, then twined frail fingers.

"What . . . is, Agatha?" she asked, uneasily.

"The terrible gossip that's going around town," Agatha Winston said. "The shameful story . . . about Louisa."

Alarm flared up suddenly in the widow Harper's face as she heard mentioned her only child. "Louisa?" she said hastily. "What about her, Agatha?"

Agatha Winston sat down on the couch with one sure motion, legs and back making a perfect right angle, face stern with righteous indignation.

"She's told you nothing?" she asked her sister.

The widow Harper's lower lip trembled. "Told me about what?" she asked, eyes almost frantic.

Miss Winston drew in a harsh breath. "I think we had better ask Louisa about that," she said. "I don't even want to speak of it until I hear what she has to say." She stood, a bleak wraith of resolution. "Come," she said.

Elizabeth Harper fluttered up. "Agatha, *please*. What *is* it?" she begged.

Agatha Winston clasped gaunt hands before her breast.

"What do you know of Mister John Benton?" she asked bluntly.

Her sister stared back without comprehension. "John Benton?" she repeated the name. "What—"

"Early this afternoon—about two o'clock I'll allow—Mrs. Van Dekker came into the shop." Agatha Winston's dark eyes probed at her sister's. "She told me something that made me shudder . . . positively shudder, Elizabeth."

Elizabeth Harper pressed trembling fingers to her lips and stared fearfully at her sister.

"I won't go into detail," Miss Winston said firmly. "The story may not even be true—I pray to heaven it isn't—but it concerns this John Benton and . . ." Her lips pressed together. ". . . *Louisa*," she finished.

Louisa Harper was dreaming. Across the lilac spread of her bed, her sixteen-year-old body lay, stomach down, chin propped up by delicately cupped hands. Her blue eyes stared vacantly out of the window. She was taking that ride again.

She had taken it a hundred times, maybe more. It was almost always the same. The petty details of its genesis were ignored. That she could not ride and was frightened to death of horses mattered little. She was out on the range again, riding, her light chestnut hair flowing in the wind, her firm body jolting with the cantering gait of the horse. The sun was bright—for now.

Then the complication, the always occurring complication. Louisa Harper's lips stirred, her mind stared deeper into her dream.

A rattlesnake, a road runner, a jackrabbit—the actual cause was not important. All that mattered was the result; her horse shying, rearing up with a head-jerking whinny, then breaking into a frightened gallop across the brush country. Her scream of terror pulsing in the hot air . . .

. . . and heard.

Her body squirmed a little, her stomach pressing slightly at the bedspread. A movement at her smooth throat. The horse galloping, galloping, her holding on with desperate fear, screaming and hysterical.

Then, out of the mist of her dream, the horseman riding, tall and erect in the saddle, his clothes dark, his hat hanging off his shoulders by its bonnet strings, his blond hair ruffling in the high wind. Closer and closer, the horseman coming, handsome face resolute, one strong hand on the reins, the other half raised toward her . . .

She kept the scene alive; it fascinated her with its terrible thunder of hooves, its pulse-quickening suspense—with the inevitability of its delicious conclusion.

Which came in a sudden command of her will. Her breath caught, her hands were numb. She felt herself swept off the bolting mount and pulled harshly against the tall rider. The horse reined up and, there they were, alone in the vast, empty range, close together on the tall man's horse.

Oh, Mr. Benton, thank you for saving me.

His eyes gentle on her, his strong arm seeming to tighten around her slender waist. Or was that imagination?

My pleasure, Miss Harper, he said. She felt the butt of his pistol pressing at her hip and it made her shiver.

The scene running, coagulating, breaking again into clarity. Sunlight driven from the sky by needs of plot, deepening shadows over the earth, gray menace swirling in the sky.

Oh, it's going to rain, Mister Benton. We'll get soaked.

I know a place where we can wait out the storm.

Rain failing, a sudden desired squall of it. A small cave in the hills, far from town. But they didn't reach the cave in time and both of them were soaked. Louisa stood by the abruptly built fire, blouse clinging wetly to her swelling form. I don't care if he sees, I don't.

You'd better take off those clothes, Miss Harper.

Why, Mr. Benton.

That smile, that throat-catching smile. *I'll look the other way. We have to get our clothes off though or we'll catch our death of cold.*

Scene changing, blurring, transition uncertain, unclear— but definite. Her in her shift, a blanket across her smooth white shoulders. Him with his shirt off; her eyes stealing across the hard-muscled bronze of his torso.

Listen to the wind. His deep, his wonderful voice. *Looks like we may be caught here quite a spell.*

I don't care.

The sudden look exchanged; beneath the blanket, her small hands trembling. I said it to him and I'd say it again.

Coffee, somehow made, the two of them drinking it in the warm cave, looking into the orange flicker of the fire, the sparks like fireflies darting up into the darkness. The hot trickle of coffee in her throat; suspense. Her young body writhed a little on the bed, throat dry, mouth dry.

The blanket slipping off one shoulder; her leaving it that way. Let him see me, I don't care. His eyes glowing in the firelight, the rain pouring and rushing outside in the black night. His hands reaching.

Sudden wild excitement *Oh, John, John!* . . .

"Louisa?"

She started sharply on the bed at the sound of her mother's frail voice in the hallway. At once, her delicate features twisted into angry lines. The cave scene went funneling down into the bottomless well of thought and Louisa looked at the door with fierce resentment.

"What *is* it?" she asked.

"May we come in, dear?"

One small fist beat down angrily on the bedspread. Louisa rolled over and sat up, her legs dropping over the edge of the mattress. She swallowed heavily, her mouth feeling feather-dry. *We?* she thought.

"Come in," she said sullenly, glancing down at herself. As the knob turned, she ran smoothing fingers over the wrinkles of her skirt.

The two women entered.

"Aunt Agatha," Louisa said, feeling a sudden dropping sensation in her stomach at the appearance of her aunt.

Agatha Winston nodded brusquely at her pretty niece, then, when her sister failed to do so, she shut the door firmly as though to close away all intruding eyes. Louisa glanced covertly at her aunt while the widow Harper came over to the bed, an uncertain smile on her face.

"What is it, mother?" Louisa asked, her eyes lowering now to avoid the gaze of her turning aunt.

"Well, dear, we—"

"We want to speak to you, Louisa," Agatha Winston said, assuming, as her natural due, the role of inquisitor.

That sinking in her stomach again. "Talk to me?" asked Louisa faintly, trying hard to remember if she'd done anything to offend her aunt. Was she supposed to have come to the shop today? No, it couldn't be that; she only worked there Mondays, Wednesdays, and Fridays in return for the financial aid Aunt Agatha gave to them.

The bed creaked as Louisa's mother sat down gingerly beside her. Louisa glanced at her with the effort of a smile trying her lips. "What is it, mother?" she asked.

Her mother smiled nervously, then glanced toward Agatha for help.

"Louisa," said her aunt.

"Yes, Aunt Agatha."

"I am going to ask you a question to which I expect an honest answer." Agatha Winston leaned forward, her beak-like nose aiming at Louisa like a spear point, her black eyes searching. "Remember, Louisa," she cautioned, "there's nothing to be afraid of as long as you tell the truth."

"Darling," murmured Elizabeth Harper, covering one of her daughter's hands with her trembling own. Louisa glanced nervously at her mother, then back again to her aunt. She didn't understand.

Aunt Agatha said, "What has John Benton to do with you?"

Louisa couldn't stop the catching of breath in her throat, the paling of cheek, the startled widening of her eyes.

"John Ben—" she began, then stopped, her voice failing. She felt her heart beating heavily and had the pointed sensation of her mind being ripped open, her most secret thoughts plucked out, naked and terrible. For a second she thought she might faint so strong was the welling of shock.

Agatha Winston straightened up with a look of vulpine self-justification on her lean face. She glanced once at the lined face of her sister, then back to Louisa whose cheeks were now coloring embarrassedly.

"W-why do you ask that, Aunt . . ." Louisa swallowed hastily, ". . . Agatha?" she finished.

"What has John Benton to do with you?"

"N-nothing, Aunt Agatha. I don't even—"

"*Louisa*." Aunt Agatha's voice threatened and Louisa stopped talking. "You have nothing to be afraid of as long as you tell the truth like the good Christian girl I hope you are."

Numbly, Louisa felt her aunt's gaunt hand fall on her shoulder.

"But—" she began.

"We expect the truth, Louisa," her aunt said.

Louisa stopped again and sat there, heart pulsing heavily in her chest.

"There was a fight this morning, Louisa," Agatha Winston said. "Between John Benton and the young man you will probably marry."

"Rob—" Louisa's voice broke off and she stared up speechlessly at the hard face of her aunt. She wanted to run from the room; go anywhere to get away from her aunt. Her throat moved in a convulsive swallow. I didn't mean it, the thought wavered across her mind, I didn't mean it at all . . .

"The facts are not clear," Aunt Agatha said in concise tones, "but it appears that young Coles was defending your honor against that . . . *man*."

Louisa felt herself drawing in, backed into a defenseless corner. How could this have happened? She'd had no idea Robby would take her joking taunt so seriously. She'd only wanted to make him angry and jealous and put some life into him.

"Darling, what did that terrible man do to you?" Elizabeth Harper asked in a faint voice, fearing the worst.

"Mother, I don't—"

"Before we go any further, Louisa," her aunt said crisply, "I want you to know that this is a very serious matter. We must have the truth. If you lie, you will be severely punished, do you understand?" She ignored the startled look on her sister's face. "This is a matter of grave importance to your very future."

Louisa looked at her aunt with frightened eyes. It wasn't a lie, her mind struggled to explain. It was only a joke, I only wanted to make him jealous. But she knew her aunt wouldn't see it that way. I didn't mean anything, she thought in anguish.

"*Did* John Benton attempt to arrange an immoral meeting with you?" Agatha Winston demanded bluntly.

Louisa pressed trembling fingers to her lips, her eyes stark with fright. "No," she murmured. "No, he—"

"Don't *lie* to us, Louisa!"

Louisa began sobbing. She felt warm tears falling across her cheeks as she sat there, shaking without control, hardly feeling the pressure of her mother's arm around her back, hardly hearing the frail voice trying to comfort her. Through the blurring prisms of her tears, Louisa saw the shapeless black form of her aunt standing over her. She wanted to tell the truth. She wanted to tell them that she'd only made it up but she was afraid of her aunt, she didn't want to be punished for lying. She was afraid of being scorned, terror-stricken at the thought of anyone knowing her secret. . . .

"When did this happen?" Agatha's voice came breaking down over her like a spray of ice.

"I don't know, I d-don't know!" Louisa sobbed and the widow Harper looked up imploringly at her sister.

"Please, Agatha," she begged, "no more. She's too upset."

"We must know the facts."

"It's not important!" Louisa blurted out suddenly, her voice rising brokenly. "It isn't important, Aunt Agatha!"

"It is *very* important," the answer came sternly. "Your honor is the most important thing in your life."

"But I didn't—" Fear broke off Louisa's words again and she slumped over, shoulders trembling helplessly.

"No, you didn't tell us immediately," Agatha interpreted her niece's unfinished sentence. "You told Robby Coles and he did what he had to do; went up against that . . . that *killer* to defend your honor. You should be grateful that your honor is so highly regarded."

"Agatha, please," begged her sister.

"Come, Elizabeth."

"I'd like to stay with her, Agatha, and . . ."

She stopped as Agatha's bony hand closed over her shoulder firmly. Agatha shook her head. "Come," she said again and Elizabeth was drawn up nervously, one shaking hand patting at Louisa's soft hair.

"Darling, don't fret now," her mother tried to comfort Louisa. "It isn't your fault, mother knows that."

"Elizabeth," Agatha said strongly, then looked down at her sobbing niece. "You had better remain in the house the rest of the day," she said. "I'll see you at the shop tomorrow morning."

Louisa raised her tear-streaked face quickly as though to speak. Then she sat staring wordlessly at her aunt. I didn't *mean* it, her mind implored but she couldn't speak the words aloud. She was too afraid of her aunt and of the punishment she would get for lying and causing Robby Coles to fight in her defense. In her mind she could almost hear the questions her Aunt Agatha would ask if she confessed. Why did you make up such a story? Why John Benton? Are you trying to say you care for that man?

No, she couldn't bear that, she *couldn't*. She sat silently as the two women moved for the door. Then the door edge had shut off the worried face of her mother and she was alone in the quiet of the room, a sense of impending dread creeping over her.

I didn't mean it, I didn't—she thought again. She'd only told Robby what she did in order to make him jealous. She'd never even dreamed that he'd take it so seriously, that he'd go looking for Benton to fight him. Robby just wasn't that kind; he was the quiet, dull kind, not at all like John Benton.

Louisa Harper sat on the edge of the bed, her sobs gradually subsiding, her breathing getting more and more even. She rubbed at the tears with shaking fingers, then stood and got a handkerchief from her bureau drawer.

She sat on the bed again, looking down at the hooked rug her mother had made for her sixteenth birthday.

Now that Aunt Agatha was out of the room, the situation didn't seem so bad. She knew she really should have told the truth but there was something about her aunt that terrified. She just didn't dare tell that she'd made up the story; especially now after she'd failed to confess it when she'd had the opportunity.

Besides—her right foot began kicking a little, thumping back against the bed—besides, it would all blow over. It wasn't *that* serious, no matter what Aunt Agatha said. Robby wouldn't go any further and certainly John Benton wouldn't; *he* was a gentleman.

The hint of a smile played on Louisa Harper's full lips and something stirred in her. There was something strangely exciting about the thought of John Benton fighting over her.

Louisa shuddered, lips parted suddenly.

The two women stood in the downstairs hall. Elizabeth Harper was wringing her hands disconsolately.

"If only my dear husband were alive," she said miserably.

"Well, he isn't," snapped her irate sister, "and we have to fend for ourselves."

Agatha Winston's hand closed over her umbrella handle with the grip of a warrior on his battle sword.

"There's work to be done," she said, her angry voice threatening in the Kellville house.

Chapter Seven

"Stop that kicking!"

Jimmy Coles' right foot stopped thumping against the chair leg and hooked quickly around the back of his left ankle as his eyes lifted in a cautious glance at his father. His fork hovered shakily near his mouth, a piece of meat impaled on its tines.

Then his father's cup slammed down furiously and made everyone at the table start.

"*Yes, sir,*" demanded Matthew Coles.

"Yes, sir," Jimmy's faint voice echoed his father's outraged prompting.

"You had better learn your manners, young man," his father said, his voice threatening slow, "or you'll feel the strap across your legs."

Jimmy swallowed the suddenly tasteless beef and sat petrified on his chair, blue eyes staring at his father. Mrs. Coles looked toward her younger son with that look of futile despair which, so often, showed on her face.

Now Matthew Coles picked up his fork and dug it ruthlessly into a thick slice of beef. Shearing off a piece with one tense drawing motion of his knife, he shoved the meat into his mouth and sat chewing it with rhythmic, angry movements of his jaw.

"In my day," he went on as though he had just uttered

his previous comment on the subject, "we valued the honor of our women. We defended it."

Robby sat picking listlessly at his food, his stomach still queasy from the brief fight. He hadn't wanted to sit down with his family at supper but his father had insisted.

"You're not eating, sir," Matthew Coles told him.

Robby looked up at his father. "I don't feel well, sir," he said quietly.

"You shouldn't feel well," his father drove home another lance. "Your intended bride is insulted and you do nothing."

"Matthew, please don't—" Jane Coles started imploringly.

Her husband directed one of his women-were-not-created-to-speak looks at her and she lowered her head, the sentence unfinished. She had been tensely worried ever since Robby had told his father the reason for the fight with John Benton. She knew her husband; knew his unyielding strength and was afraid of what he might badger Robby into doing.

"This is something which must be spoken of," Matthew Coles went on firmly. "And it *will* be spoken of. There will be no shrinking from the truth in my house. I hope I shall never see the day when men no longer defend the honor of their women. How would you like it, ma'm, if I refused to defend your honor against insults?"

Mrs. Coles said nothing. She knew that Matthew wanted no reply but preferred the advantage of asking challenging questions which were not answered. She knew it gave him the pleasure of unopposed refuting.

"No, you have no answer," said Matthew Coles with a tense nodding of his head. "You know as well as I do that when men cease to defend their women and their homes, our society will cease to exist."

Robby drank a little water and felt it trickle coldly into

his near-empty stomach. He hoped his father would go on ranting at his mother, beleaguering Jimmy—anything except stay on the subject of Louisa and John Benton. He'd been on it all afternoon at the shop where he'd insisted that Robby perform his usual tasks, ill or not.

"That a son of mine," said Matthew Coles grimly, "should be afraid to stand up for the honor of his intended bride." He shook his head. "Especially since the poor girl has no family man to speak for her." He shook his head again. "In *my* day . . . ," he mused solemnly, probing at his beef with fork stabs.

"May I be excused?" Robby asked.

"You may not, sir," said his father. "The meal is not over."

"Does your stomach still hurt, dear?" Mrs. Coles asked Robby gently.

An attempted smile twitched at the corners of Robby's lips. "I feel better, mother," he said.

"Is there anything I can get for—"

"Don't coddle the boy!" her husband broke in furiously. "Are we raising daughters or sons? It's no wonder he's too cowardly to face John Benton, the way you've coddled and protected him!"

"Matthew, he *did* tell John Benton to leave Louisa alone," she said, the faint spark of resistance born of her defending love for Robby.

"Is that what you call defending honor!" shouted Matthew Coles, his face suddenly livid with fury at being contradicted. "Getting hit in the stomach and whining like a dog all day!"

Jane Coles looked disturbedly toward Jimmy who was staring at his father, his slender body unconsciously cringed away from Matthew Coles' imperious presence.

"Matthew, the—"

"What is this—a house of *women*!" her husband raged on. "Why don't you teach them how to cook and sew!"

"Matthew, the boy," his wife pleaded, a break in her tired voice.

"Don't tell me about the boy! It's time he learned the place of a man in his society!" His head snapped over and he looked accusingly at Jimmy. "Don't think you're going to live your life without fighting," he said to the white-faced boy. "Don't think you're going to get away without defending the honor of your women."

He leaned forward suddenly, neck cords bulging, dark eyes digging into the young boy.

"Tell me, sir," he said with thinly disguised calm, "what would you do if a man insulted your mother?"

"Matthew," his wife begged in anguish, "please . . ."

"Would you just sit by and let the insult pass? Is that what you'd do?" He finished in a sudden burst that made Jimmy's cheek twitch.

"N-no, sir," the boy mumbled.

"Speak up, sir, speak up! You're a man, not a woman, and a man is supposed to be heard!"

"*Yes*, sir."

"Is that what you'd do; let the insult pass?"

"No, no," Jimmy said hurriedly.

"No, what?"

"No, I wouldn't let the—"

"*No, sir.*"

Jimmy bit at his lower lip, a rasping sob shaking in his throat.

"Woman!" cried Matthew Coles. "A house of women!"

"Matthew . . ." His wife's voice was weak and shaking.

Matthew Coles drew in a deep, wavering breath and sawed savagely at his meat. He crammed it into his mouth and started chewing while his family sat tensely in their places, unable to eat.

"*Stop that sniveling,*" Matthew Coles said in a low, menacing voice. Jimmy caught his breath and hastily brushed aside the tears that welled in his eyes, dripping down across his freckled cheeks.

"Eat your food," said Matthew Coles. "I don't buy food to be wasted."

Jimmy picked up his fork with shaking fingers and tried to retrieve a piece of potato which kept rolling off the tines. He bit his lip to stop the sobbing and stuck the fork into a piece of meat.

"What would you do?" his father asked.

Jimmy looked over, his face twisted again with frightened apprehension. Robby looked up from his plate, his jaw whitening in repressed anger.

"Well, answer me," Matthew Coles said in a level voice, his fury mollified by the silence of his family. "Would you let some man insult your mother?"

Jane Coles turned her head away abruptly so her sons would not see the mask of sickened anguish it had become.

"N-no, sir," Jimmy said, his stomach turning, tightening.

"What would you do?" Matthew Coles didn't look at his son. He ate his beef and potatoes and drank his coffee, all the time staring into space as if the discussion were of no importance to him. But they could all sense the threat of violence beneath the level of his spoken words.

"I . . . I don't know."

"Don't *know*, sir?" asked his father, voice rising a little.

"I'd, I'd, I'd—"

"Stop-that-stuttering."

"I'd *fight* him," Jimmy blurted out, trying desperately to find the answer that would placate his father.

"Fight him, sir, with your fists?" Matthew Coles stopped chewing a moment and looked pointedly toward his nerve-taut son.

"I, I—"

"With your *fists*?" said his father, loudly.

"I'd get a gun and—"

The hissing catch of breath in his mother's throat made Jimmy stop suddenly and glance toward her with frightened eyes.

Matthew Coles looked intently at Robby, still addressing his younger son.

"You'd get a gun?" he questioned. "Is that what you said, sir?"

"Matthew, what are you trying to—"

"You'd get a gun, you say?" Matthew Coles' rising voice cut off the tortured question of his wife. "A gun?"

"Oh, leave him alone!" Robby burst out with sudden nerve-snapped vehemence. "It's me you're after, talk to me!"

Matthew Coles' nostrils flared out and it appeared, for a moment, that he would explode in Robby's face.

Then a twitching shudder ran down his straight back and he looked down to his food, face graven into a hard, expressionless mold.

"I don't talk to cowards," said Matthew Coles.

Chapter Eight

The Reverend Omar Bond was working on the notes for his Sunday sermon when he heard the front doorbell tinkling. He looked up from his desk, a touch of sorrowing martyrdom in his expression. He *had* hoped no one would call tonight; there was so much necessary work to be done on the sermon.

"Oh my," he muttered to himself as he sat listening to his wife, Clara, come bustling from the kitchen. He heard her nimble footsteps moving down the hall, then the sound of the front door being opened.

"Why, good evening, Miss Winston," he heard Clara say and his face drew into melancholy lines. Of all his parishioners, Miss Winston was the one who most tried his Christian fortitude. There were times when he would definitely have enjoyed telling her to—

"Ah, Miss Winston," he said, smiling beneficently as he rose from his chair. "How good of you to drop by." He ignored the tight sinking in his stomach as being of uncharitable genre. Extending his hand, he approached the grim-faced woman and felt his fingers in her cool, almost manlike grip.

"Reverend," she said, dipping her head but once.

"Do sit down, Miss Winston," the Reverend Bond invited, the smile still frozen on his face.

"May I take your shawl?" Clara Bond asked politely and Agatha Winston shook her head.

"I'll only be a moment," she said.

The Reverend Omar Bond could not check the heartfelt hallelujah in his mind although he masked it well behind his beaming countenance.

He settled down on the chair across from where Miss Winston sat poised on the couch edge as though ready to spring up at a moment's provocation. Clara Bond left the room quietly.

"Is this a social visit?" the Reverend Bond inquired pleasantly, knowing it wasn't.

"No, it is not, Reverend," said Agatha Winston firmly. "It concerns one of your parishioners."

Oh, my God, she's at it again, the Reverend Bond thought with a twinge. Agatha Winston was forever coming to him with stories about his parishioners, nine tenths of which were usually either distorted or completely untrue.

"Oh?" he asked blandly. "Who is that, Miss Winston?"

"*John Benton.*" Agatha Winston rid herself of the given and family names as though they were spiders in her mouth.

"But, I . . ." the Reverend Bond stopped talking, his face mildly shocked. "John Benton?" he said. "Surely not."

"He has asked my niece, Louisa Harper, to . . ." Miss Winston hesitated, searching for the proper phrase, ". . . to *meet* him."

Omar Bond raised graying eyebrows, his hands clasped tightly in his lap.

"How do you know this thing?" he asked, a little less amiably now.

"I know it because my niece told me so," she answered firmly.

The Reverend Bond sat silently a moment, his eyes looking at Miss Winston with emotionless detachment.

"And it's worse than just that," Miss Winston went on, quickly. "It would be one thing if the incident were known only to those immediately concerned. But almost the entire *town* knows of it!"

"I've heard nothing of it," said the Reverend, blandly.

"Well . . ." Agatha Winston was not refuted. "Begging your pardon, Reverend, but . . . well, I don't think anyone would pass along gossip to *you*."

Someone would, thought Omar Bond, looking at Miss Winston with an imperceptible sigh.

"But this makes no earthly sense," he said then. "John Benton is a fine man, a regular churchgoer and, moreover, an extremely respected man in Kellville."

"Be that as it may." Miss Winston's mouth was a lipless gash as she spoke. "My niece's honor has been *insulted* by him."

The Reverend Bond rubbed worried fingers across his smooth chin and, behind his spectacles, his blue eyes were harried.

"It's . . . such a difficult thing to believe," he said quietly, groping for some argument. Agatha Winston always made him feel so defenseless.

"The truth is the truth," stated Miss Winston slowly and clearly. "Believe me, Reverend, when I tell you that if I were a man, I wouldn't be here *talking* about this shocking thing. I'd get myself a horsewhip and—"

She broke off as the Reverend raised a pacifying hand.

"My dear Miss Winston," he said, concernedly, "reason, not violence; is that not what our Lord has taught us?"

The colorless skin rippled slightly over Agatha Winston's taut cheeks. There were definitely times when Christianity did more to thwart than aid, she felt. This was one

of the times when she would have preferred a more hardened ethic; this loving humility had its limitations.

But she nodded once, tight-lipped, not wishing to alien-
ate the head of local church activities.

"I came here because I am a woman," she said. "Because
I am helpless to do anything by myself."

Christianity does not become you—the Reverend Bond
was unable to prevent the thought from shaking loose its
repressive bonds. Once again, he hid the thought behind
the mild and wrinkled facade he almost always presented
to the world.

"Isn't it possible this gossip is exaggerated?" he suggested then. "You know how some people talk. A chance
meeting between Benton and your niece might be con-
strued in an entirely false manner."

"I would agree with you," said Agatha Winston, lying,
"if it were not for the fact that Louisa, herself, verified the
story."

"Oh," he said, cornered again, "Louisa . . . herself."

"Believe me, Reverend, when I say I no more wanted to
believe this ugly thing when I first heard of it than you
want to believe it now. I'm not the sort of woman who ac-
cepts every scrap of gossip as the truth, you know that."

I do not know that, Omar Bond reflected silently, his sad
eyes on the face of Agatha Winston.

"Before I accepted one word of this terrible story, I went
directly to my niece and questioned her most carefully."

She stiffened her back, fingers tightening in the lap of
her black skirt. *The story is true,*" she declared.

The Reverend Bond licked his upper lip slowly. He
started to say something, then exhaled slowly instead while
Miss Winston sat waiting for him to call down the wrath
of church and Lord upon the head of John Benton.

"What exactly," asked the Reverend Bond, "did Louisa
say?"

The thin eyebrows of Agatha Winston pressed down over unpleasantly curious eyes.

"Say?" she asked, not certain of what the Reverend was getting at.

"Yes. Surely, you verified her story?"

"I told you," she said tensely, "I asked her if the incident were true and she said it was."

"Was she upset?"

Agatha Winston looked more unpleasantly confused. "Of course, she was upset," she said. "Her honor was insulted; naturally, she was upset. Especially when I told her how her intended husband, Robby Coles, fought John Benton in defense of her."

The Reverend Bond strained forward, his face suddenly concerned. "Fought?" he asked. "Not . . . not with . . . *guns*?" His voice tapered off in a shocked whisper.

"No, not with guns," Miss Winston said. "Although—"

The look on the Reverend Bond's face kept her from continuing but she knew that he was fully conscious of what she had been about to say.

"What I am getting at," Omar Bond continued, preferring to overlook her probable remark, "is that . . . well, Louisa is very young, very impressionable."

"I don't see how—"

"Let me explain, Miss Winston. Please."

Agatha Winston leaned back, eyes distrusting on the Reverend's face.

"John Benton is what you might call . . . oh, an *idol* in this town, is he not?" asked Bond.

"Men shall not bow down before idols," declared Miss Winston.

The Reverend Bond controlled himself.

"I mean to say, he is extremely admired. I do not, for a moment, say that I condone admiration for a man which is based primarily on an awe of his skill with instruments of death. However . . . this does not alter the fact that, among the younger people particularly, John Benton has achieved almost a . . . a legendary status."

She did not nod or speak or, in any way, indicate agreement.

"I have seen myself," the Reverend Bond went on, "in the church—young boys and girls staring at him with . . . shall we say, unduly fascinated eyes?"

"I do not—"

"Please, Miss Winston, I shall be finished in a moment. To continue: From the vantage point of my pulpit, I have seen your own niece looking so at John Benton."

Miss Winston closed her eyes as if to shut away the thought. "I can hardly believe this," she said, stiffly.

"I say it in no condemning way," the Reverend Bond hastened to explain. "It is a thoroughly natural reaction in the young. I would not even have mentioned it were it not for what you have just told me."

"I don't understand," said Agatha Winston. "Are you telling me that Louisa *lied*? That her story is a deliberate *falsehood*?"

"No, *no*," the Reverend said gently, a smile softening his features, "not a lie. Call it rather a . . . a daydream spoken aloud."

Miss Winston rose irately.

"Reverend, I'm shocked that you should stand up for John Benton, a man who lives by violence. And I'm hurt— *deeply* hurt that you should accuse my niece of deliberately *lying*."

The Reverend Bond rose quickly and moved toward her.

"My dear Miss Winston," he said, "I *assure* you . . ."

Agatha Winston brushed away a tear which had, somehow, managed to force its way out of her eye duct. A sob rasped dryly in her lean throat.

"I came to you because there is nothing my sister and

her daughter can do to defend their good name. But instead of—"

Another sob, dry and harsh.

Against his better judgment, the Reverend Omar Bond found himself standing before Agatha Winston, explaining, apologizing.

"I'll tell you what I'll do," he finally said, growing desperate with her. "I'll ride out personally to John Benton's ranch and speak to him."

"He'll deny it," Agatha Winston said, agitatedly. "Do you think he'll—"

"Miss Winston, if the incident occurred as you said, John Benton will admit it," the Reverend Bond said firmly. "That's all I can say for now. I sympathize with your situation, I most certainly will speak out Sunday against the insidious cruelty of this gossiping." He gestured weakly. "And . . . and I'll go out to see John Benton in the morning."

He was leading her to the door finally.

"Please don't upset yourself, Miss Winston," he told her, "I am confident we can work it out to the satisfaction of all."

"Oh, if only there were a *man* in our family to speak for us," Agatha Winston said, vengefully.

"I will speak for you," said Bond. "Remember, my child, we are all one family under God."

Frankly, Miss Winston did not accept that tenet of Christianity. Her mind pushed the concept aside angrily as she strode off into the night, unsatisfied.

The Reverend Omar Bond shut the door and turned back as Clara came out of the kitchen, drying her hands.

"What's wrong, dear?" she asked, concernedly.

"Offhand, I should say the qualifications for membership in the church," said the Reverend Bond with a weary shake of his head.

Chapter Nine

The hooves of the black roan thudded slowly down the long darkness of Armitas Street, headed for the square. Robby Coles sat slumped in the saddle, his rein-holding hands clasped loosely over the horn. He was staring ahead bleakly, between the bobbing ears of his mount, watching the dark street jog toward him, then disappear beneath the legs of the roan. His lips were pressed together; his entire face reflected the tense nervousness he felt.

When supper had ended, he'd grabbed his hat and gun-belt and started for the door, not wanting to listen to his father anymore.

"Where are you going?" Matthew Coles had asked.

"For a ride," he'd answered.

"You'd better not," his father said, "you might run into John Benton and then you'd have to come running home and hide in the closet."

Robby didn't say anything. He just jerked open the door and went out, seeing from the corners of his eyes his mother looking at him, one frail hand at her breast.

Then, halfway to the stable, Robby heard the back door open and shut quickly.

"*Son*," his father called.

Robby didn't want to stay. He felt like jumping on his horse and galloping out the alleyway before his father could say another word. But open defiance was not in him;

he might flare up now and then under provocation but, inevitably, he obeyed his father. He was twenty-one and, supposedly, his own man; but those twenty-one years of rigid training still kept him bound.

He stood there silently, buckling on his gun belt as his father's boots came crunching over the hard ground of the yard. He felt Matthew Coles' hand close over his shoulder.

"Son, I didn't mean to rile you," Matthew Coles said, his voice no longer hard. "It's been a hard day and I'm out of sorts. You can understand that, son."

Robby could feel himself drawing back. Whenever his father called him *son* . . .

"Yes, sir," he said. "I . . . understand."

"I didn't intend to blow up at the table like that," Matthew Coles went on. "I believe a family meal should be eaten in peace."

"Yes, sir," Robby said, thinking of the countless meals that had degenerated into stomach-wrenching agonies because of his father's temper.

"It's just that . . . well." His father gestured with his free hand. "Just that you're my son and I want to be proud of you."

"Yes, sir." The tight, crawling sensation still mounted in Robby's stomach. Don't, he thought, *don't*; his eyes staring at the dark outline of his father's head.

"I don't want to force you into anything, son," said Matthew Coles in as understanding a voice as he could manage. "You're of age and I can't make you do anything your mind is set against."

Robby started to speak, then closed his mouth without a word. His father wasn't through yet.

"I can punish your younger brother if he does something I know is wrong." Matthew Coles shook his head once, slowly. "I can't do that with you, son," he said. "You're of age and your life is your own; your decisions are your own."

Suddenly, Robby wished his father would rage again, rant and yell. It was easier to fight that.

"But I don't believe you realize, son," said Matthew Coles, his voice a steady, coercive flow. "This is a very serious matter. I couldn't talk about it at the table because of your mother and your younger brother. It's not the sort of subject men discuss over a family supper table."

Now his father's arm was around his shoulders and, as they ambled slowly toward the stable, Robby could feel his stomach muscles trembling and he had to clench his hands to keep the fingers steady.

"Son," his father said, "there are certain things a man must face in this life. I don't say these things are just or fair . . . or even reasonable. But they're a part of our life and no man can avoid them." Matthew Coles paused for emphasis. "And the most important of those," he said, "is that a man defend his home and defend his family."

But she's not my family. Robby wanted to say it but he was afraid to.

"I . . . want to do what's right," he said instead, his throat feeling dry and tight, the gun at his waist seeming very heavy. He wished he hadn't taken the gun with him. What if he ran into John Benton and Benton had a gun on too?

"Of course, you want to do what's right, son," said Matthew Coles, nodding. "You're a Coles and the men of our family have always done what's right—what *has* to be done."

They were in the darkness of the stable now. Robby could smell the odor of damp hay and hear the soft stamping of the two horses in their stalls. He heard his roan nicker quietly and it made him swallow nervously. I'll ride you when I'm ready, he thought belligerently as if the horse had asked to be ridden toward town, toward the possibility of meeting Benton.

"Sit down, son," Robby heard the firm voice of his father say. Weakly, he sank down on the wooden bench and his father sat down beside him, arm still around Robby's lean shoulders.

His father's voice kept on, seeming to surround Robby in the cool, damp-smelling blackness of the stable.

"I know that, strictly speaking, Louisa Harper is not yet a part of our family. And, if there were men folks alive in her family now, I would say no more. It would be *their* responsibility to defend her honor."

Honor. Honor—the word thumped dully in Robby's mind as he stared straight ahead, listening.

"However," said Matthew Coles, "there *are* no men left in the Harper family. There are no men left in the Winston family which was the family that Louisa's mother was born to."

I know all that, Robby thought, trying hard not to shiver. He said quietly, "Yes, sir."

"And because there are no men in Louisa Harper's family, the responsibility must shift itself to you. Since the young lady is your intended bride, you are the only one who can defend her name."

Silence then. Robby felt his father's hand pat once-twice on his shoulder as if to say—You see then, it's settled, now go out and shoot John Benton.

"But . . . well, I . . . what about what I said to Benton?" Robby asked.

"Your conversation with Benton, you mean?" his father said, without expression.

Robby's throat moved quickly. "Well . . . it was more than just a conversation, sir. I told him in . . . in no uncertain terms that if he didn't leave Louisa alone, I'd—"

"*Son*," Matthew Coles interrupted in a slow, firm voice, "the damage has been done. This is not a situation which can be settled by talk. John Benton attempted to arrange an immoral meeting with your intended bride. Son, the facts are clear."

"But, Louisa didn't say—"

"Sir?"

Robby felt his throat muscles tighten at the slight but very certain stiffening in his father's voice. But he knew he had to go on or he'd be cornered and defenseless.

"Sir, Louisa didn't say that Benson tried to arrange an . . ." he swallowed, "an *immoral* meeting."

"Son," his father said, almost sadly it seemed, "you are a grown man, not a child. For what purpose do you suppose John Benton requested a meeting?"

Robby drew in a ragged breath; answerless.

"There is only one question involved here," Matthew Coles completed his case, "and that is—do you mean to defend the honor of your intended bride or do you mean to let yourself be judged a coward—for, believe me, sir, you *will* be judged a coward and the meanest sort of coward—a man who will not stand up for his woman."

Robby's head sank forward, his heart beating heavily, his hands pressed tightly together in his lap.

"I want to do what's . . . what's right, sir," he said huskily. "But—"

"Of course you do," his father said, arm tightening around Robby's shoulder. "Of course you do, sir."

Abruptly, his father was up on his feet, looking down at Robby.

"I will leave the working out of this to you," he said. "You are a man and a man must do things his own way."

Robby tried to say something but he couldn't.

"I would suggest, however," said his father, "that, for

tonight anyway, you leave your gun at home. For if you should run into John Benton and he be armed . . ."

Robby shivered in the darkness, his body slumped on the hard wooden bench. His stomach hurt again.

"You're not in good physical form tonight," his father continued. "I think you should wait until—"

"Sir, I'll do what I think is right but . . ." Robby swallowed convulsively. "Let me . . . m-make my own plans." His voice was thin and shaking in the darkness.

His father pretended not to hear the nervous fear in his son's voice.

"The problem is yours, sir," he said in a satisfied voice. He patted Robby briskly on the shoulder. "I will say no more—to anyone." Pause. "You know exactly what has to be done."

Then his father had turned and Robby was watching the dark shadow of him moving for the yard.

At the door, his father looked back.

"Don't be too late," he said. "Remember, there's a good deal of work to be done at the shop tomorrow."

Matthew Coles turned away and Robby listened to the crunching of his boots on the ground, then the measured clumping up the porch steps, the opening and closing of the back door.

In the silence, a shaking breath caught in Robby's throat. He sat there for a long time, staring into the blackness with hopeless eyes.

Then, after a while, he stood, unbuckled his gun belt and left it hanging on a nail.

Now he was riding slowly down Armitas Street, staring ahead, his hands clenched around the horn. He didn't want to go into town; he was afraid of seeing anyone. But, even less, did he want to go into the house and see his father. Because, in spite of what had been said, Robby wasn't sure whether he was going to put on a gun against

Benton. It was simply that he didn't want to die. It was simply that honor seemed a very little thing beside life.

Robby tilted back his head and looked up into the jet expanses of the sky, sprinkled with glowing star dots. He felt the rhythmic jogging of the horse beneath him as he watched the sky.

Those are the stars, he thought. They were so far away no man could ever count the miles, much less travel them. It gave him a strange feeling to watch them and know how far away they were and how big. Once, his school teacher had told Robby that if a man could gallop a horse as fast as possible and keep on galloping all his life, he still wouldn't even travel a thousandth of the way to a star. So far away they were and he was so small and what he did was so unimportant to the stars. Why was it so important to him then?

Robby Coles looked down quickly at the darkness of the earth. It was no use looking at stars. Stars couldn't save him; he had to save himself.

He saw that his roan was walking past the first stores of downtown Kellville and his hands lifted from the horn to guide the horse right at the next intersection. He didn't want to ride into the square. Someone might see him; someone who knew.

When Robby turned onto St. Virgil Street, the horseman came out of the night toward him.

For a moment, Robby felt a cold, rippling sensation in his groin that made him twitch. It's *him*, the thought lashed at his mind. He almost jerked the horse around and fled. Then, with a sudden stiffening, he lowered his head and looked intently at the saddle horn, feeling the roan bump steadily beneath him, hearing the thud of the approaching hoof-beats. He can't shoot if I'm not looking at him, his mind thought desperately, no one shoots a man that isn't looking. His heart beat faster and harder, sweat broke out thinly on his forehead. The horse came closer. You don't shoot a man when he's not looking!—he thought in anguish—you never shoot a man when he's—

The horseman rode by without a word and Robby sagged forward weakly in the saddle, lips trembling, breath caught in his throat.

It was no use, no use; he realized it then. He couldn't fight Benton; the very thought petrified him. No matter what happened, no matter what anyone said, he couldn't fight Benton. He *wouldn't* fight him.

A heavy breath faltered between Robby's parted lips. In a way, it was relieving to make the decision. It gave him a settled feeling. Even realizing that he'd have to face his father with the decision, it made him feel better.

As he rode for the edge of town, Robby wondered what Louisa would want him to do. She certainly seemed astounded that morning when he paled and went storming from the house after she told him about Benton asking her for a meeting. No, he didn't think Louisa would expect him to fight Benton with a gun.

Yet, what if she did? He loved her and felt responsible for her. His father had been right in that respect anyway. Someone had to defend her and he seemed to be the only one to do it.

But did he have to *die* for her honor?

Robby nudged his boot heels into the roan's flanks and the big horse broke into a rocking-chair canter up St. Virgil Street toward the edge of Kellville.

The horsemen seemed to appear from nowhere. One moment, Robby was alone, riding in his thoughts. The next, three horses were milling around him and he was cringing with frightened surprise in his saddle.

"Hey, Robby," one of the young men shouted above the stirring hooves of the four horses.

Robby swallowed. "Oh . . . hello," he said, recognizing

the voice of Dave O'Hara, an old school friend of his he hadn't seen more than three times in the past year.

The horses twisted around, snorting, while Robby stared at O'Hara's dark form.

"Where ya goin'?" O'Hara asked.

"No place."

"What's that?"

"*No* place!"

"Well, come on with us then. We're headin' for the Zorilla."

Robby hesitated long enough for O'Hara to lean forward and look intently at him.

"You goin' after Benton, Robby?" O'Hara asked, almost eagerly.

It felt like someone driving a cold fist against his heart. Robby jolted in the saddle with a grunt they didn't hear because of the milling horses.

"N-no," he faltered, "I—"

"Heard what he done to your girl," O'Hara said grimly. "You ain't lettin' him get *away* with that, are you?"

It was like a nightmare—sitting in darkness on the shifting saddle, watching the three horsemen move about him in the jerky little movements caused by their restless mounts, hearing the deep-chested snortings of their horses.

"No, I'm . . . going to do what . . ." Robby's mind searched desperately for an answer that wouldn't commit him. Then he grew nervous at his own revealing hesitation and finished quickly.

"I'll do what has to be done," he said, his voice sounding thin and strengthless.

"Damn right," O'Hara said vengefully and the other two men said something between themselves. "The bastard's got a slug comin' for what he done. Him and his damn *rep*. Why'd he leave the Rangers anyhow? And, he's so brave, why don't he tote no gun?" O'Hara's voice was tight with a bitter jealousy. He was one of Kellville's young men who had made the inevitable step from idolizing Benton to envying and hating him.

Robby sat his mount numbly, hearing the voice of Dave O'Hara as if it were a million miles away.

"When you goin' for him, Robby?"

Robby bit his teeth together. "I . . ."

The three riders watching him, Dave O'Hara and the other two. When are you going for him? When are you going to die? A shudder ran down Robby's back. Then he stiffened himself.

"When the time comes," he said, his voice unnaturally loud.

The dark riders still moved around him. "Well, that's your own business, Robby," O'Hara said, "but I want ya to know we're all behind ya. Everybody knows Benton's a dirty coward who's too *yella* to tote a gun. And after what he done to your girl . . . well, there ain't nothin' more to say."

"That's right," Robby said, feeling as if he were trapped there with the three of them. "There's nothing more."

"Well how about headin' for the Zorilla with us and let me buy ya a drink?"

"No, I . . . have to get home." Loudly, forcedly. "I was just on an errand for my father."

"Oh . . ." O'Hara punched him lightly on the arm. "We're all behind ya, Robby," he said, almost happily. "Ain't a man in town that ain't behind ya. When the time comes . . ." Another punch. "We'll back ya."

They were gone in a clouding of night dust. Robby waited a moment, then twisted around in his saddle and saw the three of them spurring for the square.

How did the story get around so *fast*? Robby couldn't understand it. Only three men had seen the fight outside of Pat and Pat wasn't the kind to spread tales.

It was horrible how fast the story was traveling. And now he'd be trapped further, now O'Hara and his two friends would tell everybody that he was going to get John Benton.

"*No.*" Robby couldn't keep the shaking word from escaping his lips. No, he didn't want to fight Benton, he didn't *want* to! A shudder ran down his back and he couldn't seem to get enough air in his lungs to breathe.

Ten minutes to nine, Kellville, Texas, September 12, 1879. The end of the first day.

The Second Day

Chapter Ten

Benton was riding fence. There were only three men working for him and he couldn't afford to spare any of them for this simple but hour-consuming chore. Mounted on his blood bay, Socks, so named for the whiteness of its feet extending to the fetlocks, Benton was riding leisurely along the rutted trail that preceding fence rides had worn.

Five times during the morning, he'd stopped to fix loose or broken wires, missing staples, once a sagging post. Each time, he'd gotten the supplies he needed from the saddle-fastened pouch in which were staples, a hatchet, a pair of wire cutters, and a coil of stay wire.

Finding a fence section that needed repairs, Benton would ease himself off the bay and ground the open reins. Socks would then remain in place without being tied while his master worked. The work completed, Benton would take hold of the reins and raise the stiffness of his batwing chaps over the saddle.

"Come on, churnhead," he would say softly and the bay would start along the line again.

Benton's horse was one of the two cutting horses in the ranch's small remuda, a bridle-wise gelding that Benton had spent over a year in training. Cutting was a ticklish and difficult job, the most exacting duty any horse could be called upon to perform. It demanded of the mount an apex of physical and mental control plus a calm dispatch that would not panic the animal being cut from the herd. A cutting horse had to spin and turn as quickly as the cow, always edging the reluctant animal away from the herd without frightening it. This twisting and turning entailed much good riding too and, although Benton had ridden since he was eight, the process of sitting a cutting horse had taken all the ability he had.

Benton knew he rode Socks on jobs that any ordinary cowhorse could manage. But he was extremely fond of the bay and never demanded a great deal of it outside of its cutting duties. Riding fence was no effort for the bay. It enjoyed the ambling walk with its master in the warm, sunlight-brimming air. Benton would pat the bay's neck as they rode.

"Hammerhead," he'd tell the horse, "someday we'll all be rich and ride to town in low-necked clothes and have thirty hands workin' for us."

The bay would snort its reply and Benton would pat it again and say, "You're all right, fuzz tail."

When Benton rode the range, he wore a converted Colt-Walker .44 at his left side, butt forward. Sometimes it seemed as if it even worried Julia for him to wear a gun around the ranch.

"Honey, you want a snake to kill me?" he'd say with a grin.

"I don't want *any*thing to kill you," she'd answer grimly. "Or any*body.*"

That day, while riding fence, Benton reached across his waist and drew out the pistol with an easy movement. He held it loosely in his hand and looked at its smooth metal finish, the notches of the cylinder, the curved trigger in its heavy guard.

He often found himself looking at the Colt; it was the only thing he had that really reminded him of the old days. He'd killed nine men with this pistol in the line of Ranger duty. There was Jack Kramer in Trinity City, Max Foster outside of Comanche, Rebel Dean, Johnny Ostrock, Bob Melton, Sam and Barney Dobie, Aaran Graham's two sons; nine men lying in their graves because of the mechanism in this four-pound piece of apparatus.

Benton hefted the pistol in his palm, wondering if he missed the old days, wondering if violence had become a part of him. He slipped his finger into the guard and spun the pistol around backward and forward in the old way, then shoved it back into its holster with a quick, blurred movement of his hand. Miss it, *hell*. He was alive, he had a good little layout, a wonderful wife; one day there would be children—that was enough for any man.

He was grateful the percentages had passed over him. By Ranger standards he had outlived himself at least five times. Another month in the service, another year maybe and he would have died like the others, like the many others. As horrible as it had been, the incident with Graham and his sons had spared him that.

Benton threw back his shoulders and took a deep breath of the clean air. Life, he thought, that's what counts; killing is for animals.

He found the trapped calf near the spring. It was stuck under the fence where it had tried to wriggle through a gap caused by water erosion. Benton could hear the loud quaver of its bawling a half mile away. He nudged his flower rowels across the bay's flanks and the horse broke into an easy trot down the trail.

The calf looked up at Benton's approach, its big, dark eyes wild with fright. Its back hooves kicked futilely at the earth, spraying dirt over the long grass.

Benton jumped down from the bay, grounded the reins, and started for the calf, a grin on his face.

"Hello, you old acorn," he said. "Runnin' off to the city again?"

The calf bawled loudly and kicked again at the scoured ground.

"All right, little girl," Benton said, drawing on the gloves he'd pulled from his back Levi's pocket, "take it easy now. Poppa will get you out."

He hunkered down beside the fence and the calf complained loudly as Benton grabbed the wire that held it pinned down, the sharp barbs embedded deeply in its skin and flesh.

"Easy now, deacon," Benton spoke soothingly as he tried to draw out the barbs so he could raise the taut wire. He grimaced slightly as the calf squalled loudly, blood oozing across its spotted back. "*Ea*-sy now, little girl, we'll get you out in no time."

Fifteen minutes later, the bay was moving across the range, leading the roped yearling. Benton glanced back and grinned at the tugging calf.

"Gotta get your wounds fixed, runty," he told the yearling, then turned back with a shake of his head. The calf's mother had died the previous winter and the calf had been more trouble than it was worth since then, having to be fed because water and grass were still too heavy a fare for its young stomach and, invariably, wandering from the herd and getting lost.

"We're goin' to sell you for boot leather, acorn," Benton said lightly, not even looking back. "That's what we're goin' to sell you for."

The calf dragged along behind, sulky and complaining.

Back at the ranch, Benton led the calf into the barn and salved up its back, then turned it loose in the corral.

The rig was standing in front of the house as he walked toward it. It looked familiar but he wasn't sure where he'd seen it before. He moved in long strides across the yard and went into the kitchen. He was getting a drink of cool water from the dipper when Julia came in.

"Who's visitin'?" he asked.

"The Reverend Bond," she said.

"Oh? What's *he* want?"

"He came to see you."

Benton looked at Julia curiously. "What for?" he asked.

Julia shook her head once. "He won't tell me," she said. "But I think I know."

"What?"

Julia turned to the stove. "Well, from the way he avoided the subject, I'd say that story."

"What story?"

"About Louisa Harper and you."

A look of disgust crossed Benton's face. "Oh, no," he said in a pained voice. "*More?*"

He shook his head and groaned softly to himself as he took off the bull-hide chaps and tossed them on a chair by the door. "Oh . . . blast," he said. "What's goin' on in town anyway?"

At the door, he turned to her. "Aren't you comin' in?" he asked.

"You think I should?" she asked. "The Reverend doesn't seem to think it's anything for me to hear."

He came back to her, his brow lined with curious surprise. "What is it?" he asked. "Don't tell me you're startin' to *believe* this thing?"

Julia swallowed nervously. "Of course not," she said. "It's just that . . ."

He hooked his arm in hers. "Come on, ma," he said amusedly. "In we go."

In the hallway, he pinched her and she whispered, "Stop that!" But the tenseness was gone from her face.

As they entered the small sitting room, the Reverend Omar Bond stood up and extended his hand to Benton with a smile.

"Mr. Benton," he said.

"Reverend." Benton nodded. "Excuse the hand. I been out ridin'."

Bond smiled. "Not at all," he said.

"Sit down, Reverend," Benton said, putting Julia on a chair. "What's on your mind?"

"Well, sir," the Reverend Bond said, "I think that . . ." He hesitated and glanced at Julia.

"That's all right, Reverend," Benton said, smiling guardedly. "My wife knows all about it. Who's been tellin' *you* stories now? Louisa Harper?"

The Reverend Bond looked at Benton, mouth slightly agape. Then a sudden look of relief came over his face and he beamed at both of them.

"I'm so glad," he said quickly. "I didn't believe the story at all and yet . . ." He clucked and shook his head sadly. "Once the poison is put in one's mind, one is hard put to find the adequate antidote of reason."

Benton glanced at his wife. "I know," he said, trying not to smile. "That old suspicious poison."

He sat down on the arm of the chair. "All right now," he said seriously, "who told you this story, Reverend? Robby Coles?"

"No, as a matter of fact it was Louisa's aunt, Miss Agatha Winston," Bond said. "And . . ." he gestured with his hand, "I might add, were this not a situation of such potential gravity, I would not, for a moment, betray a confidence. You understand."

"It'll go no further than this room," Benton said. His mouth hardened. "I wish I could say the same for this damned story."

"John," his wife said quietly. He glanced down at her, then up at the Reverend with a rueful smile. "Pardon," he said, then became absorbed in thought. "Agatha Winston," he mused. "Do I know her?"

"She owns the ladies' clothes shop in town, doesn't she?" Julia asked.

"That's correct." The Reverend Bond nodded. "She came to my house last night and told me that . . . well . . ." He cleared his throat embarrassedly.

"It's quite all right, Reverend," Julia told him.

"Thank you," Bond replied. "To be terribly blunt then, Miss Winston said that your husband tried to arrange for an immoral meeting with her niece. Again," he added quickly, "I would not say such a thing in your presence were I not convinced that the story is untrue."

When Bond had repeated what Agatha Winston had told him, Benton's right hand closed angrily in his lap and his face grew suddenly taut. He sat there stone-faced until Bond had finished talking, then he said in a flat, toneless voice, "And did she say who told her this story?"

Bond nodded his head. "Yes," he answered, "she said that her niece, Louisa, told her. Or, rather, that she had heard the gossip in town and then checked with Louisa to verify the story."

"And Louisa said it was true," Benton said disgustedly.

Bond gestured with his hands and looked helpless. "That is what she said," he admitted.

Benton exhaled heavily. "Well, it's not true," he said. His eyes raised to Bond's. "Do I have to tell you it's not true?"

"I would like you to," Bond replied, meeting Benton's gaze steadily.

Benton's mouth tightened. "It is not true," he said slowly and Julia put her hand on his with an abrupt movement.

Bond's lips raised in a conciliatory smile. "I'm sorry," he said. "It wasn't that I believed you were guilty. It was just that . . . well, I felt that the situation called for such a definite statement." He leaned forward. "Very well," he said, "we'll say no more of that. What's important now is ending this gossip before it does any more harm. I . . . understand there was some physical conflict yesterday."

Benton nodded then, briefly, told the Reverend about how Robby Coles had come into the Zorilla and started a fight.

"And this was the first you heard of the matter," Bond said.

"That's right," said Benton. "The first."

"I see." Bond nodded as he spoke. "I . . . imagine, then, that it all began with Louisa telling Robby that . . . telling him what she *did* tell him," he finished hastily.

"But why?" Benton asked, irritably baffled. "Does it make any sense?"

Julia smiled a little at the Reverend Bond and he repressed an answering smile. "He really doesn't know," Julia said.

Omar Bond nodded slowly. "I believe it," he said. "Yes, I believe that firmly. Your husband is not the sort of man who indulges himself in false modesty."

"Know what?" Benton asked. "What are you two talking about?"

"What I said to you yesterday, John," Julia said. "Louisa Harper is in love with you."

Benton looked pained again. "Oh . . . come on, Julia," he said.

"I think the assumption is justified," said the Reverend. "You see, Mister Benton, you represent something to the young people of this town. In . . . all honesty," he went on reluctantly, "I must admit that I'm not sure what you represent to them is a . . . healthy thing. Needless to say, I do not, for a moment, think that you still are what they conceive you to be. No, I—"

"What's that, Reverend?" Benton interrupted. "What do they think I am?"

Bond looked embarrassed. "A . . . fearless . . . and a

very dangerous man," he faltered. "Mind you, I'm only assuming now. But I think that . . . well, they regard your skill with a gun as one of paramount achievement."

"But I don't *wear* a gun in town," Benton said stiffly. "They've never even seen me with a gun on."

"They've never seen John Hardin either," Bond countered, "but they know what he's done."

The Reverend's face grew sadly reflective. "It was people like this who . . . lined the roads for miles when John Hardin was taken to prison. People who waited for just one momentary glimpse of a man who had killed others with guns." Bond shook his head grimly. "It makes no sense—to me, at any rate—but it *is* so, let us admit it freely; now. Your reputation as a Texas Ranger is immense, Mister Benton. It caused a, perhaps, foolish young girl to become enamored of what she conceived you to be. It caused her, in a moment of . . ." he gestured searchingly with his hands, ". . . shall we say, a moment of *un*thinking delusion, to pretend out loud; unhappily, to pretend in the presence of her intended husband. Perhaps she meant nothing by it; I'm sure she didn't. It was a girlish whim, I imagine, perhaps done to make her intended husband jealous of someone—anyone. Young girls are . . . often misled by their feelings."

Bond leaned back, hands clasped in his lap.

"And I believe it was your reputation—exaggerated as it may be—that caused this event. Believe me, sir, I'm not accusing you of anything but . . . perhaps this is, in some measure, an unfortunate result of the life you formerly led."

"Reverend, is that . . . well, *fair*?" Julia asked. "My husband worked for law, for order. If he killed, it was not for the sake of killing; it was because it was his job."

"My dear lady," said Bond warmly, "I would not, for a moment, accuse your husband of being anything that he is not. That he, voluntarily, chose to put aside violence and live as a peaceful citizen, speaks wonderfully for his character. It is just that . . . well, I must repeat, I fear, were it not for the past events of Mister Benton's life, this situation would not have occurred."

"Well, this is getting us nowhere," Benton said, gruffly. "All right, maybe this Harper girl made up the story. But you said her aunt checked with her. Why didn't the Harper girl tell the truth *then*?"

Bond smiled gently. "You are not acquainted with her aunt, Mister Benton. Miss Winston, though, I cannot deny, a loyal Christian, often shows in her dealings with others more hasty righteousness than understanding. And her niece is very sensitive, very retiring. Cornered . . . frightened, perhaps, she would hardly have confessed that she . . . pretended, shall we say. You can understand that."

"I can understand it," Julia said. "John, you mustn't be angry with her. I'm sure she's more frightened than anything else with the gossip she's started."

"Well, that doesn't do me any good," Benton said. "If *she* doesn't stop the gossip, who can?"

"Perhaps you can," Bond answered.

Benton looked surprised. "How?" he asked.

"I would think that if you rode in to Kellville and spoke to Louisa Harper, spoke to her mother, perhaps to her aunt—the situation might be settled."

Benton looked trapped. "But . . . what good would that do?" he asked. "They seem to have their minds made up already."

"I can think of nothing more direct," Bond said. "If you wish, I could come along as . . . oh, say a middle party to ease tension."

"Reverend, I have a lot of work to do around here," Benton said, his voice rising a little. "I can't go ridin' off to town just like that. This is a small layout; I only have three hands beside myself and that's spreadin' out the labor pretty thin."

"I appreciate that," Bond said, nodding. "But . . . well, this situation could become quite bad. Believe me, I've seen such things happen before. I mean quite bad."

Julia looked up at her husband, her face drawn worriedly. "John," she said, "I think you should."

Benton twisted his shoulders irritably. "But, honey—" He broke off then and exhaled quickly. "All right," he said, "I'll ride in tomorrow and . . . see what I can do."

Bond looked embarrassed. "Well," he said, "I would think that—"

"Reverend, this place is creepin' with work that needs to be done! I just can't *do* it today!"

"John."

Benton looked aside at his wife, his face angrily taut. Then another thin breath fell from his nostrils.

"All right," he said disgustedly, "I'll go in this afternoon. But . . ." He didn't finish but only shook his head sadly.

"I don't think it will take long," Bond told him. "Would, uh, you like me to come with you and . . ."

"No, I'll handle it," Benton said. He managed a brief smile at the Reverend. "I'm thankin' you, Reverend," he said, "but . . . I think I can handle it myself."

Bond smiled. "Fine," he said. "Fine. I think it will all work out splendidly." He stood up. "Well, I . . . really must be getting back to town now."

"Oh, can't you stay for dinner?" Julia asked. "It's almost time."

"I'm afraid not," Bond said, gratefully. "I do thank you, Mrs. Benton, but . . . well." He sighed. "My . . . ranch, too, is overrun with work that needs to be done."

Later, over dinner, Benton shook his head and groaned to himself, thinking about all the work time he was going to lose.

"This is hogwash," he muttered.

"Are you sure you don't want me to come with you?" Julia asked.

Benton shook his head. "No, I'm ridin' in fast. Maybe I can get it settled quick and come back in time to get some work done."

Julia poured in more coffee, then stood beside the table, smiling down at her husband. After a moment, he looked up at her. A slow grin relaxed his mouth.

"I know," he said, amusedly, "get a haircut."

Julia laughed. "How did you guess?"

Chapter Eleven

He was surrounded by guns. On the wall racks behind him and at his right were rifles—a Springfield .45 caliber breech-loader, a Sharps and Hanker .52 caliber rim-fire carbine, a Henry Deringer rifle, a Colt .44 revolving rifle, a new Sharps-Borschardt .45, three 45/10 nine-shot Winchesters—all of them resting on wooden pegs, their metal glinting in the sunlit brightness of the shop, their stocks glossy with rubbed-in oils.

Across from him, behind his father's bench, was the board on which his father and he hung repaired pistols like a watchmaker hung repaired watches. Dangling by their trigger guards were five Colt revolvers, a Remington .36 caliber Navy pistol, an Allen and Thurber .32 caliber pepperbox, and three .41 caliber Deringer pistols. All of them had tags tied to them which had the names of the owner and the cost of the repair job.

On the bench in front of Robby Coles were the parts of a .44 caliber 1860 Model Colt which he had converted from percussion to cartridge fire by cutting off the rear end of the cylinder and replacing it with a breechblock containing a loading gate and rebounding fire pin. He'd only managed to get a section of it assembled all morning.

He couldn't seem to concentrate, that was the trouble. Every few moments he'd start thinking about his father or O'Hara or Louisa and his fingers would put down the part he was working on and, for a long time, he'd sit staring across the small shop, brooding.

Then, in the middle of a thought, Robby's eyes would focus suddenly and he'd find himself staring at the pistols hanging across the shop from him. He would sit there, looking at the long-barreled Colts, at their plow-handle shaped stocks, their hammers like steer horns jutting out behind the cylinder, the scimiter triggers filed to a hair.

He'd think of John Benton aiming one of them at him, squeezing the trigger. And, suddenly, he'd shudder in the warm shop and his cheek would be pale. No, he'd think, *no.* And go back to work; or, at least, try to go back to work.

But then, a few minutes later, abruptly, he'd remember the look some men gave him as he rode to work that morning. And his throat would move and the chain of thoughts would begin all over again. He'd end up staring at the pistols on the board again and shuddering. Through ten o'clock, through eleven, through—

Robby's hands twitched on the bench top, dropping the smooth cylinder as heavy footsteps sounded in the doorway. Looking up quickly, Robby saw his father coming across the floor, seeming very tall in his dark suit and hat, his face grave and still. Robby felt his hand start to shake and, around the edge of his stomach, all the muscles and tendons started tightening in like drawn wires.

Matthew Coles stopped by the bench and looked down at the litter of Colt parts across the bench top. He glanced up at Robby, his face a mask of unpleasant surprise.

"Sir?" he said

Robby swallowed. "I'm sorry, father. I . . ."

"I understand your concern with other thoughts, sir," said Matthew Coles. "However . . . we have duties to perform in life beside those necessary ones of honor."

"Yes, sir." Robby picked up the cylinder again and

started working, hoping that his father would leave it at that.

"I've just come from the bank," said Matthew Coles, removing his dark coat and hanging it up carefully on the clothes tree in a back corner of the shop. "There was talk about the Benton incident. *Hard* talk, sir."

Robby's throat moved again and his teeth gritted together as he kept on trying to work.

"I was asked by several men when you were going to settle this matter." Matthew Coles was adjusting arm garters to keep the sleeves up and away from filings and oil. "I told them," he said, "that it was your decision to make but that I assumed it would be soon."

Robby felt his stomach muscles start throbbing. Then, a bolt of terror numbed him as he felt a betraying looseness around his eyes. He forced his lips together and stared down at the bench without seeing anything, his eyes strained and unblinking.

". . . a matter of honor that needs settling," he heard the tail-end of his father's words but didn't dare reply for fear there would be a break in his voice. His hands fumbled and pretended to work on the cool metal of the Colt parts.

Silence a moment as his father adjusted the apron over his shirt and trouser front, sat down at the other bench, and looked over the disassembled Winchester.

Matthew Coles reached for the long barrel, then glanced up.

"Son, between you and me," he said, "when do you intend to settle this thing? Mind you, I'm not pushing; you're of age and I believe the final decision is yours to make. But the situation is getting more grave by the hour. I heard talk of it all over town. People are expecting this thing of you, sir. And soon."

Robby drew in a ragged breath. "Father, I . . ."

"It's Thursday today," Matthew Coles estimated. "I believe the matter should be settled before the weekend."

Robby's eyes closed suddenly as he bent over his work. A low gasp caught in his throat. No . . . *no*! He bit his shaking lower lip. He was in a corner, everyone was surrounding him, pushing him, demanding.

"I have heard that Louisa Harper is being kept in her house until this situation is cleared up. For myself, I believe that there is no other way. Certainly, she cannot face anyone in the street while the matter goes unsettled."

Stop looking at me! Robby's mind erupted, still working, head down, fingers unable to do more than fumble and slip.

"I spoke to young Jim Bonney," said Matthew Coles. "He agreed with me that your decision to face Benton was the only one possible under the circumstances. However, he also said that, if he were in your place, he would have ended the situation immediately."

Robby swallowed with effort. "Easy for him to talk," he said, without looking up. "He doesn't have to do it."

He didn't even have to look up to know the expression on his father's face. It was the one that said as clearly as if words were spoken—What has that to do with what we are discussing?

"Sir?" his father asked.

"Nothing," Robby said.

"*Sir?*" Urgency now; bilked authority.

Robby felt the cold shudder running down his back and across his stomach.

"I said it was easy for him to talk," he repeated, holding his voice tightly in check, "he doesn't have to put on a—" his throat moved convulsively. "He doesn't have to face Benton."

"I fail to see . . ." His father left the question a challenge hanging in the air.

Robby looked up quickly and forced himself to stare straight into his father's eyes. The two of them looked at each other across the shop.

"Father," Robby said, tensely, "Benton has been in the Rangers, he's killed *thirteen* men—"

"I fail, sir, to see what this has to do with the situation at hand," Matthew Coles interrupted, his voice rising steadily to the end of the sentence.

No, you wouldn't!—the words tore at Robby's mind but he didn't have the strength to speak them aloud. He lowered his head and went back to the pistol, screwing on the walnut stock with tense, jerky movements.

"Sir, I'm beginning to wonder just what you're trying to say to me," Matthew Coles challenged, putting down the Winchester barrel with a determined thud.

Robby shook his head. "Nothing. I—"

"Sir?"

He shook his head again. "It's nothing, father." He felt his heart start pounding heavily.

"Sir, I demand an explanation!"

"I told you I'd do it!" Robby shouted, head jerked up so suddenly it made his neck muscles hurt. "Now leave me alone, will you!"

He couldn't seem to get the lump out of his throat. He kept swallowing futilely while his fingers shook helplessly on the Colt parts. He kept his eyes down, sensing the look his father was directing toward him.

Rigid control; that was the sound in his father's voice when he spoke again. The sort of rigid control that only a lifetime of practice could achieve; the sort of control based upon unyielding will.

"I have already accepted your statement to that effect," said Matthew Coles flatly. "It is no longer a question of doing or not doing, it is a question of time. Let me remind you, sir, that it is not only the honor of your intended bride that is at stake. Your own honor, too, as well as the honor of our family name, is at stake." Pause, a brief sound of metal clicking on metal.

"The next few days will determine the future of that honor," said Matthew Coles.

There was silence in the shop then, a heavy, ominous absence of sound, broken only occasionally by the slight clicking sounds of his father's work, the infrequent insect-like gasp of the small files. Robby Coles sat numbly, working on the pistol. Another chance was gone; he was in deeper yet. Every time he wanted to bring up the point of whether he should face Benton at all, his father or someone would make it clear that this point was not even in question, that the only thing that mattered now was—*when*?

Robby looked up cautiously at his father but Matthew Coles was studiedly absorbed in his work. For a long moment, Robby looked at the hard features that seemed chipped from granite—a deep blow for each eye, several harsh cuts for the large dominant nose, one long, unhesitating blow for the straight, unmoving mouth.

Then he looked back to his work. While he finished putting the Colt together with quick, agitated hand motions, he thought of Louisa being kept in the house because of what had happened.

The more he thought of it, the more it bothered him. She was his girl; he loved her and wanted to marry her. It *was* his job to defend her; nothing anyone said could change that, no argument could refute it.

And, after all, no one really wanted to see him die. His father hadn't raised him twenty-one years just to push him into being killed. O'Hara didn't have any reason to want Robby dead. All the people in town had no grudge against him. It was simply that they all expected him to defend the honor of his woman and Louisa was his woman. Either he stood up for her or he lost her for good and, with her, his self-respect. It was as simple as that; the thought struck him forcibly.

It was strange how this different approach to the matter seemed to pour courage, strength, into him. Louisa was his woman. He loved her and he'd fight for her. That was his responsibility, his duty. Louisa was his intended bride, it was his job to—

The clicking of the trigger made Robby's flesh crawl.

He found himself suddenly, the assembled Colt held tensely in his right hand, his finger closed over the trigger.

With a spasmodic movement, he shoved the pistol away from himself and it banged down on the bench.

"Be careful!" Matthew Coles snapped.

Robby hardly heard his father. He sat shivering, his eyes fixed to the heavy, glinting form of the Colt, in his mind the hideous impression that, somehow, it was Benton's pistol and that he'd repaired it and put it together for Benton and it was in perfect working order now; it could fire, it could shoot a bullet.

It could kill.

Chapter Twelve

When Mrs. Angela DeWitt left the shop, Louisa came back to where her aunt sat writing in the ledger.

"Aunt Agatha?" she asked meekly, standing by the desk, her face drained with nervous worry.

Agatha Winston went on with her figures, her eyes shrewd and calculating behind the spectacles, her pen running crabbed hen-tracks of numbers across the lined page.

"Aunt Agatha?"

Agatha Winston's eyes closed shut. Beneath the mouse-fuzz of her mustache, her pinched mouth grew irked. Slowly, decisively, she put down the pen.

"What is it, Louisa?" she asked in the flinted tone that she conceived to be one of patience and forbearing.

Louisa stammered. "Aunt Agatha . . . *please*," she said. "May I—"

The jade eyes were hidden behind quickly lowered lids and Agatha Winston cut off the appearance of the world.

"You may *not* go home," she said, concisely. "There is much too much work to be done."

Louisa bit nervously at her finger, eyes pleading and lost.

"Heaven only knows," her aunt continued, "I ask little enough of your mother and yourself in return for the help I give you freely, with Christian affection." Agatha Winston sighed, head shaking once. "I'm tired, Louisa," she said. "I would like nothing better than to retire . . . and live on my small savings. But, for your mother's sake and for your own . . ." another sigh, ". . . I go on working. Asking *nothing* in return but a little help in the shop a few days out of the week." She fixed an accusing look upon her niece. "Is that so much to ask?" she said. "Is that so—stop that!"

Louisa jerked the moist, chewed knuckle from her lips and swallowed nervously.

"Is it, Louisa?" asked her aunt.

"No, Aunt Agatha, it . . . isn't that. I like to help you in the shop but . . ." She bit her lower lip and couldn't help the tear that wriggled from beneath her right eyelid and trickled down her cheek. "They all look at me so," she said, brokenly.

"And what would you like to do?" her aunt challenged. "Go home? Hide away as if you had something to be ashamed of?"

"No, Aunt Agatha, it isn't—"

"You might just as well confess your guilt as do that!"

Louisa's mouth twitched. "G-guilt?" she murmured, eyes wide and frightened.

"Yes," her aunt said. "Guilt. Is that what you want people to think; that you have something to be ashamed of?"

"*No*, Aunt Agath—"

"That's all there is to it," stated Agatha Winston firmly. "We have nothing to hide and we will not hide."

Louisa stared helplessly at her aunt.

"Let John Benton hide his face!" Agatha Winston said angrily. "Not us." She glared at Louisa, then picked up her pen. "Now . . . kindly take care of the shop until I finish my work."

Louisa still stood watching until her aunt looked up again, dark eyes commanding. "Well?" said her aunt.

Louisa turned and walked slowly down the length of the counter. She stopped at the front of the shop and looked out the window at the sunlit square.

She stared bleakly at the reversed letters painted on the glass—MISS WINSTON'S LADIES APPAREL. Then her eyes focused again beyond the letters and she looked at the plank sidewalk, the dirt square, the shops across the way. She looked a while at the motionless peppermint-stick pole in front of Jesse Willmark's Barber Shop. She thought of the look Jesse had given her when she passed him that morning with her aunt. The memory made her breath catch.

Then she saw a horseman ride by and look into the shop and she turned away quickly, her cheeks coloring embarrassedly. She hoped the man didn't see her blush. The way he *looked* at her . . .

She stood with her back to the window a long time, feeling a strange quiver in her body. She reached up and brushed away a tear that dripped across her cheek. Why did everybody look at her that way?

All during the last sale, Mrs. DeWitt had kept staring like that, always turning down her gaze a little too late to hide the curious brightness in her eyes. Never once did she say a word about the situation Louisa knew she was thinking about. She talked about shifts and stockings and corsets as if there were nothing else on her mind. And, all the time, her eyes kept probing up, then down, as if she were attempting to penetrate Louisa's mind and ferret out its secrets.

All through the sale, Louisa had tried to smile, to repeat the things about the merchandise her aunt had taught her. *Oh, yes this is what every woman back East is wearing now. This is delicate but completely sturdy. I think you'll find it will not bind or roll. This is the best material of its type on the market.* Words repeated in a nervous voice, when all the time she wanted to run away and hide.

Louisa glanced over her shoulder again and saw that there was no one in front of the shop. She turned back and looked out the window again. Far down in the south end of the square was the shop where Robby worked. Louisa looked in that direction.

All morning she'd been dreadfully afraid that Robby was going to come in and ask her if the story about Benton was really true. Every time she'd heard footsteps in the doorway or heard hoofbeats out front, her head had jerked up from whatever she was doing and she'd looked fearfully at the shop entrance, heart pounding suddenly. What would she tell him if he asked? How could she say she lied when Aunt Agatha was right there to hear the confession? She couldn't; she knew she couldn't.

He'd just have to stay away from her until everyone forgot about that silly story. They couldn't keep thinking about it forever. As long as they left her alone, it would be all right. She wished she could stay in the house until the story *was* forgotten. She didn't like people staring at her like that. It was terrible the way people gossiped and talked. All Louisa wanted to do was keep out of everyone's way until things were back to normal again.

Louisa started suddenly at the footsteps in the doorway and her body tightened apprehensively as she turned to see who it was.

Mrs. Alma Cartwright came waddling to the counter, hurriedly erasing from her plump face the curious look that had crossed it when she saw Louisa standing there.

"How are you, my dear?" she asked.

Louisa smiled faintly. "Well, thank you," she said.

"And your dear mother?" Mrs. Cartwright asked, sheep eyes looking quizzical.

Louisa swallowed and managed another smile. "Well," she said, "thank you, Mrs. Cartwright."

Mrs. Cartwright looked toward the back of the shop with forced casualness. "Oh, there's your aunt," she said, obviously disappointed that she wasn't alone with Louisa. "How *do*, Miss Winston."

Agatha Winston raised her head, smiled a merchant-to-buyer smile, nodded once, then returned grimly to her figures.

"May I . . . help you?" Louisa asked.

The gaze of her customer stabbed back at her. A smile was arranged on Mrs. Cartwright's puffy lips.

"I'd like to get a shirtwaist, my dear," she said. "Silk. For my girl. She's sixteen next week, you know."

"Oh," Louisa said, trying to sound pleasantly surprised.

She could almost feel the portly woman's eyes on her back as she fingered through the stack of shirtwaists in the drawer. A prickling sensation coursed her back, making her shudder. She drew in a quick breath and turned.

"No silk, Mrs. . . . . Cartwright," she finished weakly as the older woman forced the look of a buying customer on her face again.

"Oh. I'm sorry to hear that," said Mrs. Cartwright. "Well . . . perhaps . . . cotton?"

Louisa put the shirtwaist on the counter and stood there restively while the woman fingered it distractedly.

"This is the f-inest type sold in the market," Louisa said without expression. "You'll . . ."

She stopped as Mrs. Cartwright looked at her. The plump woman couldn't hide the look in her eyes. Aware of it, she stopped trying. She directed a furtive glance at Miss Winston, then smiled sadly.

"My dear girl," she said, behind the sympathy a probing inquisitiveness, "I've heard about this . . . terrible thing and I'm . . . I'm so shocked."

Louisa couldn't speak at first. She felt the heat licking up her cheeks again and had to press her lips together to keep them from shaking. She wanted to turn and run away but she knew she couldn't so she just stood there staring wordlessly, feeling Mrs. Cartwright's beady eyes on her, attempting to reflect compassion but conveying only a hungry curiosity.

"I'll ask my . . . my aunt to ah-show you another kind of—" she faltered, then turned away abruptly.

"But my dear, this is—"

Her skirt rustled noisily as she hurried up the counter, trying vainly to keep the hot tears from spilling any faster across her flushed cheeks.

"Aunt . . . A-Agatha," she sobbed.

Agatha Winston looked up suddenly, face a blank of consternation.

"What on earth . . ." she started, then stopped, her dark eyes staring at Louisa's anguished face.

"*Please*," Louisa begged, "I . . . I . . ." She couldn't finish.

Agatha Winston glanced up at the customer, then back at her trembling niece. "Go in the back room," she said. "*Quickly.*"

As Louisa stumbled away, cutting off a choking sob, Miss Winston moved in firm strides down the counter.

"I'm so sorry, Mrs. Cartwright," she said in a politely brittle voice. "Now what were we looking at?"

Mrs. Cartwright glanced back toward where Louisa was entering the back room.

"What did I say?" she asked. "My dear Miss Winston, I had no intention of—"

"It's nothing, nothing," Miss Winston assured hastily, plucking up the shirtwaist. "She's just a little upset. Is this what we're interested in today? Now this material is woven by the finest New England lo—"

She stopped talking and glared at Mrs. Cartwright who was looking toward the back of the shop again and acting upset.

"Mrs. Cartwright?" she asked.

The large woman looked at her, head shaking sadly. "Oh, my dear Miss Winston," she proclaimed, "my heart goes out to that poor girl."

Miss Winston stiffened. "I beg your pardon?" she said.

Again, Mrs. Cartwright glanced toward the back room. Then she leaned over the counter.

"Do you really think she should . . . wait counter when . . ." She gestured futilely. "Well . . ."

"Mrs. Cartwright, I'm afraid I do not know what you are talking about," Miss Winston enunciated slowly, torn between rising anger and the unquestioning demeanor she believed all customers merited.

Mrs. Cartwright looked unhappy. "Oh, my dear," she said in a sort of joyous agony at being involved in this moment. "We're all lambs in the Lord's flock. When one of us is led astray . . ."

She didn't finish. *Lambs*?—Miss Winston thought—led *astray*? Her eyes grew harder still behind her forgotten spectacles.

"Mrs. Cartwright, I'll thank you for an—"

"Oh, my dear Miss Winston. I feel nothing but sympathy for your poor dear niece. I would not for the world—"

"Mrs. Cartwright, what are you talking about?" Miss Winston demanded, putting aside, for the moment, the role of courteous vendor.

Mrs. Cartwright put her ample hand on the unresponsive fingers of Miss Winston.

"I know all about it," she whispered. "And it has made my heart go out to that poor, dear girl."

"What, exactly, do you know?" Miss Winston asked,

face beginning to go slack now with the rising fear that she did not know everything.

Mrs. Cartwright looked around, looked back.

"About the baby," she whispered. "The—"

"What!" Miss Winston's virginal body lurched in shock, her fingers jerking out from beneath the moist warmth of Mrs. Cartwright's hand. "What are you talking about! Are you intimating that Louisa is—"

Her hands jerked into bone-jutting fists. "Oh!" she said, absolutely dumbfounded.

Mrs. Cartwright drew back in alarm. "What have I—?"

"I don't know where you heard this vicious gossip, Mrs. Cartwright!" Agatha Winston said, eyes burning with vengeful light, "but, let me end it now—right this very moment! It is not true, Mrs. Cartwright, it is not true at all! I'm shocked that you should believe such a terrible thing of my niece! Shocked, Mrs. Cartwright, *shocked*!"

"Oh, my dear Miss—"

"No. No. I don't want to hear anymore!" Miss Winston blinked as a wave of dizziness rushed over her. Her hands clutched at the counter edge. "Please leave," she muttered. "Please, leave my shop."

"*Oh . . .*" Miss Cartwright moaned, face a wrinkle of dismay.

Miss Winston turned away. "Please," she begged. "*Please*."

When a shaken Miss Cartwright had retreated from the shop, an equally shaken Miss Agatha Winston found her unsteady way to the rear of the shop, throat constricted, eyes stark with premonition.

Louisa drew back in fright when she saw her aunt's face.

"Aunt Agatha," she whispered.

She gasped aloud as the clawing hand of her aunt clamped over her wrist.

"Tell me!" commanded Agatha Winston, her face terrible. "Is it true?"

Louisa shrank back. "What?" she asked, weakly.

"You had better tell me the truth!"

Louisa started sobbing again. "What?" she asked. "*What,* A-Aunt Agatha?"

Agatha Winston spoke slowly, teeth clenched. "*Are you with child?*"

Louisa gasped and stared blankly at her aunt, a heavy throbbing at her temples, legs shaking. She cried out suddenly as her aunt's hard fingers dug into her wrist.

"Answer me!" Agatha Winston cried, almost hysterically, her face mottled with an ugly rage.

"No!" Louisa sobbed. "No, I'm not. I'm not!"

A moment more did the two look at each other.

"Is that the truth?" Agatha Winston demanded tensely.

"Yes," Louisa insisted, tearfully. "*Yes.*"

Miss Winston released her niece's wrist and sank down weakly on a stool, chest heaving with breath, in her lap, her hands trembling impotently.

"Dear Lord," she muttered hoarsely. "*Dear Lord,*" her gaunt throat moving as she swallowed.

Louisa stood nearby, her body twitching with deep, unheard sobs. She wanted to run away but she was afraid to. Her mind swam with confused fears. With *child?*— she thought in a panic. Dear God, what was *happening*? She felt as if she were lost and helpless in a strange pit of terrors.

"Someone will pay for this," she heard her aunt muttering to herself. "Someone will *pay.*"

That was when they heard bootfalls in the shop entrance.

Louisa glanced over her shoulder to see who it was. Abruptly, she shrank back, eyes stark with fright, a gasp clutching at her throat. Instinctively, she drew to one side, away from the back room doorway.

Agatha Winston looked up, nerves about unstrung. "What is it now?" she hissed.

"It's . . . it—it's *him*!" Louisa whispered frantically.

Agatha Winston stood up quickly and stepped to the doorway.

Her thin nostrils flared, a calcification of outrage ran down her back. Hurriedly, she stepped away from the doorway.

"Stay back here," she ordered. "Don't move." Her agitated hands flew to her gray hair, to her skirt.

"Stay here," she said again, then moved out of the room and went behind the counter.

John Benton took off his hat as she approached him. He nodded his head politely and waited until she'd reached him.

"Afternoon, ma'm," he said then. "Are you Miss Winston?"

Her face was like stone. "I am," she said, controlling herself.

"My name is John Benton," he told her. "I—"

"I know your name," she said, coldly, wondering why she didn't erupt in his face. She would not admit nor even recognize the fact that she was afraid.

"You're Louisa Harper's aunt, aren't you?" Benton asked.

She said nothing. She swallowed the lump in her throat and stared at him, a trembling in her. She couldn't say anything but she wouldn't answer his questions anyway.

The politeness seemed to drift from Benton's face like a veil of smoke. His smile faded. "I'd like to speak to your niece," he said, softly.

"She is not here," said Agatha Winston.

Benton looked mildly confused. "What?" he said.

"My niece is not here," said Miss Winston slowly.

"Her mother said she was here," Benton answered.

Miss Winston's face lost color and she pressed together her trembling lips. Then she said, "Good day, Mister Benton."

He looked curiously at her hard, unyielding face. Then he glanced toward the back of the shop. "Miss Winston," he said, "I believe I saw your niece when I came in."

Miss Winston shuddered with repressed fury. "She is not here," she said, tensely.

"Now, look here," Benton said. "What are you—"

"Good *day*, Mister Benton."

"Look here, Miss . . ." He gestured. ". . . Winston," he finished, remembering after a momentary lapse. "I came into town because there's some fool story goin' around that—"

"Will you leave my shop or do I have to call the sheriff?" Miss Winston shuddered, remembering suddenly that Sheriff Wilks was out of town for the week, taking a prisoner to the city.

Benton still didn't understand. "Look here, Miss Winston," he said, "I came here because—"

"Get out of here!" The control was suddenly gone; Miss Winston's face grew dark with rage again.

Benton didn't even change expression at her hysterical demand. He stood there looking incredulously at her while, outside, on the plank sidewalk, a passing couple stopped and listened.

"Look, I've had about enough of this—"

Benton stopped talking. Miss Agatha Winston was headed for the back of the shop, her dark skirts rustling angrily. She turned the counter edge and came stamping down the length of the shop.

At the door, she stopped and turned, ignoring the couple who moved on awkwardly, trying to act as if they'd seen nothing.

"Get out of here, you . . . !" The proper word escaped her. Miss Winston pointed one shaking finger out at the square.

A moment more, John Benton looked at her uncomprehendingly. Then he made a sound of complete bewilderment, slapped on his Stetson, and walked out of the shop.

Outside, he turned impulsively.

"Listen, will you tell your niece to—"

The banging of the slammed door cut off his words. John Benton stood there looking a little dazed as Miss Agatha Winston drew down the dark shades of her shop and shut him away.

Chapter Thirteen

enton moved for his horse, not seeing the couple that stared at him, whispering between themselves. His face was tight with confusion as he swung up onto the saddle and drew Socks around. He started across the square for St. Virgil Street.

Then, halfway there, he pulled his mount around and headed for the small shop at the south end of the square. He'd try Robby then; maybe he could talk a little sense to a man. That woman—good God above! Benton shook his head amazedly, thinking about the way Miss Winston had acted. Maybe the Reverend was right, maybe this thing was getting a little bigger than it should. If it weren't, he would have ridden right back to the ranch and forgotten about it. But . . . well, he was here; he might as well try to end the thing if he could.

But with Robby, not with that Winston woman. Benton hissed slowly to himself. What a one *she* was.

In front of the shop, Benton reined up and dismounted. He tied Socks to the rack, then ducked under the bar and stepped up onto the plank sidewalk.

As he entered the small shop, it seemed to be empty. His gaze moved over the sun-speckled benches, the pistols and rifles hanging on the walls, the glass case on the front counter. That was a good-looking Colt there with its white-bone stock and shiny new metal. Benton felt the slight flexing in his fingers that came whenever he saw the well-made symmetry of the pistol he knew so well. It was so habitual, he hardly noticed it. His gaze drifted over the other pistols in the case.

He was looking at a Smith and Wesson .44 caliber six-shooter when Matthew Coles came out of the back room. Benton looked up at the sound of footsteps and met the glare of the older man.

Mr. Coles walked quickly to the counter. "State your business," he said curtly.

There was a slight wrinkling of skin around Benton's eyes as he looked inquisitively at Matthew Coles.

"Is your son here?" he asked.

"He is not."

Benton met the older man's stony look without change of expression. "Where can I find him?" he asked.

Matthew Coles was silent.

"I said—where can I find your son?" Benton repeated as if he hadn't noticed the slight.

"When the time comes," said Matthew Coles, "he will find you."

"Now, wait a minute," Benton said, the tanned skin tensing across his cheek bones. "Let's get this straight. This fool story about me and—"

"I am not interested in stories," Matthew Coles declared.

Benton took a deep, controlling breath. "I think you better be interested in this one," he said.

Mr. Coles said nothing.

"Listen, Coles, this thing isn't funny anymore."

"It is, decidedly, not funny," said Matthew Coles, his gaze dropping for a searching instant to John Benton's left hip, then raising as instantly, assured. "You have presumed too much on your popularity, Mister Benton. That was a mistake."

"If you're talkin' about that girl, you're all wrong,"

Benton said. "I never even *spoke* to her since I been in Kellville."

The thinnest hint of a smile played at the corners of Matthew Coles' mouth. "You don't have to come explaining to me," he said.

Benton strained forward a moment, body tensed, something in his eyes making Matthew Coles draw back, slack-faced.

Benton swallowed, controlling himself with difficulty.

"Where's your son?" he asked, tensely. "I want to see him."

"He does not wish to see you," Coles said.

Repressed anger seemed to ripple beneath the surface of Benton's face. "Listen, Coles," he said, "I came into town to end this fool story, not to be pushed around."

"I'm sure you didn't," said Matthew Coles, stiffly. "However, since you are no longer man enough to wear a gun you cannot very well command respect, can you?"

Again the tightening of Benton's muscles; at his sides, his fingers twitching.

"You're an old man," he said, softly. "But don't overplay it, Coles, don't overplay it."

Mindless rage flared up lividly in Matthew Coles' face. "Get out of my shop!" he ordered.

"My pleasure," Benton said, turning on his heel and starting for the door.

"You will hear from us, sir!" Coles shouted after him.

"I'm sure I will," Benton said, without looking back.

Then, at the door, he turned.

"Now listen to me, old man," he said, warningly. "Stop pushing this damn thing. If you don't, somebody's goin' to get hurt, understand? You've got a good kid. Don't push him into somethin' he's not up to. I've got no grudge against Robby and he's got no reason to hold any grudge against me. Understand? None at all. Tell him that." Benton's face hardened in an instant. "And *stay away!*"

The look was gone as quickly as it came. "I don't want trouble from anyone, Coles," Benton said. "Not from anyone."

Matthew Coles stood shaking with wordless rage behind the counter, staring at Benton's back as he went out of the shop, stepped off the plank walk, and untied his horse.

For a long time he stood there in the silence of the shop, trembling with impotent fury, his shallow chest rising and falling strainedly.

Then he went to the back of his shop and looked through the collection of new pistols for the one his son would use to kill John Benton.

Chapter Fourteen

Why do you *think* he left the Rangers?" Jesse Willmark challenged his suds-faced customer. " 'Cause he got *tired* of it? No. 'Cause he was too old? No. I'll tell you why." He leaned forward, gesturing with the sun-reflecting razor. "Because he turned yella, that's why."

"Couldn't say," the customer muttered.

"Look, ya remember the time—'bout a year or so ago, I guess it was—when they was gettin' up a posse to chase Tom Labine? You remember that?" Jesse asked, setting up his coup de grace.

"Yeah. What about it?"

"I'll tell you what about it," Jesse broke in intently. "They asked Benton t'help them. Sheriff Wilks don't know a dang thing about trailin' or 'bout anythin' for that matter. So they asked Mister John Benton t'help them out. You think he would? The hell he would! Can't do it, he says, cut me out. *Why*? Why wouldn't he help out his neighbors?"

"Maybe he didn't want to," the customer suggested.

"Hell, man," Jesse said, "I'll tell ya why he wouldn't do it." He raked the razor across the man's soap-stubbled cheek with a practiced gesture. "He was yella, that's why. He didn't have the guts to ride another posse. His nerves is gone and that's a fact."

"Could be," the customer said.

Jesse wiped the beard-flecked lather off his razor. He rubbed his pudgy fingers over the customer's cheek, rubbing in the warm soap.

"I'll tell ya somethin' else," he said, eyes narrowing. "It happens to all o' them. I don't know how—or why—but one day—" he snapped his fingers, "like that—they're yella."

He started shaving again. "They go on year after year shootin' 'em down like sittin' ducks," he said, "then, one day—*bang*—they turn yella; they get scared o' their own shadda. It's nerves what it is. Ain't no man alive can go on like that year after year without losin' his nerve."

He nodded grimly.

"And that's what happened to Benton," he said. "Mind, I ain't takin' nothin' away from the man. He was a big lawman in his day, brave as they come, quick on the draw. Course he never was as big as they painted him but—" he shrugged, "—he was a good lawman. But that don't mean he can't turn yella. That don't mean he didn't. He did—and that's a fact."

He shaved away beard from the customer's throat.

"Hard to say," the customer said, looking at the paint-flaked ceiling.

"All right," Jesse said, wiping off the razor edge again. "If he's still brave as he was, why don't he wear a gun, answer me that?"

The customer said he didn't know.

"Because he's *scared* to pack one!" Jesse exclaimed as if it were a great truth he had to convey. "No man goes around without a gun less'n he's too scared to use it. Ain't that true?"

The customer shrugged. "It's a point," he conceded.

"Sure as hell is a point!" Jesse said. "Benton don't pack no gun 'cause he's scared to back hisself up with hot lead."

The customer grunted, then sat up as Jesse adjusted the head rest.

"Then to go and do what he done," Jesse said, shaking his head. "Him a married man and all."

The customer could see the front door in the mirror.

"Jesse," he said, softly.

"I'll tell ya, it sure surprised the hell outta me," Jesse said, stropping the razor. "It's a bad thing when a man starts goin' down."

"Jesse." A warning; but too soft. The customer sat stiffly in the chair, trying not to look at the mirror.

"Specially a man like Benton," said Jesse. "Him bein' such a big lawdog and all. First he yellas out, then he starts playin' around with—"

"*Jesse.*"

Jesse broke off and looked at the customer. "What is—?" he started to ask, then saw how the man was looking into the mirror. His throat tightened abruptly as he glanced up and saw the reflection of John Benton, tall and grim-faced, standing in the doorway.

Jesse didn't dare turn. He stood there, staring helplessly into the mirror, his throat moving as he tried to swallow fear.

"I'd keep my mouth shut unless I knew what I was talkin' about," Benton said coldly.

Then he turned and was gone and a white-faced Jesse whirled to exclaim, "Honest, Mister Benton, I didn't—!"

But Benton was gone. Jesse hurried to the doorway, razor in shaking hand, and watched Benton mount his horse.

Then he turned back hurriedly to his customer, a look of uncontrollable dread on his face.

"Jesus," he said, hollowly. "You don't think he'll do anything to me, do you?"

The customer looked blandly at the slack-faced barber in the mirror.

"You don't think he'll come after me, do you?" Jesse asked, getting weaker. "Do you?"

The barest suggestion of a smile. "How can he?" the customer asked. "He's yella."

Chapter Fifteen

David James O'Hara could be a very impressive young bully when he tried. His face was lean and hard beneath a short crop of reddish hair. He moved with a catlike swiftness, swaggered convincingly, swore and gambled, wore a Colt .44 low on his hip, thonged to his leg, and spoke deprecatingly of every gunman who ever rode within a hundred miles of Kellville.

There had been a few shootings in the little town but, somehow, Dave O'Hara was never around when they occurred. He was twenty-three years old and still believed in his own courage because it had never been tried. The one man who had challenged O'Hara had left town without fighting and thus strongly increased O'Hara's opinion of himself.

It was about two-thirty in the afternoon. O'Hara was sitting at a back table in the Zorilla talking to Joe Sutton who was losing at cards and arguing.

"You kiddin', Sutton?" O'Hara said, putting down his card with a slap. "He's cold-footed. If he ain't scared o' Robby, why don't he wear a gun?"

Sutton swallowed. "Well, why don't he?" O'Hara challenged.

"He wouldn't say," Sutton answered.

"Y'mean you asked him?" O'Hara looked up in surprise from his hand.

"Yeah," said Joe Sutton, "I ast him yestiday mornin' but—"

"But he wouldn't tell ya," O'Hara finished. "Course he wouldn't tell ya. Think a man's gonna come right out and admit he's yella? Play your card."

Sutton licked his lips and looked worriedly at his hand, deeply troubled by the impending crumble of faith.

"Well, you should've seen him," he said then, looking up. "You should've seen him do the border roll and . . . and the shift. You know, tossin' his iron from one hand to the other. It was so fast I couldn't hardly see it." He swallowed at O'Hara's unresponsive stare. "That's how fast it was," he repeated weakly.

"So what does that mean?" O'Hara asked. "Anybody can do tricks with a gun when they's no one facin' 'em. I'd like t'see him do gun tricks with another guy throwin' down on him."

Sutton swallowed. "Well . . ." he said but that was all. He swallowed again and played the wrong card.

"Him and that cocklebur outfit o' his," O'Hara muttered. "He's no better'n a sheep herder." His fingers tightened on the dog-eared cards. "Livin' on his repitation, that's what he's tryin' t'do. Thinks he can play around with any girl he wants cause he has a repitation. Well, Robby'll show 'im."

Joe Sutton shook his head. "Y'think he'll really go after Benton?" he asked.

O'Hara pointed a finger at Sutton. "You bet ya damn life he will," he said. "Then we'll see how good ol' lawdog Benton is. Bet he won't even put on a gun!"

"What else could he do?" Sutton asked, faintly.

"Hide, most likely," O'Hara said. "Hide on his ranch like a yella hound."

Sutton looked pained. Then he looked up and said, "Uh-oh. Watch out."

O'Hara looked toward the doors which were just swinging shut behind John Benton's tall form.

"Whataya mean, watch out?" he said, a little more loudly than he'd intended. "I ain't afraid o' him."

Benton glanced toward them, then walked to the bar, his face hard with anger.

"Pat," he greeted the bartender flatly as the older man came up to him.

"The usual, Mister Benton?"

"Yeah."

Benton could hear the voice of O'Hara in back saying something about a shirt-tail outfit as he watched the amber whiskey being poured.

"What's goin' on around here, Pat?" he asked then, looking up.

"You mean about Robby and—"

"Yeah. What the hell's the matter with everybody? One day and it seems like half the town's out to get me."

"Well, now," Pat said casually, "little folks always like to try'n topple the big ones, it seems. It's human nature."

Benton smiled ruefully. "I'm just a little feller, Pat," he said. "No reason for anyone to—"

Abruptly, he stopped talking and glanced again toward the back table, hearing the words *cold-footed* spoken loudly. He squinted a little at the young man sitting in the shadows. He saw young Joe Sutton's face twitch in the repression of a smile, then he looked back at the bar. He picked up the glass and took a swallow.

"Who's that in the black shirt?" he asked, quietly.

"Dave O'Hara," Pat told him.

"Don't know him." Benton drank some more.

"Local loudmouth," Pat said. "He don't amount to nothin'."

Benton grunted, then put down his glass. "Pat?" he said.

"What's that, Mister Benton?"

Benton took a deep breath and let it out slowly. "What's happening around here, Pat? What's the latest on this . . ." he gestured vaguely with one hand, ". . . this thing?"

Pat made a sound of wry amusement. "You wouldn't believe it," he said.

Benton thought about the last half hour he'd spent. He thought about Miss Agatha Winston, Mr. Matthew Coles, Jesse Willmark.

"I'd believe it," he said.

"More?" Pat asked and Benton nodded, pushing the glass forward.

Pat looked up from the bottle. "The talk is," he said, "that Robby Coles is gonna come after ya."

Benton looked at him blankly. "Yeah?" he said as if he expected clarification. Then, suddenly, his mouth opened. "You don't—" He put down the glass. "You don't mean with a gun?" he asked, incredulously.

Pat shrugged. "That's the talk," he said.

Benton started to say something, then stopped and stared at Pat.

"That's crazy," he said then. "He's fryin' size, for God's sake!"

Pat said nothing. In the silence, they heard O'Hara say, "Come on, let's belly up," and then the scraping back of chair legs and the irregular thump of two pairs of boots across the saloon floor. Benton paid no attention. He kept staring at Pat, his expression still one of disbelief.

"My God," he murmured. "I never thought for a minute that . . ." Slowly, he shook his head. "But that's crazy," he said. "Would . . . would he be fool enough to do that?"

Pat shrugged again. "Couldn't say, Mister Benton," he said. "But if enough people push him . . ." He didn't finish but moved up the bar to where O'Hara and Sutton stood.

"So that's what his old man meant," Benton murmured to himself, remembering Matthew Coles' words. "My God, I never . . ."

He fingered at the glass restlessly, his face a mask of worried concentration reflected back to him in the big mirror. He shook his head concernedly.

He didn't hear the deprecating chuckle that O'Hara made. The first thing he did hear vaguely was something that sounded like, "What're ya *scared* of? *He* ain't got no gun on." But he wasn't sure that's what it was as he glanced down the bar at the two young men. John Benton wasn't used to having people discuss him slightingly when he was around and he couldn't quite believe that such a thing was happening now.

He saw the movement of Sutton's throat and how he stared into his drink suddenly. Then the insulting blue eyes of O'Hara met Benton's. Benton looked back to his drink immediately. There were enough things to worry about already. He took a deep breath and drank some of the whiskey. It threaded its hot way down his throat. Good God, what *now*? Bond was right, the thing was serious. But how did it get that way so quick? Everybody must really believe that he spoke to Louisa Harper. My God, what did they think he *said* to her? The barber talked about "playing around"; is that what they thought he was trying to do with the Harper girl?

Benton's broad chest rose quickly as he drew in a worried breath. It was bad, it was really bad. This was the first time anything even remotely like it had happened in his—

The chuckling again; unmistakable. Benton heard the words *cold-footed* again, obviously spoken, and something jerked in his stomach muscles. He looked over quickly and saw O'Hara looking at him again. Benton felt the muscles drawing in along his arms, the rising flutter of pulse beat in his wrists. Without a sound, he put down his glass, drew his boot from the rail, and started walking along the bar.

Sutton stepped back as he approached. A failing smile faltered on the young man's lips as he watched Benton with his dark, intent eyes.

Benton stopped a few feet from O'Hara, his arms hanging loosely at his sides.

"You got somethin' to say to me?" he asked, quietly.

A look of instinctive fear paled O'Hara's face. He pushed it away and forced back his habitual expression of arrogant assurance. But, when he spoke, the slight trembling of his voice belied the look.

"No," he said. "I ain't got nothin' t'say to you."

Benton's mouth tightened a little.

"If you do," he said, "say it to me, not to your friend here."

Sutton opened his mouth as if to assure Benton that O'Hara wasn't his friend but he said nothing.

"If I got anything to say, I'll say it," O'Hara replied trying to look belligerent.

"Good," Benton said. "That's fine."

Then he saw the slight dipping of O'Hara's gaze.

"No, I don't have a gun on," he said abruptly. "But don't let that bother you." He could feel the anger rising inside him like a fire, creeping along his arteries and veins. His temper was going; he was getting sick and tired of people looking to see if he was armed before they said what they really meant.

"I don't talk to no one who—" O'Hara hesitated momentarily, looking for words a little less insulting, "who don't wear no gun," he finished, realizing then that he couldn't afford to hesitate.

"Listen, *flannel-mouth*," Benton said, "I've had about enough from—"

"Don't call me that!" O'Hara flared up impulsively, his voice rising shrilly. "God damn it, I'll—"

"You'll what!" Benton snapped in a sudden burst of rage. "What!"

O'Hara hesitated a split second, then lunged down for his pistol. Benton's arm shot out.

"*Hold it!*"

They both twitched into immobility and looked across the bar to where Pat had a big army pistol aimed at O'Hara's chest.

"Put it away, boy," Pat ordered. "Would ya draw on an un-armed man?"

The look of sudden surprise on O'Hara's face was changed to one of frustrated rage.

"Sure!" he said, loudly. "Sure! Get a bardog to save ya! You're too yella t'save yourself!"

His voice shook thinly as he raged and, hearing it, the tension seemed to drain off inside Benton. For a moment, he looked at O'Hara without expression. Then a thin smile relaxed his mouth, a brief chuckle sounded in his chest.

"If you ever see me with a gun on," he said, amusedly, "you just say that again."

"I'll never see ya with a gun on!" O'Hara went on, furious at the lost advantage. "You ain't got the guts t'put a gun on!"

Benton turned away casually.

"Robby Coles'll kill ya!" O'Hara said loudly. "He'll *kill* ya, Benton!"

Benton turned back quickly, face tight. "Shut your mouth, boy," he said in quiet menace, "or, by God, I'll belt on a gun right now; is that what you want?"

O'Hara had the self-preserving sense to glare speechlessly at Benton until the tall man had turned away. Joe Sutton watched Benton walk back to where his glass was.

"Thanks Pat," Benton said quietly. "He might've killed me."

"He might've at that," Pat said, pouring.

Benton threw down the new drink. "Well, I'm goin' back to the ranch," he said clearly. "I've had enough for one day."

"What about . . . ?" Pat didn't finish.

"Who, Robby?" Benton shrugged and made a disgusted sound. "The hell with it," he said quietly. "I've done all I'm goin' to do for one day. I'll just stay on my spread till the damn thing blows over. One thing sure." He put down the glass with a gesture of finality. "Robby's not goin' to come after me with a gun. You know that."

Pat said no more but he looked dubious.

When the swinging doors had shut behind Benton, O'Hara looked up.

"Lucky for him he's got a bardog watchin' over him."

"Lucky for you, too," Pat told him.

"But he said—" Joe Sutton started.

"Sure," O'Hara said, bitterly. "Sure, he said he'd belt on a gun. What gun? Did he have one with him? Was he gonna make one outta the air?"

"Oh, shut up, O'Hara," Pat said casually and the young man glared at him, tight mouth trembling.

Sutton looked into his foamy beer. He wasn't sure. He didn't want to believe O'Hara, he wanted to believe that Benton wasn't afraid of anything. And yet O'Hara was right, Benton *didn't* have a gun and it was easy to talk when you had nothing to force you to back yourself up with. And, besides, Benton said he was going back to the ranch. If Robby Coles was out to get him, why did Benton go back to his ranch? And why didn't he wear a gun?

Joe Sutton shook his very young head. He didn't understand.

Chapter Sixteen

Late afternoon. Miss Agatha Winston stalked again, a clicking of dark heels, a snapping rustle of skirt. But where the previous day it had been Davis Street, today it was Armitas. Where the previous day she had been headed, stiff-legged and shocked, for the house of her sister, this day she was, infuriated and vengeance-bound, headed for the house of Matthew Coles. She was still in black, however, she still carried, in one gaunt-handed grip, her black umbrella and, in her eyes, there still burned the fire of inflexible outrage.

At the gate which led to the Coleses' house, Miss Winston paused not a jot but unlatched, shoved, stepped in, and slammed behind. Beneath her marching heels, the gravel crunched and flinched aside, the porch steps echoed with a wooden hollowness, the welcome mat was crushed. Miss Agatha Winston grasped the heavy knocker and hurled it against the thick-paneled door, then stood stiffly in the almost twilight air, waiting for acknowledgment.

A moment passed. Then, inside, a labored trudging of footsteps sounded. The door was drawn open slowly and the care- and time-worn face of Mrs. Coles appeared.

"Miss Winston," she said, her tone caught between polite surprise and apprehension.

"Good afternoon," Miss Winston announced. "Is Mister Coles at home?"

"Why . . . no, he's still at his shop."

Grayish lips pursed irritably. "Is your older son at home?" Miss Winston asked.

"Why, no, Robby is at his father's shop too," said Mrs. Coles.

"Do you expect them home soon?"

Jane Coles swallowed gingerly. "Why . . . yes, they should be home . . . very soon."

"I see. I'd like to wait if you don't mind," said Miss Agatha Winston.

"Oh." Mrs. Coles smiled faintly. "Of course," she said and then, after a moment's hesitation, stepped aside. "Won't you . . . come in, Miss Winston?"

"Thank you." The black-garbed woman entered and stopped in the center of the hallway rug.

"Won't you . . . come into the sitting room?" Jane Coles invited. "They'll be home soon now."

Miss Winston nodded once and walked into the sitting room followed by Mrs. Coles, who walked on the rug as if it were a carpet of eggs.

"Please," said Jane Coles in her nearly inaudible voice, "sit down, Miss Winston."

Miss Winston, with one slowly modulated dip, settled down on the couch edge and, drawing her umbrella to the tip of her black shoes, leaned her hands upon the handle.

Mrs. Coles stood near the hall door, a smile faltering on her lips. She knew exactly what Miss Winston was there for but she could not, for a moment, speak of it. As a result, she stood quietly, a sick churning in her stomach as she tried to smile at the forbidding face of the other woman.

"Would you . . . care for a cup of tea?" she asked, suddenly, embarrassed by the silence.

"No, thank you," said Miss Winston.

Mrs. Coles stood there, looking awkward.

"Please," Miss Winston said, finally, "don't feel obligated.

If you have work to do, please do it. I'll be perfectly all right here."

"Oh." A pleasant smile strained for a moment on the pale-rose features of Matthew Coles' defeated wife. "All right." She swallowed. "They . . . should be home very soon," she assured.

"Yes," said Miss Winston. "Thank you. I'll just wait here."

"All right." Mrs. Coles backed off, smiling, her insides tied in great knots of dreading. "I'll . . . get back to my . . . my work then," she said. Another smile, another almost imperceptible movement of her throat. "If you . . . want anything," she said, "I'll . . . I'll be in the kitchen."

Miss Winston nodded, not having smiled once since she came to the door. She watched the small woman turn and fade out of the room and heard the weary trudge of Mrs. Coles' feet moving down the hall and then the swinging open and shutting of the kitchen door.

She still sat rigidly as before in the silence of the room, her eyes straight ahead, focused only on the resolution of her inner thoughts.

In the hall, the brass-plated pendulum swung in slow, measured arcs and the ticking of the clock tapped metallically at the air. Miss Winston shifted a trifle on the edge of the horsehair couch, her nostrils dilating slightly with an indrawn breath. Her eyes focused a moment on the room and she saw, across from her, a gold-framed family photograph hanging on the wall.

There was Matthew Coles, dominating his family in light and shadow as in actuality—standing, dark-suited, face a Caesar-like cast, the hand he held on the shoulder of his seated wife appearing less as an encouragement of love than as a force pinning her down.

Mrs. Coles sat in stolid patience, on her emotionless face only hints of the charm and beauty that had once been hers. Next to her sat the gangly, freckle-spotted Jimmy

Coles, his discomfort at being stuffed into low-neck clothes clearly visible.

And, behind him, stood Robby, his face sober and youthfully good-looking, both hands resting on the back of his younger brother's chair.

Miss Winston's eyes shifted up again to the imperious challenge of Matthew Coles' face. Fine looking man, she thought, *fine; decent.* Her throat moved and she made haste to ignore the rising flutter of something unwanted by her virginal system. She drew in a tense breath and stared into her thoughts again, stirring up the mud-thick waters of righteous anger.

She was still sitting like that when the two horses came clopping up the alleyway, when the back door opened and shut and the commanding voice of Matthew Coles sounded in the house.

Quiet talking in the kitchen. Then, footsteps. Miss Winston looked up as Mr. Coles crossed the room, hand extended.

"Miss Winston," he said gravely and they shook cold hands. Behind, in the hallway, Robby lingered hesitantly.

"Good afternoon, Mister Coles," Agatha Winston said. Their hands parted.

"Mrs. Coles said that you wish to speak to me."

"To you *and* your son," Miss Winston amended.

Mr. Coles looked into the coal-dark eyes of Miss Agatha Winston and saw a message of rock-like determination there. Then he turned quickly and, without a word, motioned in his son.

Robby entered restively, trying to smile at Miss Winston but failing. He knew why she was there and the thought terrified him.

"Good afternoon . . . Miss Winston," he said, his voice cracking.

She nodded once, recognizing his presence.

"May we sit?" Mr. Coles asked and Miss Winston gestured with one hand. "Please," she said.

Matthew Coles and his son sat down.

"Now," said Mr. Coles, "I believe I know why you're here."

"I'm glad," Miss Winston said, with one curt nod. "I'm glad someone in this town recognizes the gravity of this ugly situation." She was thinking with particular deprecation of the Reverend Omar Bond.

"We have recognized it, Miss Winston," Matthew Coles assured her. "Believe me, ma'm."

Robby sat on the chair, feeling numb, a cold and ceaseless sinking in his stomach. No, he thought. No. It was all he could think. No. No.

"Then I think it's time a course of action was settled upon," said Miss Winston. "This cannot be allowed to go on any further."

"I agree with you," said Matthew Coles. "I agree with you entirely." He nodded grimly, thinking that here was a woman who spoke his language, who thought as a woman *should* think—with clarity, with decision.

"Well, then . . ." said Miss Winston.

"My son, Robert," said Mr. Coles, "realizing that it is his responsibility as your niece's intended husband, has agreed to defend her honor."

Miss Winston nodded in agreement.

"And," Matthew Coles went on, "to use force against Benton unless a complete and public apology is made."

Robby bit his lip. "But, I—" he started, too weakly to be heard. He leaned forward, the blood pounding in his head. He hadn't agreed to anything like that. He watched the two of them with sick eyes as they planned the use of his life.

"Apology?" said Miss Winston with a coldly withdrawn tone.

"Well," Mr. Coles explained, "I am not a man to shirk the truth, ma'm. But neither am I a man to advocate violence unless it is absolutely necessary. Mister Benton was in my shop today disclaiming any responsibility in this matter."

Miss Winston looked shocked. "But you didn't believe him?" she said, tensely.

"Naturally not," Matthew Coles assured her. "However . . . we must allow for all possibilities other than violence, ma'm. I believe John Benton to be guilty as charged. But, if he is willing, before the public eye, to confess his guilt and repent, I . . . see no reason why violence should not be avoided."

Matthew Coles leaned back, thinking himself a quite reasonable and impartial man.

"But if he said he didn't do it," Robby suddenly broke in, "he's not going to apologize!" His voice was nervously excited as he spoke. His hands were cold and shaking in his lap.

"Sir," Matthew Coles declared firmly, offended at this outburst as reflecting on his parenthood, "the conditions as stated are unchangeable. Either Benton admits his guilt and repents . . . or violence must, unavoidably, be used upon him."

Robby felt himself shake as a wave of nausea swept over him. I'm not going to die!—the anguished thought cut through his brain—I'm *not*!

"One moment," Miss Winston started heatedly, "all this talk of admission and, and of apology is no longer reasonable. This afternoon I took my niece home in a near-hysterical state. She will be compelled to remain there until this terrible thing is settled. Not by her mother, not by me but by gossip! She's been driven from the streets by scorn!"

Matthew Coles looked indignant and shocked.

"In my shop this very afternoon," Miss Winston went

on, furiously, "a customer—I won't mention her name—asked me—bold as you please!—if it were true that Louisa was—" she swallowed reticence, withdrawal, ingrained shame of all things physical, "—was with child!" she finished, her voice a whisper of passionate outrage.

Matthew Coles stiffened as though someone had struck him violently across the face. Robby looked suddenly blank.

There was shocked silence a moment, then the low, teeth-clenched voice of Matthew Coles rolling out slowly.

"Naturally," he said, "this puts an entirely new aspect on the situation."

"But . . . but Louisa never said that—" Robby started.

"It no longer matters what Louisa said!" Agatha Winston cried out vehemently. "What matters is that her reputation and the reputation of our entire family is being dragged through the mud!"

Robby flinched at her angry words and stared at Miss Winston speechlessly.

"Unless you stand up for my niece, she'll never be able to lift her head in Kellville again! She will be shamed, her mother will be shamed, and I'll be shamed!" Miss Winston's voice broke and she began sobbing dryly, hoarsely.

"My dear Miss Winston," Matthew Coles said quickly, jumping up from his chair, a fiercely accusing glare thrown at his son.

Miss Winston fought for control, hastily and ashamedly brushing away the hot tears that sprang from her eyes.

"We're shamed, *shamed*!" she sobbed miserably.

From where he sat, motionless and numb, Robby could see the whitened pulsing at his father's jaw, the tense set of his mouth. He looked down at the weeping Miss Winston for a moment. Then, before his father could say a word or look toward him, Robby stood with one wooden motion. He couldn't feel his hands or his feet, only the blood pounding so hard at his temples that he thought his veins would burst and spatter blood across his face.

He didn't know if it was courage or cold, drained terror. But his mind suddenly recognized the situation in all its clarity—Louisa driven into hiding, the town leering at her, picking at her reputation with insulting fingers.

"Don't cry, Miss Winston," he heard a strange, unnatural voice say in his throat.

Miss Agatha Winston looked up at the grim-faced young man and it seemed for a moment to Robby as if both she and his father were old and helpless and that it was up to him alone to settle the matter.

"Louisa will be defended," he heard the words go on as though he stood apart, listening. "Her honor will be defended. I'll stand up for her."

"*When*?" his father asked and it seemed a perfectly reasonable question in that moment, a question spoken from necessity.

"Tomorrow," Robby said. "Tomorrow I will."

His brain seemed to be hanging in a great, icy emptiness, like some crystalline machine suspended in a winter's night, bodiless—clicking and moving of itself, divorced from all fear and trepidation. There was a responsibility to be assumed, nothing else mattered. Manhood required it and he must live or fall by the demand. Tomorrow he would fight John Benton in the only way it could be done.

Robby Coles knew his father was shaking his hand strongly but he didn't feel it and he hardly saw it.

Chapter Seventeen

N o, sir," John Benton said over the supper table that night, "I admit I'm still a tenderfoot when it comes to cattle ranchin' but one thing I do know; you're not goin' to get as strong a cowhorse lettin' 'em graze. Feed 'em grain; they earn it. They're a lot better workers for it."

Lew Goodwill shrugged his thick shoulders. "Well, I guess that's up to you, boss," he said. "Most outfits I rode with, though, let their hosses graze."

Benton took a drink of his hot coffee, then put down the cup. "No, grain makes harder muscles," he said. "Gives 'em more endurance, I know that for a fact."

Julia brought more biscuits to the table and sat back down to her supper without a word. She probed listlessly at her meat, the fork held apathetically in her fingers.

Benton noticed how she toyed with her food and reached across the broad table to put his hand on hers. She looked up with a faint smile.

"Honey, stop worryin'," he told her. "Nothin's goin' to happen."

Her smile was unconvincing. "I hope so," she said.

Merv Linken made a wry face as he chewed his beef. "Ma'm, you ain't got nothin' to fret about. Robby Coles ain't bucklin' on no iron against yore husband." He made a mildly scoffing sound. "That'd be like tryin' t'scratch his ear with his elbow."

Julia tried to appear reassured but was unable to manage it.

"Saw the Reverend ridin' out o' here, this mawnin'," Lew Goodwill said, looking up from his food. "What'd he want?"

Benton always wanted his men to feel as if they were part of the family and, as a result, there were few secrets among them.

"Yeah, what'd that ol' sin-buster want, anyway?" Merv asked, his leathery face deadpan, his light blue eyes fixed on Julia.

"Merv, you stop that," Julia scolded and the deadpan changed to cheerful grinning. Julia tried not to smile back but couldn't keep from it.

"You're a terrible man, Merv Linken," she said, the corners of her mouth forcing down the smile. "There's no hope for you."

"He came out to say I should ride into town and clear it all up," Benton told Lew Goodwill when his wife had finished. "You know the rest."

Lew shook his heavy head. "Darndest thing," he said, "makin' such a fuss over nothin'."

"It's something to them," Benton said. "They're usin' both barrels on me."

"Well . . ." Julia looked worried again. "Well, shouldn't we go in and try to settle it then? We could have the Reverend get everyone together in his house and . . ." She hesitated. ". . . well, clear it up," she finished.

"Honey, I told ya the way they all acted," John told her. "They just about threw me outta town. Even the barber's spreadin' lies about me." He exhaled disgustedly. "Then when that kid, that—what's his name?—O'Hara tried to fill his hand on me . . ." He shook his head grimly. "I've had enough, Julia. I'll just stay out here on the ranch and let 'em all stew in their own juice till they cook themselves."

"But, what if Robby comes after you?"

"Ma." John looked patiently at his wife. "Can you feature that? Can you feature that little feller puttin' on a gun and comin' after me?"

Julia looked down at her plate. "You know what his father is like," she said, quietly. "You know what Mr. Coles said."

"He was riled," Benton said, grinning. "I called him an old man and that bristled him." The two other men chuckled. "No, Coles isn't goin' to push his own boy into the grave," Benton finished.

"I . . . suppose."

Julia still played with her supper, finally putting down the fork altogether and drinking some coffee. Then she got up and brought an apple pie to the table and cut thick slices of it for the three men.

While she cleaned the supper scraps onto the hound dog's plate, she heard the three men talking about bits. None of them sounded concerned, least of all her husband. And Benton wasn't the type of man who hid his worries very effectively.

Julia thought to herself. John was probably right. There was a lot of fuss, yes, but Robby Coles knew John's reputation and couldn't possibly consider trying to fight him with a . . .

But what if he *did*, what if he was *forced* to? Julia stood by the pump, staring across the kitchen at her husband. What if Robby *did* come after him?

Julia Benton closed her eyes suddenly and did the only thing she could think of at the moment. She prayed; but it wasn't out of fear for her husband's life, it was something else.

Chapter Eighteen

t was dark in the room, silent. Out in the breezeless night, crickets rasped like a thousand files grating on metal. A block away, she heard the muffled trotting of a horse as someone rode home late from town. The hoofbeats faded, disappeared, and the curtain of dark silence settled once again over the street, the house, the room in which she lay, sleep-less, on her bed.

In the back bedroom, in the bed so painfully large for her, her mother dozed fitfully, mumbling and whimpering in her sleep. Her husband had been dead eight years now but Elizabeth Harper still slept in the outsize four-poster, cold, restless, and lonely. She had never been quite the same since the funeral. They had, almost literally, buried her in the cemetery with her husband.

At least her spirit was there in the ground with his resting bones. Since his death, she had never been quite up to coping with life; and this affair about Louisa and Benton and Robby Coles and everybody else had completely unhinged her. Weeping, she regarded it, attempted to deal with it, able to think of how simple it would be if her dear husband were alive.

Louisa rolled on her stomach and gazed out moodily at the great tree in the front yard which stood etched against the moonlit sky like a black paper cutout. She rested her chin on her small hands and sighed unhappily.

Now she had to stay in the house until it was all settled. She didn't mind not going to the shop, she liked that part of it. But not being able to do anything else at all, that she didn't like; being cooped up with her doting, moist-eyed mother. And all because of that stupid story.

Louisa rolled on her back abruptly and squirmed irritably on the sheet. She raised up her feet and kicked off the blankets, her flannel gown sliding up her legs with a sighing of cloth as she kicked.

She didn't pull it back down again but lay there in the darkness, feeling the cool air on her flesh. She closed her eyes and tried to summon up the vision of that ride again.

She couldn't. Her aunt had ruined it, ruined everything. Whenever Louisa thought about it now, her aunt's gaunt, accusing face would materialize in her mind, blotting out the dream. She couldn't envision John Benton anymore without summoning up attendant visions of Robby, of Benton's wife, of her mother, her aunt, of the glittering-eyed Mrs. DeWitt, Mrs. Cartwright and all the women who had come to her aunt's shop to see her and gloat and imagine things.

Louisa felt her cheeks getting warm and she turned quickly and pressed her face into the cool pillowcase. Terrible women! She wasn't going to be like them when *she* grew up.

She felt the air settle like cool silk over her bare calves and thighs as she lay there. It was such an awful thing, gossip. All she'd wanted to do was make Robby a little jealous, get him to do something besides talk in monotones and be boring. Granted, she hadn't chosen her words too wisely but she hadn't meant any harm. And now . . . Louisa blew out a weary breath and felt the heat of it mask her face.

What was going to happen now? she wondered. Aunt Agatha had spoken about someone paying but, after all, what could Aunt Agatha do? Of course, Robby had gotten very angry and maybe he'd do something. Nothing really dangerous, though. No one would dare try to fight John Benton, that was certain.

Relieved at the acceptance of that, Louisa rolled onto her back again and stared up at the ceiling. Oh, well, so she stayed home a few days. What difference did that make? At least she wouldn't have to work in Aunt Agatha's shop and be stared at by those awful women.

With child. The thought came suddenly and Louisa's throat moved and, for a moment, she could hardly breathe. She knew whose child they meant and she knew how children were begotten.

"*John.*" She whispered it within the shell of dreams she suddenly withdrew to.

Chapter Nineteen

It was nearly midnight. The brass hands of the hall clock hovered a breath apart as Jane Coles closed the door behind herself and moved silently along the hall rug.

At the door to Robby's room, she hesitated a moment, holding the robe closed at her throat. She stared down at her frail fingers curled around the cool metal of the doorknob and there was a slight clicking in her throat as she swallowed.

Then, after a moment, her hand slipped from the knob and fell against her leg and there was a loosening of muscles around her mouth. She turned away.

After a step, she hesitated again, her face tight with nervous indecision. She stood there silently in the cool hall, looking with hopeless eyes at the door to her and Matthew's bedroom, visualizing the immobile bulk of her husband stretched out on the bed, his mouth lax, the firm authority of it gone with the teeth that lay submerged in water on the bedside table, his snores pulsing rhythmically in his throat.

Her lips pressed together suddenly and she turned back. Her fingers closed over the doorknob and, with silent quickness, she entered Robby's bedroom.

The pale moonlight fell across the empty bed.

Jane Coles caught her breath and felt a sudden harsh sensation in her stomach as if her insides were falling. Then she turned and hurried out of the dark room and down the hall and stairs, a cold hand clamped over her heart.

In the downstairs hall she stopped, then, abruptly, leaned against the wall and listened with a drained weakness to the sound of Robby clearing his throat in the kitchen, the attendant sound of a cup being placed onto its saucer.

After a moment, she drew in a long breath and pushed away from the wall.

As she came through the swinging door, Robby looked up with a nervous jerk of his head, the dark pupils of his eyes expanding suddenly. She saw his Adam's apple move and a nervous smile twitch on his lips.

"Oh . . . it's you, mother," he said.

Jane Coles smiled at the only person in the world she really loved, for some reason, never having been able to feel the devotion toward Jimmy that she did for her older son.

"Can't you sleep, darling?" she asked, walking up to the table where he sat, seeing a thin drift of steam rising from the coffee cup in front of him.

Robby swallowed. "No, I . . ." He didn't finish or pretend he had a finish for the sentence. He lowered his eyes and stared into the cup.

Jane Coles shuddered. She loved Robby so much and yet she could never speak to him nor get him to speak to her. There was always a barrier between them. Maybe, Jane Coles had sometimes thought, it was because Robby needed someone strong to love and encourage him and she was weak, vacillating, without resources. No wonder then he couldn't confide in her and seek out her judgment. No wonder then he could do no more than love her as his mother and avoid looking for anything else in her.

"Are you hungry, son?" she asked.

"No . . . mother, I'm all right."

She stood there, wordless, the smile fixed to her tired

face, wanting desperately to speak to him, to have him need her sympathy and love.

Impulsively, she drew out a chair and Robby looked up in poorly veiled surprise as the chair leg grated on the floor. His mother smiled quickly at him and sat down, feeling the pulsebeat throbbing in her wrists. The sickness of despair was coming over her again. Robby was her own son, the only one she really cared for and yet she could not speak of a situation which might lead him to his death.

She swallowed and clasped her hands in her lap until the blood was squeezed from them. She *had* to speak of it.

"Son," she said, her voice a strengthless sound.

Robby looked up at her. "What, mother?"

"You . . ." She looked down quickly at her white hands, then up again. "You've . . . made up your mind?"

"About what, mother?" he asked quietly.

She didn't say anything because she knew he was aware of what she spoke about. She looked at him intently, feeling as if the room and the house had disappeared and there were only the two of them sitting in some immeasurable void together—waiting.

"Yes," he said then and she saw how his fingers twitched restively at the porcelain cup handle. He opened his mouth a little as if he were going to go on, clarifying, explaining. "Yes," he said again.

Mrs. Coles felt as if someone had submerged her in icy, numbing water. She sat there staring at her son, feeling a complete inability in herself, feeling absolutely helpless.

She blinked then, forcing through herself the demand to think, to act.

"Because of Miss Winston's . . . *visit*?"

Robby turned his head away a moment as if he wanted to escape but, after a few seconds, he looked back at her briefly, then at his cup.

"Because of everything," he said.

She stopped the trembling of her lips before she spoke again. "Everything?" she asked.

Robby took a long drink of the coffee and she watched the convulsive movements of his throat muscles. She was about to tell him not to drink coffee or he wouldn't sleep but then she got the sudden idea that if he didn't sleep and was exhausted the next day, his father might not demand anything of him. She remained silent.

Robby clinked down the cup heavily.

"Mother, it's got to be done," he said, his voice tightly controlled. "There's no other way."

The dread again, complete and overwhelming, like a crawling of snakes over her and in her. "But . . . why?" she heard herself asking faintly. "Surely, there's . . ."

Robby twisted his shoulders and she stopped talking, feeling a bolt of anguish at the realization that she was only making it worse for him.

"Mother, there's no other way," he told her in an agitated voice. "If I don't do it, Louisa will never be able to lift her head again in Kellville."

That's his father talking, the thought was like an electric shock in her brain. She stared at him helplessly a moment but then knew suddenly she had to go on because, if she didn't, his decision would remain the same.

"But . . . John Benton didn't admit to doing what . . ." her shoulders twitched nervously, ". . . what they said he did."

"It's not enough, mother," Robby said, almost angrily now. "Can't you see that? The whole town believes he did it and . . ." he punched a fist on his leg, ". . . and Louisa is suffering for it. I have to speak for her, mother, can't you see that I have to?"

She sat in the chair shivering, staring at his tense young

face, knowing that he was trying desperately to hang on to his resolve, feeling, in her body, a twisting and knotting of sick terror for him.

"No . . ." she murmured, hardly realizing it herself. In her mind a dozen different questions flung about in a weave of stricken panic. But you didn't ask Louisa if it were true, did you? Why should John Benton do such a thing? Why do you believe everything they tell you? Why do you let them all make your decision for you? Robby, it's your *life*! There's only one! A rushing torrent of words she could never speak to him in a hundred years.

"What are . . . what are you going to do?" she asked, without meaning to.

They were both silent, looking at each other and Jane Coles could hear the clock in the hall ticking away the moments.

Then her son said, "There's only one thing."

Her hand reached out instinctively and closed over his as a rush of horror enveloped her.

"No, darling!" she begged him. "Please don't! *Please!*"

Robby bit his lip and there was a strained sound in his throat as if he had felt himself about to cry and fought it away. He drew his hand from her quickly, his face hardening and, for a hideous moment, Jane Coles saw the face of her husband reflected on Robby's pale features.

"*There's nothing else, I said,*" he told her tensely.

"But not with—!" She broke off suddenly, afraid even of the word.

"Yes," he said and she could see clearly how hard he was trying to believe it himself. "There's no other way a man like him would understand. It's all he deserves. He won't apologize or . . ." He saw the straining fear on her face and his voice snapped angrily. "I believe Louisa! She wouldn't lie to me! Not about something like this. It's my duty to . . . to defend her honor."

"Oh dear God!" Jane Coles slumped over, pressing her shaking hands to her face. "Dear God, it's your father talking, it's not you. It's him, him! Oh, dear God, dear *God* . . ." The tears ran between her trembling fingers.

Robby sat there stiffly, staring at his mother with half-frightened eyes, desperately afraid that he was going to cry too. He leaned back in the chair looking at her with an expression in his eyes that shifted from resolution to pitying contrition and back to resolute strength again.

"You don't have to cry, mother," he said, feeling a twinge at the cold sound of his voice. "I'm not afraid of John Benton. I . . . I'm not a little boy anymore, mother, I'm twenty-one."

His mother looked up with an anguished sob. "You're not old enough for this!" she cried, almost a fierce anger in her voice. "You mustn't fight him, son, you mustn't!"

She kept crying and, for some strange reason, Robby felt suddenly remorseless and cold toward his sobbing mother. There was no strength in her, the thought crept vaguely through his brain, there was only weakness and surrender. He was a man now and he had a job to do. He was going to do it no matter what happened.

He wished it was morning so he could buckle on his gun and get it over with. He found to his astonishment that he actually *wasn't* afraid of Benton now, that he wanted only to get the job over with. Louisa was his intended bride; someday she would be his wife. His father was right; he had to defend her, now and always, it was his responsibility. When men stopped fighting for their women, the society *would* fail, he was certain of it.

"Go to bed, mother," he said in a flat, emotionless tone, "there's nothing to cry about."

Jane Coles sat slumped on her chair, still weeping, her thin shoulders palsied with sobbing. Robby sat looking at her as he would look at a stranger. He felt cold inside, hollowed out by determination, drained of fear, empty of all but the one resolution he knew he had to obey.

He had said tomorrow. Tomorrow it would be.

Slowly, consciously, his fingers closed on the table top; they made a hard, white fist.

Twelve twenty-one, the end of the second day.

The Third Day

Chapter Twenty

Julia was just putting the rack of loaves into the hot oven when the hound began barking outside the kitchen door at the muffled drumming of hoofbeats. Pushing up the oven door, she moved quickly across the floor toward the window and looked out.

A sudden weakness dragged at her and she caught at the windowsill, her heart suddenly pumping in slow, heavy beats as she saw who it was.

The chestnut gelding was reined up to a careful stop before the house and stood there fidgeting while the hound cringed nearby, ears back, head snapping with each hoarse, excited bark it gave.

"*Benton!*" Julia heard Matthew Coles call out and her stomach muscles shuddered at the sound.

"No," she murmured without realizing it, gasping to draw breath into her lungs.

"Benton!" Coles shouted again, his voice sharp and demanding. Julia stared out at him, hoping desperately that he would think no one was home and ride away.

Then Matthew Coles started to dismount and she pushed from the window and opened the door with a spasmodic pull.

Matthew Coles twitched back, face whitening.

"I am unarm—!" he started to cry out, then broke off with a tightening of his mouth when he saw it was her.

"Where is your husband, Mrs. Benton?" he asked quickly, trying to cover up his momentary panic. The hound dog backed toward Julia as she stood in the doorway.

"Why do you want to know?" she asked, weakly.

"Mrs. Benton, I expect an answer."

She drew in a shaking breath. "He's not here," she said.

"Where *is* he?"

She swallowed quickly and stared at him, feeling sick and dizzy.

"Mrs. Benton, I demand an—"

"Why do you want to know?"

"That is not your concern, ma'm," said Matthew Coles.

"It's about Louisa Harper, isn't it?" she asked suddenly.

His face hardened. "Where is your husband, ma'm?" he asked.

"Mister Coles, it isn't true! My husband had nothing to do with that girl!"

"I'm afraid the facts speak differently, ma'm," Matthew Coles said with imperious calm. "Now, where is he?"

"Mister Coles, I beg of you—listen to me! My husband had nothing to do with Louisa Harper, I sw—"

"Where is your husband, Mrs. Benton?"

"I swear to you, Mister—"

"Where *is* he, Mrs. Benton?" Matthew Coles asked, his voice rising.

"Why won't you listen to me? Don't you think I'd know?"

"Mrs. Benton, I demand an answer!"

"What are you trying to do—kill your son?!"

The hint of a smile played at Matthew Coles' lips. "I don't believe it's my son you're concerned for," he said.

"Who else would I be concerned for?" she answered heatedly. "You don't think he'd have a chance against my husband, do you? For the love of God, stop this terrible thing before—"

Matthew Coles turned on his heel and lifted his boot toe into the stirrup.

"Mister Coles!" Her cry followed him as she took a quick step into the morning sunlight, face pale and tense.

He said nothing but swung up into the saddle and pulled his horse around.

"You've got to believe me!" she cried. "My husband didn't—"

The rest of her words were drowned out by the quickening thud of the gelding's hooves across the yard.

"*No!*" She screamed it after him.

Then she stood there in the hot blaze of sunlight, shivering uncontrollably, watching him ride away while the hound dog stood beside her, whining.

Suddenly she started running for the barn on trembling legs, breath falling from her lips in gasping bursts. Then, equally as sudden, she stopped, realizing that she didn't know how to hitch up the buckboard for herself. She stood indecisively, halfway between the barn and the house, her chest jerking with frustrated, frightened sobs.

Chapter Twenty-one

Well, them damn churnheads is in the bog again," was the first thing Joe Bailey said as Benton and Lew Goodwill rode up to him.

"Oh, for—!" Benton hissed angrily. Then he shrugged. "Well . . . stay here with the rest of the herd and Lew and I'll fetch 'em out."

"Okay, boss," Joe Bailey said and Benton and Goodwill rode off toward the mud hole, stopping off at the small range shack for short-handled shovels.

"It's this damn heat," Lew said as the two of them dismounted by the bog. "They try to get cool and all they get is stuck."

Benton grunted and they walked across the rilled ground toward the almost dry spring. As they walked, they saw the two steers struggling in the wire and heard the bellowing of their complaints.

"Sure. Tell us your troubles," Benton said to them under his breath. "If you weren't so damn mule-headed, you wouldn't get *stuck* in there." But he knew it was really because he didn't have enough men to keep a closer watch on the herd. How could one man keep tabs on two hundred head?

As they came to the edge of the mud hole, Benton and Lew unbuckled their gunbelts and lay them on the top of a boulder.

"Let's get the wrinkle-horn out first," Benton said.

"Right," Lew said and they struggled out into the viscous mud toward the older steer with its wrinkled, scaly horns. Benton gritted his teeth as the smell of hot slime surrounded him.

"Oh, *shut* up!" he snapped as the steer bellowed loudly, trying, in vain, to dislodge its legs.

Quickly, with angrily driven shovel strokes, Benton dug around the steer's legs. The steer kept struggling, sometimes sinking deeper into the hot, reeking muck, its angry, frightened bellows blasting at Benton's eardrums.

Once, its muzzle crashed against Benton's shoulder as he straightened up for a moment and knocked him onto his side, getting his Levi's and shirt mud-coated. Jumping up, he grabbed hold of the scaly horn and shoved the steer's head away with a curse, then started digging again.

Finally, he'd freed most of the front leg and, stepping over the back leg, he started working on that quickly so the mud wouldn't come back around the free leg. On the other side of the struggling steer, he heard his own curses echoed by Lew Goodwill.

"Damn fool!" Lew snapped. "Stop *fussin'* so!"

As he dug, trying to breathe through his clenched teeth, Benton felt great sweat drops trickling down the sides of his chest from his armpits. He kept digging, plunging the shovel point in and hurling the black mud away with angry arm jerks. It's times like this—he thought—when I wish I was back in the Rangers where the only thing a man has to worry about is getting shot.

He hadn't slept much the night before. Julia had kept talking about Robby Coles and he was still thinking about it when he fell into an uneasy doze.

He dreamed that Matthew Coles was tying him to a hitching post while Robby stood nearby, waiting to fire slugs into him. When the first bullets had struck, he'd jolted up on the bed with a grunt, wide awake.

Then Lew Goodwill had ridden in from the first night watch and said he thought there better be another man to help Joe Bailey on the second watch because there was some electric lightning in the sky and the herd was getting spooky.

Benton had dressed and ridden out to the herd and stayed with Joe a couple of hours until the lightning was gone. Then he'd ridden back to the house. In all, he'd gotten about three hours of sleep.

"All right, get on your horse," he said to Lew.

"Ain't finished the back leg, boss."

"I'll get it, I'll get it," Benton snapped. "Get on your horse."

"Okay." Lew slogged out of the mud hole and moved up to where his horse was tied. He cinched up the saddle as tightly as the latigo straps could be drawn, then led the animal down to the edge of the mud hole.

"All right, toss in your rope," Benton said.

Lew lifted the rope coil off his saddle horn and shook it loose, then tossed one end of it to Benton who tied it securely around the steer's horns. While he did that, Lew fastened the other rope end around his saddle horn and drew it taut. Mounting then, he backed off his sturdy piebald until the lariat was taut.

"All right," Benton called, "drag her out!"

The piebald dug in its hooves and started pulling at the dead weight of the steer. Dust rose under its slipping, straining legs and the muscles of its body stood out like sheathed cables. In the mud hole, Benton shoved at the steer from behind, trying to avoid the spray of mud from its flailing legs but not always succeeding.

"Come on, you wall-eyed mule!" Benton gasped furiously as he shoved the steer, his muscles straining violently.

Slowly, the steer was pulled loose and dragged up onto hard ground. When they tailed it up, it charged Benton and he had to make a zig-zag dash for the bush. Then Lew chased the steer off and they went back into the mud for the second one.

By the time they had that one out, they were both spattered with mud from head to knee and caked solid below that. They sat in the shade a little while, panting and cursing under their breath.

They were sitting like that when the gelding came over the rise. "Who's that?" Lew asked.

Benton looked up and sudden alarm tightened his face. "My gun," he muttered, and stood up quickly as Matthew Coles spurred his gelding down the gradual slope and reined up.

"What do you want?" Benton asked, realizing that Coles was unarmed.

"I'm here as second for my son," Coles said, stiffly.

"You're what?" Benton squinted up at the older man.

"You will be in town by three o'clock this afternoon to defend yourself," stated Matthew Coles.

Benton stared up incredulously. "What did you say?"

"You heard what I said, sir!"

Benton felt the heat and the dirt and the exhaustion all well up in him and explode as anger. "God damn it, get off my ranch! I told you that girl lied! Now—"

"Either you come in like a man," Matthew Coles flared, "or my son will ride out after you!"

Benton felt like dragging the older man off his horse and pitching him head first into the mud hole. His body shook with repression of the desire.

"Listen," he said. "For the last time, you tell your kid that—"

"By three, Mister Benton. Three o'clock this afternoon."

"Coles, I swear to God, if you don't—"

Matthew Coles pulled his horse around and rode quickly up the incline as Benton started forward, his face suddenly whitening with fury.

Benton stopped and watched the older man ride away.

"He's loco," Lew Goodwill said then and Benton glanced over at the big man. "He's tryin' to kill his own kid," Lew went on. "He *must* be loco."

Benton walked away on stiff legs and stood by the boulder buckling on his gunbelt. What was he supposed to do now, he wondered. Did he stay out on the ranch and wait to see if Robby Coles really would come after him? It was what he felt like doing. Without any trouble at all, he could convince himself that the kid wasn't going to commit suicide.

But he didn't try to convince himself. He stood there worriedly, staring at the crest of the slope where Matthew Coles had disappeared.

Finally, he exhaled a heavy breath and groaned because he knew what he had to do. "Oh . . . *damn!*" he muttered to himself and started in quick, angry strides for his horse.

"I'll be back as soon as I can," he told Lew. "Tell Merv and Joe I . . ." Another disgusted hiss of breath. "Tell 'em I have to go into the damn town again."

"Take it easy, boss," Lew said and Benton grunted a reply as he started up the slope.

As he swung into the saddle, he ran his right hand across his brow and slung away the sweat drops on his fingers. Then he nudged his spurs into the horse's flanks and felt the animal charge up the incline beneath him.

What do I do first? The thought plagued him as he galloped for the ranch. Should he try Robby first or his father, Louisa or her aunt or her mother, the Reverend Bond or maybe even the sheriff? He didn't know. All he knew was that things were too damn complicated. Some stupid little girl makes up a story about him and, in two days, everybody expects him to defend his life.

It was hard not to let them have their way. Certainly he was fed up enough just to let it happen the way they wanted. But then he knew again that killing Robby wasn't the answer. Robby wasn't any villain to be killed; he was only a pawn.

Why did I leave the Rangers? He was asking himself the question again as he rode up to the house and jumped off his horse.

Julia was in the doorway before he'd even tied up the panting mount.

"John," she said breathlessly, staring at his mud-spattered clothes.

"It's all right," he said quickly as she ran to him.

"*Oh*." She swallowed and caught his hand. "Mud. I thought—" She swallowed again and didn't finish. "What happened, John?" she asked instead.

He told her briefly as he went into the house, pulling off his mud-caked shirt and starting to wash up at the pump.

"What are you going to do?" she asked, apprenhensively.

"Go into town," he said. "No, I'm not takin' a gun with me," he added quickly, seeing the look in her eyes. "I'll try talkin' reason to them again." He dashed water in his face and washed off the soap. "There must be *one* of them that'll listen to reason. I sure can't see shootin' that kid over nothin' at all."

"I want to go with you," Julia said, suddenly.

"No, I'll get there faster by myself," he told her.

"John, I want to go," she said again and this time it wasn't just a request. He looked over at her as he lathered his muddy arms.

"Honey, who's goin' to feed the boys? They gotta have their chuck, you know."

"They can manage by themselves one day," she said. "I'll leave the food on the table."

"Julia, there isn't that much time."

"Then I'll leave a note telling them where everything is," she argued. "If there isn't much time, it's even more important that I go with you. There may be a lot of people to see and two of us can do more than one. And—besides— the women are more likely to listen to me than you." She spoke quickly, submerging the rise of dread in a tide of rapid planning.

Benton hesitated a moment longer, looking at her intent face. Then he turned away with a shrug. "All right," he said, wearily. As she sat down to write the note, she heard him muttering to himself about how the ranch was going to go to hell because of all this lost time.

"We'll tie Socks behind the buckboard," she said, looking up from the note, "then, when we get into town, we can separate and get more done that way."

"Well, there isn't much time," Benton said, looking at the clock, "it's almost eleven now. It'll take till quarter of twelve to reach town even if we push it."

"He didn't set a time, did he?" she asked, her voice suddenly faint.

"Three," he said.

"This afternoon?" She knew even as she said it that it had to be that afternoon. "Oh, dear God."

Benton grunted, then turned from the pump. "I'm goin' to change clothes now," he said. "Will you get Socks and the dark mare outta the barn? I'll put the other one away before we leave."

He headed for the bedroom.

"John," she said suddenly when he was almost out of the kitchen. He looked back over his shoulder.

"John . . . promise me that . . ." she swallowed, ". . . that whatever happens you won't . . ." She couldn't finish.

They looked at each other a long moment and it seemed as if the great conflict in their life and marriage were a wall being erected between them again.

Then John said, "There's no time to talk now," and left her staring at the place where he'd been standing. She listened to the sound of her pencil hitting the floor and rolling across the boards.

Chapter Twenty-two

The two women sat in the front room. They both had yarn and needles in their laps but only one of them was knitting; that was Agatha Winston. Her sister sat without moving, her limpid eyes unfocused, on her face a look of disconcerted reflection.

Miss Winston looked up. "You'll never finish the shawl like that," she said, curtly.

Elizabeth Harper's hands twitched in her lap and her gaze lifted for a moment to the carved features of her sister.

"I can't," she said then, with an unhappy sigh.

Agatha Winston's thin lips pressed a grimace into her face and she went back to her knitting without another word.

In the hall, the clock chimed a hollow stroke and then eleven more. Elizabeth Harper sat listening, her hands clasped tightly in her lap, her eyes on the calmly moving fingers of Agatha Winston. Noon, she thought, it's noon.

"How can you be so—?" she began to say and then was halted by the coldness in her sister's eyes.

Miss Winston put down her work. "What is happening," she said, "is beyond our control. It had to be this way. John Benton made it so." She picked up her work again. "And there's no point in our dwelling on it," she said.

Elizabeth Harper stirred restlessly on the chair. "But that poor boy," she murmured. "What will happen to him?"

"He is not a boy, Elizabeth."

"But he's not . . ." Mrs. Harper looked upset. "Oh . . . how can he hope to do anything against that . . . that awful man?"

Miss Winston breathed in deeply. "It is what he has to do," was all she said. "Let's not talk about it."

Elizabeth Harper looked back at her hands, feeling her body tighten as she thought about Robby Coles going against a man who had lived by violence for—how many years? She bit her lip. It was terrible, it was a terrible thing. If only her dear husband were alive; he'd have found a way to avoid violence. Indeed, he'd have raised Louisa so strictly that this terrible thing would never have happened in the first place. She'd been unable to control the girl since Mr. Harper died. Oh, why was he dead, why?

She brushed away an unexpected tear, looking up guiltily to see if Agatha had seen; but Miss Winston was absorbed in knitting.

Three o'clock, Mrs. Harper thought. Less than three hours now. It was terrible, terrible.

"You're . . . certain he said—?" she started.

"What?" Agatha Winston looked up irritably.

Elizabeth Harper swallowed. "You're . . . sure he said three o'clock?"

"That is what he said," Miss Winston answered, looking back to her work. She'd met Matthew Coles that morning on the way to her shop and he'd told her that Robby was going to meet John Benton in the square at three o'clock that afternoon. After she'd heard that, she'd gone immediately to her sister's house to see personally that Louisa remained in the house all day. Naturally, she'd have to leave the shop closed all day too.

"What is it?" she asked, pettishly, hearing Elizabeth speak her name again.

Mrs. Harper swallowed nervously. "Don't you . . . think we should tell Louisa?"

"Of course I don't think we should tell her," Miss Winston said sharply. "Hasn't she enough to be concerned with without worrying more?"

"But . . . what if Robby . . . ?" Mrs. Harper dared not finish the sentence.

Miss Winston spoke clearly and authoritatively.

"We will not think about it," she declared.

Upstairs, Louisa was standing restively by the window, looking out at the great tree in the front yard. She'd come up to her room shortly after breakfast when her Aunt Agatha had arrived at the house. Since then, a strange uneasiness had oppressed her.

What was Aunt Agatha doing at their house? She hadn't missed opening her shop one day in the past twelve years—outside of Sundays, of course. No one was more strict in her habits than Aunt Agatha. No shop owner could have been more religious in his hours. At nine, the shop was unlocked, dusted, and prepared for the day's business. At twelve it was shut for dinner, at one, reopened, and, promptly at five, it was locked up for the night. Now, *this*—Aunt Agatha sitting down in the front room with her mother. They'd been there almost three hours now . . .

. . . *as if they were waiting for something.*

Louisa bit her lower lip and her breasts trembled with a harsh breath. Something was wrong, she could feel it. But what could be wrong? Certainly Robby wasn't going to . . . no, that was ridiculous, he knew better than that. Maybe something was happening but not that, it couldn't be that. Maybe Robby and his father were going out to ask John Benton about the story she'd told. That was bad enough—

the idea made her sick with dread of what would happen if Aunt Agatha found out she'd lied.

But that was all, that was the worst that could happen.

Then why was Aunt Agatha downstairs with her mother? Why hadn't Aunt Agatha spoken more than a few words to her that morning, suggesting, almost as soon as she was in the house, that Louisa go up to her room?

Louisa turned from the window and walked in quick, nervous steps across the floor, her small hands closed into fists swinging at her sides. For some reason, her throat felt constricted and she had trouble breathing. For some reason, the muscles in her stomach felt tight as if she were about to be sick—even though there was no reason for it.

She sank down on the bed and forced herself to pick up her embroidery. Then, in a few moments, she put it down on the bedside table again and stroked restless fingers at the skirt of her gingham dress.

No, there was something wrong. No matter how she tried to explain things to herself, she couldn't find any good reason for Aunt Agatha to be there. Not if everything was all right, not if the story she'd told was being forgotten. No, there was something—

Louisa started as she heard the sound of hooves out front, the rattling squeak of a buckboard. Quickly, heart beating, she jumped up and hurried to the window.

Her breath caught as she saw John Benton's wife climbing down off the buckboard in front of the house and, unconsciously, a look of apprehensive dread contorted her face. With frightened eyes, she watched Mrs. Benton open the gate and shut it behind her.

Suddenly, she jerked back as Mrs. Benton glanced up at the window. She pressed herself against the wall, feeling her chest throb with great, frantic heartbeats. Why was

Mrs. Benton here? Louisa fought down a sob and dug her teeth into her lip. Fear welled over her like rising waters. Mrs. Benton was going to tell Aunt Agatha the truth and then Aunt Agatha would know everything. She brushed away the sudden tears spilling from her eyes.

Then she stiffened against the wall as the front doorbell tinkled. She stood there, petrified, listening.

Downstairs, there were footsteps.

Suddenly, Louisa found herself pressing off her shoes and rushing across the room to open the door, then moving stealthily into the hall. As she edged cautiously for the head of the stairs, she heard the footsteps halting at the front door.

"*Oh!*" She heard her mother gasp and then the footsteps again and the almost inaudible sound of her mother and aunt talking guardedly. Louisa crouched down by the bannisters and listened, her chest twitching with panic-stricken heartbeats.

Footsteps again—her aunt's; she knew they were Aunt Agatha's, there was something about the way Aunt Agatha walked. Louisa's hands froze on the bannister she was clutching and there was a clicking in her throat.

Downstairs, she heard Aunt Agatha clear her throat. Then the doorknob was turned and her aunt was saying, "Yes?" in that cold, unreceptive way she had.

"*Oh.*" Mrs. Benton sounded surprised. Then she said, "Miss Winston, I'd like to talk to your sister."

"Oh?" Aunt Agatha's voice was still chilled and unwelcoming.

There was a moment's pause, then the hesitant voice of Mrs. Benton saying, "May . . . I come in?"

Aunt Agatha drew in a quick breath. "I'm afraid not," she said and Louisa felt a cold shudder run down her back. "My niece is indisposed," Agatha Winston added and Louisa felt the skin tightening on her face.

"Miss Winston, please. I don't believe you realize what's happening."

Her aunt's voice hard and controlled, saying, "I know exactly what is happening." Louisa didn't realize that she was holding her breath as she pressed her paling cheek against the hard bannister. *What's happening?* The words dug at her.

"Well, then, you must know how serious it is," Mrs. Benton said, "This terrible thing has to be stopped before it's too late."

"It *is* too late, Mrs. Benton," Agatha Winston's voice said.

"But it isn't," Julia Benton said quickly. "It can still be avoided."

Another pause. Louisa drew in a quick, wavering breath, listening intently.

"Miss Winston, you simply must—"

"Mrs. Benton," Agatha Winston interrupted, "I'm afraid there's nothing I can do to help you. The situation is quite out of my hands. I . . . don't like to say it but—well, your husband should have considered the consequences before he—"

"But that's the whole point, Miss Winston!" Julia Benton exclaimed, "He didn't do it! He's had nothing to do with your niece—*nothing*!"

Louisa's eyes closed suddenly and she felt herself shivering helplessly. Now everyone would know, now she'd be punished. Oh God, I want to die! she thought in an agony of shame—I want to *die*!

"I would like to believe that," her aunt said to Mrs. Benton then, "but I'm afraid it's gone too far for that."

"Too far?" Julia Benton sounded stunned. "How can it have gone so far you won't listen to the truth?"

Louisa felt numbed as she pressed against the bannister, her fingers clutching whitely at it. She heard her aunt say, a little less assuredly now, "I told you, Mrs. Benton, the matter is out of my hands."

"It's not out of Louisa's hands!"

Louisa gasped. Now, she thought in terror, *now* Aunt Agatha would find out and everyone would know . . .

But her aunt said, "It is out of her hands too," an undertone of anger in her voice.

"Dear God, what's the matter with everybody!" Julia Benton burst out. "Do you all want Robby killed!"

Up on the landing, Louisa couldn't breathe suddenly. She felt as if her heart had stopped, her blood had ceased to flow, as if every function of her body had stopped in that instant. On her drained face, a look of utter horror froze.

Robby *killed*?

She hardly heard her aunt speak out angrily, "How dare you accuse us of that!"

"What else can I say when you won't listen to facts!"

"I think you'd better go, Mrs. Benton."

"I must see Louisa."

"I've already told you—!"

"I know what you told me! But I'm not going to stand by and watch that boy killed over nothing!"

Louisa flinched at the word, her lips trembling and cold. I didn't know, I didn't know—the words stumbled in her shocked mind—oh God, I didn't *know*.

Now, downstairs, her aunt suddenly cried out, "You're not coming in here!"

"Miss Winston, you don't know what you're doing!"

"I am in full sympathy with your concern, Mrs. Benton," Miss Winston said, her words tightly articulated, "but I cannot allow you to upset my niece any further. If you want to argue with anyone, argue with Mister Coles and his son. The matter is—"

"Miss Winston, there isn't time!"

"—in their hands now, not ours!" Miss Winston finished her sentence loudly.

"Miss Winston, Louisa is the only one who can—"

The loud slamming of the front door cut off Julia Benton's frantic voice and made Louisa start violently, her hands tightening spasmodically on the bannister. Downstairs, she heard a drawn-in breath rasp in her aunt's throat, then a choked sob. The doorbell rang insistently.

"Go away!" Agatha Winston cried out in a broken voice. "You're not welcome here!"

Suddenly, Louisa pushed herself up and moved around the bannister railing, desperately thinking—I've got to stop it!

The sight of her aunt drove her back and a whimper started in her throat as she drew away from the head of the stairs. No, no, I have to tell her!—she thought in terrified anguish.

She whirled and ran down the hall, her feet soundless on the thick rug. Pushing open the door, she shut it quickly and silently behind herself and rushed across the room toward the window.

As she reached it, she saw Julia Benton moving for the gate. Her mouth opened and she tried to call to her but the sound would not come—it froze in her throat. In her mind a flood of frightened thoughts drowned resolve—Aunt Agatha finding out, Robby finding out, John Benton finding out, the whole town finding out . . .

A sob broke in her throat and her hands clutched desperately at the windowsill. But I have to tell! she thought, agonized, I can't let him be *killed*!

"Mrs. Benton!" she called. But the call was a strangled whispering and, with sickened eyes, she watched Julia Benton get in the buckboard.

Then Mrs. Benton looked at the house, her face white

and shaken. Louisa raised her hand suddenly. "Mrs. *Benton*!" she said, a little louder but not loud enough.

Julia Benton tugged at the dark reins and the horse pulled the buckboard away.

"No!" Louisa couldn't keep from crying out. She clapped a shaking hand over her mouth and whirled to face the door. Had Aunt Agatha heard her? She stared at the closed door for a full minute, lips shaking, her eyes stark with dread.

Aunt Agatha did not come up. Louisa leaned back against the wall weakly, her mind confused with a tangling of thoughts. What was she going to do? Oh God, what was she going to *do*?

Out in the hall, a wall clock ticked its endless beat while the minute hand moved slowly for the number six. In ten minutes, it would be twelve-thirty.

Chapter Twenty-three

e's out of town," Benton told her when they met at the foot of Davis Street.

Julia stared up at him blankly. "Out of town?" she repeated in a faint voice.

"That's what the deputy said."

"But . . . for how long?"

"Three days yet," John said gravely. "He's takin' a prisoner to the Rangers." On the plank sidewalk, passing men and women glanced at them and tried to hear what they were saying.

"Well, what about the deputy?" Julia said. "He can stop it, can't he?"

"Well—" John started to say, then glanced over suddenly at the sidewalk where two men looked away and walked off quickly along the planks toward the Zorilla Saloon.

Mouth tightened, Benton dismounted and tied Socks to the back of the buckboard. A thin-wheeled rig came crackling up Davis Street and was guided around them. From the corners of his eyes, Benton saw Henry Oliver looking at him curiously.

Then the rig turned left into the square and Benton climbed up on the seat beside Julia.

"He won't do anything," he told her. "Too many people

are for it. Guess this thing is bigger than we thought. Half the town knows about it, looks like."

"But . . ." Julia stared at him, dazedly, trying to think but unable to, ". . . what are we going to do?"

John didn't even bother shrugging. "I don't know, ma," he said quietly, looking at his hands. "I just don't know." He looked up at her. "What happened at the girl's house?"

"Her aunt was there," Julia said.

"She wouldn't even let you *in*, I expect," John said grimly and she started to say something but didn't. They sat there in the motionless buckboard, trying to ignore the passersby who stared at them.

"Well, let's not just *sit* here," John said abruptly. "Here, you want me to drive?" He reached for the reins, then glanced up irritably at a passing man who was gaping at him.

"Give me the reins, Julia," he said tersely.

She looked over at him. "Where are we going?" she asked, worriedly.

His mouth opened a little as if he were about to speak, then he hesitated and blew out a tired breath.

"Where *can* we go?" he asked her.

"Well . . ."

"We'll have to go back to the ranch," he said.

"John, we can't."

"Julia, what else is there to do?"

"Can't we see the deputy sheriff again? He has to keep the peace; it's his job."

"Honey, the job's no bigger than the man. Catwell's just a store clerk with a badge on. He's not goin' to stand up against half the town. He's not the kind."

"But we *can't* go back, John," she said, more heatedly. "We've got to stop it somehow."

"What would you suggest?" he asked, his voice flat and unencouraging.

"I don't know," she said, trying to get control of her scattered thoughts. "But we have to do something."

John shrugged and let his hands fall to his lap and he sat there staring at his mud-caked boots.

"I almost think you want this—" Julia started to say, then stopped as he looked over quickly at her. "I'm sorry, I'm sorry, John," she said hastily. "It's just that . . ."

She pressed her hands together. "Can't we . . ." She hesitated and then said quickly, "We'll go talk to Robby."

"Honey, you heard his old man this morning," John said. "Did he sound like he was open to reason?"

"We'll talk to Robby, not his father."

"Same thing," he said, disgustedly.

"John, we have to do *some*thing," she said slowly and tensely. "You know we have to."

He let go of the reins and pressed his lips together.

"All right," he said curtly. "All right, Julia. But not much more. You understand? *Not much more.*"

With a nervous twitching of her hands, Julia shook the reins and the buckboard lurched forward into the square.

Chapter Twenty-four

Louisa stood at the head of the stairs, looking down, one hand pressed at the bosom of her dress, the other clamped tightly on the bannister railing.

They were still down there. They weren't talking but Louisa knew they were there and knew she'd have to walk by the front room to get to the kitchen and the back door.

She lowered one foot nervously and shifted her weight to the first carpeted step with a cautious movement. The stair creaked a little and Julia stiffened, her eyes fastened to the doorway below that led to the front room.

There was no sound. Julia brought the other foot down and stood on the top step, legs cold and trembling. Suddenly, she became conscious of the ticking clock and she glanced over at it, her throat moving.

Twenty minutes to one. There was so little time.

She moved down another step silently. I should tell Aunt Agatha, the thought oppressed her, Aunt Agatha could stop it.

But the idea of telling her aunt made Louisa's stomach turn. She couldn't do it, she just couldn't, she'd rather tell anyone else.

Besides, she rationalized weakly, Aunt Agatha had said it was out of her hands. No, she'd have to tell someone else.

But who?

Louisa moved down another step, her lips twitching as the wood crackled in strain beneath her. I should have taken my shoes off! the thought burst in her mind. What if they heard her? What if they came out in the hall and saw her on the stairs? What would she tell Aunt Agatha; what *could* she tell her?

Louisa stood fixed to the step, heart thudding in heavy, irregular beats. She bit her trembling lip. No, I have to do it! she told herself, fighting off the instinct to rush back to her room and hide. I have to, I just *have* to!

She swallowed the obstruction in her throat and moved down another step, her hand sliding noiselessly along the bannister railing, then clamping tightly as she lowered herself. Another step; another.

She froze involuntarily. Down in the front room, her aunt was clearing her throat.

"Are we having dinner?" she heard Aunt Agatha say.

"If you . . . want some," the pale voice of her mother replied. "I'm . . . not hungry, myself."

"*I am*," said Aunt Agatha.

Louisa shuddered and stood there rooted, expecting at any moment to see her aunt come walking out of the front room.

But there was only silence below. Louisa thought she heard the clicking of knitting needles but she wasn't sure. I have to get out! she thought desperately.

She moved down another step, lowering her foot cautiously, testing her weight on the carpeted wood. Another step. She stopped and tightened as a horse galloped by in front of the house and she thought it was going to stop. She closed her eyes a moment and drew in a heavy, nervous breath. Why wasn't there a back stairway?

"The nerve of that woman," she heard Aunt Agatha say.

"She's just—" her mother started and then said no more.

"Defending him like that," said Agatha Winston in an insulted voice. "The very idea; after what he did."

No, no, I mustn't cry, I mustn't—Louisa begged herself, reaching up hastily to brush aside the tears. Why did she ever tell Robby that story—*why*? She drew in a rasping breath and then cut it off sharply, her eyes widening in fright.

No sound in the front room. She moved down another step and it creaked beneath her.

"Louisa?"

She felt a bolt of panic stun her heart as her aunt's voice probed up at her. She stood there mutely, shivering without control as her aunt came out of the front room, carrying her knitting.

"What is it you want?" her aunt asked.

"I . . ." Louisa stared down dumbly at her.

"Well?"

Louisa tried to speak but there was no sound.

"Speak up, child!"

"I'm hungry." Louisa heard herself blurt out the words.

Her aunt looked up at her suspiciously a moment, then said grumpily, "Oh."

Turning, Aunt Agatha went back into the front room. Now! Louisa thought frantically and she ran down the steps on trembling legs.

"You can't be *that* hungry," Agatha Winston said, coming back into the hall, this time without her knitting.

Louisa felt a sudden cold sinking in her stomach and her legs were numb under her as she walked toward the kitchen, Aunt Agatha following behind her, saying, "Elizabeth? Come along, it's dinner time," and her mother answering, weakly, "Yes . . . Agatha."

Chapter Twenty-five

Julia drew back on the reins and the mare stopped in front of the shop. She pulled back on the brake and stood up. John helped her down without a word, his face hard and thin-lipped. She didn't speak to him as they walked, side by side, across the dirt, then stepped up onto the roofed-over plank sidewalk. John's hand released hers and he opened the door of the shop for her.

The bell over the door tinkled and Matthew Coles looked up from his bench, his face tightening as he saw who it was. Slowly, with carefully controlled movement, he rose and came walking to the front counter. He said nothing, he didn't even look at Benton.

"Mister Coles," Julia said.

"Well?" His voice was hard and unpleasant.

"Mister Coles, this thing has gone far enough," Julia said, trying to sound calm. "It must be stopped—*now*."

The expression on Matthew Coles' face did not change at all. "Stopped?" he asked as if he were actually curious.

Julia Benton swallowed and Benton pressed his lips together over clenched teeth.

"Mister Coles, my husband is not guilty of what he's been accused. I'll say it again, Mister Coles. He is not guilty. Louisa Harper *lied*."

Only the slight tensing of skin over his cheekbones

424   RICHARD MATHESON

betrayed what Matthew Coles felt. His tone remained the same.

"I'm sorry," he said. "We do not believe that."

Julia Benton stared at him, speechless. It's true, she thought, realizing it then in sudden shock, dear God, it was true! They didn't *want* to believe; no one did.

"Of course," Matthew Coles said sonorously, "If your husband wishes to make a public apology and then vacate his ranch, that is something else again."

"Listen, Coles," Benton's deep voice broke in suddenly. Matthew Coles looked over at him, his expression just sly enough, his head just tilted enough to give him a look of arrogant aplomb.

"Yes, Mister Benton," he said.

Benton felt an old, almost forgotten beat churning up in his stomach, an almost forgotten tightening of his right arm muscles.

"I'm givin' it to you straight, Coles," he said tensely, leaning forward slightly. "If you don't stop your kid, he's goin' to get blown apart." Julia gasped but Benton kept on. "You hear me, Coles—I said *blown apart*," he went on. "I'm not foolin', so listen to me."

"I'm listening," Matthew Coles said.

"This whole damn thing is a mistake," Benton said, slowly and distinctly. "Beginning to end it's a mistake. I don't know Louisa Harper, I never spoke a word to her in my life. That's *it*, Coles and that's all I'm sayin'—and all I'm takin'. Don't push your kid into this, Coles. Don't do it. You'll be sorry."

Matthew Coles tried to swallow without showing it.

"Is that all?" he said.

"That's all," Benton said.

"Mister Coles," Julia said, her voice pleading, "I beg of you . . ."

Benton said, "Come on, Julia," his voice low and curt.

Her eyes moved frantically to her husband, then back to Matthew Coles again, her lips moving slightly as though she were going to say something.

"I said come *on*, Julia," Benton said, voice a little louder now.

"John, we—"

His strong fingers closed over her arm. "Julia," he said and the way he said it, it was a command.

"Three o'clock, Mister Benton," Matthew Coles said.

Benton's head jerked around and he looked back at Coles, the edge of his jaw whitening in sudden fury.

"That's enough, Coles," he warned.

"If you are not in the square by then," Matthew Coles said, "my son will come out to your ranch and shoot you down like a dog."

Benton turned a little and his cold voice probed into Matthew Coles' ears. "You're mighty free with your son's life, Coles," he said. "I wonder if you'd be as free with your own."

Matthew Coles shuddered but immediately regained his composure. "Get out, Mister Benton," he ordered. "And be thankful at this moment that you have no gun on you . . ."

Benton almost started back after him. Then, with a twitch of muscles, he turned away. "Just remember, it's on your conscience," he said.

Benton led Julia from the shop, his hand tight on her arm. "John," she kept saying. "John. John . . ."

"That's enough, Julia," he said.

"But John, we—"

"I said that's enough," he ordered, helping her up onto the buckboard. He walked around it and climbed onto the other side.

"Do you *want* this fight?" she whispered passionately as he shoved forward the brake and snapped the reins over the mare's back.

"Sure!" he snapped at her. "Sure, that's it! That's all I've been doin' the last two days—lookin' for a fight!"

"John, I didn't mean—"

"Then, watch what you say, for God's sake!"

"John, *please*. Couldn't we go see Robby? He'd be alone at home and—"

"No," he said.

She twisted her shoulders worriedly and bit her lower lip. "Let's go see the Reverend Bond then," she said. "He might—"

"No, Julia, *no*," he said sternly. "I'm through scraping. I've had enough; I've had *more* than enough."

She sat shivering beside him, staring at his hard-set features as the buckboard rocked and rattled across the square headed for St. Virgil Street, for the edge of town.

In the church steeple, the rust-throated bell tolled and it was one o'clock.

Chapter Twenty-six

The butter, if you please," said Agatha Winston and, without a word, her sister passed the plate across the table. "Thank you," Agatha Winston said, in a tone that held no gratitude. She sliced herself another piece of bread and spread a paper-thin coating of butter on its porous surface. This she cut into four equal parts with two deft strokes of her knife.

Chewing, she eyed her sister, then her niece, neither of whom were eating.

"I thought you were hungry," she said to Louisa.

Her niece looked up a moment and Agatha Winston saw the nervous swallowing in her throat.

"I . . . guess I'm not," Louisa said.

"You'd better eat *some*thing or you'll get sick," said her aunt. She sliced off a thick piece of bread and dropped it on Louisa's plate. "Put cheese on it," she said. "It's good for you."

"I'm really not . . . not hungry, Aunt Agatha."

"Eat it," said her aunt and, after a moment, Louisa picked up her knife obediently.

"Why are you shaking so?" her aunt asked and Louisa started in her chair.

"I'm . . . cold," she said, lowering her eyes. She felt the probing gaze of her aunt on her as she buttered the bread with nervous movements. She thought she knew what her aunt was thinking—*cold; shaking; that* time of the month; something not spoken of; preferably, not even thought of.

At any other time, knowing or thinking that Aunt Agatha was thinking that would have flushed Louisa's cheek with shamed embarrassment but today it didn't seem important. There was a clock ticking away the time in the hall and there was only one thing important—to get out of the house and find someone who could stop the fight. It was strange but there was no question in her mind about telling her aunt even when she believed that it would end the fight. She had to tell someone else.

After a few token bites, she put down the bread.

"May I be excused?" she asked, wondering what time it was.

"You haven't eaten a thing," said her aunt.

"Perhaps she's . . . not well," Louisa's mother suggested timidly.

"She won't be well if she doesn't eat something."

Outside, in the hall, the pendulum was swinging; one fifteen.

"I *don't* feel well," Louisa followed her mother's lead. "May I be excused?" A plan was suddenly forming in her mind; the two of them at the kitchen table, the front door unguarded.

"You'd better go to your room," said Aunt Agatha.

"Can't I go for a—" Louisa cut off her impulsive words with a shudder.

"For what?" Aunt Agatha challenged.

"N-nothing, Aunt Agath—"

"I hope you have no plans for leaving the house, young miss," Agatha Winston said suspiciously. "You know very well you can't go out and you know why."

Louisa swallowed, feeling the pulsebeat throbbing in her wrists. She shouldn't have mentioned going out.

"All r-ight," she faltered. "I'll go up to my room."

She pushed back her chair and stood, trying to keep her face composed, trying not to think of the consequences of running from the house against her aunt's orders. "Excuse me," she murmured, her hands cold and trembling as she moved around the table and started for the door.

"I think you'd better lie down for a while," Aunt Agatha told her.

"Yes, Aunt Agatha, I will," she said, then shuddered as she realized she was lying. I don't *care*—she told herself as she pushed through the swinging door and moved along the hall rug toward the door—it doesn't matter anymore what she thinks.

"Where do you think you're going?"

At the sound of her aunt's demanding voice, Louisa's hand jerked off the door handle and twitched down to her side.

She stood there, white-faced, as her aunt stalked up to her.

"Where were you going, Louisa?"

"N-no place."

"Don't lie to me, Louisa!"

In the kitchen doorway, Louisa noticed her mother appear, her face confused and helpless.

"I was just g-going out on the porch," she told her aunt "Why?"

"I . . . just wanted some air; it's so s-stuffy in my room."

Agatha Winston looked at her doubtfully, her thin lips pinched together.

"I hope you're telling me the truth, Louisa," she said. "I hope so."

"I am, I am."

Agatha Winston gestured toward the staircase. "Go up to your room," she said tersely. "We'll discuss this later."

"Yes, Aunt Ag—"

"*Agatha*," Mrs. Harper said then and Agatha Winston

turned. For a moment, the two women looked out at each other and a questioning expression flickered across Elizabeth Harper's face. Agatha seemed to guess what her sister was thinking for she turned back to Louisa quickly.

"Your room," she said.

When Louisa had reached the top of the staircase, Agatha Winston moved to where her sister stood.

"What's the matter with you?" she challenged. "Do you want her to know? Isn't there enough to worry about already?"

"But it doesn't seem fair to—"

"Fair!" Agatha Winston burst out angrily. "Would it be fair to make her sick with worry? Would it?"

Elizabeth Harper looked at her sister and was lost in hopeless confusion. "I don't know," she murmured. "Perhaps . . . you're right. I . . . don't know. If only my dear—"

"I *do* know," snapped Agatha Winston and went back to the stairs to listen for the closing of the upstairs door.

Up in the hallway, Louisa stood leaning against the wall watching the clock pendulum move endlessly from side to side. And there seemed to be a pendulum in her chest too that swung and struck against her heart and her ribs. Back and forth hitting her heart—her ribs—heart—ribs—heart—time passing inexorably.

Her hands shook and there was a great sick churning in her stomach.

Suddenly she sobbed. "*Robby!*" His name fell like a shattered thing from her lips.

In an hour and a half . . .

Chapter Twenty-seven

She'd been silent all the way back to the ranch; silent as he unhitched the mare but left his own horse saddled and tied up in front of the house. Silent as they went into the house and found the kitchen table covered with the remains of the dinner the boys had made for themselves; silent as John went into the bedroom, silent as she stood in the middle of the small kitchen, listening to the sound of his footsteps, the sound of the clock ticking, her eyes fastened to the doorway he would return through. All this time, silent.

But when he came back in, buckling on his gunbelt, she felt herself twitch suddenly and words came.

"John, you can't," she said, "you just can't."

He stopped walking and looked at her, his face strained with unvoiced tensions. For a moment his hands were motionless on the belt buckle. Then they finished up and dropped to his sides and a heavy breath of air expanded his chest before slowly emptying from it.

"I have to," was all he said.

"But why?"

His lips pressed together a little as he stood there looking at her. Then he turned and glanced at the clock. It was almost two.

"I think you know why," he said.

He went over to the stove and opened one of the covers.

Dropping in some kindling and crumpled newspaper, he lit them with a sulfur match. Julia stood there, without a word, staring at the pistol butt bobbing slightly on his left hip as he stirred up the flames and put the coffee pot over them.

Suddenly she moved to him and her hands clutched at his arms.

"Just don't go," she said impulsively. "Just refuse to fight him."

He tried to look patient with her but it didn't work. He shook his head once, very slowly.

"But *why?*" she asked again, a tremor in her voice.

"Julia, you know why. You heard what Matt Coles said. If I don't come into town, Robby'll come out here." His head shook again. "I won't have that, Julia," he said.

"But he won't come out."

"You know different," he said calmly. "You know what's behind him, pushin'."

"But he wouldn't shoot you down in cold blood!"

"He would if his father *made* him," John said, a little more loudly now. "No, it's no good, Julia, it's just no good. I'm not goin' to set here and wait for Robby to come out lookin' for me."

"But John, he wouldn't shoot you, he's not that way."

Benton blew out a tired breath and turned back to the stove to move the coffee pot restlessly over the fire.

"Whether he shot me or not," he said, "it'd be the same. I'd be a laughin'stock."

"Laughingstock?" she said, uncomprehendingly. "I don't—"

"I could never ride into town again without bein' laughed at."

"Well who cares about that?" Julia argued. "Isn't it more important that—"

"I care," Benton said, turning abruptly, his face hard and

determined. "I didn't start this fight, Julia; you know I didn't start it. But I'm not lettin' anybody push me into a corner and make a fool of—"

"You'd rather kill, is that it?" she said sharply.

"If that's what you think . . ." Benton didn't finish up but turned slowly to the stove again.

Julia felt herself trembling with nervous anger.

"We'll move then," she said desperately. "We'll go away."

"*What?*" He looked at her incredulously. "After all the work we've put into this place? Just move? What kind of an idea is that?"

"I just don't want you to fight that boy!" she flared up at him.

His face stiffened as if he were about to yell back at her but he repressed it instantly.

"Listen, Julia," he said, "I've done everything you ever asked of me. I finally left the Rangers because you couldn't take worryin' anymore, it wasn't just the Grahams. I never wore a gun in the town, I only wore it on the ranch. I didn't even join that posse though I should have. But don't ask me to back out of this."

"You said you'd never put on a gun against anyone as long as you lived," she said in a hollow voice.

He looked at her as if he couldn't believe what he'd heard.

"Julia, what do you want me to do—forget I'm a man? Creep away from this fight? *I* didn't start the damn thing, I didn't have a thing to do with it. But, for God's sake, don't expect me to run away from it when—"

"You promised, John." It was all she could say.

"I said I wouldn't put on a gun against anybody! I never said I wouldn't defend myself! Can't you see there's a difference?"

"This isn't just anybody!" she said vehemently. "This is a boy who hasn't got a chance against you!"

"I make it that way?" he asked. "Did I tell him to challenge me?"

"It doesn't matter who challenged who! You can't fight him, that's all!"

"Julia, I'm going to fight him."

The words seemed to come from the very depth of her fear and her fury; they fell from her lips slowly and clearly.

"John Benton," she said, "if you draw your gun against that boy, it'll be murder. *Murder*!"

He looked at her colorless face a long time before turning away to the stove and saying, "That's right. It will be."

She stood there shivering, watching his steady hand pour coffee into the cup. He took the cup and walked out of the room and she listened to the sound of his boots moving through the house, then the sound of him sinking down on their bed.

Her eyes suddenly closed and she flung a hand across them as a wracking sob broke in her throat. Stumbling through a haze of tears, she moved to the table and sank down, her head falling forward on her arms, her body lurching with great, hopeless sobs.

She was conscious of the clock striking two.

Then, outside, there was a sound of turning wheels and thudding hooves. She straightened up with a gasp, a look of shocked surprise on her face. Hastily, she reached into her dress pocket and drew out a handkerchief. She dabbed at her cheeks and eyes as she stood up and hurried to the door.

It's them, the terrifying thought came suddenly. They said three but it was only a trick and they were coming at two to catch John by surprise.

Then, in the doorway, she stopped and stared out blankly at the small woman getting out of a rig with hurried, nervous movements.

Julia stood rooted there as the woman came up to her.

"Your husband hasn't gone yet, has he?" the woman asked quickly.

"No," Julia said, not understanding. "No, he—"

"Thank God," Jane Coles said fervently, then stood there awkwardly, clutching the shawl to herself.

"Come in," Julia said, feeling her heart start to throb in slow, heavy beats. What was Mrs. Coles doing there? For a second, Julia had the wild hope that the fight was canceled and Mrs. Coles was the one they'd sent with the message. But that didn't make sense and she knew it.

As she stepped aside to let the small woman enter, John appeared in the other doorway, tensed as though he were expecting the same thing Julia had expected.

When he saw Robby's mother, the tenseness left his face and was replaced by a look of startled surprise. He didn't say anything as Mrs. Coles came over to him.

"Mister Benton," she said.

He nodded once. "Missus Coles," he replied, looking down at the small frailty of her.

"I—" She said. "I . . . wanted to—to—"

"Yes?" he said.

There was silence for a terrible moment, a silence that seemed, suddenly, as if it would be permanent, holding them all fast in it.

But then Mrs. Coles' faint voice spoke. "I . . . came about . . . about the fight," she said, nervously.

Benton tightened a little but still he didn't understand. He looked down at her with confused eyes. "I . . ." he started and then waited.

"My boy is . . ." Mrs. Coles started and then suddenly it all came rushing out. "Oh, Mister Benton, don't hurt him! Don't hurt my boy!"

Benton jerked back the upper part of his body as if someone had struck him across the face; his expression was one of stunned shock.

"Don't . . ." he started to repeat her words, then broke off shakily.

"Please, Mister Benton, please. I'm begging you as his mother. Don't hurt him! He's just a boy. He doesn't know anything about g-guns or-or fighting. He's just a boy, Mister Benton, just a boy!"

Benton's lips twitched as he sought for proper words but couldn't find them.

"Mister Benton, I beg of you," Jane Coles went on brokenly and Julia shuddered, hearing in the older woman's voice a repetition of her own words to Mrs. Coles' husband a little over an hour before.

"Missus Coles, I . . ." Benton said nervously. "I . . . I didn't ask for this fight. I didn't—"

"I don't know anything about that," Jane Coles said miserably. "All I know is I love my boy and I'll die if anything happens to him."

"But Missus Coles, I just told you I—"

"Oh, please, Mister Benton, *please.*" There were tears now, running down the small woman's cheeks, and her hands were shaking helplessly before her.

"What do you want me to do?" he asked her quietly as if he really thought she could give him an answer.

She sobbed helplessly, staring at him, unable to see any part of the situation but the threat to her boy.

"Missus Coles, what do you want me to *do*?" Benton asked again, his voice rising. "Just wait for your son to *kill* me?"

"He wouldn't, he wouldn't!" she sobbed. "He's a good boy, there's nothing mean in him. He wouldn't hurt anyone, Mister Benton, not anyone!"

"Missus Coles, your own husband told me to be in town by three o'clock or Robby would come after me. What choice does that give me?"

She had no answer, only frightened looks and sobs.

"Missus Coles, I don't want this thing any more than you do. I have a life too, you know. I have my wife and I have this ranch. I'm happy here, Missus Coles, I don't want to die any more than Robby does. But I'm being forced into this, can't you see that?"

"Don't hurt him, Mister Benton," she pleaded. "Don't hurt him, please don't hurt my boy."

Benton started to say something, then, abruptly, he turned on his heel and walked away from her. At the door to the inner hall, he turned.

"You'd better go home and talk to your husband, Missus Coles," he said grimly. "He's the only one that can stop this fight now. I'm sorry but my hands are tied."

"Mister Benton!"

But he was gone. Julia moved quickly to the trembling woman and put an arm around her.

"You've got to stop him, Missus Benton," Jane Coles begged. "You've got to stop him from hurting my boy."

Julia looked at her with a hopeless expression on her face. Then she sighed and spoke.

"You'd better go see your husband, Missus Coles," she said softly. "He *is* the only one who can stop it now. I'm . . . I'm sorry." She fought down the sob. "You . . . don't know how sorry I am."

"But he won't listen to me," Mrs. Coles sobbed. "He just won't listen to me."

Julia closed her eyes and turned away.

"Please go," she muttered thickly. "That's all there is. Believe me, that's all there is."

When Jane Coles had climbed into her rig like a dying woman and driven away, Julia walked slowly into the silence of the bedroom. John was sitting on the bed, his head slumped forward, his hands hanging loosely and motionlessly between his legs. On the bedside table his coffee stood cold and untouched.

He didn't even look up as she came into the room. Only when she sat down beside him did he turn his head slowly and meet her glance. His eyes were lifeless.

Then his head dropped forward again and his voice, as he spoke, was husky and without strength.

"I'm tired, ma," he said. "I'm awful tired."

Slowly, her arm moved around his back and she pressed her face into his shoulder.

"I know," she murmured. Her eyes closed and she felt warm tears running slowly down her cheeks. "I know."

Chapter Twenty-eight

He tried to sit down and rest but there seemed to be a spring in him that coiled tight every time he sat down. First the tension would affect his hands and feet, making them twitch. Then his shoulders would twist with a tortured restlessness, his hands would close into white-knuckled fists, and the turbulence in him would show in his eyes as a haunted flickering.

Then, abruptly, he'd be on his feet again, pacing back and forth on the sitting room rug, the fist of one hand pounding slowly and methodically into the palm of the other. His gaze would flit about the room from one object to another as though he had lost something and was making a rapid, futile search for it. His boots scuffed and thudded on the thick rug and there was no rest in him.

Robby dropped down onto the couch for the twenty-seventh time and sat there feeling the coils drawing in again. His chest rose and fell with quick, agitated breaths as he stared at his hands.

On the bottom step in the hall, his brother sat peering between the bannisters, the freckles on his face standing out like cinnamon sprinkled on milk. He watched Robby start to his feet again and begin pacing.

"When you gonna fight him?" he asked.

Robby didn't answer. He breathed as if there were an obstruction in his throat.

"Robby?"

"Three o'clock. L-eave me alone."

"Where, Robby? Are ya goin' out to his ranch?"

Robby's teeth gritted together as he stopped and looked out the window at the street.

This was Armitas Street, Kellville, Texas. It was his town, it had dozens of houses and hundreds of people and stores and stables and horses and life and future. Yet in— how long?; he glanced nervously at the hall clock and saw that it was five minutes after two.

In less than an hour it might all be taken from him.

Might be? What question was there? He couldn't draw a gun like John Benton, he couldn't fire half as quickly or accurately. He'd never even gotten the hang of cocking the hammer after each shot; he'd always fumbled at it.

He jammed his teeth together to stop the chattering. Oh, good God, he was going to die! The thought impaled him on a spear of frozen terror. He jammed his eyes shut and felt a violent shudder run down his back.

"Robby, where are ya gonna?"

"I said, leave me alone," Robby muttered.

"What did you say, Robby?"

"I said—! Oh . . . *never mind.* Shut up, will ya?"

"But where are ya gonna fight him?"

"In the square! Now will ya leave me alone!"

Jimmy sat staring at his pacing brother. He wished he was big enough to fight somebody with a gun like Robby. Maybe he could fight his father.

The vision crossed his mind with a pleasant tread—him and his father facing each other in the square, guns buckled to their waists. *Awright pa, fill yer hand*! Sudden drawing, the blast of pistol fire, his father clutching at his chest, him re-holstering his pistol and running to his mother. *It's all right now, ma, it's all right. I killed him. He's dead now and he can't hurt us no more.*

His eyes focused on Robby who was on the couch again. He looked over at the clock.

"There isn't much time," he said, helpfully.

Robby forced his lips together, eyes staring at the floor.

"Robby, there isn't much time."

Robby stood up with a lurching movement and went to the window again. He stood there tensely, punching slowly at his cupped palm. Jimmy sat there listening to the dead smacking sound of the fist hitting the palm.

"Robby, there isn't much—"

"Will you *shut up!*" Robby screamed at him, whirling, his face contorted with rage. Jimmy felt a sudden jolting in his stomach and drew back from the bannister quickly.

"I was only—"

"Get out of here!" his brother yelled. "I'm sick of lookin' at ya!"

Jimmy sat there rigidly, thinking how much Robby looked like his father when he was mad.

Robby started for him. "I said—get outta here," he warned, his voice a strange, unnatural sound.

Jimmy pushed up to his feet and ran up the steps, a sudden dryness in his mouth. At the head of the stairs, he stopped and glanced back. Robby hadn't come out into the hall; he could hear him down in the sitting room, pacing again.

Slowly, he settled on the top step and looked down the staircase. He wished he could wear a gun like Robby.

In the sitting room, Robby jumped up from the couch as a thudding of horses' hooves sounded outside. It's *him*—the words exploded in his mind as he ran for the window, his heart like a frenziedly beaten drum. He felt his legs almost buckle as he moved and he grunted in shock as he caught his balance.

There was no horse in the street. Robby drew back from the window with a frightened sucking in of breath. Did

Benton ride into the backyard, was he going to *trap* him? Robby dashed for the table and, with nerveless fingers, jerked the Colt from its holster and backed away, his eyes wide with apprehension.

The back door slammed shut and there was a heavy clumping of boots in the kitchen. No, it couldn't be Benton, he wouldn't come in like that. It was his father, it *had* to be his father. He mustn't let his father see him like this, shivering, standing here with his pistol out-thrust and shaking in his hand. But what if it *was* Benton? Oh God, oh God, I *can't!*—he thought, choking on a repressed sob.

"Where are you, sir?" he heard his father's voice then and, hastily, he put the pistol down on the table and sat down.

"I'm, I'm . . ." he began, then braced himself. "*Here*, father," he said, not realizing how loudly his voice rang out in the house.

Matthew Coles entered the room, carrying a box with him.

"Where is your mother?" he asked.

"I . . . I don't know," Robby said, still sitting there, feeling as if a great weight were settling on him.

"Well, did she go out?"

"Y-yes," Robby faltered. "She . . . she just went out in the . . . rig."

"In the rig?" Matthew Coles said in displeased surprise. Robby didn't reply. He watched his father put the box on the table.

"Well, we'll settle that later," Matthew Coles said grimly. "There are more important things to be discussed now."

He opened the box and took out the pistol in it.

"I've brought you that new Colt," he told Robby. "Since you seem to have some difficulty with hammering. The double action in this model should take care of that. I don't believe you'll need more than two shots, will you."

The last sentence was not spoken as a question.

Robby watched as his father broke open the cylinder and spun it. He heard his father's grunt and then watched him break open the seal on a new box of cartridges. Carefully, Matthew Coles inserted a cartridge into each chamber, then spun the cylinder again. He looked into the barrel from the back, then grunted again, satisfied. Jerking his hand, he snapped the barrel back into place and spun the cylinder with one thumb.

"Yes," he said. "Yes, that will do fine."

He slid the Colt into Robby's holster and forgot about it. Pulling out a chair, he sat across from his son.

"Now," he said, "as to Benton's mode of fighting. I've spoken to several men who claim to have seen him fight once in Trinity City. According to them, he wears his pistol—a Colt-Walker single action, I might add—wears it on his left hip, stock forward, using a cross draw. Furthermore," he went on, "there is reason to believe he's very much out of practice. After all, he's been away from it a long time."

I've never been near it—the words moved across Robby's brain but he didn't speak them. He sat staring at his father, his eyes unblinking, his entire body feeling numbed and dead.

"These men further claim that Benton never fires at a distance of less than thirty feet. So that, I believe you may be able to seize an advantage over him by drawing your weapon at a greater distance. Your accuracy is good enough for that; especially with the better rifling in this—" he gesture toward the gun in the holster, "—weapon."

Robby swallowed the heavy lump in his throat. No, I'm sorry, he thought, I'm not going to do it. But, again, he said nothing. He sat stiffly, listening to his father plan his life away while, under the table, his nails dug into his palms without him feeling it.

"I believe you'll find much less in this battle than you

expect, sir," Matthew Coles went on confidently. "John Benton has been away from gunplay a long while. Furthermore, I think we've seen ample evidence that he's lost his nerve. In particular, his attempts to back out of this meeting. Then, of course, there was the time he refused, point-blank, to aid the men of our town in that posse. Yes—" Matthew Coles nodded once, "—it's clear that the man is no longer what he once was."

Robby's throat was petrifying. It came slowly, starting at the bottom and rising as if someone poured cement in his mouth and he kept swallowing it. He shuddered, his hands twitching in his lap.

"As to having the issue settled in the town rather than out of it, well, I believe you can understand that. This entire matter can be settled only when the people of the town see that you are willing to defend the honor of your intended bride. They must see it; for the sake of all concerned."

Silence a moment. Matthew Coles drew out his watch and pressed in the catch. The thinly wrought gold cover sprang open and he looked calmly down at the face. His head nodded once with a curt motion and he closed the watch and put it back into his pocket.

"It's time," he said, looking at his son with a sort of pride. "Shall we go, sir?"

Robby didn't answer. There was something cold and terrible crawling in his stomach as he stared at his father.

"Sir?" asked Matthew Coles.

"I—"

His father stood up with one, unhesitant motion. "Are you ready, sir?" he asked like a general asking his troops if they were ready for suicidal battle.

Robby found himself standing up even though he didn't want to. He started for the door on numbed legs.

"Your weapon, sir," Matthew Coles said, his voice slightly acidulous.

"Father, I—"

"Put on your weapon, sir," Matthew Coles said, calmly.

I've got to tell you!—Robby thought in agony of speechless terror. But he found himself moving back to the table on legs that felt like blocks of stone, he saw his hands reaching for the belt.

It weighed a hundred pounds; his shaking hands could hardly lift it.

"Come, sir, there's no time to waste. We want to be there before three."

Robby put the gunbelt around his back and fumbled at the buckle. As he did, he stared down at the butt of the new Colt and thought about drawing it against Benton. He thought of walking across the square toward the tall ex-Ranger, of trying to outdraw a man who had killed thirteen outlaws; thirteen men who, themselves, could have outdrawn Robby without trying.

Thirteen!

He couldn't help it. His fingers went limp suddenly and the unfastened belt and holster thumped loudly on the rug.

"Be careful, will you, a—"

Matthew Coles broke off suddenly his mouth gaping as he stood there staring with incredulous eyes at the tears that were scattering across Robby's cheeks and listening to the hoarse, shaking sobs his son was trying, in vain, to control.

"What is the meaning of . . . ?" Again, he couldn't finish. His head moved forward on his shoulders and he peered intently into the twisted face of his son, staring at the trembling lips, the wide, glistening eyes, the quivering chin.

"What is the meaning of this, sir?" he asked, heatedly. "Explain yourself this very—"

"I-I-I c-can't, I *can't*, father! Please, p-lease. I can't. I . . . j-j-just can't."

"What?" The word came slowly from Matthew Coles' lips, rising with anger.

"I can't, I c-can't. He'll kill me, he'll k-*ill* me, father. I'm a-f-*fraid*." Robby didn't even try to brush away the tears that laced across his cheeks and dripped from his chin and jaw.

"Can't, sir?" Matthew Coles was having trouble adjusting to this. "Can't? What are you saying to me? There is no question of—"

"I won't *do* it!" Robby cried suddenly, his voice cracking. "I *won't*! I'm not gonna die f-for nothing!"

His father seemed to swell up before him and Robby stepped back, nervously, a rasping sob in his throat. Matthew Coles looked at him with terrible eyes, his hands twitching at his sides.

"Pick up your weapon, sir," he said in a slow, menacing voice.

"No . . . n-no," Robby muttered fearfully, his chest jerking with uncontrolled breaths.

"*Pick up your weapon.*"

"No. No, I can't, father, I *can't*!"

"You have given your word, sir," Matthew Coles said, his voice quivering as he repressed the volcano of fury within himself. "You have promised to defend the honor of your intended bride. Everyone is waiting, sir, everyone expects it. Pick up your weapon and we'll say no more of this."

Robby backed away another step, shaking his head with little, twitching movements. "No," he muttered. "No, I . . ."

"Pick up your weapon!" his father shouted, his face growing purple with released fury. He took two quick steps across the rug and clamped his rigid fingers on Robby's arm. Robby winced as the fingers dug into his flesh. He stood there staring at his father, his head still jerking back and forth, his lips moving as if he were trying to speak but couldn't.

"You cannot back out of this! This is something you have to do, do you understand! It's a matter of honor! If you do this thing to me, there will be no place in this house for you! Do you understand *that*!"

"F-f-father, I—"

"*Are you going to pick up that gun and come with me!*"

Robby tried to answer, to explain but terror welled over him again and he started to cry harder, his shoulders twitching helplessly, his throat clutched with breathless sobs.

"*No!*" he cried out and his head snapped to the side suddenly as Matthew Coles' broad palm drove stunningly against his cheek. The room seemed to blacken for a moment and Robby stumbled back, clutching at his cheek with one hand, his eyes dumb with shock.

"Coward!" his father screamed at him. "Coward, coward, *coward*! My own son a coward!"

Matthew Coles lurched away toward the hall, his face a mask of near-mad rage. At the doorway, he twisted around.

"When I come back tonight I want you gone! Do you hear me, *gone*! I don't want a coward in my house! I won't have one! Do you understand!"

Robby stood there, shivering without control, staring with blank eyes at his father.

A moment more his father looked at him.

"Swine," Matthew Coles said through clenched teeth. "Filthy little coward. You should have been a girl, a little girl cooking in the kitchen—hanging on your mother's apron strings."

Then Matthew Coles was gone in the hall and Robby heard the front door jerked open.

"By tonight!" he heard his father shout from there. "If you're still in my house then, I'll throw you out!"

The door slammed deafeningly, shaking the house. Robby slumped down on the couch and covered his face with shaking hands. Trying to fight off the deep sobs only made them worse. He couldn't control anything. He sat there trembling helplessly, hearing his father gallop away outside, the sound of the gelding's hooves drowning out the noise of the turning wheels.

Suddenly, Robby looked up and caught his breath. Jimmy was standing on the bottom step, looking at him. Robby felt himself grow rigid as he looked at his younger brother. He couldn't take his eyes off Jimmy's face and couldn't help recognizing the look of withdrawal and disappointed shame there. He opened his mouth as if to speak but couldn't. He didn't even hear the back door shut.

He stood up nervously and walked on shaky legs to where the gunbelt was. Bending over, he picked it up and held it in his hand, seeing, from the corners of his eyes, that Jimmy was still there. It's true—the words lanced at him—it's true, I am a coward, I *am*!

That was when his mother came in.

She stopped for an instant in the hallway, her eyes on Jimmy. Then she looked into the sitting room. When she saw the dazed, hurt look on Robby's face, she started toward him.

"Darling, what *is* it?" she asked, hurrying across the rug, her arms outstretched to him.

Robby stepped back. His mother rushing to embrace him, in his mind the lashing words of his father—*You should have been a girl, a little girl cooking in the kitchen, hanging on your mother's—*

"Oh, my darling, what happened?"

It was the sound in her voice that did it; that sound of a

mother speaking to her little boy who she never wants to grow up and be a man.

"No!" he said in a strangled voice, suddenly twisting away from her arms and running toward the hall, the gunbelt clutched in his cold hand.

"Robby!"

He didn't answer. He saw the face of his younger brother rush by in a blur and then he was flying down the hall and into the kitchen, the frightened cries of his mother following him. He was on the porch, jumping down the steps and running into the stable where his horse was already saddled.

As he galloped out of the stable, his mother rushed out onto the porch, one thin arm raised, her eyes dumb with terror.

"No, Robby!" she screamed, all the agony of her life trembling in the words.

As he started down Armitas Street for the square, Robby began buckling on the gun.

Chapter Twenty-nine

*T*wo fifteen. She stood in the leaden heat of the sun, shivering fitfully while she watched the shape of her husband dwindle away. She stayed there until he was gone from her sight. Then, slowly, with the tread of a very old and very tired woman, she walked back to the house.

She shuddered as she stepped into the relative coolness of the kitchen and her eyes moved slowly around the room as if she were searching for something.

In the middle of clearing the table, she suddenly pushed aside the stack of dishes and sank down heavily on a chair. She sat there, shivering still, feeling the waves of coldness run through her body. We'll have to move now—the thought assailed her—we can't possibly stay here with a murder on our conscience; we just can't.

Her right forefinger traced a straggly and invisible pattern on the rough table top and her unblinking eyes watched the finger moving.

Suddenly, her head jerked up and she felt her heartbeat catch. A horse coming in.

Julia pushed up with a muttering sound of excitement in her throat. He was coming back; he wasn't going into town! Her footsteps clicked rapidly across the kitchen floor and she jerked open the top half of the Dutch door.

It was like being drained of all her energy in an instant. Dumbly, she stood there, watching Merv Linken as he rode over to the bunkhouse, reined up, and dismounted. When he'd gone in, she turned away from the door slowly, unable to control the awful sinking in her stomach.

A moment later, she was running across the hard earth toward the bunkhouse, her blond hair fluttering across her temples.

Merv looked up in surprise as he bandaged his right wrist.

"Ma'm?" he asked.

She stood panting in the open doorway. "Will you hitch up the buckboard for me, Merv?" she asked breathlessly.

"Why . . . sure, Miz Benton," he said.

"What, what happened to your wrist?" she asked vaguely.

"Snagged it on some barbed wire," he said. "It's nothin'."

"Oh." She nodded. "Will . . . you do it for me right away, Merv?" she asked. "I have to get into—"

From the way the skin tightened over his leathery face, Julia realized suddenly that he knew.

"I just passed him," Merv said grimly. "He didn't say nothin' to me. Nothin' at all. Didn't even look at me."

Abruptly, he tore off the end of the clean rag he was bandaging his wrist with and started for the door without another question.

"I'll have her ready for you in a jiffy," he told her.

Ten minutes later, she was driving out of the ranch on the lurching, rattling buckboard, headed for Kellville.

For her husband.

Chapter Thirty

It was like some endless nightmare. She'd keep moving into the hall, past the clock and over to the head of the stairs; but, every time she did, her aunt would be down in the sitting room, talking to her mother. Louisa would come back along the hall rug, past the clock, and into her room once again. It happened that way again and again, always the same except for one thing. Every time she passed the clock, it was a different time. *Two ten—two fifteen—two twenty-one—two twenty-seven—*

Oh, dear God! She stood shaking at the head of the steps, wanting to scream, her cold hands clutching at the bannister. She had to get out, she *had* to! Only a little more than thirty minutes were left now. She bit her lower lip until it hurt and her breast shook with unresolved sobs.

I'll tell Aunt Agatha, I'll tell her I lied, I'll tell her to stop the fight. I have to, I just have to! And she'd go down one step, meaning to rush downstairs and tell everything and save Robby.

But, after one downward step, she'd freeze and be unable to go any farther. She'd never been able to talk to her aunt in her life. Her aunt was remote from her, a bony-faced, dark-garbed stranger. Tell *her* that she'd lied? Tell *her* that she was in love with John Benton and had made believe that . . .

She backed up the step again, lips shaking, tears forcing their way from her eyes and dribbling down her pale cheeks. She hurried back to her room, looking at the clock as she passed. Before she reached the door, she heard the tinny resonance of the clock chiming the half hour. In thirty minutes.

Thirty *minutes*!

She stood alone in her room, looking around desperately for the answer. She had to tell someone—but first of all she had to get out of the house.

She moved to the window quickly. Could she climb down the trellis? No, she'd fall and hurt herself. And, even if she managed to do it, surely they'd hear her climbing down.

A whimpering started in her throat and she turned restlessly from the window. But I have to do something! The thought filled her with terror. She couldn't just let Robby die!

She ran to the door, thinking she might climb down from her mother's window in back. But there was no ivy trellis in back, she suddenly remembered. She'd have to jump then. But it was too high—she'd kill herself. The whimper rose. Oh . . . no, *no*. Oh, God, help me to stop it—please, please . . .

The minute hand was moving away from the six now. Louisa stared at it with sick fascination. I can see it moving now, she thought dizzily, they say you can't really see a clock hand but I can—

Oh, God, it's going to the seven! I have to *do* something!

She ran to the head of the stairs. Her stomach was tightening, she was starting to feel sick. I have to do something, I have to stop it, I *have* to. She pressed her shaking hands together, staring down the steps toward the front door.

I have to!

Suddenly, she felt herself running down the stairs, making no effort to be quiet, her shoes thudding quickly on the carpeted steps.

Before she reached the bottom step, Aunt Agatha came hurrying from the sitting room.

"Where do you think you're going?" she demanded.

"I have to stop it," Louisa gasped.

"Stop it?" her aunt said, questioningly. "I don't see what—"

"Aunt Agatha, it's my fault—mine! Please tell them to stop. I didn't mean to . . ."

She stood there trembling, thinking—there, it's said, I've *said* it and I don't care as long as Robby is safe.

"Louisa, go to your room," Aunt Agatha said.

Louisa didn't understand. "But I said—"

"I heard what you said."

"But we have to stop it!"

"Stop what?"

"The fight!"

Aunt Agatha's lips pressed together. "I *thought* you'd found out about it," she said. "If you'd remained in your room as I told you, this wouldn't have—"

"But, Aunt Agatha, we have to stop it!"

"I'm afraid that's not possible."

"But it's my fault, Aunt Agatha! I made up the story; I didn't tell the truth!"

Aunt Agatha's eyes closed a moment. "I understand, Louisa," she said calmly. "It shows you have a good heart. But I'm afraid it's too late now."

Louisa didn't understand. She stared at her aunt incredulously. "But . . ." she murmured.

"I'm sure we appreciate your wish to prevent violence, Louisa. However, there is no alterna—"

"But it's *my fault*!" Louisa burst out, tears springing from under her eyelids. "I made up the story! John Benton never even *spoke* to me!"

"Go to your room, Louisa."

"Aunt Agatha!"

"Louisa, this instant . . ."

Louisa couldn't believe it was true. She stared at her aunt dazedly, feeling her heart beat in great, rocking jolts.

Abruptly, she turned to her mother who had come into the hall. "Mother, you have to—"

"Lou-isa!" Agatha Winston's voice was metallic. "That will do."

"But you have to—"

"Go to your room, I said!"

"You're not going to—?" Louisa began in a faint voice.

"Louisa, if I have to say another word, you'll remain in this house for a month," Agatha Winston stated.

"Darling, please don't make it worse," her mother begged.

Louisa backed away, her eyes stricken with horror at what she'd done.

Then, suddenly, she lurched for the front door and jerked it open. Before her surprised aunt could jump forward to grab her, Louisa had run out onto the porch.

"Lou-*isa*!" Aunt Agatha's sharp cry followed her as she fled down the path and flung open the picket gate.

"Oh, my dear—please," her mother pleaded in a voice that no one heard.

Agatha Winston ran as far as the gate, her lean face masked with outraged surprise. There, she stopped and watched Louisa running frantically down Davis Street toward the square.

In the hallway, she put on her bonnet with quick, agitated motions. "She's lost her mind," she muttered, paying no attention to her distraught sister. "She's taken leave of her senses. Made it up, in-*deed*! Does she think a *lie* is going to stop this fight?"

She hurried from the house, leaving behind a weeping Mrs. Harper, standing in the hallway, trembling and thinking if only her dear husband were alive.

Twenty-two minutes to three.

Chapter Thirty-one

It was exactly twenty minutes to three when the Reverend Omar Bond came out of the white-steepled church on the way to his adjoining house and saw John Benton riding slowly up St. Virgil Street toward the square.

"Oh, Mister Benton," he called, stepping out into the street.

Benton glanced over, then when he'd seen who it was, he tugged a little at the barbit, reining the bay to a slow halt. The Reverend Bond walked up to the horse, smiling up at Benton.

"Afternoon, Reverend," Benton said to him.

"Good afternoon, Mister Benton," Bond answered. "My apologies for stopping you. I just wanted to find out how things went yesterday."

Benton looked down in surprise at the dark-suited man. "You don't know?" he asked.

The smile faded. "Know?" the Reverend said, disturbedly.

"I'm to meet Robby Coles in the square at three o'clock," Benton told him.

"Meet him," Bond repeated blankly.

Then it struck him. "Oh, dear Lord, no!" he said in a shocked voice. "In *one day*?"

Benton didn't say anything. He drew out his watch and looked at it, his expression unchanged.

"But it must be stopped," Bond said.

Benton's mouth tightened. "It's no use talkin' to anyone, Reverend," he said. "Nobody wants to listen. They want what they want and that's it."

"Oh, *no*, Mister Benton," Bond said, arguing desperately. "This meeting must not take place."

"It's too late, Reverend," Benton said quietly. "There's not much more than fifteen minutes left."

"Dear God, it *must* be stopped," said the Reverend in a tight, unaccepting voice. He raised his hand to shade his eyes from the sun as he looked up at Benton. "Come with me to Louisa Harper's home," he asked. "She will surely confess when she hears that there is a life at stake."

Benton looked restless. "Reverend," he said, "I been all through this. Yesterday I came in like you asked. I tried to talk reason with these people. And this mornin' both Julia and I came in. The girl's aunt wouldn't even let my wife in the house. Nobody would listen."

"But surely they don't realize—"

"Reverend, they *do* realize," Benton said. "It doesn't matter to them. They don't care, they don't *want* to believe I didn't do what they said. They want blood, Reverend." Benton's lips tightened for a fraction of a second. "They'll get blood," he said.

"Oh, no . . . *no.*"

"I have to go, Reverend," Benton said.

"The sheriff, then!"

"He's out of town, Reverend. I'm sorry. I have to go now."

"Is there *no* one?"

"No one, Reverend."

"There is you, Mister Benton. I beg of you to reconsider."

"Reverend, I have to be in the square by three o'clock," Benton told him firmly. "I'm sorry." The coldness left his voice then. "Believe me, I'm sorry, Reverend. I didn't ask for this thing. I did everything I could to stop it, I swear to that. But—" his head shook slowly, "it's no use."

"I'll go to Louisa," Bond said quickly. "I'll tell her. She *must* confess her lie!"

Benton said nothing but his gaze moved restlessly up St. Virgil Street toward the square.

"Mister Benton, can't you hold this thing off? Can't you prevent it from happening until I can reach the girl?"

Benton shifted in the saddle. "Reverend, they said three o'clock," he said. "I'll do what I can but . . ." He shrugged with a hopeless gesture.

"Then . . ." Bond looked carefully at the tall man, his mind a twisting rush of conflicts. "Mister Benton I . . . I know nothing of these things, nothing. But . . . well, you have a reputation for . . ." he struggled for the words, ". . . for accuracy and . . . and quickness with your . . . your weapon."

Benton looked down expressionlessly at the churchman. "What do you mean?" he asked guardedly.

"I know this may be unreasonable but . . . isn't it possible for you to—to merely *wound* young Coles? Even if you cannot avoid the meeting in time, couldn't you end it without taking his life?"

Benton looked down with a tense expression.

"Reverend . . . you don't know what you're asking me." He rubbed a hand across his sweat-streaked brow and wiped it on his Levi's. "Beggin' your pardon but . . . well, you just don't know what a gunslingin' is like. It's not somethin' that . . . that *lasts*. It's not somethin' you can play with. It happens too fast, Reverend, too damn fast."

Bond stood there, looking up blankly at the worried face of John Benton.

"And . . . well, besides that," Benton said grudgingly, as if he felt he must be understood, "I've been away from it a long time. I haven't drawn a gun on anybody in more than eight years—and gunslingin' is somethin' you have to keep up with or you lose the touch."

He gritted his teeth, seeing that he wasn't getting across to Bond.

"How do I know how fast Robby is?" he asked. "What if I go into this meanin' to crease him and then he out-draws me before I even get the chance?"

"But, surely . . ."

"No, I just can't take that chance, Reverend," Benton said. "If I was in practice—yes, I might do it but . . . not now."

He hesitated, then started in again, his voice rising. "Reverend, hittin' an arm or a leg in the split second a gun-slingin' takes is hard enough t'do when a man's with it every day. But I been away from it over *eight years*." He shook his head. "I just can't do it, Reverend, I . . . just can't. I want to live too—just like him."

"Well, will you try to keep the fight from starting until I can reach Louisa Harper then?" Bond asked in a hurried, anxious voice.

"Reverend, I . . ." Benton exhaled heavily. "I'll try," he said. "But you'd better hurry."

He tugged at the reins then and the bay moved off toward the square.

Bond rushed up the path to his house and into the hall, his eyes seeking for the clock as he entered. Two forty-seven.

Thirteen minutes.

"Oh, dear Lord," he muttered in a choked voice as he headed for the kitchen.

"Omar, what is—?" his wife started to ask as he dashed toward the back door.

"No time!" he cried and then was gone.

When she appeared on the porch, he was trying feverishly to get the bridle on their gray mare and attach the animal to the rig.

"Omar, what is it?" she asked, anxiously.

"Benton and young Coles going to fight in the square at three!" he gasped, his fingers fumbling at the leather.

"Oh, no," Mrs. Bond murmured.

"I'm going to Louisa Harper's house to try and stop it!" Bond told her.

A minute and a half later, he was whipping the mare out the alley and the rig was groaning as it turned onto St. Virgil Street and headed for Davis Street.

Mrs. Bond went back into the kitchen, shaken by the sight of her husband so upset, so white.

When the front doorbell jangled suddenly in the stillness, Mrs. Bond dropped the wooden spoon she was stirring with. Before the clatter had died in her ears, she was in the hallway, moving on skirt-whipping legs toward the door.

Her eyes widened as she saw who it was.

"Where's the Reverend?" Louisa Harper gasped.

Mrs. Bond knew about the affair and a succession of emotions jolted through her as she stared at the flushed, perspiring face of the young girl—shock first, then confusion, then excited resolve, then a sudden dread as she realized that Omar had said *three o'clock.*

"Quickly, child," she said. "The story you told. It wasn't true, was it?"

Louisa draw back a little, staring at Mrs. Bond with a startled expression. "Where's the Reverend?" she asked in a thin, frightened voice.

"Child, he's gone!" Mrs. Bond answered quickly. "He went to see you. We must hurry! That story—it wasn't true was it?"

Louisa still stared, her chest jerking with laboring breath.

"Child, there's no time! There are only minutes left!"

"No!" Louisa sobbed. "They have to stop! I didn't tell the truth. John B-Benton didn't speak to me."

"Will you repeat that to Robby Coles?" Mrs. Bond asked desperately, glancing toward the clock. *Two fifty-one.*

Louisa bit her shaking lips and stood there panting, the hair straggling across her forehead.

"Child, for the love of God! Will you repeat it?"

"Yes!" Louisa burst out. "Yes, I will, I will!"

"Quickly then!" Mrs. Bond grabbed her hand. "We'll have to run!"

They started down the path, the two of them, rushing for the square. In the empty hall the minute hand edged toward the eleven. *Eight minutes—seven minutes, fifty-nine seconds—seven minutes, fifty-eight seconds—seven minutes, fifty-seven . . .*

Chapter Thirty-two

He was tired. He tried to sit up straight in the saddle but he couldn't. His muscles ached; his arm muscles and the muscles in his shoulders and back—they all ached from digging and pushing the cows from the bog.

But that was only the immediate fatigue. There was the lack of sleep from the night before too. And all of that was only the surface of the endless undercurrent of exhaustion he'd felt since he'd bought the small ranch with his Ranger earnings and tried to make a going thing of it. Life in the Rangers hadn't prepared him for it. Life in the Rangers had been a hard one but more because it was dangerous than anything else. And danger didn't make the body ache with weariness.

He was near the square now. He took out his watch and opened it.

Seven minutes to three. He eased the bay over the side of the street and reined up. No point in leaving Socks anywhere near the square where a stray slug might hit him.

Benton dismounted and started tying up. He watched his tanned hands as they wound the leather rein twice around the rough wood of the hitching bar, then looped it under. His hands didn't shake but that didn't mean anything; that was just learned habit. He could be twisted in knots inside and none of it would show in his hands or his face. That was the way he was.

He finished tying up the horse now and stood there a
moment, looking at Socks with a sad smile. There was a
tightness around his lower stomach starting. It came to him
as a sudden jolt that he was nervous.

He swallowed and patted the bay's muzzle.

"See you, churnhead," he said softly, then stooped down
and moved under the hitching rack and stepped up onto
the sidewalk.

He stood there, looking around. The street seemed to be
deserted but he knew that people were watching him from
their windows. From the corners of his eyes he noted the
momentary flutter of a window shade across the street and
his mouth tightened. He started walking for the square, his
hands swinging in short, tense arcs at his sides.

About five minutes now, he thought. Robby would probably be in the square already, waiting with his father. Benton took a deep breath. He wished it was Matthew Coles
he was meeting. That wouldn't bother him so much.

He tried not to think about it. He tried to convince himself that there was nothing he could do; that it really *was*
out of his hands. He was defending himself, that was all.

But he knew it wasn't so. It was a lot more than that. He
didn't want this fight, he didn't want it at all. Robby was
just a kid. Julia had been right; he didn't want to believe it
but there was nothing else he could do. It would be . . .
*murder. John Benton, if you draw your gun against that
boy* . . . He blinked and tried to drive away her words.

Now he saw the square. It was strange to see it so empty.
The last time he'd seen an empty square was in Trinity
City. That was the time Jack Kramer had been waiting for
him. That one had been easy. He'd hated Jack Kramer and
he'd been in top condition. Kramer went down with two
slugs in his chest before he'd even gotten a chance to draw
his two Colts.

No use thinking of that now. This wasn't the same. He

didn't hate Robby Coles, he didn't hate him at all. He felt
sorry for—

No! He fought that off too. It didn't matter what he felt,
he told himself, he was still fighting for his life. If he didn't
get Robby, Robby would get him. It was as simple as that.

If only he could forget Julia, if only he didn't keep
hearing what she'd said. *John Benton, if you draw your
gun against that—*

He stopped abruptly and caught hold of himself. Drawing out his watch, he snapped open the cover. Three minutes. Well, there was no point in planning on Bond getting
to the girl in time. Benton swallowed dryly. Did he dare
wait and not be in the square at three? Maybe if he could
stall a little longer, Bond might . . .

No. That was impossible too. They had said three and
it was no use fighting himself. Maybe it was pointless,
maybe even stupid but when three o'clock came, he had to
be in the square. It was the way he was and there was no
way to change it now.

He put the watch away and took out his pistol. Opening
the cylinder, he took a cartridge from his belt and filled
the empty chamber. One of these slugs—the thought
came—is going to kill Robby Coles.

Or *was* it?

He shuddered as he slid the pistol into its holster and
started walking again, his mud-caked boots thudding on
the plank sidewalk. What kind of question was that? He
didn't understand where it had come from. And yet it was
true—he didn't know how fast Robby was. He'd never given
it a thought; it just never seemed as if it were possible
that . . .

And yet it was, of course. Benton felt a cold sinking in
his stomach. I've been away from it too long, he thought,
I'm starting to worry about it. That's what happens when
you're away too long.

He shoved the thought aside. How could Robby possibly outdraw him when all he did was work in a shop all day? No, he was going to die.

Benton's throat moved as he thought, once again, of Julia's words. And he wondered, as he approached the square, if it were possible to do what Bond had asked. At one time, it might have been simple. But he hadn't drawn on anyone in a long time. Could he possibly . . .

His chest shuddered with forced breath. Too much thinking, he told himself angrily, too damned much thinking! He tried to blank his mind to all thought but one: There was an armed man in the square, waiting to kill him.

He stopped at the end of an alleyway that led to Taylor Street. He squinted toward the sun-drenched square. They'd expect him to come down St. Virgil Street because it led out of town to the trail.

Abruptly, he moved into the shaded length of the alley. Maybe he'd come out where they didn't expect him. They might not see him right away, it might put more distance between them. That might save a minute and give Bond a chance to get back with the girl. It was worth a try anyway.

He was halfway down the alley when the two of them entered it from the other end. The second they saw him, they froze in their tracks.

Benton didn't stop. He kept walking until he was fifteen feet from them, then he stopped. He paid no attention to Joe Sutton; his eyes were fastened to the stiff features of Dave O'Hara.

"Well?" he said.

O'Hara swallowed and tried not to move his hands.

"I told you if you ever saw me with a gun on, you could say it again," Benton told him.

O'Hara swallowed convulsively.

"What do you say, little boy?" Benton snapped. "I haven't got all day."

O'Hara's lips started shaking. His dark eyes stared petrified at Benton.

"All right, unbuckle your belt," Benton ordered.

"Huh?"

"You heard me."

With cold, shaking fingers, O'Hara fumbled at the buckle until it came loose. He let the whole belt drop to the ground with a crash.

"Pick it up," Benton told him, standing motionless, his hands hanging loosely at his sides.

O'Hara bent over obediently and picked up the belt.

"Now drop it in that trough," Benton told him.

O'Hara started to say something and then changed his mind. Biting his lip, he moved on unsteady legs to the trough while Joe Sutton watched incredulously, taking it all in.

"Drop it in."

The belt was released and it made a loud splash as it hit the water. They all heard it thump as it hit the bottom of the trough.

"You're not big enough for a gun yet, sonny," Benton said coldly. "Don't let me see you with one anymore."

His eyes shifted to Sutton and he looked at him a moment without saying anything.

He didn't have to say anything.

Without another word, he walked past the two of them and turned left at the end of the alley, a thin smile playing on his lips. *Flannel mouth*, he thought.

Then the smile was gone and he walked in long, regular strides until he'd reached the foot of Taylor Street.

John Benton stepped down from the sidewalk and walked out onto the edge of the square.

His eyes moved slowly around the edge of the square until they settled on the two figures far across from him, standing in front of their gunsmith shop.

Benton felt his heart start pumping heavily and he pulled out his watch. Two seconds after three o'clock. He was on time.

He'd stand right there, the idea came. He wouldn't move; then it would take Robby longer to reach him and maybe Bond could get back in time to stop it.

He put his watch away and took a deep breath. Far across the square, Robby Coles left the side of his father and started walking slowly toward Benton.

Benton felt his fingers twitch and then felt that indicative tensing of his right arm muscles.

But it was different. A look of tense uncertainty flitted across his face. The heat of anger wasn't there, the confidence-inspiring knowledge that the man he was about to face deserved to die.

His heartbeat faltered. It's different, he thought, it's *different*. He hadn't even conceived it could be like this. It had always been so definite before, so clearly defined. He'd had a job to do and there had been a badge on his chest that gave him the permission to kill. And, deep inside he'd known that, if he killed, the man who died deserved no more.

Until the Grahams . . .

He almost backed away. There was a cold lacing of sweat across his brow and Julia's words hit him again. *It'll be murder. Murder!* His throat moved nervously and he began to look around for Bond. He had to get to the girl in time, he had to!

Desperately, he tried to tell himself it was self defense, he was forced into it. But he couldn't convince himself. And now his hands were shaking, something that had never happened before. Dear God, how could he fire on someone he had no reason to fire on?

He felt a shudder run down his back. *It'll be murder.* He blinked and brushed away the sweat drops that ran into his eyebrows and over his upper cheeks. One salty drop of it ran into his mouth. He clenched his teeth and looked across the square at the approaching figure of Robby. How far away was he? A hundred yards? No, less, less.

He stood there rigidly, throat tightening as he watched Robby come closer. Go back, he thought suddenly, go *back*! Again his glance fled to all the street openings of the square, searching. Where was *Bond*!

His eyes shifted again. How far now? Seventy-five yards. No, it wasn't that far.

Should he turn and leave? What could they do? By the time they found him, Louisa could be forced to tell the truth.

No. He couldn't do that, he knew he couldn't. It didn't matter how desperate he was not to fight Robby, he couldn't run. It just wasn't in him to run. But what was he going to—

All right! His face grew taut in the instant he made his decision and, with a slight lurch, he began walking across the wide square toward Robby.

There was no noise at all. It was so quiet, the sound of his boots pressing down on the earth sounded clearly. He walked slowly and unhesitantly, eyes focused on the approaching boy.

Now he could see Robby's face. It was tight and without expression of any kind—a white mask of rigidly held determination.

Sixty yards now, fifty-nine, eight, seven. Benton felt his arm muscles tightening, readying. I've got to let him draw first, he ordered himself, *I've got to let him draw first*.

His boot heels crunched over the hot, dry ground, his eyes were fastened to the hands of Robby Coles.

Fifty yards.

Benton suddenly tensed as Robby's hand flew up to his pistol and he fought down the instinct of muscles to draw at the same time.

The roar of the Colt cracked a million jagged lines of sound in the silence of the square. Dirt kicked up two yards in front of Benton. Good God, what's wrong with him?—the question lanced across his mind. It was an easy shot.

He had his hand on his pistol butt just as the second blast of gunfire sent echoes rocking through the square. Dirt kicked up at his feet and he heard the slug whine ricocheting into the air.

The gun was in his hand then, suddenly. He stopped walking and twisted himself a half turn so he could extend his arm and aim. The third shot roared and he saw Robby's lips jerk back from clenched teeth as the bullet struck him in the right arm. He saw Robby's gun fall and hit the ground and, slowly, he lowered his arm.

Then he stiffened again, his breath catching. Robby had fallen to his knees and was trying to pick up the pistol, his face twisted with pain and terror.

The pistol fell from Robby's numbed right hand and, with a sob that Benton could hear, Robby grabbed at the Colt with his left hand. And, as Robby looked up, it seemed to Benton, in that instant, that he could see, in Robby's eyes, the same agonized dread he'd seen in Albert Graham's eyes just before he'd shot him.

Benton's shout filled the square.

"*Robby! Leave it alone!*"

But Robby had already thrown up the pistol, forced back the hammer and fired again. Benton heard the slug whistling by his right shoulder and, jerking up his pistol automatically, he thumbed back the hammer and fired.

The shot was too rushed, too shaken. The bullet only creased the edge of Robby's left arm and he was so numbed by fear that he didn't feel it. He jerked at the trigger and the silence was shattered again.

Benton staggered back with a startled grunt as though

he'd been struck across the chest with a club. The Colt slipped from his suddenly lax fingers and, before it hit the ground, another slug drove into his chest, knocking him back further. With a sharp gasp, he fell to one knee, face dazed, dumbstruck eyes staring at the white-face boy who was sitting on the ground fifty yards away, the Colt still clutched in his left hand.

Then the square began to waver before his eyes and there was a terrible burning in his chest. Blinking, he looked down at himself and saw red blood spilling out between his clutching fingers. He tried to speak but he couldn't; his throat was clogged.

He looked up again dizzily and watched the wave of blackness rush at him across the square, break over him, followed by another and another.

That was when the buckboard reached the square. The woman in it dragged back the reins and braked suddenly, standing up. The people coming out from behind locked doors could see the look of stupefaction on her face. They watched how she half climbed, half fell from the buck-board and started walking across the square, then broke into a stiff, weaving run.

They saw too, the Reverend Bond's wife come rushing down St. Virgil Street with Louisa Harper. They watched the white-faced girl as she stood on the edge of the square, staring open-mouthed at the four figures on it. And they wondered.

He was still on his knees when Julia reached him. Both his arms were crossed tightly over his chest and stomach like those of a little boy who had eaten too many green apples and fallen sick. His blood was running over his arms and dripping on the ground.

She stood before her husband for several moments, one hand covering her lips, in her throat a sickened moaning as she looked down at him.

Abruptly, then, she gasped his name and fell to her knees beside him.

Slowly, in tiny, jerking movements, he raised his face to her. It was the face of a man who could not understand what had happened to him. For almost ten seconds, he stared at her, eyes dazed and unmoving, mouth hanging open.

Then, without a sound, he fell against her, dead.

She held his body in her arms, her face distorted by grief, dry sobs stabbing at her throat, hands stroking numbly at his back. She would remember for the rest of her life how it felt to have his warm blood running across her hands like water.

Fifty yards away, a father was leading his son, speaking to him in a stiff, proud voice.

"You're a brave boy," he said. "You did what had to be done. You're a very brave boy. We're all proud of you."

He failed to notice the look his son directed at him; one of sickened hatred and disgust.

He only became aware of what his son was feeling when Robby jerked his left arm free and staggered away, moving past Louisa without a word, his face a rigid mask of pain as he strode unevenly across the square.

It was three minutes after three P.M., September 14, 1879. The end of the third day.